accident-prone

THE ORDER OF RAVENS AND WOLVES

T.L. HODEL

For Dylan, (you know why) and the best PA's ever.
Affinity Author Service and Julia Murray, you deserve an award for
trying to organize my chaos.

This book contains is a dark romance and contains violence, profanity, references to child abuse, humiliation and bullying, non-consensual and dubious-consensual sexual situations, suicide, PTSD reactions, alcohol and drug use. If you are a reader sensitive to such material, this may not be the book for you.

This is the fourth book in the series book three is Happenstance

THE ORDER OF RAVENS AND WOLVES TITLES

KINGS:

- Louis Kessler (King go Kings)
- Dean Whitley
- Sebastian Creswell
- Dr. Martin Creswell
- Ryker Hudson

KNIGHTS:

- Micha Kessler (Future king of kings)
- Mason Kessler
- Logan Hudson
- Parker Whitley
- Preston Whitley
- Silas Creswell
- Finn Creswell

Name Pronunciation

- Micha: Mike - ah
- Ryker: Rye - cur
- Silas: Sye - lass
- Riley: Rye - lee
- Paisley: Pase - lee
- Derek: Dare - ick
- Marnie: Mar - knee
- Trina: Tree - nah
- Logan: Low - gan
- Mason: Mase - on
- Preston: Press - ton
- Parker: Park - er
- Finn: Finn
- Junior: June - your
- Shelby: Shell - bee
- Naomi: Nay - oh - me (bitch)
- Chase: Chase
- Tanner: Tan - er
- Amy: A - me
- Ava: A - va
- Whitley: Witt - lee
- Kessler: Kess - ler
- Creswell: Cress - well
- Mathers: Ma - th - ers
- Grier: Gr - ear
- Harper: Har - per
- Louis: Lou - is
- Lana: La - na
- Sean: Sha - awn

Playlist

'"Nothing Else Matters' by Metallica
'Twice' by Christina Aguilera
'Blue On Black' by Five Finger Death Punch
'If Everyone Cared' by Nickelback
'What It's Like' by Everlast
"Lost Cause' by Billie Eilish
'Voodoo' by Godsmack
'Heaven Knows' by The Pretty Reckless
'Rockstar' by Nickelback
'Down To The River To Play' by Alison Krauss
'Move Along' by The All-American Rejects
'All I Know So Far' by Pink
"Bodies' by Drowning Pool
'Dead And Gone' by T.I ft. Justin Timberlake
'Shivers' by Ed Sheeran
'Heat' Kelly Clarkson
'It' Not Over' by Daughtry
'Station' by Lapsey
'Cat's In The Cradle' Ugly Kid Joe
'Drunk' by Ella King

TEN YEARS AGO:

My nose crinkled as my dad hugged my mom and kissed her cheek. Adults were so gross. They were always holding hands and stuff. Didn't they see the cooler of snacks was beside them?

I wanted a snack, but I wasn't going to go over there. Then my mom would kiss my cheek. Eww. She'd been all lovey since she got back from making her movie.

I'd watched the last movie she made. My dad said I couldn't watch this one, though, cause I was too young. I was always too young. When I got bigger, I was going to watch all the movies and do the other things I wasn't allowed to, and no one could stop me.

"Silas! Put those down." My dad waved his finger at the feathers in my hand, "They're dirty."

"Stop it, Martin. They're just feathers." My mom reached up and touched my dad's cheek. "Let Silas have his fun."

Yeah, let me have my fun.

I wouldn't say that out loud, or else I'd lose my game. Or worse...I'd get the belt.

"Do you know how many diseases birds carry?" My dad's firm eyes swung my way. "Put them down, now."

With a sigh, I opened my hand and let the feathers flutter to the ground. It took me forever to collect those. When I grew up, I was going to have all the feathers, too. I'd sprinkle them on my furniture so when my dad came over, he'd have to sit on them.

My dad's brow rose when I just stood there glaring at him. "Go play."

Those were my feathers. I frowned and crossed my arms.

"We can go home if you want."

Instead of arguing, I stomped my way back over to the sandbox, where Mason and Harper were playing with my cousin, Finn. It took all morning for Mom and me to convince my dad to come to Cherry Lake, and we'd just gotten here. I didn't want to go home. Why were adults so bossy?

My lip curled at Mason's mom. She was still standing on the docks, staring out at the water. She was so weird.

The lake was busy today. Kids were everywhere while the adults laid around. Even Logan was here, and he never came to Cherry Lake. Everyone was happy, except Mason's mom. She was just standing there by the water. Not moving, or sticking her foot in it, or anything.

"Why is she doing that?"

"I don't know. Maybe she's trying to find that mermaid guy...."

Mason's head tipped up as he squinted against the sun, "what was his name?"

"King Triton?"

I rolled my eyes at Harper's answer. "Did you guys watch that movie again?"

Every time I went over to Mason's house and Harper was there, that movie was playing in the background. He said it was because Harper liked it, but I think he liked the mermaid's red hair. It wasn't even close to the same red as Harper's hair. Hers was darker, and it shone in the sun and bounced when she ran. It was also really soft when I pulled it.

Harper's brother ran by, yelling, "I got it!"

Clutched tightly in his raised fist was a swimsuit top, flapping around like a flag behind him as he ran. Actually... it would make a good flag, and we needed one for the sandcastle. Maybe Sean would drop it?

That idea got squashed when his mom ran after him. "Sean Douglas Callaghan, you get your ass back here right now!"

I'm not sure who's suit Sean had snatched, but their mom didn't seem happy about it. Oh well, I had other things to worry about.

Like my cousin.

"No, Finn." I sprang across the sandbox and grabbed the rock out of his hand before he could stick it in his mouth. "Why do babies have to eat everything?"

"Oral exploration is a key development stage for kids Finn's age."

We all cocked our heads at my dad's answer.

"What's that mean?" Harper whispered.

"Don't ask," I warned her. "Then he'll explain it."

Harper smiled and said, "Thank you, Mr. Creswell," because none of us wanted him to tell us more.

My dad nodded at Harper.

"You're welcome, dear," which was when I let out the breath I was holding. I don't know how many times we'd all had to sit down and listen to my dad talk.

According to him, it took four thousand pounds of force to break a femur. Neither Mason or I knew what a femur was, but we'd been looking for one ever since.

"Finn ate my truck the other day." Mason stood up and flipped the bucket we were loading with sand over.

"Really?" I grimaced as the bucket slid over the mound inside. Our first three attempts failed, so we made sure it was really full this time. "What did you do?"

He shrugged. "I played with Micha's."

Harper and I both stopped and stared up at him.

"You played with Micha's stuff?"

Mason scowled down at me. "Why wouldn't I?"

"But..." Harper's brown eyes went wide. "It's Micha's?"

"So? Micha's my brother. I can play with his stuff."

My eyes narrowed at my best friend. "You didn't ask him, did you?"

"I don't haveta ask him."

I bet Micha wouldn't say the same thing. He didn't let anyone touch his stuff, and when someone did, he wasn't nice about it. In fact, Micha was just plain mean.

Right now, he was on the other side of the beach, pushing a little girl with black hair in the sand. I didn't know who she was, but I kind of liked her. Once she was on the ground, she lifted her foot and kicked him, making Micha crumple and fall down beside her.

Maybe we should ask her to join our monster-hunting business? Mason and I hadn't come across many monsters. So far, we've saved people from mostly iguanas and a few spiders, but we did protect a few people from a vampire.

The guy that cooked at Mae's was really pale and only came out at night. So we hid garlic all over the place. That girl might make a good monster hunter.

I looked up as the girl swung her hand and slapped Micha in the face. Two seconds later, he pushed her down and kicked her in the side.

Then again, maybe not.

Micha was mean, but he wasn't a warlock or vampire. He was better than Logan, I guess.

I turned to the right, watching a blond little boy sneak up on a woman enjoying the sun. Each step he took caused a drop of water to slosh on the sand from the red bucket in his hands.

If the woman was sleeping, she wasn't anymore when Logan tossed water on her back. She shot up screaming and completely forgot about the bathing suit top she had undone. Which Sean swiftly swooped in and snatched.

My brows pulled together as I watched the bouncing mounds on her chest. What was the fascination with those? Once a boy hit a certain age, it was like boobs were all he could think of—even my dad stared at them. I didn't get it. One thing was for sure, I'd never like them.

"That's five!" Logan yelled and took off before she could chase him.

If she did think about going after him, she stopped once he ran up to his parents. Couldn't blame her. I didn't like his parents either. Well, I liked his mom, but his dad...

Ryker's green eyes met mine from across the beach, sending a shiver up my spine. The corner of his mouth curled, making me quickly turn my attention back to the sandcastle. I didn't like that smile. Bad things happened when I saw it. Things that hurt and made me feel icky.

Don't look at the Boogeyman. That's when he comes for you.

Maybe that's why Mason's mom was acting weird?

None of the adults knew. She did, though. I'd seen the Boogeyman coming out of Mason's mom's room. My mom was always saying that I could tell her anything, but she didn't know. The Boogeyman could hide in the shadows and had magic.

That's why Mason's eyes were green. He cast a spell on him, so every time his mom looked at him, she would remember.

Never talk about the Boogeyman.

"Silas…" Harper's hand pressed against my back. "Are you okay?"

I kicked my foot out and muttered. "Mason sucks at making sandcastles."

He didn't suck. I just couldn't tell her why I was mad. If Harper and Mason knew, then the Boogeyman would come for them. Naomi told Ava, and then Ava was in the hospital for a long time.

I was young, but I still remember Parker crying. He thought she was going to die. Mason, Harper, and I cast a spell so that wouldn't happen. As long as that box stayed buried in my backyard, Ava would be okay.

"I don't suck," Mason argued.

Just then, Finn's little hand reached out, grabbing a handful of the sand mound that came out perfect. I should've been mad at my cousin. We'd finally got it right, but I was kind of happy he wrecked it. I wanted to wreck something.

"Your dumb cousin keeps breaking it." Mason huffed and dropped down with his arms crossed.

Harper tipped her head, causing her red hair to sparkle in the sun. "I think he's cute."

Finn giggled out a babble and threw dirt at her.

"Yeah, real cute." Mason snorted.

"He is cute." I didn't really think he was, Finn was always drooling and had barely any hair, but he was my cousin. It was my job to stick up for him.

"You better learn to like babies, Mason Kessler." Harper leaned forward and swept Finn's hand clean. "Cause I want three."

"Threeeeee," Mason whined and fell back.

I snickered because as much as he wanted to argue, he wouldn't. He was taking his job as Harper's future husband very seriously. Which meant that he had to give her all the babies she wanted cause babies were the girl's job.

Mason better make sure he had lots of food for the stork. My dad said babies came from the mom's tummy, but they had to get in there somehow.

"Yup." Harper nodded. "Two boys and a girl, so they can be the bestest friends, like us."

Mason and I both gagged. Girls were so sappy.

"Okay, but we have to name one Scar," Mason pointed out. "That's a cool name."

It was a cool name.

Harper nodded and then added, "But the girl's name will be Buttercup."

"Buttercup? Eww." Mason shook his head. "I like Xena. She had a sword."

I sighed and rolled my eyes, though I agreed with Mason. Xena was better than Buttercup. I bet none of the other people around us were arguing over something so dumb.

Cherry Lake was busy today. There were lots of people out enjoying the clear blue sky, including a bunch of people I didn't recognize. Probably what my dad called 'tourists?'

I wasn't sure what a tourist was, but my dad didn't like them. They made him say bad words. Since I got to spend the money in the swear jar, I was okay with it.

"Silas," my mom called. "Do you guys want a snack?"

"Snack?" Mason jumped up and sprang over to my parents with a smile on his face. "Yes, please, Mrs. Creswell."

"Hey, she's my mom. I get the first snack."

My mom frowned. "Remember your manners, Silas." Why should Mason get the first snack? I was her son. It was her job to feed me, not him.

"But..."

She cut me off with a look. The same one she gave me when we had company over, and I had to be polite. Why did I have to be polite to guests? They came to our house. They should be nice to us. And Mason wasn't a guest. He was at the same beach as us. We were all guests here.

"Stupid manners," I grumbled and kicked some sand as I walked over.

I flopped down and ate my granola bar because Mason got the last pack of fruit snacks. He smiled at me as he popped the last one in his mouth.

I was gonna tell Micha he played with his truck.

"I think we need a seashell for the sandcastle," Harper said while grabbing another rock out of Finn's hand.

Stupid baby.

"Why?" Mason's lip curled. "It's broken."

"But we can make it not broken with a seashell."

Mason looked at me, and I looked at the half-formed sandcastle. No shell was going to fix that. There was a big baby handful taken out of it.

"Okay," Mason sighed when Harper looked over at us. "I'll get you a seashell."

I jumped up before he could. "I'll get it."

"Nuh," Mason shook his head. "I'm gonna be her husband. It's my job."

"I'm gonna get a better one. Then she's gonna marry me instead of you."

His mouth opened as his head flew back, and he gasped with wide eyes.

Shouldn't have taken the last pack of fruit snacks.

"I saw her first."

I crossed my arms. "Doesn't matter, cause I'm gonna get a better shell, and penguins pick who brings them the best rock."

It was true, and he knew it was true. We'd watched that show together.

Mason stomped his foot. "She's my penguin, not yours."

"Not if I find a better shell."

"You're not my best friend anymore!" He took off to the beach, looking for shells.

"Good!" I yelled back and went the other way. "Best friends don't eat all the fruit snacks!"

I wandered around the beach forever, looking for a shell. Most of the ones I found were too small. I was about to give up when something glinting in the sand caught my eye. I knelt down and swept the dirt away. Underneath was a perfect shell.

The outside was crisp white, but the inside was a shimmering orange with little bits of red. Harper was definitely gonna like my shell better. I'd never seen one this color.

Standing up, I looked down the beach to where Mason was still looking and sighed. Harper was his. I couldn't take her away from him even if he did eat the last fruit snacks. I should give him the shell to give to her.

Two steps later, I stopped. Not far from me, there was a girl digging a hole. She had the prettiest eyes. So dark they were almost black, with little flecks of silver.

I tipped my head and watched the sun shine down on her blonde hair, casting a halo of light around her. Was she an angel? She looked like an angel in her pink bathing suit.

Mason had his wife pick, and my dad said Micha did too, but I didn't have one. I looked down at the shell in my hand. Maybe she could be my wife?

I walked over and smiled down at her. "Hi."

My heart skipped when she looked up at me. She was really pretty. Had those super pink lips the girls in the movies my dad watched had. Pouty, and a little bit wet. I tried to hide and see more.

My dad always caught me and kicked me out of his room, but I'd never forget the way those girls stared at the men in his movies. The way their eyes shimmered—this girl's eyes were shimmering.

"I'm Silas."

She didn't say anything, just stared up at me. That was okay. She was probably nervous. It wasn't every day that you met your husband.

"I found this for you."

Her eyes rolled down to the shell I held out for her as her lip curled. She was definitely nervous. I should explain to her how it was. Then she could relax.

"Penguins bring their wives a rock, so I'm giving you a shell."

Her gaze snapped back up to mine, making me smile. I liked it when she looked at me.

"I don't want your stupid, dirty shell."

I gasped and stepped back from her snarl. She must be one of those tourists my dad talked about cause she didn't sound like me when she talked. That must be why she was being like this. She didn't know how things worked around here.

"You will take it," I explained while trying to mimic my dad's firm tone. "I'm your husband, and you'll listen to me."

"No, you're not!" She stood up and glared at me. "I don't want you. My husband will be better."

Be better? My dad was always saying that to me. Be better, Silas, do better, be the best.

My hands fisted, but I didn't get to do anything because she reached forward and shoved me down on the ground before I could.

"No one will want you," she sang and spun around.

My eyes narrowed on a small pink triangle on her neck as she skipped away. Know who had marks like that? Witches. And there was only one way to get rid of witches.

My fingers dug into the warm sand. I'd show her. I'd become the best at everything. Then I'd find that little witch and burn her.

As kids, we thought the world was filled with magic—Santa, the Tooth Fairy, even the Boogeyman. Everything was wondrous and mystical. Mom kissed our booboos better, and Dad could take on the world because he was the strongest man in ours.

Then we grew up, and that magic fractured. Dad was just another man with a chip on his shoulder, and Mom's kisses didn't heal our wounds.

They made more. Our parents' flaws became reasons to hate them because they failed at the one job they had—preparing us for the world.

"Good fight." Some guy slapped Mase's shoulder as we made our way through the crowd.

Mase shrugged away from him and marched up the stairs. "Whatever you say."

I shook my head and followed him.

Reality was the universe's sucker-punch, and Mase had been hit harder than any of us. There wasn't mysticism and wonder around every corner. There were no fairies hiding in the garden or fat, jolly men bringing us presents.

The only thing we found around that corner was a dirty alley full of deception. That's all childhood was—a lie.

"We need to find another place." Mase swung open the doors to 'Grey's Records' and stepped out in the parking lot. "That was too easy."

"There is no other place," I grumbled.

Grey Montego, the owner, was a kindly seventy-year-old man. I used to come in and talk music with him. The man knew his stuff, and it was hard to find anyone that still appreciated the classics.

Now his son Ryan ran the place. Though he'd managed to increase the record shop's profits, I doubted his old man would be impressed with the underground fighting ring he was running out of the basement.

A fighting ring that Mase had already worked his way through.

It was the fourth this year.

"There's no more *here*." Mase tipped his head in my direction." But in New Haven…"

"You're fucking kidding, right?"

"What? How's it any different than this neighborhood?"

I cocked a brow at the rundown building we just came out of and the street full of potholes. The dockside neighborhood in Ashen Springs wasn't the best. Though, I did welcome the salty ocean air over the smell of sweat and blood in Grey's.

I shook my head at the spark of mischief in Mase's green eyes. The guy got off on crossing the line. Hitting on other guy's girlfriends, showing up at Sean Callaghan's going away party, and then this.

Guys like us weren't welcome in this neighborhood. Not that anyone could say shit about it. We owned this town. A point we proved when we helped Micha clear out Riley's block a couple years ago. A few of the local gangs, however...

My gaze shifted from a group of guys standing around a red pick-up to another group on the corner. The street light above them flickered, highlighting the lines of disdain etched in their faces. Each one sported a green bandana, either hanging out of the back pocket of their jeans or wrapped around their upper arms.

Both of the groups were glaring at us, but the members of the gang, Hades Hounds, would shoot us in the back if they thought they could get away with it.

And this shit was tame compared to New Haven.

My mother was an actress, my Grandpa, a governor, and Mase's old man was Louis Kessler. In New Haven, that would bring us one of two things—a ransom-kidnapping or a violent death. A town founded by addicts and criminals wasn't a safe place for anyone, including the addicts and criminals.

"New Haven is not an option, Mase."

"Why not?" He shrugged. "Might find a challenge there."

"If by challenge you mean surviving a knife in the gut...." My brow arched at him. "Then sure. We'll find a lot of challenges there."

"I have connections in New Haven."

Really?

"Your drug connections are the exact reason we are staying the fuck away from that town."

Mason's hand flew to his chest. "I haven't touched the stuff since I got out."

As far as I knew, that was true. Since he got out of rehab, I'd been watching him like a hawk, and I hadn't seen any drugs. Alcohol, on the other hand.

"And what about last week?" I tipped my head at him. "I saw you drink that beer at the bonfire."

"It was one beer," he said with an exaggerated sigh.

"One beer is too many for an alcoholic."

He threw his head back and rolled his eyes. Mase didn't like being lectured. Too fucking bad for him. Someone had to make sure his dumb ass didn't end up back in rehab.

"What are you, my dad?"

I snorted. "Your dad would've locked your ass back up."

"Please don't send me back there." He spun around and cupped my cheeks, squishing them together, while he sang, "I swear I'll never touch the devil's nectar again."

Asshole thought everything was a joke. Screwing around in rehab and wanting to drag me to New Haven. In about five seconds, he wouldn't have to worry about finding a challenge in some skeezy underground fighting ring because I'd knock him the fuck out.

"Get your fucking hands off me."

My fist balled as the corner of Mase's mouth curled. I knew that look. It was usually followed by a kiss. If this fucker's lips came anywhere near me…

"Hey, Kessler!"

We both cocked a brow and turned our heads. Well, Mase turned mine. Fucker still had his hands on my face. The guy sitting on the tailgate of the red pick-up hopped off and threw his finger up.

"I lost a bet because of you."

Mase tipped his head and sized the guy up.

Fuck.

I recognized that twinkle in his eye.

"Aww, look buddy." He squeezed my cheeks, making my lips pucker. "I think someone's upset."

"Get the fuck off me," I snarled and slapped his hands away.

Prick.

I eyed the nametag on the guy's coveralls as he stormed forward and hissed. "You owe me a grand, Kessler."

Al, who apparently worked at Max's Gas and Gulp, was not happy. And the best part? Guess where Max's Gas and Gulp was. New Haven. Great.

Mase shot me a wink and folded his arms over his chest. I knew exactly what he was thinking. The guy and his friends weren't as big as Mase or me, but they were big enough. And there were four of them.

"That's funny." Mase leaned over and peeked around the guy's shoulder to see a wide-eyed woman gawking out the back window of the truck. "I don't remember ordering some second-rate used pussy." He cocked a brow at me. "Did you?"

Motherfucker.

His comment was enough to make the other three guys push off the truck and march across the parking lot with Al.

"Remind me to kick your ass later," I growled under my breath.

Mason smiled and nodded at the angry men. "Get in line, Buddy."

I should let them kick his ass. If he was anyone else, I would. But I knew how fucked up Mason Kessler really was. The world didn't just eat him up and spit him back out. It shat all over his very existence.

His mother was a piece of shit. His girl betrayed him, and everyone else hid the truth from him. Micha could wrap it up in whatever pretty bow of protection he wanted. The truth was, we all fucking lied to him. Including me.

I was fourteen when I put everything together—the green eyes and Logan's abnormal protection of Mason. Don't get me wrong, Logan protected us all, but not like he did Mase.

And did I say anything to him? No. I kept it to myself. I didn't want to break his heart. Harper took care of that when we were ten.

Besides, how do you tell someone they're the spawn of the Boogeyman?

"I'm going to get my money back, Kessler."

"You hear that, Bubby? He's gonna get his money back."

I set my bag down and rolled my neck. "Yeah, I fucking heard it."

Asshole.

Being who we were, stress was a natural part of life. Do this, do that, go here, be there. Add all the Order responsibilities on top, and you had a powder keg ready to blow.

Logan didn't give a shit and exploded whenever he felt like it. Micha pent everything up. Parker pretended to be the good boy, and Preston…well, nobody really knew what Preston did.

My unnatural stress level came from my best friend, who I was definitely going to smack around after this shit.

Mase glanced over his shoulder and sang, "Remember the four 'A's."

"Go fuck yourself," I muttered back.

The four 'A's were a running joke between him and me. It was something his old man once told us—tips for handling the overwhelming situations we would be put in—but the only overwhelming situations we had were fucking Lou and the Order rules. That, and my dad, which was a whole other matter.

'A' number one was adapt.

That one was usually mine because I was the one that needed to adapt to whatever fucked up shit Mase started.

Once, we woke up in Nova Scotia. No clue how we got there, but there we were on some island, surrounded by a bunch of Canadians. That was a fun conversation to have with my old man when we got back.

"No one talks about my sister." Al puffed his chest out as they all stepped up to us.

All four were more focused on Mase than they were me. Then again, they'd just watched him pound their champion into the ground. They'd be stupid not to keep their eye on him.

"Wow, you New Haven fucks really do like to keep it in the family. Tell me…" Mase rolled his shoulders back and leaned forward. "Does she spit or swallow?"

Now came the second 'A.' Avoid, which was what Mase did when Al's fist swung through the air. Faster than a man his size should be able to move, Mase ducked down out of the way, spun around, and grabbed the guy to the left of Al.

In one graceful move, he brought his leg up, cracked the prick's face on his knee, and twisted to face off against another fucker.

Dipshit flew back unconscious with blood streaming from his broken nose.

Just like that, we had the third 'A.' Alter.

Instead of four against two, it was three. And number three didn't look too keen on continuing.

Al roared and jumped on Mase's back, clawing at him like a fucking girl. One elbow in the ribs put a stop to that. Mase reached behind him, grabbed Al's collar, and flipped him over his shoulder. Leaving him groaning on the ground next to his friend.

Number two's attack was put to an end by a solid clothesline from me. After that, number three held his hands up in surrender, which brought us to the final 'A.' Accept.

I looked around at the three pricks on the ground. One was hunched over, coughing from my hit. Another one was down for the count, and Al was still struggling to catch his breath.

"Come on," I scooped up my bag and tugged on Mase's arm. "It's done. Let's go."

And because Mason Kessler was a supreme dick, he reached in his pocket and tossed a hundred dollar bill down on Al.

"Come find me if you want to collect the other nine hundred."

I threw my bag in the back of my Hummer and climbed in behind the steering wheel.

"See," Mase said, plopping down in the passenger's seat. "We could totally handle New Haven."

"Yeah," I snorted, "because that gas jockey and his idiot friends are the worst that place has to offer."

He shrugged. "We took them out easy enough."

"That might have something to do with the fact that they were drunk."

I could smell the beer on them. That, and no one in their right mind would challenge Mase after they saw what he did to that guy tonight. I'd seen Mase in a lot of fights, but I'd never seen him go off on someone like that.

Fighting was his way of letting off steam. That wasn't the issue. Everyone had coping mechanisms. The problem came when said mechanism didn't work anymore. And Mase was one sideways glance away from imploding.

Harper was my first clue. Yes, he was a prick to her—to be fair, she deserved it—but it was always the typical bully crap.

Lately, he'd been seeking her out, hunting through the school halls just so he could make her life hell. Bastard even showed up at her house when I had to do a project with her. Not that I particularly cared how he treated her. I just wanted to get the work done.

Things got worse after prom. Logan said Lana made Parker take Harper since she was still in the hospital. I'm not sure what happened that night, but whatever it was…changed Mason. He hated Harper before. Now he fucking loathed her.

I dropped Mase off and headed home, more than happy to put this night behind me. The relief I felt pulling in the driveway lasted about point three seconds. There was a moving van parked down the street.

No one was out moving anything. Then again, it was close to

midnight. While I was curious about my new neighbors, that wasn't what caused my brows to furrow.

A long neck and a large feathered body ran down the sidewalk.

Was that a fucking ostrich?

I rubbed my eyes and stared down the sidewalk. Sure enough, there were two long legs running at mach speed, bouncing a big feathered butt. That wasn't even the weirdest thing. The damn thing was wearing a pink eye-patch with a sparkly flower on it.

How did I know this? The motherfucker twisted its long neck and glared back at me as it continued running. I was standing in my driveway, being stared down by a goddamn pirate ostrich.

Did Mason put acid in my drink again?

I glanced down at the water bottle in my hand and back at the bird. The fucker was fast. Ran right past a car, which squealed to a stop so the driver could stick their head out the window.

His eyes landed on me, as mine landed on him. A silent confirmation passed between us.

Yeah, that's right. I saw it too.

Should I go over and talk to him? Or go inside and pretend that none of this happened? I didn't get to make the choice. As I lifted my foot to take a step, someone crashed into my back.

We both toppled on the ground in a tangle of limbs. I managed to roll with it, pushing off the cool grass to roll my body over the other, a reaction that was now instinct—side effect of having Mason Kessler for a best friend.

"Fuck sakes," I growled, already at my limit of shit dealing tonight. "Watch where you're...."

All words were lost the instant I saw the girl underneath me. She was fucking gorgeous—full pink lips, a long ponytail full of platinum hair. But it was her eyes that had me entranced. Dark, sparkling onyx orbs that had a slight purple tinge in the moonlight. They were also oddly familiar...

She twisted her head and murmured, "Oh shite," when the hair caught in my watch yanked her neck back.

Fuck me. She had an accent. Normally British accents grated on my nerves, but hers…

While she worked to untangle her hair, I braced my palms on the ground and lifted myself up. There wasn't much to her nightgown.

White fabric with little flowers on it, thin enough that I could see the silhouette of the hourglass figure underneath. My gaze slid over the curve of her hip and up to her pert little tits.

"Sorry about this." Her warm breath skimmed across my skin, sending goosebumps shooting up my arm.

"No problem."

And it really wasn't. She could stay under me all night long. Hell, if it weren't for my dad and our precious family reputation, I'd fuck her right here in front of all my neighbors.

I might anyway. The longer she wriggled on the grass, the harder I got. It was damn near impossible not to press in on her.

And then she had to go and lift her flushed face and smile up at me. "Almost done."

Let me just say, that right there—the way her face lit up—I'd kill a man to see that shit.

I couldn't help but feel disappointed when she finally freed herself. I wanted to keep her chained to me. Do things to her that no girl who smiled like that should have done to them. She slid back and sat up, making my fingers dig into the ground, so I didn't grab her neck.

Until now, I'd never gotten why Mase had it so bad for Harper. Yeah, she was good-looking when she wasn't hiding, but she was so small.

This girl wasn't as small as Harper, but she was smaller than

Riley. I could hold her down with one hand and fuck her with the other.

"Sorry," she gave me another one of those smiles. "Someone left the bloody gate open, and Andi got out."

Was that her boyfriend? I'd fucking kill him.

"This might sound a little odd, but have you seen an ostrich?"

I didn't hear what she said because I was too busy clenching my jaw at the small triangle-shaped birthmark on her neck. I'd seen one like it before, on a little girl at the beach.

Wait...

My head tipped as my eyes rolled over the girl sitting in front of me. The platinum hair, the dark eyes, and the accent. Son of a bitch! The sound of her voice slapped me in the face like a punch in the gut.

"So, have you?"

"Have I what?" I growled back at the little witch who'd haunted the back of my head for ten years.

'My husband will be better.'

My old man said that to me all the time, but it was her words that drove me to do just that. Be better—at school, in the Order, and at being a son. I even became better at handling Mase. No one could calm him down like I could.

Her pink lips parted, making me want to slap the shit out of her with every word she spoke. "Have you seen her?"

"Have I seen who?" Maybe if I could silence the source, then the voice that echoed in the back of my mind every time a girl ran from my dick would stop?

'No one will want you.'

"Andi," she tilted her head and peeked up at me through thick lashes. "My ostrich?"

That look made my rage burn hotter. The witch that haunted my thoughts was right here. Invading my life with chaos and a fucking ostrich. The worst part was the aching need rolling through my balls.

"Nope." I jumped up to my feet and glared my disdain down at her.

She stayed where she belonged, on the fucking ground, eyeing me skeptically. "Are you sure?"

"Nope, didn't see no ostrich." I crossed my arms and arched a brow, challenging her to say something or call me on it. Give me a reason to hurt her. "Maybe you should take better care of your animals."

That, she didn't like. Her pretty face twisted in a scowl.

"My animals are well looked after."

"Uh-huh?" I leaned forward a little and softly growled, "I'd hurry if I were you. I hear ostrich meat is pretty good."

I had a gun upstairs. I could find that fucker and grill up some burgers before the night was done.

"You don't have to be a cunt."

Little witch had no idea how much of a cunt I could be. She'd find out, though. There was one good thing about the ghost of my memory becoming real.

I couldn't hurt a ghost.

"Happy hunting," I sang and walked inside the house. Payback was a bitch.

"You don't scare me," she called back before I slammed the door.

Her comment made me smirk. Mason Kessler wasn't the only asshole in this town. I was just *better* at controlling my wrath. There'd never been anyone I wanted to unleash it on. Until now.

Burn, little witch, burn.

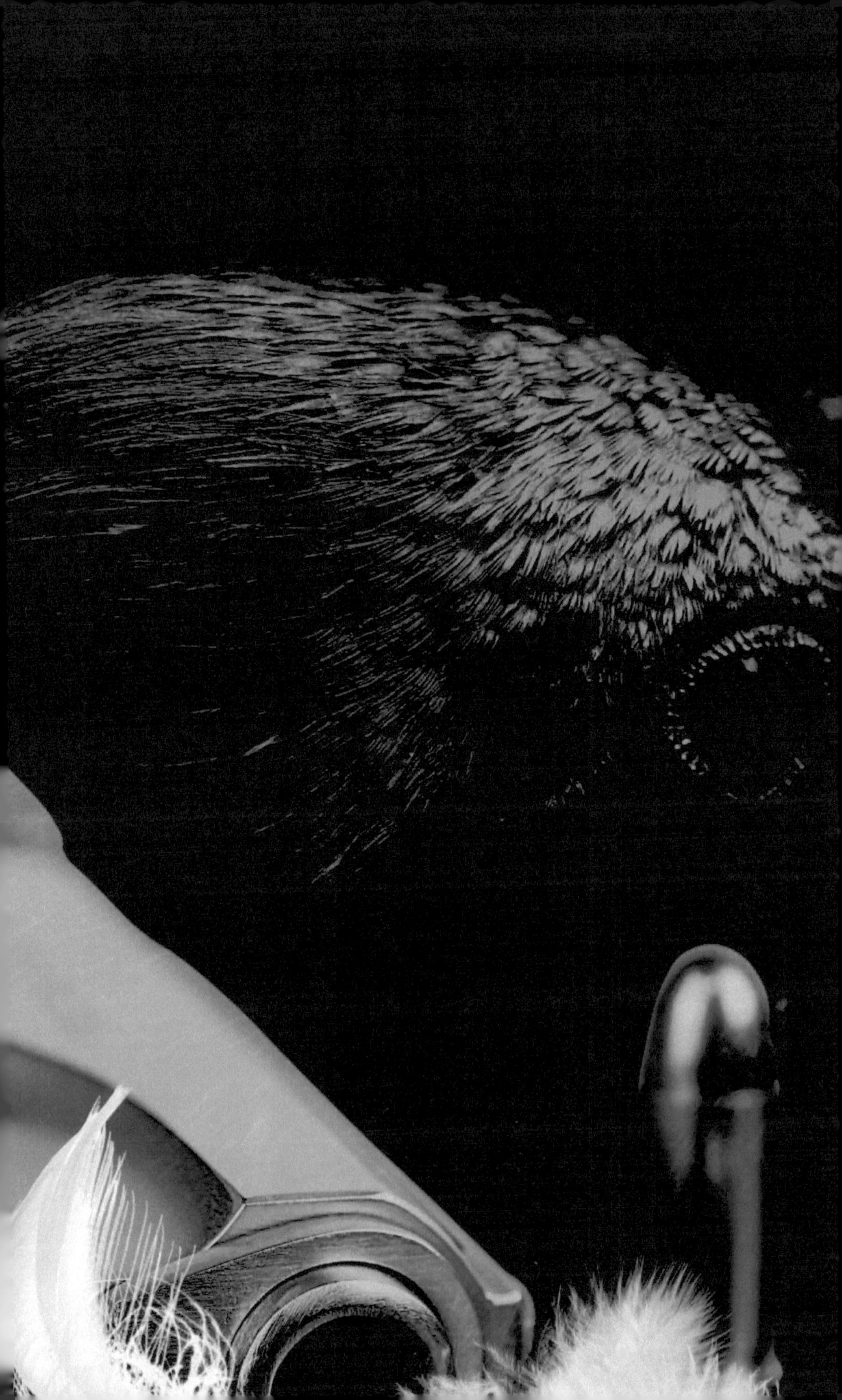

Chapter 2
Star

Star

There was one thing all teenagers wanted—popularity. It made no difference what they said or how they acted. Everyone wanted to be adored. Worshipped by their peers as if they were royalty.

I had that. Back home, I was the shite. When a new fashion trend went around school, it was because I started it. I was the queen, and they were my subjects. My world was perfect.

Until it wasn't.

An encounter in my school's bathroom changed everything.

When the dust settled, I woke up in a new world—no longer blinded by my stupid teenage aspirations. People didn't adore me. They were afraid of me. None of my friends were there for me, because I didn't *have* any friends. Just people who pretended to be my friends.

That's all popularity was.

A beautiful mirage in the desolate desert of adolescence, and everyone wanted a sip of that water. Feeling that cool rush of power flowing through your veins was addictive and poisonous. I became blind to everything else. It didn't matter who I hurt—status was the only important thing.

Now, I spent my nights chasing Andi, our ostrich, through the streets.

My yawn was cut off by a foot being crammed in my mouth. I groaned as my brother Ash's toes wriggled along my tongue.

What the hell did he walk in?

I swept Ash's foot off my face, smacked at the bitter taste in my mouth, and blinked my eyes open. My baby brother wasn't the only one curled up next to me. The twins were down by the foot of the bed. Cedar was sleeping across my legs while Elm hugged my hip —three little heads full of thick dark curls.

The fourth head was snoring loudly in my ear. Will had the same pale shade of blonde that I did, along with the curls of our other brothers. Cy was the only one not in the bed. I could hear him, though.

Carefully slipping out of my brothers' grasps, I sat up and peeked over the footboard. Cy was lying on the floor with his mouth open, his head thrown back over one of my teddy bears. Wisps of platinum hair framed his sleeping face, highlighting the rosy spark in his cheeks.

While he looked like a sweet little cherub, I knew better. The arsehole genes were strong in the eldest of my little brothers. Cy was only ten and already had a rapport with bobbies back home.

"Star?" Ash yawned and stretched his legs, wiggling his little toes. "Is it morning?"

"Yes, it's morning." I smiled as his bright, sparkling eyes

blinking open. "Why are you in here? I thought you liked your room?"

Ash was the first to tear through the house, searching for the bedroom with the puppy wallpaper Mum told him about. I assumed he found it because we didn't see much of him for the rest of the night.

"You were screaming," Will grumbled and ducked his head under my pillow.

I was?

Cedar rolled over and kicked his leg out, hitting Elm in the shin. "El said we had to protect you from the Sandman."

"I did not." Elm reached out and slapped him in response. "You were worried about the Boogeyman, not me."

Ash's eyes flew open. "Was the Boogeyman after you?"

"Ash," I pulled my baby brother on my lap and swept back the curls on his forehead. "There's no Boogeyman."

I tried telling him that this summer, and he believed me. Until Cy made him watch '*Hellraiser.*' Now, not only did Ash fully believe in monsters, but he thought a Rubix Cube was the key to hell.

He grabbed onto my shoulders, digging his little fingers in with urgency. "Was it the guy with the pins in his head?"

I shot sleeping Cy a dirty look and shook my head. "No."

It was someone worse. A ghost I wish I could leave in the past.

"Who was it?"

Me.

I sighed and changed the subject. "Do you know what day it is?"

Like the innocent child he was, Ash immediately brightened up and forgot all about 'evil pin man,' as he called him.

"Moving day?"

We got here too late last night to move anything, so we fed the animals and went to sleep. Well, everyone else did. I fought sleep and the memories that haunted my subconscious as long as I could.

"That's right." I gave my brother an exaggerated eye roll and groaned. "It's too bad everyone is still sleeping."

That's all I had to say. Before the last word left my mouth, Ash was bouncing around the bed, elbowing and kicking the twins to wake them up. Will, he was a little more gentle with, gently shaking his shoulders while yelling in his ear.

By the time he was done, I was snickering at six angry eyes. All of them were the same light golden hue as our Mum.

Cy and I were the only ones that got our father's dark color. They suited Cy. Little bastard was constantly picking on our brothers. On occasion, he'd get on my nerves. I was older though, and had no problem smacking him.

Which I was tempted to do right now. Especially after Ash's pin man comment. It turned out, I didn't need to, because Ash climbed over the foot of my bed and dove down onto Cy's chest.

Cy shot up, coughing, "You little shite."

"Morning," Ash sang, kissed him on the cheek, and ran out of the room.

He might only be three, but he was smart enough to know not to stick around.

Cy immediately jumped up and took off after him. "Get back here, you little bugger!"

My other brothers weren't far behind. After all, there was action to see. The only one that didn't scream and run down the hall to join in the chaos was Will. He waited until everyone else was gone and turned his worried eyes my way.

"Are you okay?"

I gave him a little smile. Will had been worried about me since that day. "Yeah, I'm okay."

I wasn't. Probably never would be, but Will was only eight. He didn't need to worry about me.

He nodded and left me alone to sigh and glance around my room.

This move was supposed to be a fresh start, according to my parents. Rebirth in a new country and a town where no one knew what happened. Why Ashen Springs? This was the last place we vacationed before the twins and Ash were born.

Mum always talked about coming back to the quaint little seaside town. Guess she got her wish, but it didn't matter where we went.

Ghosts never died.

"Star, breakfast is ready."

"Okay Mum," I called back. "I'll be down in a minute."

Knowing how excited Ash was to get this day started, I quickly washed up, brushed my teeth, and got dressed.

If I didn't hurry, he'd come back up here, and considering his morning probably wasn't off to a good start—and depending on if Cy caught him or not—I didn't want to disappoint him further.

He was the only one that was too young to remember what happened. As far as Ash was concerned, I was sick and in the hospital for a bit, and that's how I wanted to keep it. The trick was keeping Cy's mouth shut.

While Mum and Dad fed the animals, I took care of the boys. Quiet and our house didn't go together. My parents ran an exotic bird sanctuary back home, and a few of the former residents were still with us. Besides Andi, the ostrich that had lost her eye in a fight, we had Eilane, an antisocial penguin.

We had Craig, a cockatiel that only spoke in Spanish. We never did figure out what he was saying because we didn't speak the language.

Harry was a hedgehog that Will found in a ditch barely alive, and Roger, our peacock, couldn't control his hormones. Not necessarily a bad thing if he didn't have a fondness for human men.

Any of these animals might seem strange to other people, but they didn't grow up in the house I did. My parents never grew out of their hippie phase. They simply perfected it.

My legal name was Star Moonbeam Chadwick. All my brothers were named after trees: Cypress, Willow, Cedar, Elm, and Ash, and every ounce of cleaning products, skin cream, shampoo, or make-up, was homemade.

I couldn't complain about it. My parents' natural, free-love life-style made them quite a bit of money. And it all happened by chance. Mum was only sixteen when she had me. Dad was seventeen.

They were out for dinner one night when Mum took me in the bathroom to change me. There was another woman in there, and her baby had a bad rash. So Mum gave her some of the cream she'd made.

A few days later, the same woman, who happened to be royalty, showed up on our doorstep. The Chadwick line was born after that. Dad had a running joke where he referred to me as their million-dollar baby. I chalked it up to the one thing that seemed to be constant in our lives. Chaos.

"Oh, bloody hell, Star!" Mum called from the inside of the moving truck.

Why we had a moving truck that we had to unload ourselves was beyond me. Dad said it built character. I said it built tension in muscles and strained my back.

"Yes, Mum?"

I ran up to the truck, peeked inside, and almost burst out laugh-ing. The only part of Ash's face not covered in a thick layer of white cream was his light eyes.

"Look, Star." He clapped his hands together, splatting the cream on his palms. "I found cream."

"I see that," I chuckled and briefly wondered if I should tell him said cream was meant to go on babies' arses?

Mum huffed out a sigh and glanced over at me. "Can you clean him up?"

I nodded, reached out for Ash, and stopped when a shiver ran down my back. Suddenly, I had the overwhelming feeling of being watched. I tried to ignore it as I lifted Ash into my arms but glanced over my shoulder anyway.

Standing down the street, leaning against a deep crimson Hummer, was the cunt from last night. His piercing crystal eyes followed my movements as I marched across the front yard.

Ash peeked his head over my shoulder. "Who's that?"

An arsehole who threatened to eat Andi.

"Our neighbor."

"Is he nice?"

No.

I smiled down at the innocent spark on my brother's cheek. "I don't know? Maybe?"

Deciding to focus on the sweet boy in my arms rather than the cunt staring at me, I headed into the house.

Much to Ash's dismay, I ran him a bath. A cloth wouldn't do anything but spread the thick cream around. He, naturally, didn't want to get in. A few boats, and a lot of bubbles, convinced him otherwise.

Instead of joining the twins' wrestling match that I could hear them having in the backyard, Will came in and kept us company. He preferred things calm. Based on the yelling wafting in through the window, calm was not what he'd find out there.

"Who left the gate open?" Dad yelled. "Where's Roger?"

I sighed. Apparently, calm wasn't what he'd find in here, either.

"Go," Will took the cloth out of my hand and nodded at the door. "I'll watch him."

Any other eight-year-old I wouldn't trust, but Will was very mature for his age. Mum claimed that he had an old soul. I couldn't really argue with her. Last week, I'd caught him reading Hemmingway. The worst part was, he understood it better than I did.

Though Roger was kind of my bird—we'd come to an understanding after an argument over the last scone—I hesitated when Ash smashed a handful of bubbles in Will's face.

"Are you sure?"

Ash laughed while Will sighed and swept off the bubbles.

"Yes." He gave Ash a dirty look. "We'll be fine. Go," which I did before Ash did something else, and I felt too bad leaving Will alone with him.

Roger didn't listen to anyone but me, so if he had gotten out, then whoever tried to bring him back would be in for a fight. Moving was always rough. Mum and Dad didn't need to worry about anything other than getting our new home set up. A thought that made me stop and knit my brows.

The old me would never have cared about how hard things were. The only things she was concerned with were the latest designer labels, and what her friends were doing.

Sorry, her so-called friends. None of them came to see me in the hospital. The only people to visit, besides my family, were the parents of the girl who put me there.

That's when I decided that the Star everyone knew never came out of that bathroom.

I blew out a breath when I rounded the corner and walked into the backyard. Roger's pen was unlatched and wide open. He was always breaking out of that thing.

I told Mum to get him a better pen. But did she listen? No. And now I was on a bird hunt again. At least Roger didn't run as fast as Andi.

In fact, it didn't take me long at all to find him. I stopped and eyed Roger. His tail feathers were spread as he danced in front of a cute lad with green eyes. That wasn't what made me curse under my breath. It was the lad standing next to him with his arms folded across his chest.

Why couldn't Roger run down the street like Andi? Why did he have to go over there? I sighed and shook my head. Whatever that arsehole said or did, it wouldn't be close to what I deserved. Mum always said that karma got its payment. Maybe he was mine? Still…

I watched the lad's jaw twitch as Roger continued his dance. He didn't just act like an arse. He looked like one, too—thick black hair, with a piercing gaze, and a tanned complexion. My eyes landed on some black ink peeking out of the sleeve of his navy t-shirt. It looked like the tip of a wing.

I didn't notice the third lad, holding on to a pram, until the one with green eyes leaned towards him and said, "How do you turn down a peacock?"

"Fucked if I know."

The third lad was taller than the other two, with blond hair and light eyes that were more grey than blue.

After what happened last night, I was kind of iffy about going over there anyway. Then again, what were the chances that my neighbor was actually an arsehole?

I mean, I did knock him over. Who wouldn't be grumpy if some strange girl crashed into them? And he did have a bird tattooed on him. So, he couldn't hate them, right?

Just go and get it over with.

"Bloody hell, Roger," I yelled, not because I was mad at Roger, but because it made me feel more confident. "Sorry about that," I snatched his leash off the ground and tried tugging him away. "He used to have room to run."

I was really missing our country estate right now.

Green eyes stepped forward with his hand held out. "Hey, I'm Mason."

Maybe they were nicer than I thought?

"Star," I said, accepting his hand.

"Star isn't a name," my arsehole neighbor growled, "It's a thing."

Even more confusing than my neighbor's apparent hatred was the embarrassment burning in my cheeks. Despite having an odd name, I liked it. How many other Stars were people going to meet?

"This grumpy fucker here," Mason smiled at the arsehole and threw his arm around his shoulders, "is Silas."

So his name was Silas. Would've been nice if he told me that. Say, last night when we were on the ground, tangled around each other.

Be nice, Star. Remember, he could've had a bad day.

I sighed internally and held out my hand. "It's nice to meet you."

Silas glanced down at my open palm and then promptly marched into the house and slammed the door.

I shook my head and muttered, "Well, he's a bit of a cunt, isn't he?"

"Actually," the lad pushing the pram cocked a brow at the closed door, "he's not usually that bad."

I beg to differ.

"Don't lie to the girl, Parker. Silas has always had a stick shoved up his ass." A smile I wasn't sure I liked spread across Mason's face. "So, Star, what school are you going to this year?"

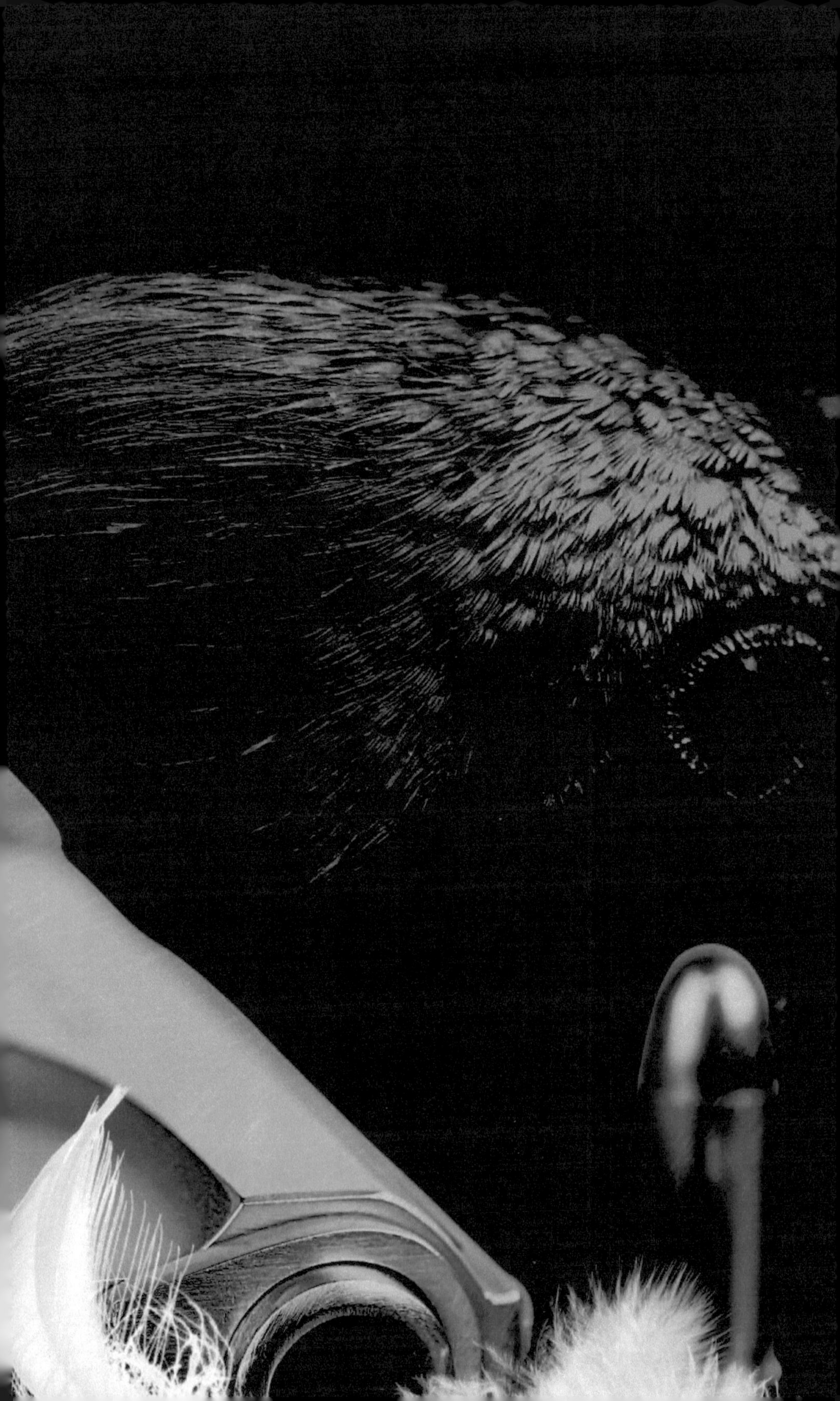

Grumbling under my breath, I opened the oven and pulled out the cookie sheet. Stupid arsehole neighbor. I tried to be nice, and the cunt wouldn't even shake my hand. What the hell was his problem? I stared down at the freshly baked cookies.

What the hell was my problem?

Half the night, I laid awake in my bed, thinking of friendly things I could do. Why? Who cared if some guy named Silas didn't like me? Did it really matter?

Hate wasn't new to me. Back home, I was public enemy number one. When anxiety stopped me from being able to go to school, people showed up at the house.

I wasn't the only one affected by the fallout from my actions. My brothers were picked on at school. The twins were taunted endlessly, and Cy and Will were cornered more than once.

Cy being the one to fight back, ended up getting it worse. He was always a little moody, but now I was the one that got his angry glare.

I couldn't blame him. We had to uproot and move from our home to come here—a strange town in a foreign country. And it was all my fault. If I had been nicer…

'No one wants you here.'

'Pathetic.'

'Useless.'

'Kill yourself.'

My palm flattened on my chest, fingering the scar through my sleep shirt. My family wanted to escape, and perhaps they could. It was my sin, not theirs. It'd been almost nine months, and I could still feel heat cutting through my flesh.

All the candles and incense in the world couldn't take away the charred scent of smoke in the air. The soft tick, tick, tick of thick crimson drops falling on the cool tiled floor constantly rang through the back of my head. That wasn't something I could outrun.

The only reason I didn't curl up and let my ghosts win was that I made a promise to two people who should've never wanted to talk to me in the first place. I'd be a better person.

The kind that made peanut butter, chocolate chip cookies for the tosser next door. Because everyone had bad days. Though in Silas's case, I'd say it was more like a bad week.

"Look what I found." Mum walked in and dropped a box on the island. "One of your brothers put them in the trash."

I focused on carefully scooping up my cookies off the pan and into a tin I had ready. "I threw it out."

"Honey… these are all your trophies." I could feel Mum's eyes boring into the back of my skull.

"I know."

"Star…"

I spun around and cut her off. "I don't want them."

"Alright." Mum's lips parted with a long sigh.

The first couple of missed dance classes, Mum and Dad, didn't question. When I dropped out of all my competitions, they started to get worried. But that was old Star. She was the one who cared about trophies and dancing. New Star would find something else. I dropped the last cookie in the tin and smiled. Maybe baking?

"Are those my peanut butter biscuits?"

Mum made the best cookies. This recipe was my favorite.

I nodded. "They're for the lad next door."

The instant the words left my mouth, I regretted it. Mum's eyes lit up as a smile curled her lips.

"The lad next door? Is he cute?"

Yes.

"Can't I do something nice for our new neighbor?"

"You can do plenty of *nice* things for our neighbor."

"Mum!" I gasped. "I barely know the him."

"Do you know his name?"

"Yes. It's Silas."

"What more do you need to know?"

The sad fact was Mum was completely sincere when she said that. I had a theory about promiscuous teenagers. While all my friends grew up with conservative parents that didn't want to believe their children were doing dirty things in the dark, mine pushed me to do them, and I was pretty sure I was the last virgin in my class.

"Your father and I are worried about you, Star. You're seventeen and haven't had any boyfriends." I groaned as her finger waved through the air. "It's normal for a girl your age to have a little fun."

I sighed and dropped my face in my palm. "I'm not having this conversation with you."

"Alright," Mum grumbled, clearly irritated that I refused to talk about my non-existent sex life with her. "At least take this and have some fun with the lad."

I eyed the bag of marijuana she dropped on the counter.

Good lord.

"I'm not supplying the neighbor with drugs."

"It's a plant, Star," Mum rolled her eyes, "Hardly what I would consider drugs."

That was the problem. Other than the really hard stuff like cocaine and heroin, my parents didn't consider much 'drugs.' They would drop a tab of acid on occasion when they didn't have the boys, of course. They were responsible in that aspect.

"Mum," I rested my elbows on the counter and leaned in a little closer to her. "Most parents don't contribute to the delinquencies of their children."

As if my day couldn't get worse, Dad chose that moment to walk into the kitchen.

"Who's delinquent?"

"Star baked biscuits for the lad next door." Mum sat back and smiled, which prompted Dad to give me the same cheeky look.

"Just remember what I said about foreplay."

That was one very detailed and entirely disturbing conversation that was permanently burned in the back of my skull. And one I didn't care to add to.

Before either of my parents could elaborate, I said, "I have to go," and ran upstairs to get dressed.

It was so bloody hot here.

I managed to throw my hair up in a messy bun, put on a pair of shorts, and a pink tank-top without being interrupted by my parents, who had been known to follow me.

After I grabbed the tin of cookies, I rushed out the door and counted my blessings. Until Dad stopped me on my way out and passed me a handful of condoms.

I couldn't give them back to him or drop them because then Dad would follow me and give them to the tosser I was meeting. He'd done it before.

So, not only was I about to face off with someone who despised me, but I had a pocket of prophylactics. Because while love was free, so were diseases.

My heart picked up as I looked from my car to the edge of our property. This wasn't a suburban neighborhood where our neighbors were right next door. It was a ten-minute walk to the next driveway.

That was also ten minutes I could take to hate my life before I knocked on the cunt's door. Exactly why I chose the slower route. I may have even dragged my feet, doubling the time it took to get there.

It also gave me time to admire Silas's house. Ours was nice, but his was extraordinary—white walls with black shutters and two marble pillars framing the front door.

What I did notice was how perfect everything looked—neatly cut grass, lined up rows of flowers, along with trimmed hedges and trees. Neat, clean, and cold. I didn't see any personal touches. There were none of the imperfections that made a house a home.

We'd been in ours for less than three days, and the twins had already started building a fort in the backyard. Ash christened the walls with a black marker, and Will put up the family flag the boys made last year in the front yard.

Heck, even Mum and Dad had their tacky wicker swing hung up on the deck. A family lived in my house. I don't know who lived here.

I stepped up to the door and gave myself a pep talk.

Okay, Star, you can do this. Remember to be polite and smile.

With one more big breath, I straightened my shoulders and pushed the doorbell. A melodic chime rang through the air, causing my heart to flutter.

It felt like I stood there forever before the door was opened and not by the arsehole I expected. The boy standing on the other side could be a mini version of Silas.

He had the same black hair and crystal eyes. Even his chin had the same sharp angles, though his mouth didn't wear Silas's tight grimace. It was spread in a big smile.

Well, he's not scary. I can handle this.

"Hi," I sang and held out my hand. "I'm Star, your new neighbor."

His eyes lit up as his smile grew. "Hi, I'm…."

"Finn, who are you talking to?"

Crap. I knew that voice.

A second later, a familiar grumpy scowl appeared behind the boy.

"This is Star," Finn looked up at him. "She's our…."

"I know who she is." Silas pushed him away from the door and cut him off. "Go pack your shit."

Finn's shoulders dropped. "Do I have to?"

"Yes."

I really wanted to roll my eyes at Silas's snappy tone. Instead, I silently cursed his name.

"Bye, Star," Finn smiled at me and waved, "It was nice to meet you."

I waved back. "Bye, Finn."

At least someone here had manners.

Once he was gone, Silas crossed his arms and leaned against the door. "What do you want?"

I was suddenly struck by how much bigger he was than me. I couldn't see past his shoulder into the house, and I had to lift my chin to meet his gaze.

Not something I was keen on doing, but it was better than watching his chest press against the fabric of his shirt. The ridges underneath were making me think things I shouldn't be.

Like how solid he felt when I crashed into him. The heaviness of his body on mine and how he first looked at me with heat in his eyes. Then he opened his mouth.

I cleared my throat and straightened up a bit–which did not make me feel any bigger. "I think we got off on the wrong foot."

He didn't say anything. Just stood there glaring at me.

Awkward.

"I brought you a peace offering."

Peace wasn't what I got when I went to hand him the tin. My complete and utter mortification was apparently the universe's plans for the day. Something fell out of my pocket as I shifted. The foil packet hit the ground with a soft flap that froze my heart dead in my chest.

Silas cocked a brow as humiliation burned a hot trail down my cheeks and across my chest.

"That's not…." I died a little bit when another one fell out.

Panic rocketed through my system. I wanted to scoop them up and run away, but I couldn't move, just talk. Which was so much worse.

"Those aren't for you… My dad… I mean… I would never…"

My mind screamed at me to shut up, but my mouth wasn't listening. I did, however, manage to get down on the ground and stuff the condoms back in my pocket.

"Please don't think… I wouldn't come here… I've never had sex before."

My lips stopped spewing out excuses as a slow clap rang out in the back of my head.

Way to go, Star. Tell the gobshite you're a virgin.

Instead of laughing at me–which was what I expected–Silas rolled his eyes back up to mine. The heat burning inside his crystal gaze had me swallowing back the nerves fluttering through my system.

"As tempting as your offer is, Crumpet," he tipped his head as he slowly raked his eyes down my kneeling form. "You couldn't handle me."

My mouth fell open.

This arrogant…

Nope.

I took an internal breath, wiping away that familiar wrathful feeling, and moved to stand up. Silas crouched down and stopped me by placing his palms on the deck and caging me in his arms. He was so close I could smell the mint from his toothpaste on his breath.

"I didn't say you could get up. I like the way you look on your knees," he leaned in and whispered in my ear. "Stay there like a good little bitch, and I might consider taking you up on your offer."

"The only thing I came to offer you," I shoved the tin in his chest, "is this."

He cocked a brow down at it. "What's in there? Lube?"

"No!" I snarled. "It's biscuits, you arsehole."

"I'm not interested in your biscuits, Crumpet." He pushed himself up and took a step back. "Now get the fuck off my deck."

That's it. Clearly, he had no plans of returning my kindness, so there was no point in trying anymore.

"If you want to be a cunt…."

That's as far as I got because he slammed the door. I sat there for a second, stunned, before getting up to leave. Finn's sweet smile made me pause and set the tin down on a bench near the door. He shouldn't be punished because Silas was a cunt.

I walked back home, thanking god that he was just a neighbor. That was something I could avoid.

I'd never been more wrong about anything in my life.

Chapter 4
Silas

The little witch showed up at my door with fucking biscuits. What the hell was that? Who the fuck gave their neighbor biscuits? The condoms… now, that shit was funny. It almost made her visit worth it.

If I could just shake the image of her on her knees from my head, then everything would be fine. But no, apparently, my mind liked the way she looked up at me, all red-faced and embarrassed. And so did my dick.

I grunted and adjusted myself. My jeans were cutting into my nuts, I was so hard. If this bitch continued invading my space, I was gonna need two things. A meditation ritual, and bigger pants. If Jasmine wasn't in another state at college, I'd give her a call.

Then again, there was always Amy. Masochistic bitch enjoyed

driving herself down on my shaft. The only thing that kept me away from her was the fact that Logan had fucked her three ways from Sunday. That, and her pretense for dragging some other girl along. Who usually ran the other way when I whipped my shit out.

'No one will want you.'

My hands balled as I gritted my teeth. That voice had gotten louder over the past couple of days. Every time I looked out the window at that fucking house, I wanted to burn it down. I wanted to hear her scream. Humiliate Star, and taunt her like she had me for the past ten years.

Something crashed above me and rolled along the floor. I sighed and pinched the bridge of my nose. My vengeance would have to wait. Apparently, Finn was having another tantrum.

He'd been acting out since I spoke to him yesterday. I got it, Finn was pissed, but I didn't know what else to do. Every night, he'd scream for hours, and I tried everything–woke him up, fought to calm him down, even took him for weekly therapy sessions with Lou. None of it worked. It just wasn't enough.

My dad wanted to send Finn back to his school, so his intelligence wouldn't be wasted. That's all he was concerned about—keeping the family prodigy a prodigy. Because, in his words, *'Finn would get over it.'*

That was the problem.

I never got over it, and my cousin's brain didn't work like other people's. As I got older, the horrors of my childhood became distant memories I could ignore.

Some things I forgot, and others I became disconnected from—Finn didn't have that luxury. His eidetic mind wouldn't let him forget anything. Every breath, word, and touch replayed in his brain as clear as the day it happened.

Logan's old man was dead. It was finally over.

That's what everyone said. They didn't get it, though. The day

Ryker took Finn, he became immortal. The boogeyman of our childhood would forever be the living monster in Finn's head.

Ryker may not be walking around anymore, but he still won. As long as my cousin was alive, so was a part of him.

"I hate you!" Finn screamed down the stairs. "I wish I'd died with my Mom and Dad!"

I knew it was a guilt trip. Didn't mean it wasn't working. Every word he spewed dug a little deeper, twisting at the fractured parts of my soul. I wished I could keep him here, but that would only make me feel better. It wouldn't do shit for him. As much as it killed me to admit, I didn't know how to fix Finn. Or even help him, for that matter.

A bellowed scream echoed down the stairs as something else crashed on the floor. I almost wanted Star to come back. At least Finn was smiling when she was here.

It'd been almost a year, and his screaming only got worse. The only time he did sleep soundly was when Junior was around. I don't know what the kid did for my cousin, and I didn't care. If he ever needed me, I'd be there. No questions asked.

"All you want to do is pass me off on someone else!"

I scrubbed a hand down my face and glanced up the stairs, dreading the fact that I had to go up there. Lou would be here any minute.

I needed to make sure everything was packed. But that look on Finn's face killed me. The disappointment and anger in his normally sparkling eyes reminded me of how I failed him.

The ache in my chest grew when I headed up the stairs and was met with my cousin's frown. I leaned over and cocked a brow at the shattered lamp on the floor behind my cousin.

"That make you feel better?"

Finn huffed and stomped his foot. "No."

The black lamp with gold embroidery was one of the few things that had survived the fire at Finn's house, and the last undestroyed item he had of his father's. Until now.

"Want me to fix it for you?"

"Yes." His shoulders slumped, signaling that whatever tantrum he was having was over. Now, he just looked defeated and sad. "Silas."

I cursed internally when his gaze met mine. There was that look again. "Yeah?"

"I don't want to go."

"I know," I reached out and tousled his hair. "But you have to."

"Why?"

Because I don't know how to help you.

"Aren't you excited to be around Junior and Maggie more?"

My change of subject seemed to work. Finn brightened up a bit.

"Maggie got a new tea set."

"I know," I chuckled. "You told me."

He told me everything about Shelby's little sister, like Maggie's favorite color was pink, she liked cats and dogs and took two lumps of sugar in her tea. The last one I learned myself when Mase forced me to attend a tea party. Megan Grace was a sweet girl, but holy crap...

Between my best friend and my cousin, I knew way more about that girl than I cared to. Thankfully, I didn't have to hear it from Junior as well. In fact, I was pretty sure he hated her.

My hand twitched as I looked over Finn's head at his suitcases. He had them scattered around the room instead of ready to go in one spot. My cousin was a genius, but his disorganization was starting to pick on my last nerve.

"Did you pack everything?" I asked while placing his suitcases by the door.

"Yes. Oh, wait..." Finn proclaimed and took off down the stairs. "I forgot my watch."

Not sure why he put so much stock in that thing. Ever since Lana gave him that old watch, he carried it around like a security blanket. Lost his damn mind last week when we went out and he couldn't find it. He wouldn't even let me touch it.

I blew out a breath and headed down the hall to my room for a little peace. My thoughts were a jumbled mess. Was I doing the right thing? Should I have tried more? Would Finn hate me forever?

Uncle Sebastian trusted me with my cousin's care. Would he have wanted me to give him to Lou? If anyone could help him, it would be Lou, right?

I couldn't help but feel for Parker and Lana. I was struggling with a twelve-year-old, and they had two helpless babies that literally couldn't survive without them.

How did they know if they were doing the right thing? One wrong choice could fuck someone up for life. No seventeen-year-old should have to make these kinds of decisions.

My old man was pissed when our lawyer read my uncle's will. Fuck, even I was shocked. Why me? Why was I given guardianship of Finn? I was still a teenager, for fuck sakes. I glanced down at the letter in my hand. I'd been reading it all morning and still had yet to find an answer.

Dear Silas,

If you're reading this, it means your aunt and I are gone. I'm sure you have questions. I'd like to start by apologizing. Our choice was in no way meant to cause friction between you and your father, which I'm sure it is.

Finn is all that's left of us now, and while I

love my brother, his main concern will be for the family's reputation. You, my boy, have always loved your cousin and have gone above and beyond for him. That's why he's your responsibility now.

Take care of Finn. Show him that duty isn't all there is to life, and remind him that, despite our many flaws, his parents loved him.

We know you'll do what's right for our son, Silas, and remember a name is only as important as the family that comes with it.

Your loving uncle,
Sebastian

Uncle Sebastian was wrong. Giving me guardianship of Finn didn't cause friction between my old man and me. It caused full-blown screaming matches. Because I was still a minor, and he was my parent, he thought that meant he had control of Finn.

That was the exact reason the courts assigned us a social worker to help handle things until I was eighteen. She thought signing Finn over to Lou was a great idea. The man was a shrink, after all, and well respected.

Mason may hate his dad with his rules and Order bullshit, but I knew he'd do what was best for Finn. He did it for Mase. It didn't matter how many times Mase fucked up or rebelled. Lou was always there.

Every call he got, whether it be from Ashworth or the cops, Lou showed up. He didn't send someone else or tell them he'd deal with it later. He dropped what he was doing and went there himself. That said a lot. In all the years I'd been in school, my parents attended one parent-teacher meeting.

I dropped the letter on my desk and picked up Lucy. She wasn't as high-end as some of the other guitars in my room, but Lucy was my favorite. An old red acoustic Gibson I saw sitting in a thrift store window when I was a kid.

My dad complained when I begged him to buy her. The guitar was beat-up and missing strings. Nowhere near the state of the shiny new toys I had, but I had to have her. Looking at her now, no one would know the condition I'd found her in.

My fingers moved, strumming the strings as I sat down on the edge of my bed. Lucy purred notes through the room, calming my angered soul. I sang my rage out and finally felt some sense of peace.

Until I looked out the window.

Across the back yard, a set of pink curtains were thrown back, revealing a bedroom. The flowery bedspread and wallpaper weren't what caught my attention. My sole focus was on the British crumpet staring out her window.

At first, I thought she could see me too. She was looking over here, but not at me. I knew that glint in her dark eyes. Little Star was staring at something only she could see.

Her eyes closed as she pressed her forehead against the glass. It was such a stark contrast to how I'd seen her carry herself that I couldn't stop staring. Mason used humor and violence as a shield. When that wasn't enough, he turned to alcohol and drugs.

I tipped my head and scanned Star's slumped shoulders. "What ghosts are you hiding from, Crumpet?"

Suddenly Star opened her eyes, spun around, and clicked on a radio next to her. I watched as she began to move her body, hips swaying, while her arms lifted to pile hair on top of her head.

My gaze traveled along her curves to that slender neck I wanted to wrap my hands around. I could almost feel her pulse beating against my fingers.

This wasn't the first time I imagined the look in her eyes while I choked the life out of her. But it was the first time my dick joined in on the fantasy. It twitched, wanting to feel each graceful glide and fierce pop of her hips. Hear the sounds that would come out of her mouth while her face twisted as I made her take every last inch of my shaft.

I tried to look away and find something else to concentrate on, but the longer she danced, the more mesmerized I became.

The little witch was good. Seductive, even. Maybe she wanted me to take her. Use that tiny body and vent out the last ten years of pent-up rage. It was tempting as hell to do. There was one problem, though.

I fucking hated her.

My gaze shifted over to the radio and then back to Star as she dipped her head, twirling her hair through the air like a majestic platinum curtain.

I wonder what song she's listening to?

I shifted Lucy on my lap and plucked at her string, trying to find a beat that matched her rhythm. Was almost there, too, when Mase came waltzing in.

"Hey man. Whatcha doing?"

I grumbled under my breath. Just fucking great. If Mason caught me spying on my neighbor, he'd never let me live it down.

"Did you forget how to fucking knock?"

Mase shrugged. "Wouldn't be the first time I caught you jerking it."

One time this motherfucker walked in on me, and know what he said? *'That's why your arms are so big. It must take some serious muscle to work that thing.'*

I shook my head, wondering why I was his best friend and set Lucy down on my bed.

"You're a pain in my ass."

"I love you bro, but Mason Kessler doesn't swing that way."

I knew someone who would argue with that statement.

"What about Par—" I stood up and stopped, cocking a brow at the familiar tin in his hand. "What is that?"

"Cookies." Mase smiled and crammed one in his mouth.

Biscuits, you mean.

"And Parker was a drunk experiment."

Sure he was. "All three times?"

"What is it scientists say?" Mase lifted his green eyes to the roof while grabbing a fucking cookie. "Trial and error?"

He lifted the biscuit to his mouth, biting into it like my nerves were biting into the back of my brain.

"Where did you get those?"

"On the deck."

"You often eat cookies you found on the deck?" I couldn't believe she left them. Did the little witch think I was going to run over and thank her?

"These are the first ones I've found," Mase shrugged while chewing on another. "Gotta say, they're pretty damn good."

Sure they were. They looked homemade to me. Who knew what she put in them.

I made the mistake of glaring over my shoulder at Star, who was now rummaging through a box.

Mason honed in on my glance like a fucking panther. His lips curled as that mischievous spark poured into his eyes.

"Playing peeping Tom, are we?"

"Fuck off, I'm not peeping," I growled. "Her room is right fucking there."

"Is that why you were staring out your window when I walked in?"

"It's my fucking window." I could stare out it if I wanted to.

The smile on Mase's lips spread. "You like her."

"Like to slap her around maybe," I snorted.

"I knew you were into some kinky shit."

Oh, for fuck...

"Where's your old man?"

He waved his hand over his shoulder, mocking me with the chocolate chip goodness clutched in his grasp. "Outside, talking to your girlfriend's parents."

"She's not my...." I sighed when he popped a cookie in his mouth. All his fucking chewing was starting to piss me off. "Can you stop eating those?"

"Why?"

Because they're my fucking cookies!

My brows knit. What the fuck did I care if Mase ate them? They were just some stupid cookies the neighbor girl made. Let him have them.

"Could it have anything to do with this?" Mason held up a folded piece of paper with a smiley face drawn on it and proceeded to open it up and read it. "Dear Silas, I'm sorry if my bird caused you any problems." He paused to give me a sly look. "Is her bird causing you problems, buddy?"

My face dropped. _I'm gonna kill him._

He cleared his throat and continued. "I hope we can move past this and be friends. Respectfully yours, Star."

I scoffed out a snicker. Respectfully, my ass.

"Isn't that sweet. She wants to be friends," Mase sang while folding the note back up. "And you know what they say about friends... they can come with benefits."

"Did you forget to take your crazy meds today?"

"I'm not the one that wants to bang the girl next door."

That would depend on his definition of that term. Harper had that sweet, innocent, 'don't hurt me' look going on. Some might call her the girl next door. And besides, I didn't want to bang Star. I stole another glance through my window.

Well, maybe a little.

"Just say it." He stepped forward, waggling his head with each word, "I. Want. To fuck. Her."

I crossed my arms and stood my ground. "I don't know what you're talking about."

His gaze dropped down to the hard-on I couldn't hide because my dick was too fucking big.

"You sure about that?"

Motherfucker.

"Give me those," I growled, snatching the tin out of his hand.

"Hey," Mase whined. "Those are my deck cookies."

No, they're not. They're mine.

"Get the fuck out of my room." I shoved him towards the door.

He rolled his eyes and sauntered out, singing, "Geez, someone's moody."

I muttered under my breath and followed.

By the time we got downstairs, Lou was coming in. He straightened his suit jacket and glanced quickly at Mase, who grumbled something in response. Based on the frazzled look on Lou's face, and the way Mase's hand twitched, I'd say they got in yet another argument on the way here.

Things between them had never been great. Lou was strict, which Mase actively rebelled against.

Things got worse when he found out who his biological father was, and without Micha there as a buffer, the Kessler household was basically Chernobyl waiting to blow. And that wasn't counting the fact that Shelby wanted nothing to do with her soon-to-be stepdad.

How Lou managed to keep things from affecting the younger kids was beyond me. As far as I was concerned, the man was a miracle worker, which was exactly what I needed.

I looked over at Finn, who was peeking around the kitchen doorframe. He was almost a teenager but looked so much younger. There was a wide-eyed, scared expression on his face that pulled at my heart.

I opened my mouth to call him over but stopped when Lou held up his hand.

"Hello, Phineas. Are you ready to go?"

Finn's eyes narrowed, making me scrub a hand down my face. The destructive, childish version of my cousin was back.

"I'm not going anywhere."

"That's a shame," Lou said. "Megan will be disappointed."

"She will?" and just like, the anger Finn was openly displaying washed away. "Why?"

Lou explained, "She's been working on your room all morning."

"Well," Finn tightened his lips and let out a sigh, "I wouldn't want to disappoint her."

I stood there stunned, watching Lou and Finn converse. He'd turned my cousin's mood around so flawlessly he made it look easy. Maybe I was doing something wrong?

By the time they were done, Finn was not only excited to go, but Lou had somehow convinced him that it was his idea. He rushed up the stairs to help bring his bags down while jumping around like it was Christmas morning.

While it was refreshing to see him like that, I still wasn't sure if sending him with Lou was the right thing. That, and I didn't want to let him go.

Any doubt I had fled when Finn ran over to me and threw his arms around my waist.

"I don't hate you, Silas."

I choked back my tears and smiled down at him. "I know."

"You'll come visit, right?"

"Of course I will." God himself couldn't keep me away. I swung my eyes Lou's way and added, "This is only temporary."

I knew Lou wouldn't keep Finn away from me. When we signed the papers, he insisted that I was kept in the loop on things like if the school had an issue with my cousin.

They'd not only call Lou but me as well. I still needed the reassurance, which Lou gave me with a nod, while Finn waved and skipped out the door. He was excited to see Maggie. That didn't mean it didn't hurt a little that he left so happily.

Watching him go was gut-wrenching. I wanted to grab him and pull him back in. Instead, I reminded myself that I was doing this for him. So Finn could get better, sleep at night, and maybe kill the monster in his head.

Once Finn was out of sight, Lou walked over to me and put his hand on my shoulder. "There's something I'd like to discuss with you before I go."

Mason scoffed out a snicker and shook his head. Guess he knew what his old man wanted to talk about, and he wasn't too impressed with it.

"Don't start, Mason," Lou blew out a breath of exhaustion that I knew all too well. "We had this discussion already."

"A discussion requires two people's points of view, *Lou*."

"I'm your father," Lou snapped back at him.

Mase had been calling his old man by name since he got out of rehab. We all tried talking to him about it. His only response was, *'He's not my father, remember.'*

Micha was worried about him. Hell, we all were. Mason was

headed down a dark path that started with Harper when we were ten years old. The only thing I could do was be there to catch him when he fell. And he would fall. Hard and fast.

Mase's green eyes narrowed on Lou. "Last I checked, we didn't have any DNA in common."

"I'm still your father, just like Megan will be your sister."

"There's a difference," Mason growled and stormed into the kitchen. "She never lied to me."

I couldn't help but feel for Lou as he released another long sigh and pushed his fingers through his hair. I'd worn that same look of defeat.

"Come, Silas," Lou placed his hand on my back and steered me into the sitting room. "Let's talk."

Chapter 5

Silas

My fingers tightened around the steering wheel. Mason's cocky smirk was pissing me off. I wasn't in the mood for his shit. I was still trying to deal with not being able to see my cousin for a couple weeks. Lou said I needed to give Finn space to settle in.

Logically, it made sense, but school started today. I should be the one dropping him off and making sure he was okay. Finn didn't do well with change, and Midgarden wasn't like his old school. Junior and Maggie would be there, but…

Mase flopped his head back and sighed. "What's taking so long?"

"Since when are you in a hurry to get to school?" I nodded at the guard, who waved us through Ashworth's gate.

"What? I wanna get my learning on, is all."

He wanted to what?

I shifted my gaze and was met with that stupid fucking smile again. Don't get me wrong, there were plenty of things Mason got excited about—school was not one of them.

In fact, this was the first year I didn't have to drag his ass out of bed. When I pulled up, he was waiting outside, bright, chipper, and ready to go.

"What the fuck are you up to?"

"Moi?" Mase sang in an innocent tone. "Why would I be up to anything?"

Because you're an asshole.

"You're always up to something."

"True," he said with a nod. "But maybe this time, I'm just excited for school."

I laughed outright at that statement.

"What? I happen to have set goals for myself. They're important to my recovery, you know."

Uh-huh.

He set goals alright. His first year at Ashworth, his *'goal'* was to bang every girl on the swim team. The second year, it was to drive our Physics teacher into early retirement. Last year, he set his sights on Mrs. Grier. He had yet to accomplish that goal.

"Don't bullshit me, Mase. I know you're up to something." I pulled into the parking lot and eyed his crisp, freshly pressed uniform. "You're wearing your tie."

"I always wear my tie."

Like fuck he did.

"Wrapping it around your wrist doesn't count."

He smirked and shot me a wink. "But it does give me a solid argument."

That argument was that his tie was indeed worn and visible, as per Ashworth's dress code guidelines. Wearing them on his nuts didn't count as visible, no matter how many times he whipped down his pants.

"Edith didn't argue it," he pointed out.

To which I argued, "She was just tired of seeing your junk."

The rest of us referred to Ashworth's receptionist as the Ice Queen. Not Mase. Calling her by first name went with his unaccomplished goal. Just once, I'd like to see Mrs. Grier take him up on one of his many sexual offers. Someone needed to catch him off guard.

"Mason," I let out an exasperated sigh. "This is the first day of school."

He cut me off with a slap on my back. "It sure is, buddy, and I can't wait to get shit started."

Unimpressed, I watched him hop excitedly out of my Hummer. Shit is exactly what I'd be walking into—why was I friends with Mason Kessler again?

"Come on," Mase bent over and looked in at me with sparkling green eyes. "Time to get this show rolling."

Show? Fucking great.

I let out a breath and silently asked God to grant me serenity before I got out and followed Mase into Ashworth. I swear, if there was another barber shop quartet, or strip-o-gram, somewhere around here, my best friend wasn't going to make it through his first day.

Surprisingly, we made it through the front doors without anything jumping out. When I walked down the first hall unscathed, I even started to think that maybe Mase really was excited.

It was our senior year, after all, and Micha wasn't here. He was at college in Miami. Meaning, for once, Mase wouldn't have to live in his shadow.

Mason loved Micha, he really did, but every time someone

referred to him as Micha Kessler's little brother, his jaw twitched. Even I had to admit it was nice to be the older ones for once. We were no longer the tag-a-longs to the kings of the school. We *were* the kings.

We rounded the corner, and I stopped and cocked a brow. Leaning on the wall next to my locker was Lana. She looked down at her watch and blew out a huff of air, puffing her cheeks out.

Was everyone in a hurry today? A better question was, why the hell was Parker's wife waiting for me?

I wasn't babysitting again. The twins were cute and all, but there was something fucking wrong with their son.

Innocent baby, my ass. I saw hell when I looked into Weston's eyes. That kid made me believe in the Anti-Christ.

"Shit," Mase glanced warily around the hall, "you see Riley anywhere?"

Fuck sakes, here we go again.

Why was he still refusing to talk to her? Mase told me what Ryker made him do. Clearly, Riley was over it. Don't know why he was so conflicted. It wasn't his fault. If anything, Mase saved her. Who knows what Ryker would've done otherwise?

"Riley's not exactly the hiding type," I pointed out.

The first day I met her, the girl crushed my nuts. She didn't warn me or tell me to fuck off. She just walked right up, grabbed my sac, and squeezed. The last thing Riley would do was hide from Mason.

"Then what is Lana doing here?"

I shrugged. "Fucked if I know?"

We didn't have to wait long to find out. The second she saw us, Lana rushed forward. "Oh my God, you guys took forever to get here."

Okay?

"Well," she stretched her neck and glanced over our shoulders, "where are they?"

Mason looked just as confused as I was. "Were we supposed to bring someone?"

I shrugged my shoulders in a silent 'I don't know.' If we were, no one told me.

"Oh my God," Lana threw her arms up. "Riley and Shelby."

What the fuck was she talking about?

"What about them?"

"Yeah, Lana banana," Mase agreed. "You're not making much sense here. It's okay." He grabbed her hands and held them firmly while saying, "You just need to calm down and take a breath. Say it with me. Woosah, woosah."

Lana's face dropped with each deep breath Mason took. I might not be the first person to hit him today.

"You good?" Mason tipped his head at a very unimpressed Lana before releasing her hands and waving his own with a very calmly spoken, "And go."

She clicked her tongue and looked up at me with a sigh. "Where are Riley and Shelby?"

"Why would I know?"

"Mason lives with Shelby."

"So?" Mase and I replied in unison.

"Wait… they didn't come with you?" She flipped her dark hair over her shoulder and glanced around. "Damnit, I have to go help Mr. Wagner in five minutes, and I have the best news to tell them. Well, probably not the best news for Riley, I doubt she'll care, but Shelby definitely will."

"Uh-huh?"

Could I walk away?

I wasn't dating her, so why should I have to listen to her? Lana was pretty, and she'd never been anything but nice to me, but the motormouth was Parker's department. He's the one that knocked her up.

"So anyways, there's a couple new students this year, I mean, besides for the freshmen, obviously."

Why is she still talking? Did she think I cared?

"There's this guy and a set of twins that start next week, but the real exciting one…." Lana stopped and cocked her head at Mase. "Are you wearing a tie?"

Okay, that I cared about—I knew I wasn't crazy. Fucker was up to something.

"What?" Mase whined, "Is it that unusual to see me with a tie on?"

Lana eyed him suspiciously while I crossed my arms and arched a brow.

Mase dropped his shoulders with a groan. "Did it ever occur to either of you that maybe I want to start the year off right?"

Lana believed that about as much as I did.

"Sure," she said with an eye roll. "Anyways, I gotta go. If you see the girls, tell them I'm looking for them."

I'll get right on that.

She rushed off down the hall and called out, "And don't tell them about Star Chadwick."

"Whatever you say," I waved and lifted my foot to take a step. *Hold up.* "Did she say…"

That stupid smirk on Mase's mouth grew, spreading across his face, while his eyes lit up.

Son of a bitch.

He was definitely planning on starting the year off with a bang, alright. *Prick.*

"Motherfucker. That's why you were so pumped to get to school. You wanted to see my face when that witch walked down the hall."

"What?" He scoffed, snorted, curled his lip, then gave up his fake objections and nodded. "Yeah, pretty much."

"You could've told me."

Mason threw his head back in a loud laugh.

I was definitely going to be the first person at Ashworth to hit him. Had my fist ready to go, when someone pranced around the corner.

Wrath blazed through my veins as I honed in on Star's face buried in a piece of paper. My teeth ground at the sight of her fingers clutching tightly to the schedule. A schedule for *my fucking school.*

She continued to walk, heels clicking on the floor as her shapely legs glided her along.

As if my day couldn't get any worse, Mase had to remind me of another problem.

"Damn bro, she looks pretty good."

I'd seen that same skirt and shirt on countless girls, and it never looked like that. Each step she took caused the red plaid fabric to bounce off her hips in a tantalizing way. I wasn't into the schoolgirl thing—until now.

"You should fuck her in the storage room."

"I'm not gonna fuck her," I growled back.

"Huh?" Mase tipped his head to roll his eyes over the girl walking our way. "Can I fuck her then?"

Before I had time to think about it, I grabbed Mason's collar and tightened my fist. The only thing that stopped me from knocking the smug grin off his face were the words he quietly spoke.

"Careful buddy, someone's watching."

Still clutching Mason's shirt, I twisted my neck. Not more than a foot away stood Star, staring up at me with shock sparkling in her wide eyes.

"What the fuck are you looking at!"

Star reared back and squeaked. A small, barely audible squeak that shot straight to my dick. I couldn't escape this girl. She invaded my dreams and caused chaos in my neighborhood with her fucking birds. Now she was walking around my school. As if she belonged here.

Well, fuck that!

"What's wrong, Crumpet? Cat got your tongue?"

"I… Uh…" her lips parted with gasps and broken words, "I… what…."

"Didn't they teach you how to talk in England? It's not that hard." I let go of Mase's shirt and clapped my hands in front of her face. "Speak!"

Satisfaction filled my chest as the shock on her face morphed into anger.

"You don't have to be an arsehole." Her accent was thicker when she was angry, which wasn't doing my hard-on any favors. "It's not my fault you lads are having a lovers' spat."

A few quiet snickers echoed down the hall as a smirk spread across my face.

It's on, now.

"No need to be jealous, Crumpet," I bent over to growl in her ear, "I'm as likely to fuck him as I am you."

She stepped back and scoffed up at me. "I don't want you to do anything to me."

"I'm not the one that showed up at your house with a pocket full of condoms."

People in the hall gasped, causing a bright red hue to crawl across her skin, tainting her cheeks and chest.

"Wait…" Mase interrupted, "when you say pocketful?"

"There weren't that many," Star whispered while glancing around.

"They were falling out of your pocket," I pointed out, enjoying the way her mouth fell open.

I liked her like this—shocked and nervous while teeming with anger.

"Damn girl," Mase whistled, "How many dicks have you seen?"

I answered for her. "Apparently, she's a virgin."

"Hey!" Star yelled, then quickly quieted down when a few people turned their heads. "That's personal."

"Had no problem sharing it with me."

"That was… I didn't mean…." Her little foot stomped against the floor.

As much as Mason Kessler pissed me off, sometimes I really loved my best friend. No one could get under someone's skin like Mase could. When he saw an opening, he took it.

"Don't take your virgin frustrations out on us, Sweetheart." Mason held up his hands and cocked his head. "It's not our fault no one back home wanted to take the plunge."

Most girls would be dying of embarrassment by now. That's not what Star's body said. She was blushing, but her shoulders were rolled back, and her head held high. What I really found interesting was the expression that flashed across her face. It was the same confident sneer popular girls wore.

"I didn't want to take the *plunge*," she snarled, finger quoting the word 'plunge.'

"Ah," Mase breathed. "So you're a prude. Got it."

She shrieked, "I am not!"

Guess she wasn't concerned with causing a scene anymore. I glanced down at her fingers digging into the palms of her hands. Then again, girls like Naomi never were. But which one was she? The bitch, or the smiling girl with the sunshine spark in her cheek?

"I have to agree with her," I cocked my head and raked my gaze down her body. *How far am I gonna have to push you, little Star?* "After all, she did offer herself to me."

"I did…" Star stopped, took a deep breath, and reset her calm expression. "You and your wanker friend can toss off. I don't have to bloody well take this."

I grabbed her arm when she tried to march past me and leaned down to growl, "That's where you're wrong. Look around. These are my people. Not yours."

The hall was quiet because everyone around was watching us. Ninety percent of them had already picked a side, and it wasn't hers. Realization settled in Star's features with a loud swallow. She might've been someone at her old school, but she was in my world now.

"Welcome to hell, Crumpet."

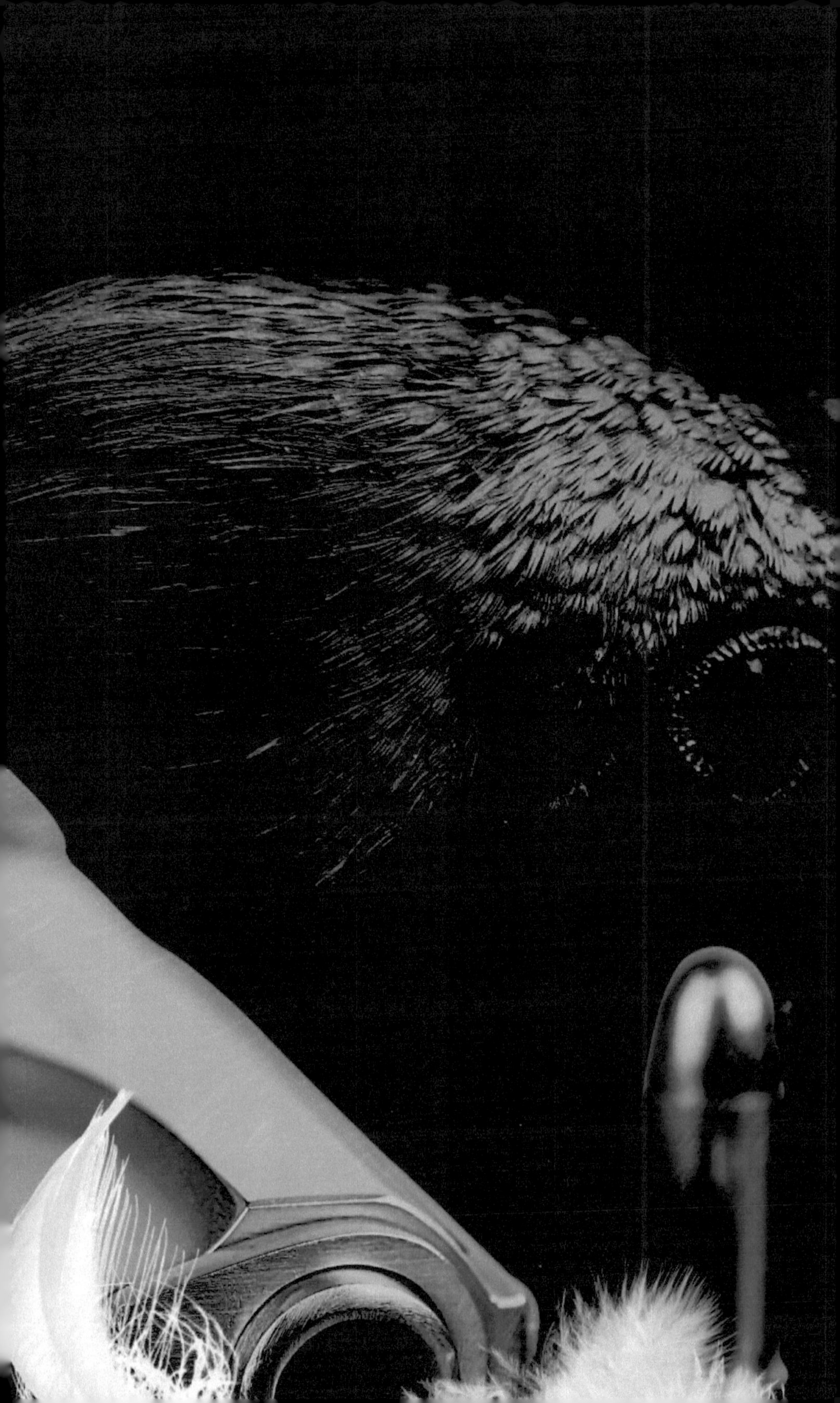

Chapter 6
Star

Ashworth Academy resembled a castle, with a beautiful brick wall and a carefully landscaped exterior. Not much different from my school back home. It was the atmosphere, and people inside that confused me.

I was having a hard time remembering the American terms for everything. Class, not lesson. Teacher, not tutor, and schedule, not timetable. When I asked someone for directions to my next lesson, they stared at me like I was an alien. I suppose I was, a bit. Definitely felt like I was one.

I watched a group of girls dressed in cheerleader uniforms stroll past me and enter the canteen. Not a single one of them bothered to glance my way.

Not everything was different. I was just as much of an outsider here as I was the last few weeks in England. It was amazing how quickly my supposed friends turned on me.

Things were better that way. If anyone should be bit in the arse by karma, it was me. Penance wouldn't come from sympathy or compassion.

Penance shouldn't come at all.

"Are you alright?"

I looked away from the red canteen doors and up to the kindly smile of Ashworth's dean. No, not dean. Principal.

"I'm okay," I reassured him and turned back to the doors I was staring at. "Just taking a minute to right myself."

"Has someone been giving you a hard time?"

Was someone giving me a hard time? I had to suck back my snort to that question. This morning had taught me two things. That someone did indeed reap what they sowed, and that Silas Creswell was the vessel of my penance.

He was in two of my three lessons. So far, he'd tripped me, pushed my books off my desk, and whispered numerous taunts in my ear. In short, yes, someone was giving me a hard time. But I deserved it.

"No Sir," I smiled up at the dean. "Everyone has been very polite."

"That's good. I don't want any of the troubles you had last year affecting your comfort here."

My hand rose to brush over the scar on my chest. Troubles? That was one way of putting it.

He placed a hand on my shoulder and said, "If there's anything you're worried about or afraid of, please, don't hesitate to come and see me." Before walking down the hall.

There was only one thing I was afraid of—I sighed and tipped my head.

The ghosts on the other side of those doors…

. . .

"Look at that." Tatum tipped her chin at a girl shuffling across the floor with a tray in her hands. "Someone got a new sweater."

Ugh. Emily. She was so pathetic. Did she really think those little rainbows on her sweater were cute? No wonder she couldn't get a date. She walked around with her head hung, refusing to look people in the eye. I suppose it saved me from having to see her face. She was still tainting my world with her plainness, though.

Tatum and Christina cackled out a "moo" as Emily came closer.

My eyes flew from the brown hair hanging in lanky locks down to the mountain of food on her tray. It was my duty to help her. The last thing Emily needed was to put more food in that oversized body.

Slipping my foot out, I caught her scuffed-up shoe and yanked her foot out from under her.

Emily flew forward, flinging the contents of her tray as she toppled on the ground.

"Oops," I sang. "You should watch where you're going, Emily. You might've gotten my new shoes dirty."

My friends laughed while I arched a brow at the chocolate milk staining her sweater. That was one problem solved.

The tears were already streaming down her face when Emily pushed herself up and muttered, "Why do you hate me?"

"Oh Emily." I smiled and bent down to tap her cheek. "You don't matter enough for me to hate you...."

You don't matter enough? What kind of person says that to someone? Me, that's who. A vile, wretched thing that didn't deserve to walk this earth. Yet here I was.

Sucking back my guilt, I straightened my shoulders and pushed my way into the canteen. Prepared to face whatever repercussions were waiting for me inside.

Surprisingly, the scene before me wasn't too dissimilar to what I was used to—various groups sat around neat and tidy tables while others moved through a line to collect their lunches.

A few things did throw me off, such as all the varsity jackets. There weren't many sports teams back home. School wasn't the place for that.

That appeared to be the opposite in America. In the short time, we'd been in Ashen Springs, I'd heard more people talk about the football team than anything else. And I still had yet to see anyone kicking around a ball.

Once I had my lunch, I spun around and stopped. Dread chilled my veins as I stared across the canteen at the face of a ghost.

No, not a ghost.

I tipped my head and scanned the curtain of deep red hair, hiding the eyes of a small girl tucked in the back corner. Her shoulders slumped forward as she picked at her food with an exaggerated sigh. She was sad, hiding, and alone.

Just like Emily.

My feet lifted and carried me over to her before I knew what I was doing. I was drawn to her, pulled by a need to do things right this time. If I could help someone, instead of hurting them, then maybe I could become the person I promised to be.

"Hi. I'm Star."

All I did was greet her, but when the girl lifted her chin, and I saw those big doe-like eyes, I would've thought someone slapped her. She wasn't just beaten down. She was bloody well broken.

Something told me she didn't like people getting too close to her, so I nodded at the seat across the table. "May I sit here?"

"Um," she glanced nervously around, then quickly ducked her head while whispering, "Okay."

She didn't say anything when I pulled the chair out and took a seat. Nor did she speak as I settled in. She just sat there, hand tightly gripping her fork, as if she was afraid I was going to lunge across the table.

I reached out to touch her hand and calm her but pulled back when she jerked away. Perhaps it would be better just to talk?

"Do you have a name?"

She shuffled away from my voice. "Um. Harper."

Harper. That was a pretty name for a pretty girl. Why was she hiding herself? She had gorgeous thick curls and beautiful doe-like eyes. Normally, girls like her were beating the fellas off. So why was this one sitting by herself? It didn't make sense.

What Harper reminded me of were the abused birds Mum and Dad had at the sanctuary. Not the ideal teenage girl everyone admired.

Figuring conversation was a good place to start, I opened my mouth but was interrupted when a tray was slammed down on the table

"Who the hell are you?" A girl not much bigger than me dropped down in the seat next to Harper and glared at me. "Why are you sitting here?"

Before I could answer the angry expression on her face, a tall blonde sauntered up and rolled her eyes.

"Relax, Rye, not everyone has malicious intent." She stopped and cocked a brow down at me, "Right?"

I nodded in agreement and took a second to study the girls. The blonde one I'd seen in English class. I assumed she was a cheerleader or something. She had that blonde bombshell look, with sparkling cinnamon eyes and flawless make-up—a lot like the girls I used to call friends.

I glanced over at the blazing dark blues eyes of the one called Rye. I wouldn't be surprised if that one had a knife hidden somewhere. If anyone should be worried about anyone having ill intentions, it was me.

The blonde sat down beside me and smiled, "I'm Shelby."

"Star," I said while eyeing the other one.

She was sitting really close to Harper, who was obviously uncomfortable with it.

"Don't mind Riley," Shelby waved her hand. "I'm convinced she has a permanent case of PMS."

I was inclined to agree.

"So, what made you leave England and come to our little town?"

How did she know I was from England? I'd barely said five words to her.

"You're in my chem class."

"Oh." That explained it, I guess.

Though I didn't understand why they had three separate classes: physics, biology, and chemistry. Back home, we did all of that in science. Wouldn't it be easier to have one lesson, instead of three? But what did I know?

I would've graduated already back home if I hadn't missed half the year. Here, eighteen was the normal age. At least I wasn't older than the other kids in my grade. I thought 'grade' was what they called it?

My attention was diverted when yet another girl joined us. This one had a beautiful caramel complexion and a full head of thick curls.

Also, Harper didn't seem as wary about her. She even smiled a touch when the girl plopped down on the other side of me.

"Oh my God, guys, you'll never guess what happened this morning." She dropped her tray on the table and tossed a grape in her mouth. "So, there's this new British girl in school…."

"Um, Lana." Harper shifted her gaze at me and then back to who I assumed was Lana.

"It's okay to call her British. I checked," Lang sang with a hand twirl.

I'm not sure if it was considered politically correct in America, but I had no problem with it.

"Anyways," Lana sighed. "Word around school is that she got in a little tiff with none other than Mason Kessler and Silas Creswell."

I couldn't help but notice the way Harper flinched when Lana said Mason's name. Maybe he was her ex. Or perhaps he used her and then tossed her away. A lot of blokes my age seemed to do that —part of the reason I had yet to travel down that path.

This time it was Shelby that tried to stop the girl from talking. "Lana…"

But Lana wasn't having any of it.

She just kept on going, singing, "I know. Silas is usually so quiet. Maybe he doesn't like British people or something."

Could be possible. It would explain why he hated me for no reason.

"And that's not the best part…."

"Lana!" All three of the girls called out.

"Calm down," Lana sighed. "I'm getting there. The girl that made straight by the books Silas come out of his shell is none other than Star Chadwick." She sat back, proud of herself, and took a bite of her sandwich. "As in, Chadwick cosmetics."

Shelby's eyes lit up as her mouth dropped. "Your parents own Chadwick cosmetics?"

Lovely. There went my secret identity as the common girl from England.

"Oh my God." Lana jumped back in her chair as if she was startled to see me sitting there. Right beside her. Literally less than a foot away. Lord help the person relying on her to pay attention. "Why didn't you guys stop me?"

Harper dropped her face in her hand, Shelby rolled her eyes, and Riley sighed.

"Do me a favor Lana, before you sit down, give the area a quick scan." Riley waved her hand over the table, "Maybe do a head-count. You know, see who's here before you start talking."

It was Lana's turn to roll her eyes. "I'm not that bad."

"You said my dad was hot," Riley growled.

Shelby looked past me to Lana. "And called me psycho."

"You're dating Logan," Lana muttered. "You can't blame me for thinking something was wrong with you."

I'm not sure who Logan was, but Riley seemed to agree.

She lifted her hand and pointed at Shelby, "She has a point."

Shelby opened her mouth like she was going to say something, then shut it and nodded her head, which made me kind of curious about this Logan fella. Had to wonder about a guy whose girlfriend questioned her own sanity for being with him.

Speaking of questioning one's sanity...

All eyes seemed to turn to the two lads entering the canteen—Silas and his tosser friend. They strutted in like peacocks, proudly displaying their feathers. Heads held high, with their shoulders back, not bothering to give anyone a second glance.

I used to walk into a room the exact same way. As if everyone else should be honored that I'd graced them with my presence. There was one person here that wasn't honored that these two cunts join us.

I glanced over at Harper, who had not only gone back to hanging her head but was also trembling. A large part of me wanted to wrap her up and hide her where no one could hurt her. But hiding wouldn't do anything. Emily tried to hide.

"I've heard so much about your American burgers, I think I'll try one after school. Would you like to come with me, Harper?"

I couldn't help but smile at the shocked look on her face.

"Harper doesn't go out," Riley chimed in.

"Why don't you let her answer for herself?"

The table fell silent as the fork fell out of Riley's hand, and she sat up. "Listen, new girl...."

"No, you listen, I wasn't asking your permission. I was asking Harper if she would like to join me."

Lana muttered, "Shit."

Shelby sucked in a gasp, and Riley sat back and crossed her arms while eyeing me up.

I didn't care what they thought. Harper wasn't a child. She was perfectly capable of taking care of herself. She just needed a little help realizing it. Though Riley did scare me a bit.

After what seemed like an eternity, Riley finally spoke.

"I like you, new girl." She bent over and dug back into her food. "Don't make me stab you with my fork."

Just when everyone started to relax, and I thought everything was okay, Riley shot out of her chair and yelled, "Oh no you don't!"

When I glanced over my shoulder to see who she was glaring at, I saw Mason's green eyes widen.

"If you think you're going to ignore me all year, Mason Kessler, you've got another thing coming. Now, get your ass over here."

Mason stopped mid-stride and glanced down at his empty wrist. "Oh shit, would you look at the time."

"Don't you dare," Riley warned.

That look in her eyes would make me second guess leaving. Not Mason.

"Sorry spitfire, I gotta get to the closet," Mason smiled and started backing towards the door. "Don't want Sandra to start blowing someone else."

He was out the door and down the hall before Riley could call out, "Son of a bitch." After which, she took off after him.

I was definitely afraid of Riley.

My eyes locked on an icy-blue glare across the room.

And maybe a wee bit of someone else.

"You did what?"

My Dad was there when I got home. Said he wanted to see how Finn's first day was. 'Bullshit' was what I said. There were only two reasons my old man ever came home.

Because my mother was here, or to lecture me. This time, it was to try once again and convince me to send my cousin back to his other school, which was when I told him Finn was staying with Lou.

"Go and get him," my old man demanded.

Needless to say, he was less than impressed.

I folded my arms over my chest and leaned back against the marble countertop. "No."

Shocked that I had the gall to flat out deny him, my old man reared back. My parents weren't used to hearing me say no. I did what they wanted. Got good grades, took the courses my old man told me to, and kept the public family image pristine.

The Creswell's weren't just part of the Order. My grandfather was in politics, and my mom was away in Hong Kong filming her next movie, putting both of them in the public eye, along with the rest of us. Scandals brought unwanted attention to everyone.

Two years ago, a picture of my grandfather with a married woman had surfaced, and I couldn't escape the reporters. The meeting was perfectly innocent. The woman was merely a friend of his, which the media spun into a torrid tale of affairs and lies. Grandpa hadn't talked to her since.

So, yeah, I gave a shit about family image, but what was going on with Finn had nothing to do with image. And even if it did, I didn't fucking care. He was my responsibility. I'd do whatever it took to help him. Something I decided the third night I sat up trying to stop him from screaming.

"You don't have the right to decide this."

"Actually, I do," I pointed out. "Uncle Sebastian left me rights to Finn. Not you."

The esteemed Dr. Creswell was three things, controlled, demanding, and calm. Yet his jaw still clenched at my statement.

"Well, I'm your father," he let out a breath and straightened the cuffs of his shirt. "And you're not eighteen yet."

His calm, cool demeanor was crushed with six words. "That's why I gave Lou guardianship."

"What?" he shrieked. "This is… Silas… You can't…."

I sat back and watched his face redden with each word. Did I want to give Finn over to Micha's old man? No. Was he going to hate me for doing it? Probably. I kind of hated myself. But anything was better than letting my father call the shots. There'd be no coming back for Finn if that happened.

He may be a doctor, but he didn't know shit about the mind.

Know what his response was when he found out what Ryker did to me? *'Can't change it now.'*

"Silas," he finally stopped sputtering and pointed an angry finger at me. "You're going to go and get your cousin and cancel the guardianship right now!"

"I can't. As you pointed out, I'm still a minor."

And minors couldn't sign legal documents. Hence why I got Finn's social worker to co-sign the guardianship papers.

"Exactly my point. You can't sign your cousin over."

"Unless," I interrupted. "Gina signed the form as well."

My father's mouth opened, sputtering unspoken words. That was something we both knew he couldn't argue. Gina's sole job was the care and wellbeing of Finn. I highly doubted any court would go against the decision of the professional they assigned.

"Good luck getting him back from Lou," I sang and stormed up the stairs.

Don't know why I was so upset. I knew this was coming, knew he'd be pissed when I told him about my cousin. Who had a name—Finn. He wasn't only known as my cousin or Dr. Creswell's nephew.

I bet that my old man didn't even know that Finn's favorite color was yellow or that he had an irrational fear of spiders. And he wanted to decide his life.

Fuck that.

"Get back here, Silas," my dad called out. "We're not done."

"I've got school tomorrow, *Dad*." According to him, senior year was my most important. I needed to do my best and make the family proud.

What would that be like? Making someone proud? More specifically, my father?

When I was a kid, I tried to get him to smile with my music, but that was a waste of time because music wouldn't get me anywhere in life. Then I'd bring home tests, all which were in the high nineties.

He'd ask me why I didn't get a hundred. No matter what I did or how much *better* I became, I just couldn't seem to get that puffed-up 'he's my son' look.

Pfft, better.

That word haunted me almost as much as the voice constantly calling it out.

Don't worry, little witch— I'll show you just how much better I am.

"Fine, we'll talk about this tomorrow," my old man barked out. "I'm going to Cindy's."

"That's right, go hide out with your whore."

He didn't exactly give me much to be proud about either.

I stood inside my room, balling my hands to stem the rage boiling inside as I listened to his car drive away. My old man was a walking contradiction. Telling me to keep the family image clean while he was out fucking around.

My mother was just as bad. She slept around too. And the really fucked up part, they both knew about it. I heard them one night discussing their sexual escapades. They could do whatever they wanted.

Why the fuck couldn't I?

Snatching Lucy off her stand, I began plucking away, pouring an angry, unrhythmic tone through the room. But no matter how hard I pulled on her strings or what song I sang, I couldn't shake the need to destroy something.

So, that's what I did.

I set Lucy back in her spot and then drove my fist through the wall. Twice. And finally, I felt some relief as my skin tore with the plaster.

Then her voice drifted into my ears. Carried by the wind blowing through the open window.

"Mum, you forgot to lock up Roger."

I marched across the room and glared into the backyard next door. Star was chasing around that fucking peacock while the damn pirate ostrich squawked loudly.

How many goddamn birds did she have? I counted two pens, three cages, and some weird igloo-looking thing.

Two dark-haired little boys wielding sticks ran past Star, screaming like motherfucking banshees.

"Don't you hurt each other with those things." Star waved an angry hand at them. "Do you hear me… Cedar! Elm!"

I cocked a brow. She was fucking kidding, right? Cedar, Elm, and Star? Who the fuck were their parents? The hippies from hell?

Star returned to chasing the bird around, darting across the yard while the peacock scratched at the ground and ducked away as if he was amused by her frustration. Okay, that bird might be alright.

I tipped my head and watched the light hair bounce off Star's back.

Her, however…

My fist tightened, reigniting the ache crawling across my bloody knuckles. What would she look like with red painted on her face? I dropped my gaze to a deep crimson drop sliding across my skin and imagined licking the same drop off her cheek. Then again…

I lifted my head to stare back out my window.

There was another kind of blood I could taste—the pure, innocent flavour of a broken virgin. That was one road I'd never traveled down. My dick was too big. Some experienced girls had trouble, and I always thought I'd be too painful for a virgin. But that virgin…

I slid my gaze down the curve of Star's hip and back up.

I wouldn't mind hurting her.

Fuck.

I grunted and adjusted my stiffening cock. I couldn't shake the thought from my head. The way Star would look with her bottom lip pushed out in a pout and tears streaming down her face.

I didn't just want to hurt her, I wanted to feel it. Hear her cry while I tore my own pleasure from her body.

The setting sun cast a glow across her face, making me think back to that flash of bitch queen I saw in her expression. What was she trying to hide?

I didn't have time to contemplate the answer to that question because my phone went off. Ringing *Frozen's* 'Let it Go.' Fucking Mason. Last week he changed my ringtone to Peter Pan's theme song. I rolled my eyes and shook my head before answering the call.

"What?"

"What's wrong, buddy," Mase snickered on the other end. "Don't like your new ringtone?"

Why hadn't I hit him yet?

"Whatcha doing?"

"Wondering why I'm your friend," I grumbled back.

"Aww," I could see that stupid mocking frown on his face. "Did I interrupt peeping Tom time?"

"Shut the fuck up."

"Hey, I'm not the one playing creeper next door."

Pinching the bridge of my nose, I released a sigh. "What do you want?"

"Are you watching her right now?"

My gaze found its way back to Star, who was bent over the peacock now. Whatever she was doing, I hoped she did it a little longer. Goddamn, that was a firm ass.

"You are, aren't you?" Mase sang in a teasing tone.

"I'm hanging up now."

"No, wait," he called out. "I'm bored. Let's do something."

I could handle a distraction. "Like what?"

"We could go to Ricky's?"

Ricky's was a rundown bar near the docks. I didn't mind it. There was a pretty relaxed atmosphere there, and no one gave us shit. But I preferred going on Fridays when they had a live band. Sometimes I'd even get on stage and play with them.

"Nah, I'm not really in the mood for Ricky's."

"Okay," Mase sighed. "We could go to the springs. There's always a couple chicks hanging around."

Mase's idea of a good time involved one of two things—alcohol or pussy. Whatever. It was something to do.

"Mum..." Star stood up and brushed her hands on her shorts. "I'm going to the market."

"Or, let's see." Mase clicked his tongue. "Logan's in town. We could give him a call."

Logan Hudson was not the first person I would choose to hang out with—I never knew what that crazy bastard would do. However... I stopped and smirked as Star threaded her fingers through her hair. There was one thing Logan was a master at.

"Yeah, give Logan a call."

"What do you have in mind?" Mase smiled.

"You still got those masks?"

Chapter 8

Star

$\mathcal{I}$ could see why Mum liked this town so much. Driving around through the downtown, I couldn't help but notice the beautifully quaint details in the architecture. All of that was enhanced by Ashen Springs' various beaches and lush green plant life.

This place reminded me of one of those artsy towns I saw in travel brochures. The ones with clear blue skies that Craig used to say he was going to move to after graduation.

When everything happened, Craig was one of the few people that came to visit me. I missed my dance partner and felt bad for ignoring his texts and letters, but I was never a good friend. In fact, I was downright mean. He was better off without me in his life.

Just like I'd be better off without this heat.

A sigh of relief blew past my lips as I opened the window,

letting the wind whip across my face. How did people survive these sticky, heavy temperatures? One of these days, I was going to sweat to death. Even the salty ocean air didn't help. I'd pull over and jump in the lake if I knew how to swim.

That was something I should probably look into—there were so many bodies of water around here. Heck, ninety percent of houses had a pool. Even if it would be nice to have something cool to dip my toe in, I was happy Mum managed to find one without a pool. Having a one around Ash and the twins was just asking for something bad to happen.

I turned to glance at the lake passing to my right. Moonlight shimmered off the water's edge, tempting me to pull over and find some relief. Mum and Dad would be getting the boys ready for bed right now. Meaning the house would be utter chaos—the twins running around half-naked while Ash played a game of hide-and-seek.

It wouldn't be the end of the world if I took my time getting home.

Sighing, I continued on my way. As much as I'd like to miss our nightly commotions, I had to get home. Will would stay up waiting for me. Every night, he and I cuddled and read a book. This week's choice was *'A Tale of Two Cities.'*

I brushed the sweat off my brow and turned my Sunfire around the corner. Shouldn't it cool down at night?

A blinding flash of black darted out on the road. I screamed, feeling my heart leap out of my chest, and slammed on the brakes. My tires squealed to a stop against the asphalt as the thing smacked off the hood of my car. The loud bang echoed through the air, along with the pulsing whoosh in my ears.

Oh God, I hit it!

The night stilled as I sat there, tightly gripping my steering wheel. I could hear the quiet rustle of the trees to my left, mingling with the soft lapping of water to my right. But all I could see was the dark, empty road ahead. I held my breath, waiting for a deer or another animal to jump up and run off.

Nothing.

Beyond my own trembling, there was no movement whatsoever.

My gaze dropped to my headlights cutting through the darkness. Maybe it was just a ghost, and I didn't hit anything? Except ghosts haunted your mind, not the road. Taking a breath to calm my nerves, I slowly slid forward and peered over the dash.

There was definitely something there. Whatever it was, it didn't look like an animal. There was no fur or accusing eyes staring back at me. A shiver ran down my spine.

Dead brown eyes with a trickle of blood gliding over the open lifeless orbs.

I squeezed my eyes shut and shook my head. "Calm down, Star. This isn't that bathroom. You're fine."

But I was pretty far from bloody fine. Alone, in the dark, with something on the road in front of me.

Something I hit.

Once again, I peered over the dash. My hand slapped over my mouth, muffling a gasp. The shiny black blob wasn't a blob at all. It was a boot. Dear God, I didn't hit something.

I hit someone!

I flew out of the car and rushed forward so fast that I tripped over the boot and fell face-first on top of the unconscious form. Afraid of hurting them further, I sprang back, smacking my tail bone on the hard asphalt.

The person remained motionless. Shouldn't they groan, or whimper, or something? I tipped my head and eyed the form—pulling my gaze along the black robes, hood, and gloves. There wasn't a single drop of blood, no twisted and mangled limbs, or even the sound of labored breaths.

Come to think of it...

Lifts were one of the hardest things for dancers to pull off. If I learned anything from the many failed attempts over the years, it was that falling on someone hurt. Yet, I was cushioned when I fell on this person.

I pushed my leg out and carefully nudged the figure. The entire thing moved with my foot. Whatever this thing was, it was far too light to be a person.

I crept closer and gingerly reached out to grab their shoulder. My fingers dug into the soft mass. Definitely not a person. That didn't make me feel any better. Because that meant someone intentionally placed it in my path.

Before I lost my nerve, I flipped it over, which was when the hairs on the back of my neck rose. The eerie face inside the hood was drawn on a pillow. It stared back at me with a crooked smile while the warm breeze whistled through the trees and skimmed across my neck.

"Boo."

I screamed and lurched forward along with my heart, then spun around to see who was there.

The road was empty.

"Bloody hell, Star, get ahold of yourself."

There was no one there. I was just hearing things. It wouldn't be the first time ghosts talked to me. Then again—I glanced at the dummy on the ground—someone did have to throw that thing.

I stood up and scanned the forested area to my left and the lake to my right.

"Very funny, you bloody twats. Now come on out before I call the bobbies... I mean, police."

You're in America, Star, not the UK.

There was no response. No movement in the shadows or whispers in the dark. Just the faint chirp of crickets and the croaks of frogs. I suddenly felt extremely exposed, standing out in the open with the beams lighting up my legs. Anyone could be hiding out there.

I took one last look around and backed towards my car, where I could safely tuck myself behind locked doors.

I was wrong. There'd be no safety for me because when I spun around, my blood ran cold. There was a figure dressed all in black, standing next to the open driver's door. And it was a lot bigger than me, by at least a foot. But it was the mask that made me stop dead in my tracks.

The only hint of humanity in the featureless white face, with sunken-in eyes and no mouth, was a pair of sparkling green orbs staring back at me.

I only knew one person with eyes that color.

"Mason, is that you?"

He said nothing, just cocked his head as if studying me. My fear was no longer the issue. My anger was. I'd met some arseholes in my time. Heck, I was an arsehole, but even I had never gone as far as making someone think they ran over a person.

"This isn't funny! I should have you arrested for this." I stomped my foot against the road. "Throwing this thing in front of my car. You should spend a night in jail!"

The only response I got was a quiet snicker, which did not settle my nerves at all. If anything, it spiked the adrenaline rushing through my veins.

When the figure lifted his arm, splaying his hand on the windshield, all I could taste was the bitter flavor of fear rising in my throat. The 'fuck' inked across his knuckles was like a punch in the gut.

Mason didn't have any tattoos. Not that I could remember, anyways.

"Mason?" I croaked out, praying I was wrong.

The figure winked one of those sparkling eyes. "Try again, sweetheart."

Shite.

That deep tone, I did not recognize. Meaning… This man wasn't Mason!

The voice in the back of my head screamed, 'run,' and that's exactly what I did. Until I turned around and saw another figure down the road. This one was wearing a similar faceless mask. Before I had a chance to think about it, I dodged to the left and sprinted for the trees.

All I could think as I sprang over discarded branches and pushed deeper in the foliage was, '*this is how girls in horror movies die.*' But did I turn around and go back? No. I allowed my racing pulse to carry me further into danger, which was exactly what my tormentor wanted.

Something I realized when the quiet night sky echoed with a loud guitar riff. That was followed by the eerily taunting scream of a familiar song. I would never look at Guns n' Roses, *Welcome To The Jungle* the same way again. I just prayed it wouldn't be the last song I ever heard.

Panicked, I searched through the trees for a way to go. I couldn't tell where the music was coming from or the sound of laughter and footsteps. It felt like it was all around, filling the tops of the trees while bouncing off the ground. I didn't know what to do, so I stopped and watched the area around me. Couldn't run from someone I couldn't see.

That was not the best choice I could make.

Dread poured through me when my back hit something hard.

Hot breath trickled past my ear with one word, "Boo."

Instinct drove me, throwing my elbow back into his gut. After which, I rushed forward, only to crash into another figure, who shoved me back into someone else. I was surrounded by three of them, with nowhere to go.

I looked from one to the next, taking note of what I could. All of them had to be over six feet, and two of them had green eyes, while the third had blue.

It wasn't much to tell the police, but it was something and who I would be calling after this. Whatever this was.

"Alright, you pricks." I lifted my tiny fists and braced my feet on the ground. "Let's go."

Was I terrified? Lord yes! But whatever they were going to do to me, I was sure as hell going to make them earn it. I took a few self-defense courses back home.

"She's a fighter," Green Eyes Number One chuckled, "I like it."

Green Eyes Number Two tsked. "Put your claws away, sweetheart. Ours are bigger."

That was the one who was getting it first. Not because he was a smart arse—which he was—but because I knew that cocky tone. Mason Kessler. I lunged forward, slamming my foot against his knee.

"Ah shit," he muttered and bent forward, allowing me to jab my fingers into his windpipe.

Green Eyes Number One keeled over laughing, giving me an opening I happily took. One strike, that's all I managed to get. My fist landed in his side, which was when he grabbed my arm and spun me, locking his arm around my neck.

The truly terrifying part was that he didn't so much as flinch when I hit him. And I hit him hard.

"You're lucky my girl's waiting for me," he tsked in my ear. "Or I'd show you how to really inflict some pain."

I glared back and snarled, "I feel sorry for her."

I swear I could see him smile behind that creepy mask.

"Aren't you a fun little toy? Too bad you're not mine to play with." I cringed away from the feel of latex cooling my cheek when he leaned in to growl, "You're his."

I looked past Mason coughing on the ground to the last one, standing a foot away, with his arms crossed. His intense blue glare penetrated into my very soul. I could feel the hatred coming off him, and when he stepped forward, I knew I was in shite.

Before I could react, Green Eyes Number One shoved me towards my remaining assailant. I slammed into his chest and was assailed with the fresh scent of citrus and rosewood.

"Silas?" My brow furrowed.

Silas tore the mask off his face and smirked down at me. "Boo."

"Oh my God!" I smacked his chest. "Was this your sick idea of a prank?"

I was fuming. My neighbor had been a thorn in my side since I got here, and I'd never been anything but nice to him.

"You can't do that to people!" I took another swing, but he caught my wrist and pulled me up against him.

"I think you'll find there's a lot I can do." His fingers speared in my hair, roughly yanking my head back, so I was forced to meet his gaze. "Especially to you."

"What did I ever do to you?"

His blue eyes narrowed, "You should be more worried about what I'm going to do to you."

I felt his threat in my very soul. He didn't just want to torment me. He wanted to destroy me. A tear-streaked face flashed through my mind. Sad eyes that had lost all spark of happiness. Perhaps I deserved it?

I stared up at the scowl on his face and whispered, "Okay."

"What do you mean, 'okay?' " Silas's brows knit.

"I mean, do what you're going to do."

I deserved it.

"Well, fuck." Mason coughed and pushed himself off the ground. "I thought you'd put up more of a fight. Way to be a killjoy, sweetheart."

There was no point in fighting against karma. The devil always got his penance.

Silas's hand dropped out of my hair as he took a step back to study me for a second before confidently stating, "She'll fight."

No, I wouldn't.

"I just have to find the right button." He took a step forward, causing my throat to bob with a loud swallow. "Isn't that right, Crumpet?"

"Do what you want." I insisted, prepared to take whatever punishment he had planned.

My confidence lasted as long as it took for him to lift his hand and trail his finger over my collarbone. The instant his warm touch grazed the swell of my breasts, I reacted. Slapping his hand away and giving him what he wanted.

His thick lips curved in a crooked smirk that made my stomach flip. "There we go."

The smart thing would've been to stand my ground, straighten my shoulders, and refuse to give them the response they wanted. That's not what I did. Instead of being smart, I chose the stupid action of spinning around and bolting.

My doom came when Green Eyes stuck his foot out, tripping me. Thankfully, all my years in dance allowed me to roll out of it and protect my face. Unfortunately, my taste of luck was short-lived.

Before I could spring back on my feet, Mason seized my hands, stretching my arms out, while Silas crawled over my back. By the time I sucked the air back into my lungs, I was trapped.

Silas pressed his weight down on me and brushed his lips across my ear. "Look around, Crumpet, I could slit your throat and leave you here to rot. No one would ever find you."

A tear slid down my cheek because he was right. My parents and brothers would never know what happened to me. They'd spend the rest of their lives searching, thinking that I ran away. I might be dead, but they would be destroyed.

"Don't worry. I'm not going to kill you…yet."

"Let me go! And I won't tell anyone." I pleaded.

"Tell who you want," Silas growled. "No one will give a shit."

My parents would, and so would my brothers. I may not have much, but I had them. And they were all I needed. If nothing else, I had to make it through this for them.

A familiar voice roared through my system, drowning out the guilt and spiking my survival instinct.

Pull your knickers up, Star. He's just some teenage twat. Don't take his shite.

My chin lifted, rolling my glare up to a smiling Mason. "Are you gonna go first, or let your friend have me?"

"Oh no," Mason tipped his head with a chuckle. "This is his rodeo."

"Of course it is," I scoffed back at him, "You seem like the following type."

That made his jaw twitch.

There was something my assailants didn't know about me. Even if I hadn't learned that Mason Kessler had an older brother, I would've known. He had the classic signs of a younger sibling who was over-compensating. Walking around with his chest puffed out like he had something to prove.

I might not be able to beat them physically, but I could read them. And sometimes, words did more damage. They destroyed Emily.

Green Eyes barked out a laugh. "Aw, look at that. She does have some fight after all."

"What are you laughing at?" I rolled my face along the dirt floor to sweep my gaze over Green Eyes' chuckling form. "Let me guess. Daddy issues?"

He instantly stopped laughing and tipped his head down at me. The rage burning in his glare told me I'd hit the nail on the head.

He tipped his chin at Silas. "If you don't shut her up, I will."

"Go ahead, Silas," I twisted my neck to glance over my shoulder. "Shut me up."

One-touch—that's all it took to make the old Star fall back into the recesses of my mind.

Silas smirked and slipped his hand under my shirt. Sliding his warm palm over the curve of my hip. I sucked in a breath, attempting to stop the shiver wracking my body. But he felt it, and so did Mason.

"Oo, I think she likes that," Silas sang while leaning down to press his firm chest against my back. "Do you like that, little Star?"

"No," I whimpered and pressed my face into the ground.

All I could feel now was the heat coming off his body. How heavy he felt pressing against me. And it was doing things to me. Making me feel things I didn't want to feel. Not for him.

His soft mouth skimmed along the nape of my neck, pulling a gasp from my lips. Mortification burned a path across my skin as I silently cursed myself and Mum.

Because she was worried that I hadn't explored my sexuality yet, she brought home videos. I ignored most of them, but there was one that I watched. One scene, in particular, fascinated me.

A girl at camp, running through the woods from four guys. I was fascinated by the fear in her face as they chased her, and then again when they caught her and her expression twisted in pleasure. Now my body was reacting because of that movie.

Why couldn't I have normal parents who tried to dampen my teenage hormones?

Mason laughed. "I think she wants you to fuck her here, buddy."

"No." Silas sat up and let out a breath. "The only time she'll see my dick is when she's choking to death on it."

And then they were gone, just as fast as when they came— leaving me alone to wallow in my shame.

That little witch haunted me all night. I couldn't shake the way she felt under me. Every twitch, huff, and tremble lingered on my fingertips. It didn't matter where I went—the sweet smell of her fear tainted the air.

Our little game in the woods was supposed to blow off some steam, not build it up. I went to bed with a stiff cock, and woke up with a harder one.

My morning wasn't any better. The first thing I saw when I dragged my ass out of bed was Star. She was prancing around in front of the window in nothing but a pink shirt.

On the upside, I was finally able to take care of my problem. Ten strokes later, my satisfaction exploded in a fury that still had my knees shaking.

I sat back, kicked up my feet, and sipped my coffee. Part of me was starting to think Star really was a witch. I fucking hated her but couldn't stop staring at the purple underwear she had on today.

Breasts should not look that good. The creamy, supple mounds of flesh cradled perfectly in lace fabric made my mouth water. And don't even get me started on the thong wrapped around her hips.

My only regret was that she didn't put those on in front of the window. She did everything else out in the open, so why not get dressed? Last night, I watched her dance with tears streaming down her face. It was hauntingly beautiful like her.

My head tilted, sliding my gaze over Star's flat stomach. The little pink star tattooed above her belly button made me snort.

How fucking cute.

There was something incredibly sexy about a girl with tats. Not too many, otherwise no one could admire their curves without being distracted. But a few cute little tasteful ones…I found myself scanning her exposed skin, wondering if she had any more.

The window wasn't big enough for me to see below her hips. That, or she was too short—sure didn't act short, though. What the fuck was she thinking, raising her fists like that? Someone as small and easy to control as Star didn't stand a chance against one man, let alone three.

Some might call her brave. I called it stupid. How many times did Riley's mouth get her in trouble, and Star was shorter than her. Not by much, mind you, but still…

Girls like them needed to be taught their place. Otherwise, they'd get hurt. Micha did it for Riley. Well, he kind of did. At least she didn't go around crushing guys' nuts anymore.

Took me weeks to stop tasting bile in my throat after that. Preston would've cut her hands off. Micha's lucky I didn't hit her.

Once again, I glanced through the window. She was in dire need of humility lessons. Lucky for her, I was more than happy to play teacher.

"Silas, are you still here?"

I dropped my head back and groaned.

Great. Dad's home.

School didn't start for another hour, but fuck it. No time like the present, right?

"Just about to leave," I called out while taking one last look out the window.

See you at school, Crumpet.

I left my room and headed down the stairs, hoping to avoid the old man. Apparently, he had other ideas.

He stepped in front of me at the bottom of the stairs, cutting me off. "Where are you going?"

"School." I arched a brow at the navy tie around his neck. He was dressed for work, all prim and proper in a suit. What the hell was he doing here? "Don't you have a practice to run?"

"It can open a little late."

I scoffed. *Yeah, right.*

The last time he opened up late, it was because an accident held him up. I had to listen to him bitch about it for weeks. God forbid some poor fucker had a bad taste of luck that inconvenienced my old man.

"Fine," he rolled his eyes. "I forgot my phone last night."

That's more like it. Dr. Creswell always came before Dad.

"Better hurry," I shook my head and shouldered past him. "Don't want to keep your patients waiting."

"Silas wait...about your cousin?"

Should've seen that one coming. He probably spent the last two days trying to find some legal argument to get his hands on Finn. The great Martin Creswell didn't like to lose. Especially to Louis Kessler.

Our King of Kings wasn't doing a proper job, according to my father. He should have a tighter leash on his son. Mase would disagree. His life was spent fighting against the leash his old man kept tightening around his neck.

"I think we should talk about your decision."

"There's nothing to talk about." I grabbed my bag and stepped outside before he could say another word.

He didn't follow me. And why would he? I wasn't sick or in need of medical assistance. Aside from his patients, the only other person to attract my father's attention was his slut receptionist.

I wonder how keen he'd be on sleeping in her bed if he knew Mase fucked her every Thursday while he was going over the books? An ongoing date that I'd arranged.

One thing the Order taught us was that everybody had skeletons in their closet, that they'd do just about anything to keep hidden.

A few more pictures and my father's mistress would have a sudden need to change careers. Just like Mr. Thompson did last year. We enlisted Jasmine for that one.

I thought back to the first time I saw Star in her bedroom. The way that spark faded from her eyes as she stared out the window made me wonder one thing—who or what was she hiding from?

Whatever it was, I'd find out. There was one problem with hiding skeletons in a closet. Eventually, someone will open the door.

I pulled my keys out of my pocket, then stopped, arching a brow. A kid was standing next to my Hummer. A boy around Finn's age. Maybe a little younger.

The sun was glinting off his platinum hair as I scanned the grey slacks and vest of a uniform. The same one my cousin wore to school.

"You lost, kid?"

He lifted his chin and narrowed a pair of dark eyes. "You made my sister cry."

His sister? Who the fuck...

It was then that I realized who this kid was. I should've seen it before. The resemblance was uncanny. Same light hair, dark eyes, and fair complexion as a certain little witch. How many fucking brothers did Star have?

"Look kid, I'm not in the mood for your shit."

"I don't give a shite what you're in the mood for. Nobody makes my sister cry."

Thinking he was joking, I almost laughed. But the little fucker was completely serious. Kind of respected that. It took a lot of balls for someone his age to stand up to a guy like me. Maybe there was hope for someone in that fucked up family.

"What's your name, kid?"

"Cy."

At least it wasn't a fucking tree.

"You better leave my sister alone."

"Oh yeah?" Returning his glare, I crossed my arms and barked out. "What the fuck are you going to do about it?"

His eyes locked on mine, sending a chill down my spine. I wasn't disturbed. I was used to that. I grew up with Logan, and there was no telling what that crazy bastard would do.

Staring into this kid's eyes unsettled me, which was worse. Exactly two people had made me feel that sensation of wrongness crawl across my skin—Preston Whitley and this kid.

"This your ride?" Cy asked, tipping his head at my Hummer.

"Yeah. So?"

The last thing I expected was for him to pull out a knife. It wasn't enough to make him look threatening. He did manage to shock the shit out of me when he looked me directly in the eye and stabbed the blade in my tire.

"What the fuck?"

"Stay away from my sister," he warned again.

The air hissed out, pulling on the rage I kept locked away. This motherfucking kid just slashed my tire. And not like other kids would do it. Slinking around at night, when no one could see them. No, this son of a bitch wanted me to see it.

He stabbed that shit right in front of me without a goddamn care in the world. If he thought I made his sister cry last night, just wait until I got my hands on her today.

"I don't think you're hearing me." Cy did it again—pulled the blade out and stuck it through the rubber a second time. Making extra sure my tire would flatten. "Leave my sister alone."

Fuck Star. I was going to kill her brother instead.

"You little…"

He was saved by the sound of a female voice.

"Cy!"

The kid went from devil to angel in point two seconds. Pocketing the knife, he washed a rosy spark in his cheeks before a woman ducked her head through the shrubs. Their mother, I guessed, based on the almost white hair.

"There you are." She stole a quick glance at me and then waved at the kid. "Bloody hell, Cy, didn't you hear me calling?"

"Sorry, Mum. I was just letting our neighbor know he had a flat tire."

This little shit.

I was too stunned by the bright cherub-like smile on his face to say anything. Even if I did say anything, this bitch wouldn't fucking believe me. I barely believed it.

Right now, the motherfucker literally looked like one of those innocent kids painted in churches. For fuck sakes, his eyes were twinkling.

"Well, it's very nice to see you being helpful, but we're going to be late." She disappeared back the way she came, calling out, "Come on."

"Coming Mum." He skipped after her and paused long enough to glare back at me while dragging his finger across his neck.

I stood there staring at my flat tire with my mouth open.

Did that just fucking happen?

* * *

Some days, I despised Ashworth's uniform. Today was one of those days. It was especially hot out. Students trickled across the parking lot, fanning themselves in an effort to escape the sun bouncing off the asphalt, while Mase and I stood by my Hummer.

I looked over at his half unbuttoned shirt to the tie wrapped around his wrist. At least some things were getting back to normal.

Mase smirked and threw a wink my way. "You wanna lick my pecs?"

"Fuck off," I grumbled and scanned the parking lot.

"What the hell is wrong with you? I've been talking about the fine piece of ass I got last night, and you haven't said two words. You're not even paying attention."

My brow rose. "When do I ever pay attention?"

Guess what Mase did on Thursdays? And then again on Friday and Saturday? He might take Sunday off. Every weekend, there was only one thing on my best friend's mind. Getting his dick wet.

Quite frankly, I was surprised there were still girls in this town that he hadn't defiled.

"Well..." He tipped his head up, squinting against the bright morning sun. "You did shake your head last week when I told you about that chick I banged after the fight."

"That's because you're an asshole."

Beating his opponent to a pulp in the ring wasn't enough for my best friend. No, he had to fuck his girlfriend right after. Way to drive the nail in further.

Why was I friends with him?

"One could argue that she was the asshole in that situation." He shifted his gaze my way. "I didn't come on to her."

He had a point. What kind of girl decides to fuck the guy that just beat the hell out of her boyfriend? There was only one word to explain that situation. Fucktastophy.

"And man, did I use that asshole."

I groaned and rolled my eyes.

"See," Mase threw his finger up. "That's what I'm talking about —you're extra grumpy. Well, you're always grumpy, but today it's like someone pissed in your cornflakes."

Oh, for fuck sakes.

I leaned back against my Hummer and crossed my arms. Mason, of course, wasn't going to let it go. He smirked up at me while nudging me with his elbow.

"*Did* someone piss in your cornflakes, buddy?"

"You could say that." My eyes narrowed on a Sunfire rolling into the parking lot. "Some kid slashed my tire."

Most people would ask who the little shit was or if I caught his ass.

Not Mase. He just let out a loud "Ah," and nodded his head. "That's why you were late."

"I wasn't late," I barked out.

His green eyes rolled. "You were late for you."

He had me there. But to be fair, I had to be early to drag his ass out of bed. That fucking kid was going to get it.

My eyes locked onto the thick head of platinum hair climbing out of the Sunfire.

Maybe someone else would get it instead.

"Do you have any idea how long I waited under the covers with that super soaker?"

Wasn't sorry I missed that. Last time the fucker put blue dye in the water. I suppose it was better than pink.

"Too bad," Mase snickered. "I would've loved to see the look on your face."

Whatever.

I rolled my eyes back to Star while he continued to talk about his wasted ambush plan. Her lips were extra plump today and glistening with a pink sheen. That's not what I was staring at—all that light hair on her head was piled up, exposing her neck.

I tipped my head, following the delicate lines to the beating rhythm next to her birthmark. How hard would that pulse when my hand was wrapped around her throat?

Star continued walking across the parking lot, drawing my attention to someone else. Riley and Shelby were by the front doors, with Logan leaning back against the wall. I'd say, by the look on his face, his girl was in the middle of another talking tangent.

The only other person who could spew out as many words as Shelby was Lana. When those two got going, no one knew what was going on.

The second Shelby saw Star, she grabbed Riley's hand and skipped over to her. Which was when I smirked and nudged Mase.

"Check it out," I nodded at Logan, slowly following his girl, "who do you think will hit him first? Star or Shelby?"

Logan's face was hidden behind a mask last night, but that smug fucker wouldn't be able to keep his mouth shut. His eyes were already twinkling.

My parking spot was close to the front of the school, something I was appreciative of when they met Star at the bottom of the stairs.

Shelby smiled, Riley groaned, and like the asshole he was, Logan chuckled. "You look a lot better without the branches and leaves in your hair."

Star's face dropped as charged forward with her finger raised. "You!"

Shelby's brows knit. "You two have met?"

"This bloody tosser and his wanker friends chased me through the woods last night."

"Calm down, sweetheart. We were just having a little fun."

"Fun," Star shrieked. "You made me think I ran over someone."

Shelby's eyes went wide. "Logan! Why would you do that?"

Don't know why she was surprised. If anyone should know how unhinged Logan was, it was her.

Mase leaned back and crossed his ankles. "Star and Shelby are the least of his worries."

He tipped his chin at Riley, who did not look impressed. Then again, when did she ever? Which got me thinking…

I scanned her black ponytail and thought back to the night Mase confessed what he considered his darkest sin. That's why he wouldn't talk to her because every time he saw her, he was reminded of how much he enjoyed what he did.

It wasn't the girl he got off on. It was the act. An act I was starting to wonder about myself.

"You ever do it again?"

Mase's lip curled in confusion. "Do what?"

I answered him by nodding at Riley. It didn't take him long to catch my meaning.

He folded his arms over his chest and let out a breath. "Why?"

"Just curious." I shrugged and swung my eyes back to Star.

I had to do something, or these constant hard-ons were going to kill me. But did I have to do it with her?

"I've played around a bit," Mase sighed. "But it wasn't the same. Their eyes didn't have that—"

"Fear?" I finished for him.

Mase's green eyes flew to mine. "Yeah?"

We stood there staring at each other for a few minutes before Mase asked me, "You sure it's not the girl that's making you ask this?"

His dark head tipped towards the blonde who turned her back to Logan, called him a cunt, and marched up the steps to Ashworth.

I shrugged. Maybe? I'd never hated anyone like I did her, and what better way to destroy someone than by taking everything pure they had?

Star twisted her neck and glanced back at us. Dark eyes glimmering with nervousness had my cock hardening. The best part came when she tripped up the last step and stumbled inside the school.

It was definitely the girl.

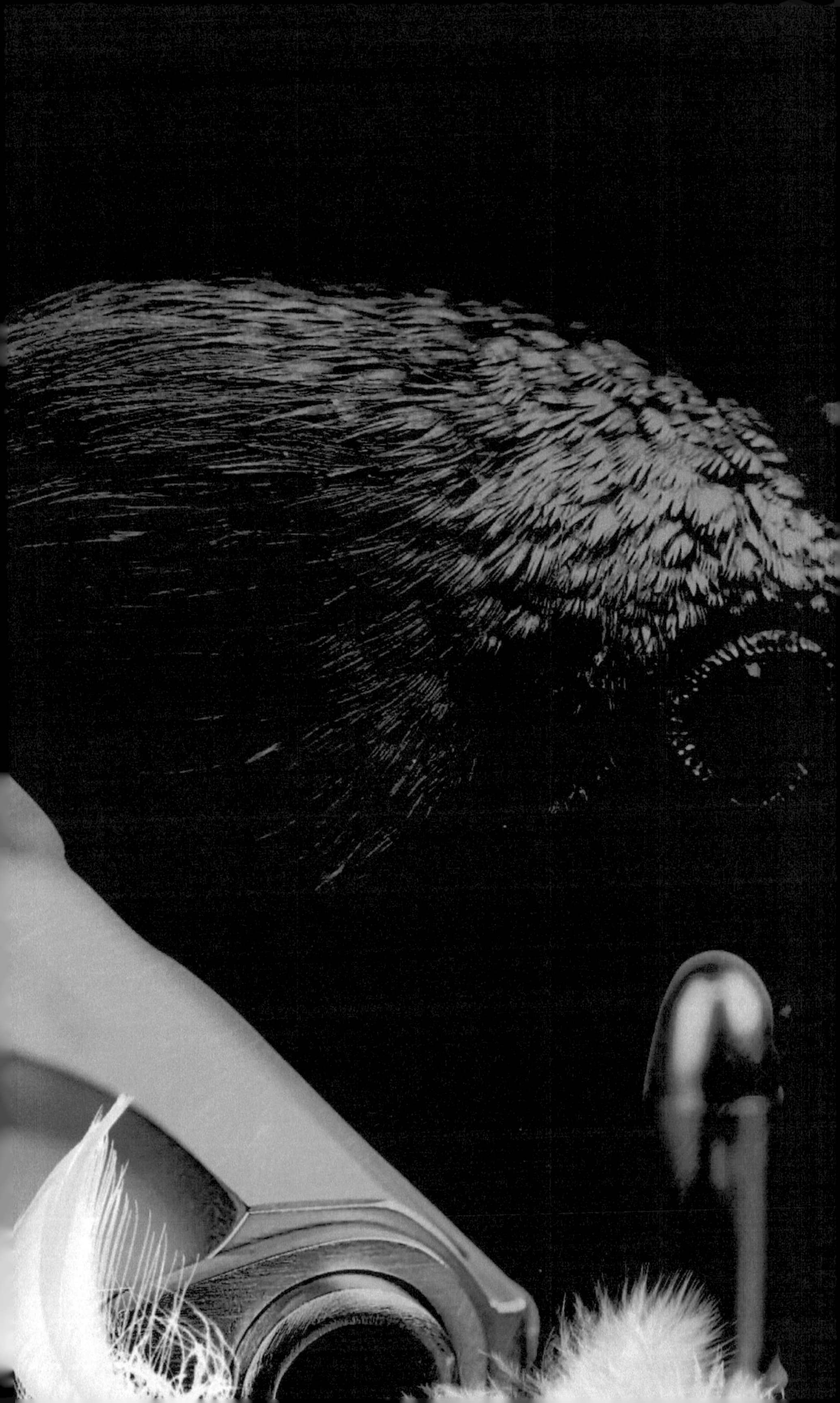

Ashworth's library was unimpressive. It had the aesthetics the rest of the school did—big cherrywood shelves, with ornate busts and paintings and comfortable deep red armchairs.

But it was small. I couldn't remember the last time I was in a library with only one floor. Then again, this wasn't the typical place I would lounge around in.

I glanced at the deep wood-paneled walls and huffed out a sigh.

Maybe that was a good thing?

My last period was study hall, which I still wasn't sure had a purpose. I'd never get used to the American school system. Why not simply send me home early, where most people studied.

An elderly woman sitting behind a desk smiled at me. "Hello, dear. I'm Mrs. Smith. Can I help you find something?"

I was oddly excited to meet a Smith. It was a very American name. I thought I'd have met more by now.

"I'm here for study hall?"

Maybe she'd be able to give me some direction?

"Ah, I see. You're the new student from across the pond."

I couldn't help but return her smile. My home country had been referred to as England and Britain. I had yet to hear anyone use that term. It was relaxing, which was nice after the day I had. Silas Creswell had become the unbearable thorn in my side.

This morning I opened my locker to find it stuffed full of condoms. In third period, he tripped me as I was slipping past him to my desk.

Then this afternoon, after lunch, he shoved me in a storage closet and locked the door. Luckily someone passed by and heard me banging. Otherwise, I'd probably still be in there.

"I take it they don't have study hall in England?"

I shook my head.

"Well," Mrs. Smith sat back. "What you're supposed to do is find a quiet place and study for tests or go over your lessons."

"What I'm supposed to do?"

"Between you and me," she leaned across her desk as if she was getting ready to tell me some big secret, "most kids just play on their phone or talk."

Ah. So study hall really did have no purpose.

"Got it." I gave her a thumbs up and looked around for a quiet corner I could play my game in.

I was dying to try out the new version of Mahjong I'd downloaded. The game might have me slightly addicted. I finished the last one in three days. It was quite an accomplishment. There were over four hundred levels.

The haunting voice in the back of my head laughed. I couldn't help but agree with my own mockery. Instead of getting out there and living my life, I was hiding at home, matching tiles in a game. But who would I go out with? I didn't have any friends here.

How far the mighty have fallen.

My eyes landed on the back of a blonde sitting at a table in the far corner.

Maybe I did have a friend?

Shelby seemed happy to see me this morning. Until that twat sauntered up, that is. A twat that just so happened to be her boyfriend.

I overheard a few girls talking about the great Logan Hudson when I stormed inside. The entire morning, his name was all I heard, buzzing down the halls and whispered in classrooms.

Everyone in this place seemed to like him. But I grew up with lads like him, flashing their charming smiles to get what they wanted. Nine times out of ten, what they needed and what they wanted were polar opposites.

Kind of like Shelby. She was a contradiction in every way. That tall, beautiful, blonde girl was born to be a model.

Yet, she had no interest in popularity. Plus, she was quite possibly the sweetest person I'd ever met and just the kind of person that shouldn't be my friend.

Straightening my shoulders, I headed over to where she was sitting and slipped into the chair across from her. "You don't mind if I sit here, do you?"

"Absolutely not," Shelby beamed brightly back at me. "I'd love the company."

I'd learned a few things in the short time I'd been around Shelby. She was a chatterbox, who for some reason, chose Riley as her best friend—I was still unsure about her, and lord help the person trapped in a room with Shelby and Lana.

Never seen anything like I did yesterday afternoon. Words were spewing across the table at faster than light speed.

By the time the bell rang, my head hurt from trying to keep up —part of the reason I chose to eat my lunch outside today.

Needless to say, I kind of expected Shelby to take the lead in our conversation. But she didn't. She just tipped her head down and furrowed her brows.

It wasn't any of my business, and I probably would've left it alone if the glint in her bright eyes didn't remind me of someone else. Sad brown eyes that didn't have anyone to talk to during lunch.

"Are you okay?" I reached across the table and laid my hand on hers. "You don't seem like yourself."

She let out a small sigh. "Can you keep a secret?"

"I'm the queen of secret-keeping." She had no idea how true that statement was.

"I think I got married."

Okay? That wasn't what I was expecting.

"What do you mean, you *think* you got married?" In my experience, that was something people tended to remember.

"Well, Logan came home to see me yesterday, which was super sweet."

That made me roll my eyes. Yeah, he did such sweet things last night.

Shelby was quick to defend him. "I know he was a jerk to you, but I swear he's not always like that. Well… he kind of is, but he has his good points. He's incredibly protective and adorable with his baby sister, but if he brings me one more unicorn, I swear to god…."

"Shelby," I called out, interrupting her.

She stopped and looked up at me, confused.

"The marriage?" I explained.

"Oh, right. So Logan came home and took me out for dinner at this superb restaurant, and I totally recommend the clam chowder. It was so good, and they have these cute little tables set on the beach, all lit up with candlelight…."

Dear lord, I've awoken the chatterbox.

"After that, we went for a walk where he told me about school and stuff, and I told him about you, because oh my god, Chadwick Cosmetics, I still can't believe it.

Anyways we somehow wound up in this chapel, which had the most adorable little girl playing the piano. And then I was married. I'm really not quite sure how it happened?"

I sucked in a breath and took a second to process everything she'd just said.

"Were you knackered?"

Shelby raised a brow. "I'm not sure what that means, so I'm gonna go with no."

"Did you drink alcohol?"

"Oh," she shook her head. "No. But can I just say… Knackered, so much more sophisticated than drunk off my ass."

I agreed with her there.

"Okay then." I paused to think, "Did you do any drugs?"

"Are you kidding? Coach would kill me."

I didn't take Shelby to be an athlete.

"So you were of sound mind and body when you took your vows then?"

She nodded.

"And you don't know how it happened?"

"That's right."

Huh?

"Yeah, I don't know what to tell you."

"See." She slapped the table. "How does someone get married, knowing they were getting married, but not knowing they got married?"

My mouth opened and then closed as I scoured my brain for a logical reason to give her. Problem was, I didn't even understand what she said. Knowing, but not knowing, yet still doing it.

"Yeah, I got nothing."

"You're where I'm at then."

If she was referring to the headache of confusion clouding my brain, then I was definitely where she was.

"Okay," I said, needing to move on before my head exploded. "Do you love him?"

"With all my heart."

My lip curled. She really loved pretty boy arsehole? To each their own I guess.

"If you love him, then you should be happy," I pointed out, hoping she was just the tiniest bit that she was confused. I liked Shelby. Her boyfriend, or husband, however…

"I know." Her chest lifted with a long sigh. "But we're so young."

"So?"

Her eyes rolled up to meet mine. "You don't think that's a problem?"

"No." I shrugged. "My mum was sixteen when she married my dad, and they're still happy as the day they met."

"Really?"

I nodded.

"Don't pay attention to statistics. They weren't designed for you, or me, or that bloke over there." I nodded at a fella across the room. "Every person's different, and so is their situation."

Something I learned far too late.

For the first time since I sat down, Shelby looked relieved. The stress melted out of her shoulders as she gave me a small smile.

"Thanks, Star."

I was only stating facts, but glad I helped at the same time. It felt nice to make someone smile instead of cry. A feeling I didn't get to enjoy long because Lana came out of nowhere, making me jump in my chair.

"Oh my God, I've been looking for you everywhere."

My face dropped in my palm as I let out a breath. I swear the girl was a ninja. I never saw her coming until her voice was ringing in my ear.

"What's up?" Shelby sang.

"Parker's been up all night with Winslow. She's teething and absolutely miserable. I want to cut out early so he can get some rest. Can you take Harper home?"

Parker? Why did I know that name? Oh wait, he was the lad with the wee ones. Was Lana his wife?

"Sorry." Shelby frowned. "I have practice. Did you ask Rye?"

Riley scared me. I couldn't imagine Harper would be too comfortable alone in a car with her.

"After last time, Harper refuses to get in a car with her," Lana let out a huff of air. "She says Riley has road rage."

I could see that.

"I could take her."

They both stopped and looked at me.

"Really." Lana's brow arched in skepticism. "You don't mind?"

"Not at all."

"Okay, I'll let her know. Thank you."

"Of course." The bell rang, signaling the end of this useless period, "Oh and for the wee one, blend up some of her favorite fruit with a pinch of cloves, and then freeze it in cubes she can suck on. Worked like a charm for my baby brother."

A large smile spread across Lana's face. "Thanks, Star."

"No problem," I said and stood up to gather my books.

Maybe America wasn't so bad after all?

* * *

Harper was waiting for me after school. Well, waiting might not be the right word. She was standing by the doors with her head hung while wringing her hands, which she was still doing. Honestly, I was a tad surprised that she got in my car.

Her desperately entwining fingers tugged at the heavy feeling in my heart. She was so much like Emily, frightened, sad, and alone.

I may not have made her this way, but I was just as guilty as the person that did. Reaching up, I grazed my thumb over the scar on my chest. Only a horrible person would hurt someone so sweet.

Or a monster.

I looked over at the curtain of hair hiding Harper's face and forced my lips to curl in a smile. "I love your hair. Is it natural?"

While the compliment was meant to strike up a conversation, I really did mean it. Harper's hair was a rich cherry red with perfect curls. The kind that most girls would pay a fortune to fake.

My brow cocked at her answer.

"I'm not allowed to dye my hair."

Parents being against tattoos or piercings, now that I could understand. But not letting their daughter color their hair... That was just odd. Maybe Harper's parents were simply more conservative than most?

I'd never seen her wear any make-up, so it would make sense. Besides, who was I to talk? How many parents encouraged their teenage daughter to shag the bloke next door?

"It's beautiful." I reached out to run my fingers through her soft curls but pulled my arm back when she lurched away. "Do you style it yourself, or does your mum help you?"

I knew it was a silly question. What girl our age didn't know how to style hair? Maybe Riley, although I'd guess that was more out of not caring than not knowing how.

"My mom is...gone."

"Does she work out of town?"

Her one-word answer made me feel like a complete arsehole.

"No."

Well shite.

A big part of me wanted to ask what she meant by gone. Did her mum leave, or had she passed on? The small breath she released made me decide to keep my mouth shut.

The last thing I wanted to do was push her deeper into her cloud of misery. Sadness and desperation seeped into a person's soul, tainting the brightness within until there was nothing left. I'd seen the crushed void left behind.

"We should go to the beach this weekend." I may have destroyed Emily, but maybe I could save Harper. "I found a lovely lake the other night."

Or rather, drove by it before a bunch of arseholes chased me through the woods.

"What?" Harper's head snapped up, eyes wide. "I can't go to the beach."

"Why not?"

"I-I just c-can't," she whispered.

"Of course you can," I argued. "Don't worry. I won't keep you out past your curfew."

She really started to panic then. "B-but... I-I... what i-if..."

I'd never seen somebody so against going out. Even Emily attended functions and wandered the shops in town. The haunting echoes of a ghost-filled my mind.

Brown eyes lying empty in a pool of blood.

If Harper was this terrified already, how long until she met the same grizzly fate?

I couldn't let that happen. Not again.

"Nonsense," I said, trying to sound calmer than I felt. "I'll pick you up Saturday morning."

"B-but..."

"Don't worry." I smiled at her and pulled into the driveway of the address Lana gave me. "We'll have a great time."

Her stark white face should've made me feel bad because I'd clearly terrified the girl, but she had to stop hiding.

If that meant I had to force my way into her life and shove some confidence down her throat, then so be it. Things might've been different if someone had done that for Emily.

My focus was no longer on Harper when I drove through a grand archway of winding ivy. The mansion in front of us was far beyond anything I expected—a wrap-around porch, courtyard to the left, with a trickling three-tiered fountain and lush green trees all around.

It reminded me of one of those plantation houses in the movie *Gone With The Wind*.

I pulled to a stop in front of the house and eyed a man sitting in a chair on the deck. He had an aura of authority around him that led me to believe he was somebody important—dressed in a clean black suit, with neatly cropped dark hair and a hard expression set on his face.

"Is that your dad?" I asked as he rose and waltzed towards us.

Harper nodded and quietly slipped out of the car. "Thanks for the ride."

It didn't take a genius to figure out that that was Harper's timid way of saying goodbye. I didn't leave, though. Curiosity had a hold of me, pulling me outside to follow.

The best way to learn about someone was to see who they lived with—everything I knew about Harper, I'd learned from other people. Like Lana, who I was pretty sure couldn't keep a secret to herself if her life depended on it.

"Hello honey." He tipped his head up and smiled at me. "Who's your friend?"

Harper stopped and slowly glanced over her shoulder. I couldn't help but notice the way her back stiffened for just a second. I was more interested in her father. He washed that smile onto his face way too fast.

"Hi." I raised my hand and walked forward. "I'm Star."

"Ah yes, I met your father in town yesterday." He wrapped his fingers around my palm and widened his smile. "Nice man."

I took the opportunity to study his doe-like eyes because I knew he was lying. He may have met my dad, but he didn't think he was a nice man. I could sense the deception in that statement. Except, I couldn't see it in his face.

Perhaps he's just being polite?

He placed his hand on Harper's shoulder and nodded at me. "Thank you for bringing Harper home. I was stuck in a meeting."

Lie.

I nodded back at him. "My pleasure. Harper is an absolute delight. I'm looking forward to our beach date this weekend."

My statement caused his fingers to tighten on his daughter's shoulders. "Doesn't that sound like fun."

Another lie.

"I should be going." I sang while glancing back. For some reason, it made me feel safe knowing my car was a few feet away, "My little brother's waiting for me."

"Well, it was a pleasure meeting you, Star." He spun around and steered Harper toward the door while singing, "And thanks again," over his shoulder.

I couldn't put my finger on it, but there was something definitely wrong with that man, and you could bet your arse I was going to find out what it was.

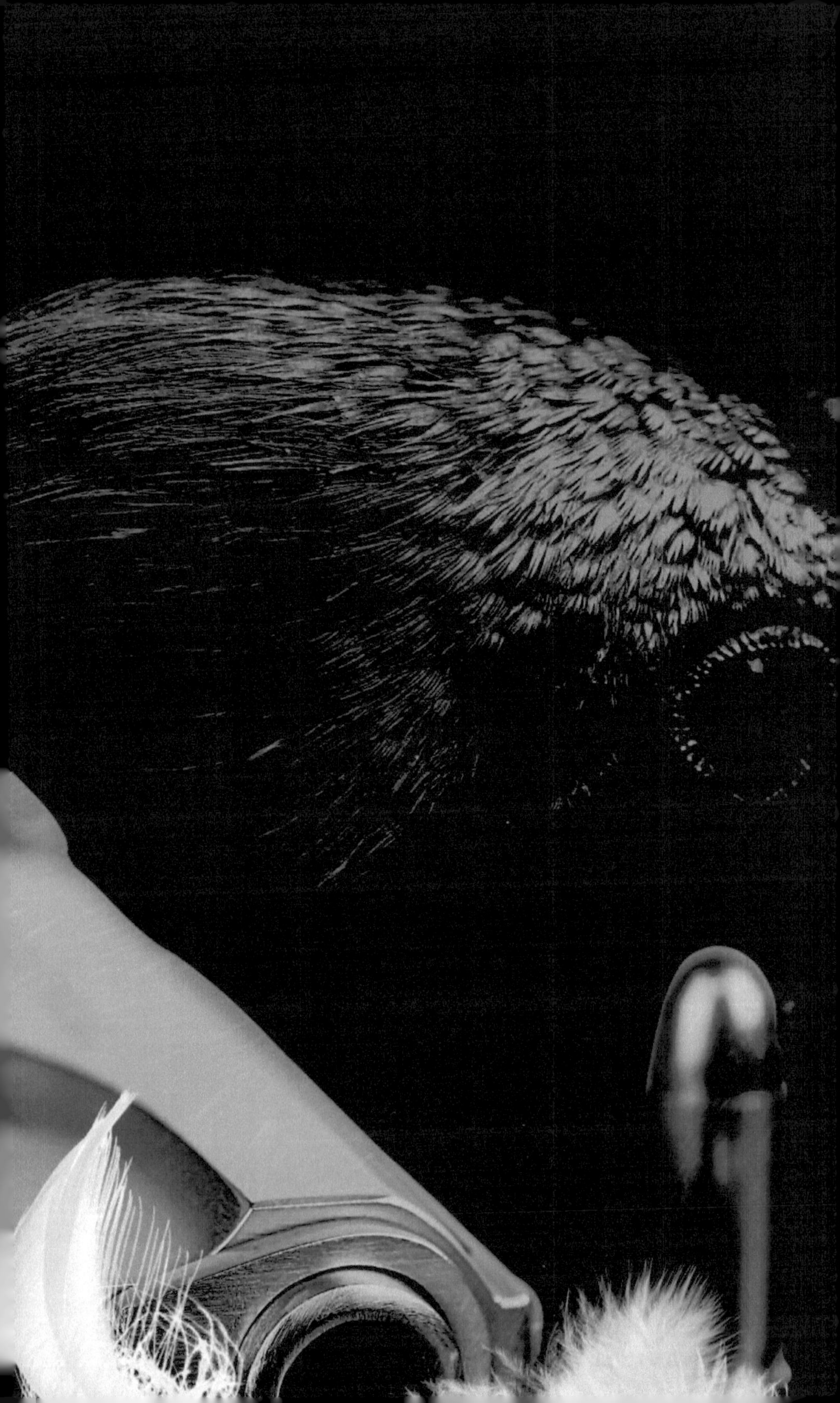

"No, no, no," I groaned and dropped my head on the steering wheel as my car sputtered to a stop.

This was the third time in two days my Sunfire stalled. The first time was yesterday morning after I picked up Harper. Lana couldn't do it because her daughter was sick, so she had to stay home.

Then again, it stalled that day when I was heading home, and now. This morning everything seemed fine, so I thought whatever my dad did to it worked. Apparently not, because now I was sitting on the side of the road, next to a forest, in a stalled-out car.

With a sigh, I pulled out my phone.

Great, no signal.

Mum and Dad needed me to get home. They got called into some emergency meeting with the realtor. Some shite about a fence being an inch over the property line. We didn't even put the damn thing up.

I let out a breath and stared at the thick trees to my left. Not a house in sight. Bugger all. Guess I was taking a trek through the woods to try and find a signal.

At least the sun was still out, and as far as I could tell, there weren't any masked arseholes hiding in the bushes.

Slipping out of my car, I darted around the front and held my phone up, praying the bars would light up and I wouldn't have to go into the thick foliage. They didn't. I shouldn't be surprised. Why would my luck start now?

Still, the forest wasn't my first choice, but other than the drop down a steep hill to my left. There was nowhere else to go. So, reluctantly, I ducked into the trees.

I got so lost wandering around, searching for a signal that I didn't realize the forest had thinned out until a loud roar cut through the sky.

My pulse picked up at the sudden sound, causing me to jump back and look around. The last time something spooked me, I was chased around in the dark.

But there weren't any masked assailants lurking in the shadows —just the breathtaking view of an overgrown field filled with purple and blue wildflowers. Now standing in the middle of the field—the forest I was afraid to enter wasn't nearly as thick as I thought it was.

I could still see the sun glinting off the red paint of my Sunfire. A sight that allowed a breath of relief to escape my lips. My heart began to settle down to a calmer rhythm until that bloody roar rocked through the air again.

I spun around, prepared to take on whoever was behind me. Instead of swinging my fists, my jaw dropped. A spray of water glittered in the skyline on the other side of what was left of a decapitated stone bridge.

I'd completely forgotten about the geysers until now. That

wasn't what made me cock my head. Of all the times Mum and Dad talked about the geysers, they neglected to mention that they were red. And not just any red, but the same thick crimson as blood.

That loud sound cut through the air again, sending my hand up to the aching scar on my chest. I stood frozen as water spewed up and fell back down in deep red crimson drops…

Drops that seeped into my shirt and trickled down my abdomen to the tiled floor.

My mouth fell open as I stumbled back from the smoking barrel, and my finger tightened on the trigger.

Bang!

"No!" I screamed and threw my hands up as the bullet sliced through my arm.

"Damn girl, calm down."

What? There were no boys in the girls' washroom!

Warm palms cupped my face, pulling me away from the ghosts threatening to suck me back into my living nightmare.

"It's okay." Warm brown eyes smiled back at me. "No one's going to hurt you."

What did he mean, 'no one was going to hurt me?'

"She has a gun."

His face scrunched up. "Who?"

"Emily."

I ducked down under the safety of my arms as another bang echoed through the air. It didn't help. I could feel the bullet tearing a burning path through my flesh, digging deeply into my side.

"Hey, it's just the geysers." The lad raised his arm and pointed at the spray of water in the distance. "See?"

I blinked and scanned the tall grass I was huddled in—grass, not tile because I wasn't in that washroom. I was in a field. My heart calmed down a bit when I swung my gaze and spotted the hood of my Sunfire through the trees.

The lad seated on the ground in front of me tipped his head. "See, you're safe."

Safe?

I let out a breath and looked around again. There were no tiles or blood. Just flowers, trees, and a concerned stranger. None of which made me feel better. The geysers went off, and despite myself, I still jumped a little. Would I ever feel safe again?

"Sorry." I gave the lad watching me a small smile and ducked my head. "I'm normally not this jumpy."

"I've seen worse." He shrugged. "The name's Tico, by the way."

"Star."

"Well, Star." He stood up and offered me his hand. "Welcome to the Causegrove."

I stared at his hand for a second before accepting his help to get on my feet. Tico wasn't overly big. Three or maybe four inches taller than I was.

That didn't take away from his appeal, though. He was positively adorable, with tousled black hair and defined muscles under his dark T-shirt.

I nodded at the name of the band sprawled across his chest. "The Ramones are my dad's favorite."

"You dad has good taste." He smiled and tipped his chin at the broken bridge behind him. "Can I offer you a drink?"

"Oh... Um..." Tico seemed nice enough, and I appreciated him helping me out.

His laugh cut off my thought.

"Oh honey, don't worry about that." He leaned in and whispered, "You're not exactly my type. I prefer a little less boob and a lot more dick on my dates."

It took a second for my brain to register his meaning. "Oh."

I found his openness oddly fascinating. I'd only met one other homosexual lad back home, and he was still in the closet. Or, at least he was until I outed him. And why did I do that? Because I was a horrible person that ruined people's lives for fun. But I wasn't that person anymore.

Or at least I was trying not to be that person.

My brows knit at a fire burning under the bridge. "Do you live here?"

"Sometimes."

What did that mean? I didn't think Tico was much older than I was. Shouldn't he have parents or a family member or someone that cared?

And then another thought struck me. What if he didn't?

"You can come to mine." I couldn't leave him out here all alone. What if he got hurt or was hungry or cold? "It's kind of crazy, I've got five little brothers, but we've got lots of room."

"Oh, don't worry about me."

"But…" someone should.

"Really." He insisted. "I sleep out here all the time."

I didn't know about that. How safe could this place really be? If I found it, then anyone could, which wasn't a good thing.

Tico let out a sigh. "If it makes you feel better, I'll go home tomorrow."

So he did have a home. Why didn't he want to sleep there?

"Okay," I said, deciding I was probably overreacting. For all I knew, this was normal American teenage behavior. "Can I get a signal anywhere around here? My car broke down…."

"Sorry, honey, the Causegrove is a dead zone. But I can have a look at your car. If you like?"

"Really?" I could've kissed Tico when he nodded.

Cars were not my forte. Up until recently, I'd never even put my own gas in my tank. My parents did that for me. They did everything. Cooked our food, cleaned up after us, and bought us anything we wanted, which I, of course, took advantage of—I was the epitome of a spoiled princess.

That didn't mean I blamed my parents for my previous behavior or what happened. My actions were mine and mine alone. But I wasn't the only one that learned a lesson that day.

"Come on." Tico grabbed my hand and pulled me through the woods to my car. "I'm not the best mechanic, but let's see what I can do."

He didn't have to end up doing anything because when I got back behind the steering wheel, my car started right up. As if nothing was wrong. I spent the next five minutes trying to convince Tico and myself that I wasn't crazy. He seemed to believe me. I, on the other hand…

The only thing I could do, as I said goodbye and drove home, was shake my head. Maybe I was crazy. Dealing with Silas Creswell was enough to drive any girl mad. Today alone, I'd tripped over my own feet, choked on a mouthful of water, and walked into a pole.

I prided myself on my dexterity and graceful manner. I won numerous ballroom dancing championships, competed in two gymnastics tournaments when I was a child and could skip down a rocky path in stiletto heels.

Yet when it came to that arsehole, I was only two things, tongue-tied and accident-prone, none of which I'd been before him.

Why did he affect me so much? I couldn't even pull into my own driveway without looking at his house. Part of me expected him to be standing outside with his arms crossed and that grumpy look on his face.

I was desperate to tear him apart and shove him back down that hole he reigned supreme over. Show everyone in school who Silas Creswell really was. As days wore on, it was harder and harder to keep the old Star at bay.

I could feel her in the back of my head, begging to get out and put that arsehole in his place. It was an all too familiar feeling that didn't get any better when I pulled to stop in front of my house.

Ash was standing next to the back fence, with tears streaming down his face.

If Cy was picking on him again...

Frowning, I got out of my car and headed my baby brother's way. "Ash, what's wrong?"

"Cy kicked my ball over the bushes." He blubbered while pointing off in the direction of his lost toy.

Our brothers were always throwing stuff around, especially the twins. I didn't see the problem.

"So, go and get it."

"Mum says we hafta stay in the yard."

It was then that I realized where his beloved ball went.

Bloody hell.

Why did we have to move in next to the arsehole king?

"Stay here," I groaned. "I'll go get it."

Ash's face beamed with excitement as I strolled around the front of the house and down the sidewalk.

First, my car stalled, thrusting me at the ghosts of the past, and now I had to sneak my way into the neighbor's backyard. All because my brother decided to be a twat. I was putting itching powder in Cy's bed tonight.

I glared up at the pristine white manor—crisp and clean like the cunt that lived there—and slunk my way down the side hedges to slip through the back gate. If I was lucky, I could sneak in, get the ball, and leave without being seen.

That didn't happen.

Rounding the corner, I was met with a crystal blue burning glare.

"Why the fuck are you sneaking into my yard, Crumpet?" Silas barked out. "Don't I get enough of you at school?"

Well, hello to you too, you bloody gobshite.

"Don't get your knickers in a bunch." I rolled my eyes at the snarl in his lip. "I'll leave as soon as I get my brother's ball."

"I hope you're not talking about this," he pulled his arm out from behind him and held up a red *Paw Patrol* ball. "Cause this is mine now."

"Vey funny." I lifted my arm, opening my palm. "Now, hand it over."

"No."

"What do you mean, no?"

"I mean no, Crumpet. Don't they have that word in England?"

The only reason he was being a jerk was to get at me. Well, I wasn't going to let him win. Not this time. That was Ash's favorite ball, and I was going to bring it home for him.

"What could you possibly want with a child's toy?" I challenged.

Instead of answering, Silas flipped open a pocket knife and stabbed it in the rubber.

My jaw dropped as I watched the cartoon face smiling at me deflate into something deformed and sad.

"You can leave now." Silas tipped his head, angering me with the curl in the corner of his mouth.

If he wanted to pick on me, that was fine. Lord knows I deserved it. But my brothers were off-limits.

"Look at the big bad bloke," I growled, charging up to get in his smug face. "Do you enjoy picking on three-year-old's?"

"I could give a fuck less about the three-year-old." He leaned in just enough so his hot breath skirted off the shell of my ear. "It's you I want to crush."

We'll see about that.

"I know what you are, Silas Creswell."

"Oh yeah." He snickered. "And what's that, Crumpet?"

I jabbed my finger hard into his chest. "You're a bloody bully."

"Is that so?" Silas's eyes glimmered as he cocked a dark brow down at me.

He could've straightened his shoulders and stepped into my space, further intimidating me with his size. But he didn't have to, and he knew it.

He could feel the fear in the air and sense the trembles I was suppressing. That taint filling my veins with shivering chills was what cunts like him ran on.

I knew this because I fed the same monster for years. He still clawed deep in my soul, asking for more torment and misery to feast on, except this time.

It was my nervousness that satiated him. Every time his lungs expanded, expanding the broad planes of his chest, my stomach flipped. Making the beast inside me purr.

"I'm not afraid of you," I stated as flashes of the woods flew through my mind.

He controlled me so easily. As if I was nothing more than a paper doll. I rolled my eyes, peeking up at him through my lashes. There was no hint of anger or hatred on his face—only amusement toying with the corner of his mouth.

"No one ever said you were smart, Crumpet." The deep tone of his voice washed over me, vibrating through the air in melodic rhythm.

He wasn't just enjoying this. He got off on it.

That's it!

"You want to bloody well play with me, you gobshite? Fine."

Something deep inside clicked as I jabbed my finger harder into his chest. "Before you know what's happened, I'll have spat you out and walked away. I eat twats like you for breakfast."

"Keep pushing me, Crumpet, and I won't just hurt you," he growled. "I'll fucking destroy you."

Not so smug now, are you arsehole?

"I can take anything you dish out."

There was a moment of silence as we stood there staring each other down. Yes, this lad was bigger than me. And yes, he could probably snap my neck with a flick of his wrist, but I was so done with his shite. I couldn't take it anymore. Not today.

"I've always wondered if it was true?"

"If what was true?" My brows knit together. Was he trying to confuse me now?

Silas bent forward and whispered, "Do all witches fly?" before slamming his palm against my chest.

The air violently left my lungs as I flew back towards the pool. Time slowed down. I saw the water coming at me. Felt the cool lick of it soaking into my clothes, and only one thought went through my mind.

At least I won't die hot and sweaty.

I'd faced the Grim Reaper's icy touch once before—I saw his skeletal hand reaching up to drag me to the underworld. I was too confused to fight then. Broken and torn up like the bullets had done to my flesh.

I might not have fought this time, either, if I hadn't seen a familiar face staring up at me. Satisfaction glinted in the ghostly image of Emily's brown eyes as I floated weightlessly toward the bottom, which was when panic overtook me.

My limbs flailed, desperately clawing to pull me out to the water's edge. But I couldn't see it, couldn't tell which way was up.

The longer I fought, the more my lungs ached, weighed down by the heaviness filling my chest.

Emily's voice throbbed through my ears, along with my heart.

'Did you miss me, Star?'

My body jerked, trying to pull me away from her voice as blackness seeped into my vision.

'I missed you.'

She was closer now. I could feel her fingers wrap around my arm.

'It's so cold down here, Star. All alone in the dark. The perfect place for a spiteful cunt like you.'

Then, she was gone. The weight was lifted off my chest, and I could breathe again. I broke through the water, coughing and sputtering as I greedily sucked air back into my lungs.

"Jesus Christ," Silas yelled and slammed me back against the wall of the pool. "You gave me a fucking heart attack!"

Gave *him* a heart attack? I was the one almost eaten by the ghost of vengeance.

"Why the fuck can't you swim?"

I tipped my chin, glared back at him as hard as he was glaring at me. "You pushed me!"

For a split second, I thought I saw a spark of guilt in his eyes, but it was gone so fast I couldn't be sure. I hoped he was guilty. He should feel like shite.

"I didn't know you couldn't fucking swim."

"That's what happens when you act like an arsehole and do things without thinking." The stupid thing was that I was more upset that he'd almost destroyed himself with the same guilt that ate me up than I was that he almost killed me.

"What would you have done if I died, huh? You think you'd be able to move on with your life? I've got news for you. I see Emily's…."

I quickly clamped my mouth shut. But it was too late. Silas not only heard me, but he honed in on one word.

"Who's Emily?"

Shaking my head, I pushed further into the hard wall digging into my back. "No one."

Silas stopped me before I could climb out of the pool. He rushed forward and placed his palms on the cement patio, caging me in his arms.

A wet lock of black hair flopped over his forehead as he tipped his head. "Who's Emily, Crumpet?"

"No one," I snarled.

He paused to search my expression, looking for some hidden clue. A clue I wouldn't allow myself to give up. Especially to him.

"If Emily is nobody, then how come you flinch whenever I say her name?"

I did not.

He leaned in and whispered, "Emily."

My jaw twitched.

Bollocks.

"You can tell me now, or I can find out on my own." He pushed back an inch and rolled his eyes down the line of my neck. "Personally, I prefer the—"

I waited for the inevitable threat, but it never came. Only the uneasy silence of whatever he was going to say sucked back with a long gasp. When he finally did speak, it came out as more of a groan than actual words.

"Fuck me."

It was wrong how incredibly sexy those words sounded. Silas may be an arsehole, but he had the voice of a god. Gravelly, melodic, and deep all at once. A small part of me didn't mind the taunts he spewed my way because I got to hear him speak.

What is he staring at?

Was my tie crooked? Did I have something in my teeth? I ironed my uniform this morning, and Mum bleached my shirt…

I faltered and felt my face pale. It felt like I just got punched in the gut.

Yes, Mum had bleached my shirt. My very wet, white shirt! And to make matters worse, it was so hot out that I took my bra off in the car. Meaning…

I glanced down at my nipples, standing proud and very visible underneath the now transparent fabric. Mortification poured down my cheeks, heating up my neck and chest.

Okay, Emily could drag me down to hell now.

"I should go."

A fine idea until I tried to pull myself out of the pool. My hand slipped on the wet stone, sending me face-first into Silas's hard chest.

"Fuck." He grunted and thrust me back against the wall by flattening his large body on mine.

My eyes widened because his chest wasn't the only thing that was hard. I could feel his cock digging into my stomach. Dear lord, how big was he? Silas was wearing jeans. I shouldn't be able to feel it. Not this well.

"Silas…"

"Shut up." His hand wrapped around my neck, choking the rest of my words into silence. "Just, shut. The fuck. Up."

That's exactly what I did.

I held my breath and shut the fuck up. Not because this man could snap my neck with a flick of his wrist, but because my body was reacting to the danger twitching in his fingers.

Fear flowed through me like molten lust, sending sparks of excitement to my core. I was going to have to have a serious talk with Mum about her *'video'* selections. This should *not* be turning me on.

But it was.

Silas grazed his thumb along my jawline as a deep groan escaped his lips. The intensity of it vibrated through my very soul.

"So fucking soft." He groaned again and leaned in, bringing his mouth a breath away from mine.

I couldn't stop staring at his lips. Full and soft, and right there. I sucked back a gasp and prayed to whatever god was listening, that this man—the one who tormented me any chance he got—wouldn't feel me shiver.

"I'm only going to say this once, Crumpet."

Was he going to kiss me?

Did I want him to kiss me?

"You have ten seconds to get the fuck off my property."

"Or?"

Shut up, Star. Don't ask questions, just leave.

"Trust me, Crumpet." His eyes rolled up, locking with mine. "You don't want to find out."

That was enough for me. I slipped onto the patio and quickly scuttled home. Not because I was scared of him and running away like a timid mouse. I was fleeing the desire, begging me to poke the hungry beast I saw glimmering in those icy-blue orbs.

That ravenous creature clawing in the recesses of my mind wanted to let Silas Creswell devour me whole. I was afraid that sooner or later, it would win.

Chapter 12

Silas

I slammed my locker shut and grumbled under my breath. This morning was the first time I seriously considered ditching school.

My old man was a drill sergeant when it came to my education, but would one day really matter? Mase did it all the time, and he still managed to get good grades.

That probably had to do with the visits he made to Janice Watkin's house. She wasn't Mase's typical type. Hell, plain would be a compliment for that girl, but she was smart.

Mase referred to her as a puppy. I believe his exact words were, *'Give a puppy some attention, and it'll do whatever you want.'*

Did I mention how much of an asshole my best friend was? Then again, so was I. The only difference was, I was better at getting away with it.

No one paid attention to the quiet guy in the corner, especially when someone else was doing his dirty work. Secrets were better than gold. It was amazing what people would do to keep them hidden.

Lieutenant Cora Jensen of the New Haven police department was a perfect example of that. She'd do just about anything to prevent the Kings from finding out she existed. Why? Who the fuck knew?

Like I said, everyone had their secrets. This one just so happened to benefit Mase and me. It never hurt to have a cop in your back pocket.

"Will you hurry up?"

I glared at Mase and stormed down the hall. "Since when are you in a hurry to get to class?"

"Aren't you the one always telling me to take my education seriously?"

I cocked a brow back at him, to which he rolled his eyes.

"Fine," he sighed. "I may have paid Clingy Kara a visit last night."

"Seriously." There was a reason every guy in school called her clingy.

"I know, I know." Mase glanced over my shoulder at Kara, who was walking down the hall with two other cheerleaders. "Can we just go before she sees me?"

I gave Mase a look and shook my head, but honestly, getting out of here sounded like a great idea. Ashworth was the last place I wanted to be today.

The schoolwork I could handle. Some subjects were boring as fuck, but whatever. I grew up getting lectures, so this shit was nothing new. I wanted to avoid this place for another reason.

My eyes narrowed on the back of someone rounding the corner in front of us.

And here comes the reason now.

I watched Star's ponytail bounce off her ass as she skipped down the hall. Tempting strands of platinum hair taunted me to do what I almost did yesterday—reach out to grab a fistful and force the little witch haunting my dreams to her knees. And I thoroughly enjoyed how she looked on her knees.

My fingers twitched, remembering how her skin felt. So fucking soft and smooth. Like a silky canvas waiting to be marked.

One thought rang through my head all night. How hard would I have to choke her to make her neck the same perfect shade of pink as her nipples.

And what was the first thing I saw in the morning? Her. Stretching in her window like a cat in heat. Fucking yoga! Now she was less than ten feet away, strutting down the hall like a goddamn succubus.

More like a witch.

Mase released a long groan. "Just fuck her already."

My jaw clenched as my dick twitched at the thought. "I don't want to fuck her."

"Oh, please." He threw his head back and rolled his eyes. "I see how you look at her."

"Kind of like how you look at Harper?" I shot back, wiping any hint of amusement off his face.

Alright, that might've been a low blow, but he deserved it.

"This doesn't have anything to do with her."

"Doesn't it?" I stopped and spun around. "I mean, you do want to fuck her."

Mase wanted to deny it. I could see the irritation curling his lip. But I wasn't his fucking brother. I knew all his dirty little secrets—what happened with Parker, what he did to that girl last year, and, most of all, what he wanted to do to Harper. Micha didn't know shit about who the real Mason was.

I did.

Mase crossed his arms and arched a brow. "You wanna do this now?"

"Yeah." I dropped my books loudly on the ground and shoved his shoulders. "I wanna fucking do this now."

"Okay, but while you're busy pounding on me." He tipped his chin down the hall. "Someone's snaking on your territory."

My glare swung over to Star and the asshole talking to her. Brandon motherfucking Torres. That son of a bitch had been a pain in our asses since we were kids. More so for Parker than the rest of us, but still…

Figured the prick would've learned his lesson after what Logan did to his brother, Noah.

We fed the cops some bullshit story about a drug deal gone wrong, which Derek Adams didn't believe. The last thing our sheriff was, was stupid. Too bad for him, we owned the cops in this town.

Though, I doubted that that particular job bothered him too much. Noah and his friend did drug Shelby after all.

The ironic part…Noah Torres survived that shit.

He might've even had a long, fulfilling life if he hadn't taken Lana. That was the first time I'd seen Micha hide anything from Logan.

After what he did to Shelby, they told him Noah was dead, and he was—now. But what Micha didn't know was how long Parker took to do the job. Never cross a Whitley. They're all fucked, and Dean—with his Mike Brady smile—was the worst.

Brandon's eyes twinkled as he reached out and laid his hand on Star's shoulder. Motherfucker was starting to piss me off.

"Aww, look at that smile," Mase sang. "I think she likes him."

"What's your fucking point?" I growled, digging my fingers into my palm to relieve some of the rage coursing through my muscles.

Mase slapped his hand on my back. "You need to do something about that shit."

Star lifted her chin and giggled, the sweet tone of it echoing through my ears like acid on an open wound.

"No, I don't," I ground out.

"Whatever." Mase waved his hand through the air. "If you want some other dick tainting your pussy, that's your problem."

"She's not mine. I fucking hate her."

"And that matters, why?" Mase argued.

My glare snapped over to him. "What the fuck is that supposed to mean?"

Mase nodded at Harper, who timidly slipped into a classroom down the hall. "You think she gives me the warm and fuzzies?"

When it came to Harper Callaghan, the only warm fuzzy feeling my best friend got was when he thought about choking the life out of her.

"So?"

"So," Mase sighed and leaned in to add, "How many guys do you see her walking around and flirting with?"

Huh?

I hadn't thought about that before. That was just how things were. Harper was Mason's, and if anyone touched her, they would die. It never occurred to me as to how that knowledge got spread around or why.

"Just because you hate her doesn't mean she's not yours." Mase shot me a look and then sauntered into the same classroom Harper disappeared into.

I stayed behind, watching Star say goodbye to Brandon, before gathering my books off the floor and heading down the hall.

On my way, I made sure to bump into Brandon conveniently, slamming my shoulder against his.

"Stay away from that one."

"Why would I do that?" The smirk tugging at the corner of his mouth tempted me to smack the shit out of him.

Instead, I smirked back and sang, "Ask your brother," while following Star into the classroom.

The first thing I saw when I walked into the classroom was Mason's smug face. His green eyes glittered as I walked over and took my seat beside him.

I could feel the satisfaction coming off him as he tilted his head at Harper, who was seated behind him with her head hung.

He didn't have to speak for me to know what he was thinking. The cocky tone of his voice saying, *'mine knows her place,'* echoed through my head, taunting me to say something in retaliation.

Except there wasn't anything I could say. Because Mason Kessler knew me just as well as I knew him, and the truth was, I did want Star. I fucking hated her, but I wanted her too. More than I'd ever wanted anyone.

That was why I was pissed off. Everything in my life was controlled and organized. I knew what socks I was going to wear on what day. Now I had a fucking peacock and ostrich living next to me, and I never knew when my dick was going to pop up and say, 'Hi.'

I glanced over at Star, sitting at the desk on the other side of me. For the first time in my life, I didn't have control, and I didn't like it.

Mase said she was mine. Like it was some simple thing. Don't like a girl but want to fuck her? You just take her. Easy peasy, right?

Wrong.

He'd been claiming Harper for years but still had yet to touch her. Why? Because he loathed the girl. Possibly more than I hated Star. No matter how hard he used Harper, he couldn't fuck away her betrayal.

The little witch, on the other hand...

Star crossed her legs under the desk, bouncing the top one in a rhythm that had my fingers tapping on my desk. Her dark eyes swung my way, making me smirk at the snarl pulling on her lips.

"Can I help you?"

I snorted.

Her? Help me?

That was possibly the funniest thing I'd ever heard.

I could help her, though. Bitch was definitely something that could be fucked out of a girl, and there was one little witch that was in dire need of a lesson.

"Good afternoon, class."

My brow rose at the hard-set expression on the elderly woman walking into the room. She wasn't our regular teacher. Guess Mr. Dawson was sick today.

"I'm Mrs. Parish, and I'll be running your sexual education class today."

Was this starting already? Last year's class was utter bullshit. They didn't teach us anything we didn't already know. Hell, the teacher spent most of the class fending off Mason's outrageous questions.

Timid thing came to school every day in a long skirt and sweater, batting her big innocent eyes. It took Mase less than three days to scare her off. Guess the final straw for her was when he asked how long he could keep a hot pepper in his ass.

My eyes rolled over the old-fashioned school marm strutting in.

Wonder how long it'll take Mase to run this one off?

As if on cue, Mase leaned over and whispered, "Is that a fucking banana?"

I snickered and shook my head at the box she dropped on the desk. This should be good.

"Before we begin." Mrs. Parish turned around and dusted her

hands off on her black pencil skirt. "Is there a Harper Callaghan here?"

All eyes turned to the back as Harper raised her hand.

"Your father hasn't given you permission to attend this class, so you're excused."

Okay, that was a little weird. Then again, Harper's dad made mine seem like a pot-smoking hippie. So, I could see him banning his child from this class. Two other people in the class also raised a brow. Mase, well I wasn't surprised to see him narrow his eyes.

He didn't like Ned Callaghan, or any of the Callaghan family, for that matter. Can't say I blamed him. Having cops show up to arrest you when you're ten years old wasn't something someone easily forgot or forgave.

The glint of suspicion in Star's eyes as Harper walked out, now that was something I didn't expect, which was why I spent most of the class watching her.

Trying to figure out the girl that moved in next door—the little witch was an enigma. One minute she acted like the sweet girl next door, and the next, she was another version of Naomi. A rich, entitled bitch that guys drooled over. Though, if Naomi could pick up on people's weaknesses like Star, she'd be unstoppable.

Ten minutes in the woods, and Star had Logan pegged. She picked up on his Daddy issues like it was displayed across his fore-head. She didn't even have to see his face.

The real question was, why wasn't she using it?

Could it have something to do with Emily? I was definitely going to have to dig into that.

Mase smacked my arm, drawing my attention back to Mrs. Parish. He pointed at a box of extra-large condoms on the desk. That's not what made my brow rise.

The teacher, a woman with wrinkles etched on every inch of her stern face, was currently rolling one of said condoms down her arm. I hadn't seen any shit like that in sex-ed class before.

"As you can see, gentlemen, none of you need an extra-large condom." She waved her finger through the air. "None of your penises are this big."

Mase threw his hand up. "I beg to differ."

Don't fucking say it.

"My friend here," with a big smile on his face, he slapped my shoulder. "Is at least a foot long."

I sighed and scrubbed a hand down my face. "I'm not that big."

After the second time, some prick in the locker room made a comment about my size, so I measured my dick. I didn't see what the big deal was. I'd had the fucker all my life, so it didn't seem big to me. Knew better now.

The seven inches I had soft was what some guys were hard. Being well endowed was not the blessing most guys thought it was.

Star shuffled in her seat as a pink tint flooded her cheeks. I couldn't help but smirk at the shock in her eyes.

Maybe it was a blessing?

"Whatcha looking at, Crumpet?"

"Nothing," she whispered.

Mase snickered. "I think she wants to see your dick."

"Mr. Kessler!" Mrs. Parish slapped her hand on the desk. "Watch your language."

"There are so many worse words than dick," he argued. "Cock, baloney pony, womb broom, custard launcher, fuckpole, love muscle, meat rod...."

I watched Star as Mase continued to spout off slang terms. She was trying really hard not to look and failing miserably, which had my dick swelling to its full eleven inches. It was fucking annoying when this shit happened.

I had to shift to alleviate some of the strain my pants were putting on my shaft. What I did like was the way Star's cheeks flushed when her gaze fell south of the border.

My head tipped to the red plaid skirt draped across her legs. I could see her muscles clenching underneath as she squeezed her thighs together.

How tightly would her legs clench if I pulled it out?

A thought that Mase gave me the perfect opportunity to act on.

"Or anaconda, which is what my friend here is sporting." His smirking face turned towards Star. "And what that one wants to see."

Star reared back, insult curling her mouth. "I bloody well do not."

"Don't be shy." I lifted my gaze to meet hers. "If you ask nice, I might show you."

Her lips parted, and I could sense the insult coming.

That's when I stood up and started unbuckling my belt.

"Then again…" Shocked gasps filled the room, none of which I cared about—there was only one person I wanted to see choke on their shock. "You're not the asking-nice type. Are you, *Star*?"

I put extra emphasis on her name, so she knew that I knew she wasn't who she was pretending to be.

"Mr. Creswell." Mrs. Parish barked out. "Sit down."

Go fuck yourself, Mrs. Parish.

"How about it, Crumpet? I only have one rule." I flicked open the top button of my pants. "Once he comes out, he gets to play."

Star's mouth fell open, and I couldn't stop imagining what her wet tongue would feel like sliding down my shaft.

Just like that, Crumpet. Keep those pretty lips open for me.

A loud bang rocked the air, silencing everyone in the room.

"Mr. Creswell!"

Ah shit.

I rolled my eyes over to Mrs. Grier, standing in the doorway with her arms crossed. Old bitch had to ruin everything.

She pointed down the hall, ordering, "Office. Now."

"Aww, man, things were just getting good," Mase whined.

Mrs. Grier waved her hand. "You too, Mr. Kessler."

"What'd I do?"

"I know you had a hand in this."

When he opened his mouth to argue, Mrs. Grier's soul-sucking glare narrowed. That was enough to make me shrug at Mase and gather my books.

"This sucks." He grumbled while following me out of the room. "Why am I always getting blamed for everything?"

Chapter 13

Star

I couldn't stop staring at the carrot stick in my hand. It was very phallic-shaped. Like something else I'd almost seen less than an hour ago.

He wouldn't have really pulled it out right there, would he? It sure felt like he was going to—reaching down to unbuckle his belt and open his pants.

No, he wouldn't have done it.

My fingers pinched the carrot. If he had, would he have been hard? I definitely saw a bulge, and if Mason's claims were right…

I thought back to the other day in the pool and the hardness I felt pressing against my stomach.

I shook thoughts of Silas with his icy eyes and possibly large package out of my head. No one was that big.

He had to be turned on, that was all. It happened to lads all the time, right? My eyes once again fell to the carrot stick.

Stop it, Star.

My hand opened, dropping the vegetable as I searched for something else to concentrate on.

"Did you see…"

"Oh my God… can you believe…"

"I know, right." *Giggle.* "Like, come on…."

My gaze shifted between Lana and Shelby. I don't think it was possible for my brain to hurt more than it did right now. It started off as a debate on which salad dressing was better, French or Italian.

Personally, I preferred the basil and parmesan dressing Mum made. Not that I could tell them that. None of us could get a word in edge-wise because they were too busy talking about…

"Can you imagine?"

Groan.

"So bad."

Well, I wasn't entirely sure what subject they were debating now. Or if it even was a debate. Bloody hell, I couldn't even tell which one was speaking.

Their words blended together in a cacophony that had my mind swirling. This—whatever it was—couldn't be normal.

I leaned over to Riley and whispered, "Should we stop them?"

"Pipe down, Rapunzel." Her lip curled my way. "You want them to drag us into this shit?"

While I didn't appreciate the attitude or sneer, she had a point.

"Did you call me Rapunzel?"

Riley shrugged. "Cut your hair if you don't like it."

My hair wasn't that long. Was it? I glanced back at the end of my ponytail resting on the seat behind me. Alright, Rapunzel, it was.

I suppose it wasn't bad, considering some of the other things I'd heard Riley call people. Some of them were right on point, like

Mason. He shifted between prick and dead man, depending on her mood.

I wasn't sure why he was so afraid of Her. She was only an inch or two taller than me, and I wasn't very threatening. But for some reason, he booked it the other way when he saw Riley coming. Then again…

Two girls wearing cheerleading outfits sauntered past the table, bumping Riley's shoulder on the way. The pencil quickly etching on the notepad in front of Riley stopped as she lifted her head and narrowed her eyes on the brunette.

"Sorry," the girl muttered and quickly scuttled away with her friend.

Alright, maybe Riley was a tad intimidating.

Thankfully, there was one sane person at the table.

Harper sat quietly next to me with her head down. The more time I spent with her, the more it broke my heart to see her hiding from the world.

I'd convinced Lana to let me be Harper's ride to and from school, so I'd gotten to know her a bit more. Not much, mind you. It was a fight just to get her to talk.

"You should let me do your hair." I smiled at Harper and swept a bundle of curls back from her face. "When we go to the beach tomorrow."

Harper ducked and shied away from me. I suppose it was progress. At least she stopped flinching when I talked to her.

Lana lifted her head and glanced our way. "You're going to the beach?"

How she heard us between the words Shelby and her were babbling, I had no idea.

"Um… I… ah…." Harper's eyes widened, reminding me of a frightened doe. "I don't know."

"Oh, stop it." Lana waved her hand, cutting Harper off before I could. "You need to get out of the house and have some fun."

I couldn't agree more. Though the emphasis Lana put on the word *need* made me question her motives.

"I agree," Shelby piped in. "You spend way too much time with your dad."

Lana's face twisted at the last statement, which made me tip my chin. Something in Shelby's words caused lines of disgust to pull at her mouth. Interesting.

"Oh." Shelby slapped her hand down on the table, making the rest of us jump. "We should all go!"

Lana said her daughter was still miserable, something I completely understood, having five little brothers. I thought the twins were bad when they were teething, but Mum and Dad barely slept when

Ash went through it. None of us really got any sleep. Thank God for nannies.

I missed the days when my parents had people, maids, butlers, and drivers to do everything. Sadly, none of them came with us. After what happened, Mum and Dad were dead set against raising another spoiled child. Couldn't say I blamed them. Look how I turned out.

Riley muttered a one-word answer, "No."

"Oh, come on." Shelby's face dropped as she let out a rather exaggerated scoff. "It's just the beach."

"Last time, you hid all my bathing suits and forced me to wear that tiny red bikini."

"Which you hid under shorts and a t-shirt," Shelby pointed out.

"That's because it was riding up my ass." I couldn't help but admire the color of Riley's eyes as she rolled them. A deep, dark blue, like the sky at twilight. "I don't care what you say, a perma-wedgie is not sexy or fun."

"You know, for once, I'd like to have a girly best friend."

"So." Riley shrugged. "Go find one."

Shelby stuck her tongue out at Riley, who returned the gesture and went back to her sketchbook. Their friendship fascinated me. I'd never seen two people more opposite, yet anyone could see how much they utterly adored each other.

"Who's going to the beach?"

We all looked up at the brunette smiling down at us, whom everyone except Harper and I seemed to know. Lana grinned, Riley muttered under her breath, and Shelby's face brightened.

"Trina! What are you doing here?"

"Destroying what's left of my day," Riley grumbled.

I guess she didn't like this Trina too much. One look at Trina's perfectly styled hair and flawless makeup job told me she wasn't the Riley friend type. Then again, neither was Shelby. Those two being friends, I understood.

For a split second, Trina's aqua eyes shifted my way. "We're starting here on Monday."

We're?

The cafeteria quieted down at the sound of the receptionist's voice.

"Trina Camile Dupire, this is not talk-time with your friends."

I was more stunned by the girl standing next to her. Other than the dapper clothing and glasses, she was a carbon copy of the girl standing at our table.

"Ugh." Trina rolled her eyes. "Coming, Grandma."

"Shut the fuck up," Riley's head snapped up. "Soul sucker is not your grandma."

Mrs. Grier's lips pressed together, "Language, Miss. Adams."

"Don't even get me started," Trina muttered and skipped off to follow her grandmother out in the hall.

Riley's shocked face turned Shelby's way. "Did you know about this shit?"

"No." She shook her head.

I left them to discuss their friend and looked over Harper's shoulder to the words she was writing down. She was hiding the little brown notebook under the table, so I couldn't quite make out what she was writing.

This wasn't the first time I'd seen her scribbling words down. Although this notebook seemed new, making me wonder if she'd filled the other one. And, if so, what was she filling them with—stories, poems maybe, or simple notes? Would she let me read them if I asked her?

Harper's timid gaze lifted my way as she quickly slapped the book shut.

Guess not.

Perhaps I could convince her to? I wasn't a big reader. The last book I read was for my lesson, and even then, I only skimmed through it. But I really wanted to know what was in that book.

Harper was such a mystery, and I couldn't help her if I didn't understand her. Something told me Mason wasn't the only reason she was sad and scared all the time.

If I could only get her to talk.

"What's your favorite book?"

This time when she lifted her head, there was a different glint in her eyes—bright and cheery.

"You like to read?" Harper said.

"Not really." I wiped the frown off my face and tilted my head. "But maybe you can suggest one I'd enjoy."

When she lifted her gaze to the roof and furrowed her brows in contemplation, I thought I might've made a breakthrough. Until that terrified look came back on her face, and she dropped her head again.

It didn't take me long to figure out why. A group of girls were coming our way, dressed in black and red uniforms. Similar to the ones I'd seen the cheerleaders wearing.

The only thing that outweighed my confusion as they took the empty chairs around our table was the deep-set scowl on Riley's face.

For a brief second, I was a little worried that she might stab the one next to her with the pencil in her hand. "Are you lost?"

Not only was the girl unperturbed by Riley's attitude, she completely ignored her and turned her smile my way.

"Hi there, I'm Tiffany, but you can call me Tif."

Riley snorted.

"Anyways…" Tiffany sighed, shooting a look over her shoulder. "I'm captain of the drill team, and you've missed three practices."

Shelby's eyes widened. "You're part of the drill team?"

I didn't even know what a drill team was.

"Are you kidding me?" Tiffany seemed almost insulted by Shelby's question. "What kind of drill team wouldn't recruit Star Chadwick? Do you have any idea how many championships she's won?"

Wait a minute… was this the dance thing Mum and Dad signed me up for, despite my insistence against it? Dancing was old Star's hobby.

"Twelve," Tiffany reiterated as if everyone here should know that.

It was fifteen, but who was counting.

I gave Tiffany—I refused to call her Tif a small smile and said, "There's been some kind of misunderstanding. I told—"

I was cut off before I could finish explaining.

"Oh no, it's quite simple, you haven't come to practice, so we decided to come to you." Tiffany waved her hand at the other members of the team, who all nodded in response.

"It's funny that you weren't this eager to recruit Harper." Lana's hazel glare snapped up to the captain of the drill team. "She can dance too."

"You can?" I looked over at Harper, who blushed and tucked her face further in her hair.

Lana nodded. "She won two swing championships when she was eight."

That, I would not have guessed, and based on the way Riley and Shelby were staring at Harper, I didn't think they would've guessed it either.

"I did the ballroom circuit," I explained to Harper. "My specialty was Latin. The salsa and tango, more specifically."

I adored the freedom I felt dancing around the room. There was nothing like it. No words were needed—just music and a body.

There were a million different ways to tell a story, but very few that could make people feel it. One simple hip swing had the power to captivate an entire audience.

Tiffany's lips curled with a groan of disgust. "Harper doesn't have what it takes."

I didn't have to see the frown on Harper's face to know it was there, which gave me an idea.

"I promise I'll come to the next practice." I threw my arm around Harper's shoulders. "If Harper comes with me."

Being included in something meant she couldn't hide.

Chapter 14

Silas

Star Chadwick was fucking everything up.

I was the ideal student. Hadn't skipped a day or gotten in trouble once. So, why was I sitting in the office next to my idiot best friend, waiting for my old man to show up and give me a lecture?

Because chaos had disrupted my life in the form of a tiny blonde. That little witch, with her tempting figure, had my mind all messed up—causing me to make bad decisions like the split-second one that ruined my perfect track record.

"I'm disappointed in you boys." Mr. Sampson scratched at the nylon covering his elbow.

I couldn't help but snort at the colorful roses decorating his arm. Who the fuck was he trying to kid?

"Especially you, Silas."

"Join the club," I grumbled.

Did I regret what I'd done? Fuck no. If I could go back, the only thing I'd change was my timing. I'd have whipped my dick out before that old cow showed up.

At least then I'd have the memory of Star's shock to distract me from the principal's nice guy crap.

Who knows, maybe Star would be the first girl whose eyes didn't widen in horror when they saw my cock? After all, she was the first girl I wanted to see with that look. The 'that thing will never fit inside me' grimace.

With the right determination, a man could pack a lot of meat in a tight little hole. And when it came to Star Chadwick, I had spades of determination.

"Tell me something, Pops." Mase tipped his chin, nodding at the fake flowers covering the principal's forearm. "What the fuck is that?"

A line of confusion etched its way across Mr. Sampson's forehead. "What?"

"That." Mase waved his finger through the air. "The fucking flowers."

"All you kids have tattoos," Mr. Sampson explained while stealing a glance at his arm.

I shook my head at the genuine look of bewilderment on his face. Personally, I didn't have anything against the guy. I just thought it was foolish for a man well into his sixties to waste his time trying to fit in with a bunch of teenagers.

Last week, he came to school in a pair of bell-bottoms because someone told him they were cool.

"No, see what we have is *actual* ink. Not a damn nylon tattoo sleeve. And it's not even a good one, at that. Roses, really?" A frown tugged on Mase's lips as his green eyes rolled up. "Come on, dude."

Mase had a point. The last thing Mr. Sampson needed was to be more feminine. The only thing his greying hair did, was make his delicate features appear more fragile. Flowers were the last thing he should be wearing. If you're gonna fake it, fake it well.

Mr. Sampson lifted his chin and confidently stated, "I've gotten quite a few compliments on these."

"From who," I asked. "The cheerleaders?"

"Well… Um…" the principal blew out a huff of air. "Your fathers should be here soon. We'll talk more then."

"Can't wait," I grumbled as he spun around and walked into his office. Probably to remove the tattoo sleeve.

I should be used to waiting around for my old man by now—either of my parents, for that matter. Mom stopped by three months ago for a couple days to say, 'Hi.' I didn't fault her for it. Such was the life of an actress. But my old man lived in the same house as me, and I saw him just as much.

Five minutes here, ten there. Maybe a quick check-in when he stopped at home to grab a change of clothes before going back to his whore's house. Honestly, I'd be surprised if he made it to Ashworth without asking for directions.

I shifted in my seat. "Why do they make these things so uncomfortable?"

"They're not so bad." Mase shrugged. "I kind of like them."

Of course, he did. The asshole spent more time in the office than he did in a classroom. The chairs in there weren't much better, but at least they had some padding. This one was worn out from the numerous asses that sat here waiting for reparation.

"We're missing lunch," I pointed out.

I could be sitting in the cafeteria right now, making a certain someone uncomfortable. Star wasn't too happy when I stared at her from the next table. I liked it, though. Liked watching her nerves come alive, making her all squirrely and flushed. Would she shift on my lap like that?

That's when another thought occurred to me.

What if Brandon was sitting with her? Putting his hand on her leg while she smiled up at him?

My fists balled tightly. That motherfucker was probably touching her right now.

"Calm down, here comes Edith," Mase sang as a quiet growl escaped my mouth. "Hey sweet cheeks, did you bring us some food?"

I didn't want fucking food. I wanted that prick's head on a stake.

"I'm busy, Mr. Kessler," Mrs. Grier let out a tired sigh. "I don't have time to deal with your shenanigans."

Mase's brows knit together. "Who the fuck says shenanigans?"

Mrs. Grier, that's who. Now can we get the fuck out of here so I can kick the shit out of Brandon?

"Language, Mr. Kessler."

"It's so fucking hot when you scold me. If I'm a bad boy, will you spank me?"

Oh, for fuck sakes.

I'd bet my left nut that if by some miracle Mrs. Grier did spread her legs, Mase would fuck the shit out of that old ass pussy to prove a point.

Thankfully, two girls strutted in behind the receptionist, saving me from whatever sickening exchange I was sure my best friend had planned. No one wanted to see that shit.

"Check it out." Mase nudged me with his elbow. "Twins."

"I can see that."

And what was more, I'd seen them before. At a party last year, by some broken-down bridge. I only remembered because the frumpy one stuck out like a sore thumb, which was saying a lot, considering Riley was there. It was kind of hard to miss the girl standing alone in a corner wearing a big-ass sweater.

Chicks like that didn't come to high school parties. They hung out in the library. Her sister, on the other hand… My eyes rolled over the skirt, barely covering the other twin's ass. She was definitely a jock bunny.

Mase's eyes twinkled as they poured over the brunettes. "I love me some fresh meat."

I rolled my eyes. They'd been here for less than a minute, and there was no doubt in my mind that Mase already had a game plan picked out for his next target. And I meant target because glasses girl was exactly his type, which was a blessing in disguise for her.

A girl like that didn't stand a chance against Mason Kessler. Half the girls in this school had already dropped to their knees for him.

"Sit over there, girls." Mrs. Grier pointed at an empty table on the other side of the room. "And I'll bring your paperwork."

Short skirt groaned. "Didn't our parents already fill that out?"

"Come on, Trina." The other one grabbed her hand and pulled her over to the table. "Grandma's just doing her job."

Oh shit.

Mase's face lit right up. "Edith, you didn't tell me you had twin granddaughters."

"How come he gets to call you Edith?" Trina whined. "And we have to call you *Mrs. Grier?* You're our grandma."

"Don't worry, sweetheart. Grandma just wants to ride my cock."

Unbelievable.

"Mr. Kessler!" Mrs. Grier shrieked, "You will watch your language around my granddaughters."

"Aww, Edith, don't get jealous."

Could I slap him? I really wanted to slap him.

"I promise." Mase shot the girls a wink, which made Mrs. Grier huff out a grunt. "I'll be on my best behavior."

He'd be on his best behavior, alright. I knew that look. Too bad. I kind of liked glasses girl and the scowl she was giving us. When

Mason Kessler set his mind on something nine times out of ten, he ended up fucking it.

May as well kiss your innocence goodbye now, honey.

"There you are." My old man walked in with Lou in tow.

Neither of them wore an expression that matched the prim and proper suits they were wearing. Guess they weren't too happy. Figure Lou would be used to it by now.

"I've been looking for you everywhere."

My brow arched at my old man. Did he expect to find me on the street corner ringing a bell for change? Last I checked, the office in Ashworth hadn't relocated in a decade.

Lou let out a tired sigh. "What did you do now, Mason?"

"He got my boy in trouble. That's what he did."

I shook my head. "I got myself in trouble."

"That's right," Mase nodded. "This asshole's the one that decided to whip his shit out in class. I just encouraged him."

No one was expecting that. Even Lou's brow rose. It didn't take my old man long to come back from it, though. That stern glare washed over his face before I could blink.

"Explain yourself, Silas."

I sat back and folded my arms over my chest. "Seems pretty self-explanatory to me."

"So you admit it?"

I shrugged. "I never denied it."

"I expected better from you."

My jaw clenched. There was that disappointment I was used to —along with that word I fucking hated. *Better.*

"This is your senior year. Colleges will be looking at you, watching everything you do. You need to shine."

In other words, stop embarrassing him and live up to the family name.

My old man huffed. "You can't afford to be pulling this kind of crap."

"Calm down," Lou interjected. "One infraction is not the end of the world. We were young and dumb once too."

"Hey," Mase cried out. "Who are you calling dumb?"

I swung my gaze over to Mase. "You filled out your last test with a red crayon."

"I happened to get ninety-five on that test."

"Only because you were fucking the teacher."

"What?" Lou arched an unimpressed brow at his son, who in turn shot me a look.

I tipped my head to my shoulder, giving Mase a silent apology.

"You see," my old man exclaimed. "We never did shit like this."

That made me laugh. According to my old man, he was the perfect student and son when he was my age, which was complete and utter bullshit.

My mother didn't come from the blue-blood breeding stock, yet he demanded I choose a wife from said line. He met her in a bar down by the docks, fell in love, and married her. And look at them now.

So much for fucking love.

"Yes, we did. We just didn't get caught." Lou paused to give Mason a pointed glare before returning his attention to my dad. "Give the boy a break."

"You're the last person I'd take parenting advice from." I could feel the animosity coming off my old man. "One son rejected an Ivy League school so he could be closer to his girlfriend, and the other is an addict and deviant."

Mase gave his dad a smug smile while I internally sighed. Not because of what my old man said, but because of the hatred he had for his. Like it or not, Lou was a better parent. Yeah, his kids were fucked up, but he tried and never gave up on them. That was more than I could say for the esteemed Dr. Creswell. I'd been called to the office once, and he was ready to write me off as a lost cause.

"What are you pissed about, Dad? That Lou is giving you parenting advice?" I rose from my chair and narrowed my eyes. "Or that he's in charge of your precious prodigy?"

"Finn belongs with us."

Bingo.

"Finn's better off forgetting we exist." I spun around and stormed out, muttering, "At least then he wouldn't have to worry about the family reputation."

"Silas, get back here."

I answered him by flipping the bird over my shoulder.

Honestly, I didn't know what got into me. I normally didn't talk back to him like this. I didn't talk back at all. Like every other member of my family, I fell in line and did what was expected.

But it wasn't just my life I had to think about anymore. Uncle Sebastian was gone, and someone had to look out for Finn.

I may not be able to fix him, but I could make damn sure my old man didn't fuck him up more.

"Hey," Mase skipped down the hall after me, "you wanna get back at your old man?"

"Why?" My unimpressed gaze slid his way. "You gonna fuck his secretary again?"

"I had something better in mind."

"Like what?" I couldn't wait to hear this.

"He still have that brandy locked away?"

"It's cognac," I argued.

"Whatever." Mase waved his hand. "Does he have it or not?"

"Yeah."

Of course, he had it. That cognac was his most prized possession.

Occasionally when I was a kid, my old man would take out his bottle of Black Pearl. He'd hold it on his lap and tell me that when I graduated from Yale with honors, we'd finally open it.

Nothing else compared to that black bottle. Not my mother. Not his Austin Martin, and not me. Over the years, it became a symbol of perfection, taunting me from the cupboard it was locked in, like a precious gem in a museum.

"I don't know about you." Mase draped his arm over my shoulder. "But I'm feeling a little parched."

A smile spread across my face. "It was dry in there, and it is Friday, so I don't have to get up early tomorrow."

The same grin crept across Mase's face. "That's true."

"You can't drink any."

I wasn't letting him use my anger as an excuse to dive back into a bottle.

"I don't have to. I'm sure there's plenty of other thirsty people that would be more than happy to help you polish off Daddy's brandy."

Chapter 15

Silas

This town held parties in one of three places, Logan's house, the beach, or on the bluffs by the hot springs.

If Lou didn't spend so much time at home, Mase would have one there every weekend. Having a shrink wander around a bunch of drunk teenagers kind of put a damper on things.

Honestly, I avoided using my house as party central because I didn't want to see the mess the next day.

Not to mention all the people that would be invading my personal space. But I had to say, I didn't mind it. Actually, I was thoroughly enjoying watching people dance around my backyard, trashing my old man's perfectly planted flowers.

I didn't even mind the two cops Mase was talking to, one of which was our sheriff, Derek Adams. Guess after being called out here three times, the Ashen Springs police department felt the need to send the big guns.

Some of my neighbors weren't too impressed with the live band. Well, they could go fuck themselves. I had a belly full of brandy and a guitar in my hand. I didn't give a fuck about anything else.

I smirked at the yellow curtains hanging in the window next door.

Well, there was one thing I cared about.

Was Star in there right now? Did she like my choice of music? The band had asked me more than once to pick something other than *Five Finger Death Punch*, but this was my house.

I'd sing what I damn well pleased. Which, at the moment, happened to be *'Blue On Black.'* Don't know why. It just happened to be the song that house brought to mind.

"Truth, lies, and in between," I sang while imagining her on the other side of those curtains.

Could she feel the depth of honesty in those lyrics? Cause I could. Especially the lies part. Star was hiding something. She knew it, and I knew it. Sooner or later, I'd find out. I just had to siphon through the many Emily's in England first.

I'll find what you're hiding, little witch, then I'll shove it down your throat.

"Alright, Silas," Derek Adams interrupted my thoughts by tapping me on the shoulder. "I'm not gonna break up your party, but you need to turn the music down."

I snorted as he motioned to my guitar. Did he really think he had any power here? Or anywhere, for that matter?

"I mean it." He reached over and unplugged my amp. "Enough with the band-shit. It's midnight, for fuck sakes."

"Run along now, Sheriff." I snatched the cord out of his hand. "Your presence isn't wanted here."

"In case you forgot, there's a new mother three houses down, whose husband I had to talk out of coming over here."

My hand froze, hovering with the plug an inch away from my amp. "Lana called?"

"No, Parker did."

"Alright, fine," I grumbled and waved the band away.

Derek let out a sigh of relief. "Thank you."

Not sure what he was so thankful for—I didn't shut the band down for him. Parker was my friend, and he hadn't gotten much sleep lately. I could more than sympathize with that.

Mase sauntered over and nodded at me. "Everything okay over here?"

"Yeah. The sheriff here was just telling me about the many noise complaints he'd gotten."

Mase clapped his feet together and snapped up in a firm salute. "Don't worry, officer. We'll keep it down."

Derek leaned back and eyed him. "Have you been drinking, Mason?"

"Why?" Mase rolled his eyes. "You gonna tell Daddy I've been downing shots?"

That was bullshit. I'd been watching him all night. But Mase didn't give a shit what anyone told his old man. In fact, he encouraged it. Pissing Lou off had become his favorite hobby.

I sighed at Derek. "He hasn't touched a drop."

Derek hesitated for a moment to study the glare Mase was giving me before nodding and walking away.

Mase crossed his arms and watched the sheriff leave. "You didn't have to say anything, you know."

"Yeah, I did."

He may not care about the hole he dug himself in, but I did. Lou wouldn't hesitate to send his ass back to rehab.

"Killjoy."

"Dickhead."

I rose from the chair I was sitting on and stumbled forward, tripping down the step of our makeshift stage. The only thing stopping me from smacking face-first into the ground was Mase's hand on my chest.

"I think you've had enough to drink."

"I'm fine," I growled and kicked the stage. "Stupid thing is wobbly."

That's what happened when something was slapped together last minute.

Mase lifted his hand, displaying three fingers. "How many fingers am I holding up?"

Was this asshole seriously giving me a sobriety test? I wasn't sober, but I wasn't drunk either, and Mase was killing the warm buzz warming up my body.

I shouldered past him and said, "Why don't you go find some pussy to get lost in."

He was disappointed the twins didn't show up. Not me. That just meant I wouldn't have to burn my sheets in the morning. I guarantee that motherfucker would use my room to sully them.

"I'm gonna get another drink."

And that's exactly what I did.

I made my way through the crowd to the table in the back littered with bottles. Most of which were empty by now. Leaving me to choose between some second-rate Vodka and the new beer Whitley distilleries just made.

I chose the latter. Cracked open a bottle and swallowed a mouthful. The name on the label made me shake my head. What the fuck kind of name was Tandem Ice? Sounded like some shit Ava would come up with if you asked me. Whatever, it tasted good.

It didn't take Mase long to take my advice. By the time I was done with my drink, he was in the pool making out with some chick in a blue bikini. I could drain that shit in the morning. Right now, I was more interested in the asshole standing by the firepit.

Who the fuck invited Brandon? Scratch that, I knew who. My gaze swung back to Mase.

Asshole.

This wasn't some Tinkerbelle costume or game Mase could use for amusement. I legit wanted to kill the fucker. The twinkle in Brandon's eye shouldn't piss me off. But it did. Same with that stupid smirk on his face. It was the same dumbass grin he gave Star.

And what did she do? She fucking smiled back at him. Was she stupid? Didn't she see how much of a moron the guy was? A better question was, why did I care?

Yeah, okay, I wanted to fuck the girl. I'd admit that. But it wasn't like she was my girlfriend or anything. Who wanted to be attached to someone they hated. Sorry, but I wasn't into self-torture. Then again, I did enjoy knocking her down a peg.

Maybe Mase had the right idea with Harper? Keep your friends close and your enemies closer. If Star was by my side, then I could really enjoy her torment. After all, you couldn't truly destroy someone if they were attached to someone else.

Pondering whether I should march over there and storm into her room, I glanced over my shoulder at the tall shrub separating our houses.

I didn't have to go that far to find the object of my desire because her wide dark eyes were staring back at me. Little witch was hiding in the shadows of the leafy branches, spying on me.

"Don't you know it's rude to spy?"

She squeaked and ducked back into the shrub.

A smirk tugged at my lips. Star wanted to play hide and seek, did she? Alright, I was game.

"Where you going, Crumpet?" I sang and deposited my empty bottle on the table before following her into the thick branches. "Don't you want to come out and play?"

Despite the music in the background, I heard her quiet, "No. Go away."

My ears sought out the sound of her voice like an addict sought out their next fix. Each syllable of that sweet tone pumped adrenaline through my veins.

"Come on, Crumpet, don't hide from me." I pushed a branch out of my way and ducked deeper into the shrub. "I'll be nice. I promise."

I couldn't help but chuckle at the derisive snort echoing through the rustling leaves to my right. The girl wasn't stupid.

"Alright, I won't be nice," I confessed. "But let's be honest, you don't want nice."

"If you come near me, I'll bloody well sac you."

I tsked and made my way closer to the sound of her voice. "Didn't work out so well for you last time."

My dick got hard just thinking about that night in the forest. The fear in her eyes as she raised her little fists, prepared to take all three of us on. That shit was fucking hot.

"I still managed to knock one of you twats down."

"That's true." I snickered. She kicked the crap out of Mason. Logan was never going to let him live that shit down. "But at the end of the day, which one of us was on the ground?"

A flash of platinum glinted in the moonlight less than two feet in front of me. So close, I could smell the sweet scent of her fear.

Star's face twisted as she searched the darkness around her. "You cheated."

My hand twitched at my side, fingers desperate to reach out and grab her. But not yet. I wanted to enjoy the way her body was shivering and soak up the way her hips swayed under those pink shorts.

"It was three against one, arsehole."

Her feet moved, shuffling against the ground and bringing her back. Closer to me. I stood there silently, watching her, as each footstep echoed through my thundering pulse.

"Hardly what I'd consider fair odds."

One last step, and she froze as her back slammed into my chest.

I leaned down and growled in her ear, "Who said anything about fair?"

Star moved to dart away, but I was faster. I grabbed a fistful of that silky hair and twisted it around my hand, pulling her back into me. Almost immediately, she sucked in a deep breath and parted her lips, preparing to scream.

Like I said, the girl wasn't stupid. She was slow, though. I clamped my hand over her mouth before a single squeak could escape.

"Ah, ah, ah," I tsked in her ear. "We don't want to attract any unwanted attention."

In an act of defiance that had my cock aching to be let out, Star released a loud muffled scream. A scream she shut off the second I took my hand out of her hair and wrapped it around her throat.

"Careful now, Crumpet, bad girls get punished." I dug my fingers into her flesh, reveling in the way her pulse fluttered against my thumb. "And you don't want to get punished, do you?"

Her muffled whimper vibrated through my pulse as she shook her head.

I took a deep breath, trying to push back how warm and soft she felt pressed against me and rested my chin on the top of her head.

"If I take my hand away, are you gonna be good?"

Star nodded, and I couldn't help but tip my nose down to inhale the fruity scent of her shampoo. Fuck, she smelled good. So good I forgot to drop my hand until she mumbled something.

"What do you want?"

"That depends." My eyes fell past the tip of her nose to the swell of her breasts, heaving with her heavy breaths. "What are you offering?"

"Silas…"

Maybe it was the alcohol still warming my blood, but I really liked the way my name sounded on her lips. I needed to put my mouth on her, absorb the saltiness of her sweat, even if it was just a taste.

"I don't want to play your games."

I slid my hand up to her chin and pushed her head to the side, so I could nuzzle in the crook of her neck.

"But I like playing with you," I purred while laving my tongue over her skin.

She was so fucking soft. I wanted to sink my teeth into her flesh and mark the spot I'd just claimed. Even better than the taste exploding in my mouth was how her whole body shuddered with a loud gasp.

Star wrapped her fingers around my forearm, tugging against the grip I had on her chin. "Let me go."

"Sure. I'll let you go." I couldn't stop running my lips over her pulse. "Just as soon as you tell me why you were spying."

"Because I heard the music." Star breathed out huskily and shifted her hips, making me groan. "I wanted to see. That's all."

Images of her body swaying in her bedroom window flashed through my mind. There was only one question I had. "Did you want to dance?"

Her back went rigid. "I don't dance."

Interesting. But her refusal to do something she clearly loved was a puzzle for another day.

"In case you haven't noticed," I slid my palm down her neck, slipping my fingers under the collar of her shirt. "I don't have very much control right now. Lying to me is a good way to lose your cherry, Crumpet."

She sucked in a shocked gasp. "But you hate me."

"And what better way to get rid of those feelings." I spun her around so she could see the seriousness in my eyes. "Than by hate fucking you good and hard."

I watched her throat bob with a heavy swallow and considered doing just that. Ripping those shorts off and pinning her to the ground sounded like a good idea to me.

"Yes," she whispered, drawing my gaze to her pouty pink lips. "I wanted to dance."

How many times had I jerked off to this girl swinging her hips? Except this time, it wasn't some jacked-up song on the radio that made her want to move.

It was the song I was playing on my guitar—not some dipshit rock star that banged a different girl every night. It was me. My music called to her soul.

The next thing I knew, my mouth was on hers. Crashing down in a growl of fury-filled hunger. Ten years of burning hatred and rage poured out in that kiss.

I claimed her mouth like I wanted to claim her soul. Sweeping in when her lips parted in shock to swallow her pants.

Star fought at first, flattened her palms on my chest with a feeble shove. That was easily remedied by pinning her wrists behind her back. One taste, and I was done. I couldn't hold back anymore. I needed to be inside her.

Right. Fucking. Now.

"Silas," Star panted out as my hand went for her shorts. "We can't."

"Maybe you can't," I trailed my mouth across her cheek to the side of her neck, "but I can."

I bit down, sinking my teeth into her warm flesh. Star cried out and shook her head, but her hips bucked up against me.

The more she protested, the harder I got until it felt as if my dick was going to burst out of my jeans. I didn't give a shit if she wanted it, it was on now, and she was going to get it.

Every. Last. Inch.

At least, that was my plan.

"Where the fuck did he go?"

Mason's voice rang through the darkness, bringing clarity back to my mind. I pulled away and looked down at Star's flushed face. The girl I hated and wanted to destroy. Not some object to desire. What the fuck was wrong with me?

"Get the fuck away from me," I growled and shoved her on the ground.

She landed ass first in the dirt and looked up at me with tears sparkling in her eyes. I didn't care. Fuck her. That's where she belonged.

"By the way," I sang while spinning around to walk away. "You taste like shit."

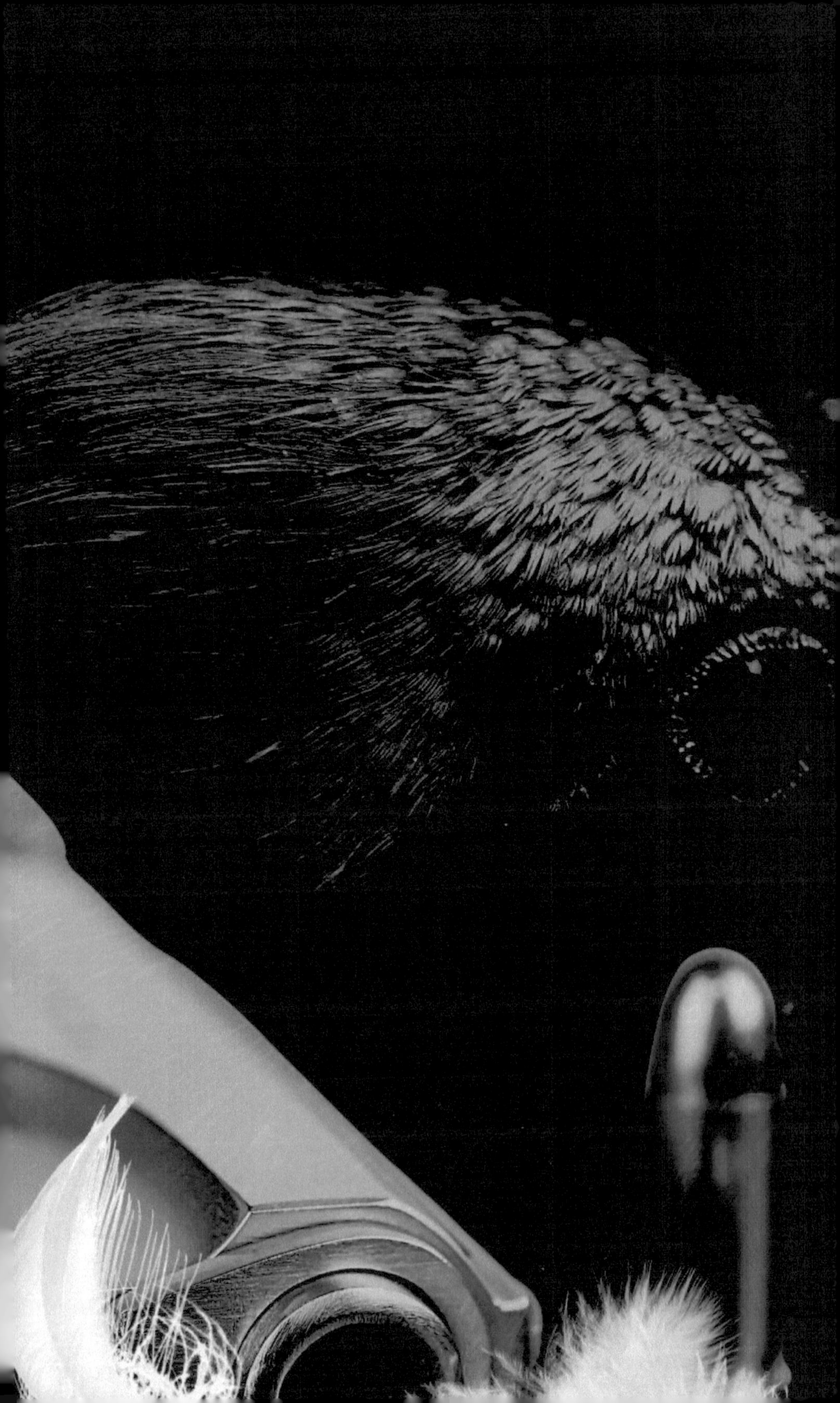

Chapter 16

Star

Two things in this world helped calm my soul, dancing and the salty, fresh scent of ocean air. When I had a particularly rough day, I'd head to the beach and lay back to let the cool mist wash over me.

It was the same scent here as it was back home, but the mist was warm. Perhaps that was why I couldn't stop those words from floating through my head.

I smiled at Harper and relaxed back in my lounger. Although her father smiled at me when I showed up at her house, he was not impressed that I was there. And less so when I dragged her out the front door. And dragged was exactly what I had to do.

I tried gently to coax Harper into coming to the beach, but after it took an hour to convince her to put her swimwear on, it became evident that a firmer touch was needed.

By the time I convinced Harper to leave, the sun would be

setting, and I really needed to get away from the house. Or should I say, the lad next door.

'You taste like shit.'

Why did that bother me so much? It was nothing more than an insult spewed from a spiteful mouth—a soft and firm mouth that tasted like a bottle of fine wine.

That's what was troubling me. Just because I hadn't shagged before didn't mean I hadn't done other things.

Back home, a girl in my position didn't get where she was without indulging in a make-out session or two.

There was nothing south of the border, but I still had enough experience to know when a lad enjoyed a kiss. And Silas was just as lost in my mouth as I was his. In fact, it was that hunger pouring off him that sucked me in.

I suppose it didn't matter. The arsehole made it clear there wouldn't be an encore performance, which I was utterly fine with— I didn't want to kiss him.

Is that why you've eaten nothing but fruit today?

That didn't mean anything. There was nothing wrong with eating a healthy diet.

You brushed your teeth three times.

Oral hygiene was important.

You touched yourself...

"Alright, that's enough."

Harper's brows knit together. "What?"

"Nothing," I waved my hand and told my thoughts to slog off. "I thought I saw a bug."

She seemed to accept it. At least, that's what I chose to assume when she shrugged and settled back in her lounger.

I did the same. Dropping my head back while trying to enjoy the sun's warm rays, but I couldn't stop staring at Harper. While it was nice to see her finally relax a bit, she was still hiding.

Except this time, she used a pair of plaid shorts and a white cotton T-shirt instead of her hair, which looked fantastic in the sun, by the way. Her red curls sparkled like divinely cut rubies.

"Your swimwear is very cute. You should show it off."

And I meant cute. Under her clothes, Harper was wearing a black one-piece decorated with little daisies. It was a suit that was closer to something a child would pick than a teenage girl, which I chalked up to the strictness of her father.

He gave me a list of rules for his daughter before we left the house. Most of which were normal parent laws. No alcohol or boys. That type of thing. It was the don't let my daughter talk to anyone else, and she better be back here in two hours, that made me cock a brow.

"I'm fine." Harper tucked herself back in the lounger and hugged her knees.

The last thing that girl was, was fine.

"Is it just you and your dad?"

"I have a brother." She released a tiny sigh and laid her cheek on her knees. "But he's gone away to college."

I rolled onto my side and looked over at her. "You must miss him."

She nodded in response.

A few people at school had mentioned Sean Callaghan. Apparently, he was quite the quarterback. I was more interested in the stories I heard about him and Mason Kessler. Whom Sean did not get along with, from my understanding. Can't say I blamed him.

I had no problem slapping around the little pissant that picked on Will last year. If Harper was my sister, I'd hate the bloke too. Hell, I did hate him, which posed an interesting question.

"Your dad seems very protective." My gaze swept across her face, reading the micro-expressions pulling on her lips. "How come he hasn't talked to the school?"

"About what?"

Harper was good at hiding everything except her emotions. She knew exactly what I was talking about.

"All the arseholes that pick on you in that place," I announced.

"It's fine."

It's not fine.

"Harper," I sighed and sat up. "I had to break you out of a locker yesterday."

Lord knows how long she'd been in there. I just happened to pass by and hear her crying.

"Why don't you say something? Are you that afraid of Mason Kessler that you won't tell your dad what's going on?"

I had my answer when Harper's face paled. And it wasn't because of what I said. It was because of who was walking down the beach. As if hell heard me call his unholy name, Mason Kessler sauntered across the sand with his green eyes twinkling. Less than a foot behind him was the devil himself.

"Have you told your parents about him?" Harper wondered while tipping her chin at Silas.

No, I hadn't. My parents had enough to worry about—Ash just hit his terrible toddler phase, the twins wouldn't calm down, and then there was Cy. He'd been in school for less than a week, and my parents already had a meeting this afternoon because he was fighting.

I loved my brother, but he gave new meaning to the word trouble. They didn't need me causing more.

Harper leaned over and whispered, "We should go."

"This is a public beach." My eyes narrowed in on Silas. "We're not going anywhere."

I'd be damned if I was going to let some arsehole chase me away from my relaxing Saturday afternoon. I was going to sit right here and enjoy the sun.

If they didn't like it, then they could leave. A thought I only became more determined to do when Silas's blue eyes landed on me.

His black hair shone in the light as he tipped his head and cocked a brow. I couldn't stop staring at the saliva glistening on his thick bottom lip. Did his mouth always look that delectable, or was it the smirk tugging on the corner that drew me in?

Stop fawning over the bloody twat.

I tried to do just that. I laid back down and focused on the light warming my skin. But I knew he was looking at me. I could feel his eyes raking over my body, soaking up every inch of my curves.

The longer I fought to ignore it, the more I could feel his caress gently sweeping down my side. Eventually, I couldn't fight it anymore. My eyes swung back over to the victorious smile on Silas's face.

He'd won. I'd done exactly what he wanted. I gave him my attention, which was so much worse when I attempted to shove away the butterflies erupting in my gut and falling out of my lounger. I flopped down in the warm sand like a sack of potatoes.

Bloody hell.

"Oh my God," Harper peeked over the edge of her lounger. "Are you okay?"

"I'm fine," I grumbled and pushed myself up.

The beach was full of people, yet it was Silas's chuckle that thundered through my ears. A world-class dancer should not be this clumsy, and I wasn't until Silas was around.

Then I walked into lockers and tripped over my own feet. I glared over at the snickering arsehole, brushed the sand off my skin, and flipped him the bird before laying back down.

That was my first mistake. The second was not looking away right after. Silas smirked as if my insolence was some sort of challenge and reached back to lift his shirt over his head. When the chiseled lines of his torso came into view, I knew I was fucked.

The lad was built better than the sculptures I'd studied in art class. Every dip and curve of his solid exterior tempted me to poke the beast buried inside him. And he knew it, too.

Tipped his chin at me as if silently daring me to touch him, which was precisely what I wanted to do. I wanted to graze my fingers over the textured black wing tattooed on his arm. Then down to the deep-set V disappearing in his black shorts.

My only saving grace came when I heard Harper squeak. She was also staring over there. Her bright brown eyes were stuck on Mason, glimmering with a feeling I knew all too well.

Guilt.

* * *

I pulled into the parking lot and looked up at the red sign saying Pop Pop's Garage. It wasn't the kind of place I would pick to bring my car, but it was the one Harper recommended. I lost count of how many times Dad looked at my car, and it stalled yet again on the way to Harper's house.

As we sat on the side of the road for twenty minutes, all I could think was, thank God someone else was with me this time. I was starting to think I was going crazy, and maybe I was.

After all, I did agree to leave the beach because I was lusting after a lad I should be kicking in the nads. One thing was for sure, I couldn't take much more of this.

I stepped out and eyed the chain-link fence at the back of the building. Cars in various states of decay sat on the other side, making me wonder if maybe I should look for another mechanic shop.

There had to be a more upscale shop in town. But would my car make it there without another stall?

With a sigh, I headed into the building. Who knows how long I'd be stranded on the side of the road next time. I didn't want to call Dad.

He'd just mutter on about girls not knowing how to take care of their vehicles. While he had a point—I did just learn how to pump my own petrol—I didn't want to hear it.

I stepped through the doors, a bit surprised at how well put together the interior was. The red walls went nicely with the black leather bench and counter. Behind the counter were various pictures.

One, in particular, caught my attention. An older man with greying hair stood beside a smiling Shelby, who was wearing the same grey coveralls. She was so beautifully done up at school. It was odd seeing a girl like that with grease on her face.

No one answered when I slapped the bell on the counter. So, I tried again, this time calling out, "Hello, is anyone here?"

When that resulted in nothing, I peeked into the garage. Other than a black pick-up propped up on blocks, it was empty. I did, however, hear laughter coming from the open back door. Already incredibly frustrated with my day, I charged over, prepared to give the mechanic a piece of my mind.

The scene outside made me stop and smile.

Seated around a picnic table enjoying a feast of sandwiches and fruit was a cute little family. Before the twins came, we'd have outings like this all the time. We'd sit in the park and enjoy Mum's ham sandwiches while running around.

Now there were too many of us for our parents to control, especially with Ash. My baby brother would go one way while the twins took off to terrorize other families. I swear those three were in cahoots.

I cocked my head and watched the woman sweep her blonde hair over her shoulder. The most adorable little boy jumped up and down as she passed him a muffin.

The big smile on his face caused his light gaze to glimmer like polished silver. I'd never seen eyes that color before. They were utterly breathtaking.

I was a bit disappointed when the man turned to look at me and didn't have the same color.

"Oh, sorry, I didn't see you there." He reared back, shock glimmering in his blue eyes.

Ice-blue, like Silas. Though, his were more crystal than ice.

Stop thinking about him!

I cleared my throat and held up my hand. "I didn't mean to interrupt."

I could come back later when I wouldn't be disrupting their picnic.

"No problem. I'm supposed to be working anyway." He stood up, kissed the woman on the forehead, and walked over. "What can I help you with?"

"I, ah…" Unsure, I glanced at the spider web inked on his neck and down to the name displayed on his coveralls.

Key? That was an unusual name. Then again, mine was Star.

"Um, my car keeps stalling."

The top few buttons of his coveralls were open, displaying the black feathers of a crow's head. Key looked more like a criminal than a mechanic to me. Or an arsehole. Silas had a raven tattooed on him. Maybe the arseholes had a thing for blackbirds?

"Does it make a sound before it stalls?"

"Not really." I blew out a frustrated breath. "It just bloody stops."

"Let me guess." He grabbed a rag from his back pocket and

wiped his hands. "After a minute or two, it starts right up again. Like nothing's wrong?"

My eyes widened. "Yes." Maybe I wasn't going mad?

"I think I know what's wrong. Take a seat." Key tipped his head, causing his blond hair to shimmer in the light. "Shouldn't take more than a few minutes."

Thank the lord.

I happily passed him my keys and watched him disappear inside. I was about to follow when the woman called out.

"You can sit with us." She smiled over at me. "If you don't want to sit alone inside, that is?"

Other than Lana, I hadn't seen many friendly faces in this town. Everyone at school seemed to follow Silas and Mason. Even Riley and Shelby were skeptical when they met me. That I understood, they were protecting Harper.

A twang rang through my heart when I thought about seeing her in the cafeteria all alone. But she wasn't alone. Not like Emily was.

If I had just...

I sucked back my guilt and forced a smile onto my face. She didn't say much as I graciously accepted her offer and took a seat. While I desperately wanted to talk to someone, to feel like I had someone in this world to count on, I was thankful for the quiet.

And then I wasn't.

My mind started to wander, wondering if this was how Emily felt all those years? Did she have anyone to lean on? A place to escape? Or did I take that all away from her?

"Don't worry." The woman bumped my shoulder. "Key will figure out what's wrong with your car."

The brightness of her green eyes struck me as both beautiful and odd. The little boy with them not only had different colored eyes, but his hair was dark. My parents were polar opposites of each other. Mum had platinum hair and light eyes, while Dad's were dark.

My brothers and I looked very different, but we all had something from our parents. Other than the woman's full lips, I didn't see anything this child had in common with his.

"He's adorable." I nodded at the boy. "Let me guess, around two or three?"

"Two and a half." She smiled, "Do you have any?"

"Lord no," I chuckled. "I have five little brothers, and trust me, that's enough to scare any woman off birthing babies."

I loved my brothers, but sometimes I wanted to kill them.

"Brother's can be hard sometimes."

Her whispered words tugged at my heart, almost as much as the deep-set lines washing over her face, lines of horrible grief and loss. I'd felt this pain in the air once before when Emily's parents came to visit me.

"Star, you are a beautiful girl with a bright future." Mrs. Perkins reached out and tightly grasped my hand. "Promise me you won't throw that away. Become the woman my Emily would've been. Let your light shine, beautiful girl."

I turned away from her tear-streaked face and stared at the monitor echoing beeps through the room because there was no light left in me—just the dark void of evil threatening to devour my soul.

"It gets better." The woman reached out and swept my hair over my shoulder. "You'll never forget them, but you learn how to move on."

I searched her gaze for deception. All I found was peace. A peace I'd never have. She may have been able to move past her ghosts, but mine were sent to seek retribution for my sins.

"Found the problem," Key announced while holding up a ping pong ball.

My brows furrowed. "A ball?"

"Put one of these in the gas tank, and it gets sucked down into the exhaust, causing your car to stall. When it floats back up...."

"The car will be fine," I finished for him.

Son of a...

He tossed me the ball and sat down beside the woman, pulling her into his arms. "I'd say someone's pulling a prank on you."

Prank, my arse.

My hands fisted. If he wanted to play with me, fine. I'd had just about enough of Silas Creswell. If no one else in this town would stand up to that arsehole and his friend, then I would. I'd tear that castle down around him while everyone watched.

Come one, come all,
And watch your king fall.

"When you said we had to go, I thought we were going somewhere fun." Mase cocked a brow at my cousin's school. "Not playtime at Midgarden."

I pulled into the parking lot and blew out a breath. Spending time at Finn's school wasn't my idea of a fun Saturday afternoon either. I'd rather be at the beach imagining what I could do to Star in that little red bikini, but here we were.

Ah well, it was probably a good thing we weren't there anymore. Star and Harper ducked out before we did, but enough people saw them there. Someone would've said something to Mase, and I didn't feel like putting out that fire. Not today.

"Don't get me wrong. I always had a thing for Miss Fawn—I'd totally tap that shit."

"Is there any shit you wouldn't tap?"

There was no hesitation in Mase's answer, "Naomi."

I agreed with him there. Was Naomi hot? Yeah. The issue came when she opened her mouth or looked at you or waved her hand in that dismissive way.

Anything she did, really. The girl was an utter cunt, that neither Mase nor I could stand. How Micha and Logan put up with her, I had no idea.

"Seriously." Mase tipped his head my way. "What the fuck are we doing here?"

"Finn got in trouble."

"Finn?"

I nodded. "That's what your old man said."

"What'd he do? Spout off the theory of relativity during nap time?"

"I don't know, but whatever it is, it can't be good." I sighed and opened the door to my Hummer. "They called a meeting on a Saturday."

Every night I went to bed wondering if Finn was still afraid. Could he sleep through the night now, or did he just hate me more? It killed me not knowing. So, when Lou called asking me to come to this meeting, I jumped at the chance.

"A meeting is nothing." Mase swung his door open. "When they keep the school open just to put your ass in detention on the weekend, now that's when you gotta worry."

Right, forgot who I was talking to.

"Come on," I shook my head and hopped out. "Your old man's probably already here."

"Oh boy. Saturday afternoon with Louis." Mase sighed and stepped out to follow me.

I wish he'd cut that shit out and just call him Dad already.

"Are you worried about what they're going to say?"

I shook my head.

Don't get me wrong, when a school called parents in on a Saturday, some serious shit went down. That didn't matter to me. I'd just have to teach Finn how to get away with it better, was all. I was more worried about the hate I'd see in Finn's eyes.

"I'm sure it'll be fine." Mase slapped his hand on my back. "I mean… it's Finn. How bad could it be?"

Last year I'd have agreed with him, but Finn wasn't that sweet little boy anymore. Ryker killed that part of him. There was no telling what someone was capable of when the boogeyman took a piece of your soul.

As Mase and I stepped into the school, all I could hope for was that Lou could help him salvage the pieces left of my cousin.

My pulse picked up as we turned down the hall towards the office. Was Finn already there, waiting to spew hatred at me? Shock had Mase and me stopping dead in our tracks. It wasn't Finn that we found sitting in one of the red chairs.

Micha tipped his chin and glared up at us. He was about as impressed to be here as Mase was to see his brother sitting there.

"What the fuck, Micha?" Mase cried out. "You can't call your brother when you get back in town?"

"Sorry," Micha rolled his eyes over to Junior, seated in the chair next to him. "I had to come in and deal with this shit."

Junior curled his lip in response. "I told—"

"Drop it, Junior. I'm not in the mood to deal with your shit." Micha dismissively waved his hand at the kid.

It was scary how much he reminded me of Lou right now—sitting there with the same angry disappointment on his face that their father gave Mase daily. Was that why Micha attached himself to the kid? Because he saw his brother in Junior's disobedient nature?

Junior huffed and crossed his arms. "You're the one that put me in school with a psycho."

No. That kid was one hundred percent Micha.

"This shit isn't a joke, Junior," Micha barked back at him, giving me flashbacks of Lou.

He'd said those exact same words to Mase more than once. Were all Kesslers born with that *'don't fuck with me'* look on their face? Mase technically wasn't a Kessler, and even he could pull off that expression.

Junior sank back in his chair and muttered, "It's not my fault you can't find your girlfriend."

That made me cock a brow. Last summer, when Riley disappeared for an hour, Micha damn near lost his mind. It turned out she was with Parker the whole time.

No one told him about that because then Parker would need a tube to breathe. Can't say I blamed him. That girl was a magnet for bad attention.

"I know exactly where she is, and as soon as this shit is dealt with, I'll hunt her ass down." Micha's jaw twitched as he muttered, "Bad reception, my ass."

"You didn't have to come." Junior's jaw mirrored Micha's twitch. "I didn't ask you to be here."

"And I didn't ask you, and Finn didn't have to stab some little shit."

"What?" Finn stabbed someone? That didn't sound like him. Did Ryker fuck him up that bad?

"I told you," Junior barked back. "He stabbed himself."

"First rule of deception, kid…." Mase dropped down in the chair next to Junior. "Come up with a believable lie."

I mean… I kind of had to agree with Mase there. Junior grew up with a crack-whore for a mother in a neighborhood full of gangs.

Figured the kid would be able to come up with something better than that.

"I'm not lying." Junior threw his finger up to point at Lou and Finn walking into the office. "Ask Finn."

I didn't know I could miss someone this much until I saw my cousin. Every fiber of my being pulled at me to rush over there and scoop him up and ruffle my fingers through his black hair until he gave me that bright shining smile that lit up my life.

But there was no smile on his face or light in his bright eyes. Just a scowl of discontent as he flopped down in one of the vacant chairs.

"Don't bother," Finn grumbled. "They won't believe us."

I wanted to believe him. I really did.

"You gotta admit, it's kind of unbelievable." I cocked my head at my cousin. "Why would someone stab themselves?"

"I don't know? Why would someone who says they love you, give you away?"

Ouch.

He may as well have punched me in the gut with that statement.

"We've been through this, Phineas," Lou huffed out a groan. "Your cousin is merely doing what he thinks is best."

Finn shot a glare my way. "Whatever helps him sleep at night."

I sighed and scrubbed a hand down my face. Maybe my old man was right, and Finn would be better off with us? At least he wouldn't hate me then.

"Don't give up now." Lou placed a reassuring hand on my shoulder. "He is making progress."

I was about to argue that this meeting said otherwise when the office door opened, and three people stepped out. The man and woman I recognized as Star's parents, but it was the little shit with the tears in his eyes that had my jaw-dropping.

Motherfucker.

"Oh good, everyone's here." Midgarden's principal nodded at the crowd in the room. "This is Cypress Chadwick."

Of course. Another fucking tree.

"The victim."

Cy sucked back a sob and rolled his dark eyes my way. This kid was not a goddamn victim. He was the prick that made victims like what he was doing to my cousin. Finn didn't do shit to him.

That motherfucker stabbed himself. There was no doubt in my mind about that.

"There won't be a meeting." I marched across the room and grabbed my cousin's hand. "Come on, Finn. We're leaving."

For the first time in I don't know how long, Finn smiled up at me as we headed for the exit. Lou stopped us before we could leave the office.

He stepped in front of me and held his hand up. "You can't go, Silas."

"The fuck we can't. That little shit is lying, and I'm not going to let my cousin take the fall."

"Yeah!" Finn yelled in agreement.

"Think about what you're doing here." Lou leaned in and added, "I'd hate to see young Finn in handcuffs."

Fuck. As much as I hated to admit it, he was right. Finn wouldn't have a record—no cop in this town dared to charge us with anything—but he'd still be arrested. Looking over at Mase, I released a heavy sigh. I knew what that could do to someone Finn's age.

"Fine." I begrudgingly dropped Finn's hand, then pointed at Cy. "Don't think I don't know what you're up to."

Cy batted his innocent eyes. "I was just trying to play with them when Junior hit me for no reason."

Did no one else see that smirk flash across his face?

"Bullshit!" Junior jumped out of his chair with his chest puffed up. "I only hit you because you hit him."

"Junior, sit down," Micha growled.

"Fuck you, Micha!"

"Mr. Alverez…" The principal wagged her finger. "I will not have that kind of language in this office."

"Oh, blow it out your ass, Mrs. Templeton."

Before Junior could be reprimanded, Micha pulled him back down and whispered something in his ear. Junior quieted down after that, and judging by the look he gave me, he was on to Cy's shit too.

Though, his attention wasn't on the little shit. It was on his parents. Who had yet to say anything in their child's defense.

I tipped my head at the mother, who had the same small frame and platinum hair as Star. Which only pissed me off more. When I swung my gaze to the father, I lost it.

He had the same glimmer of shame in his dark orbs that I'd seen so many times on his daughter. Motherfucker knew exactly what his kid was.

Unlike his parents, I had no problem putting Cy in his place.

"You little shit." I threw my finger up and charged across the room. "I will end you."

No one fucked with my cousin.

Lou grabbed my shoulder. "Silas, calm down."

"I will not calm down!" I shrugged out of Lou's grasp and locked my glare on Cy, "You fucked with the wrong family."

Cy turned on the waterworks. Crying out, "Mummy, I'm scared," while clutching onto her arm like some innocent fucking angel.

"Mummy, I'm scared," I sang mockingly back at him.

I'd give him something to be scared of.

Cy's dad stepped in front of his son and said, "I understand that you're upset, but you need to stop taking it out on my son."

Now you fucking speak.

"Your son's a fucking psycho." I locked my stare on his. "But you know that, don't you?"

They had to see it. How could they not?

"Perhaps you should wait out here, Mr. Creswell," Mrs. Templeton intervened, "While the rest of us discuss this matter."

"Agreed," Cy's dad nodded.

My eyes narrowed on him. Interesting how he didn't deny the psycho comment.

The principal shuffled everyone into the office, then shot me a look before closing the door.

"Dude," Mase sang from behind me. "You just attacked a kid."

"He's not a fucking kid," I grumbled and sat down beside him. "He's devil spawn."

I could've spent the time explaining what I knew about the kid to my best friend, but I preferred to stare at the closed door. My cousin was in there, being blamed for god knows what.

All because Cy could pull off the cherub-look better than him. One thing I could guarantee, the last person in that room that was innocent was fucking Cy.

Twice, Mase had to stop me from barging into the meeting. He tried to distract me with other topics. Some worked. Others just wound me up more. By the time the door opened, and everyone came out, I was a giant ball of frustration.

But I was calmer than I was a few minutes ago. At least I didn't want to punch the kid anymore. Can't imagine that would go over too well with his parents.

I watched the principal thank everyone and shake hands, waiting to hear the fate of my cousin, which turned out to be three days suspension. My old man was going to love that. I could hear the lecture now.

'Finn wouldn't have stabbed anyone if he was with us.'

But Finn didn't do shit. Micha knew it. I knew it. And fucking Cy knew it.

While the adults were talking, Cy skipped over to me with a fake as fuck smile on his face. "I hope we can all be friends now?"

"I know what you're up to."

"Do you really." Cy leaned in and quietly added, "Because I'm just getting started. I told you to stay away from my sister."

Like the dipshit he was, Mason loudly proclaimed, "I heard that. You just threatened him."

The only person who didn't look our way was Micha. He was too busy sizing up Cy's parents.

"Everything okay over there, Cy?" his dad called out.

Almost instantly, the kid washed an innocent spark in his eyes. "Yeah, Dad. Silas was just saying how happy he was that everything got worked out."

"That's good," his dad nodded. "Hopefully there won't be any more trouble."

Mase's jaw dropped.

Welcome to the party, asshole.

Alright. I could play Cy's game. Forcing a smile on my face, I rested my elbows on my knees and leaned in closer to the little shit.

"You're awfully protective of your sister. It'd be a shame if someone took her away from you."

Cy's gaze snapped back to mine. "The same could be said about your cousin."

Was I really having a stare-down with a ten-year-old right now? The really fucked up part was Cy's lack of fear. I could seriously fuck this kid up, and there wasn't a single flicker of hesitation on his face.

Even Preston had some sense of self-preservation. It was disturbing, to say the least.

"Come on, Cy," his mom waved at the office door, "time to go."

"Okay, Mum," he happily sang and left with her. But not before he whispered, "Remember, if you fuck with mine, then I'll fuck with yours."

Once again, Mase's jaw dropped. "Holy fucken shit."

Holy fucken shit was right.

"What are you gonna do?"

A smirk spread across my face as I watched Cy skip away with his parents. "Destroy the thing he loves most."

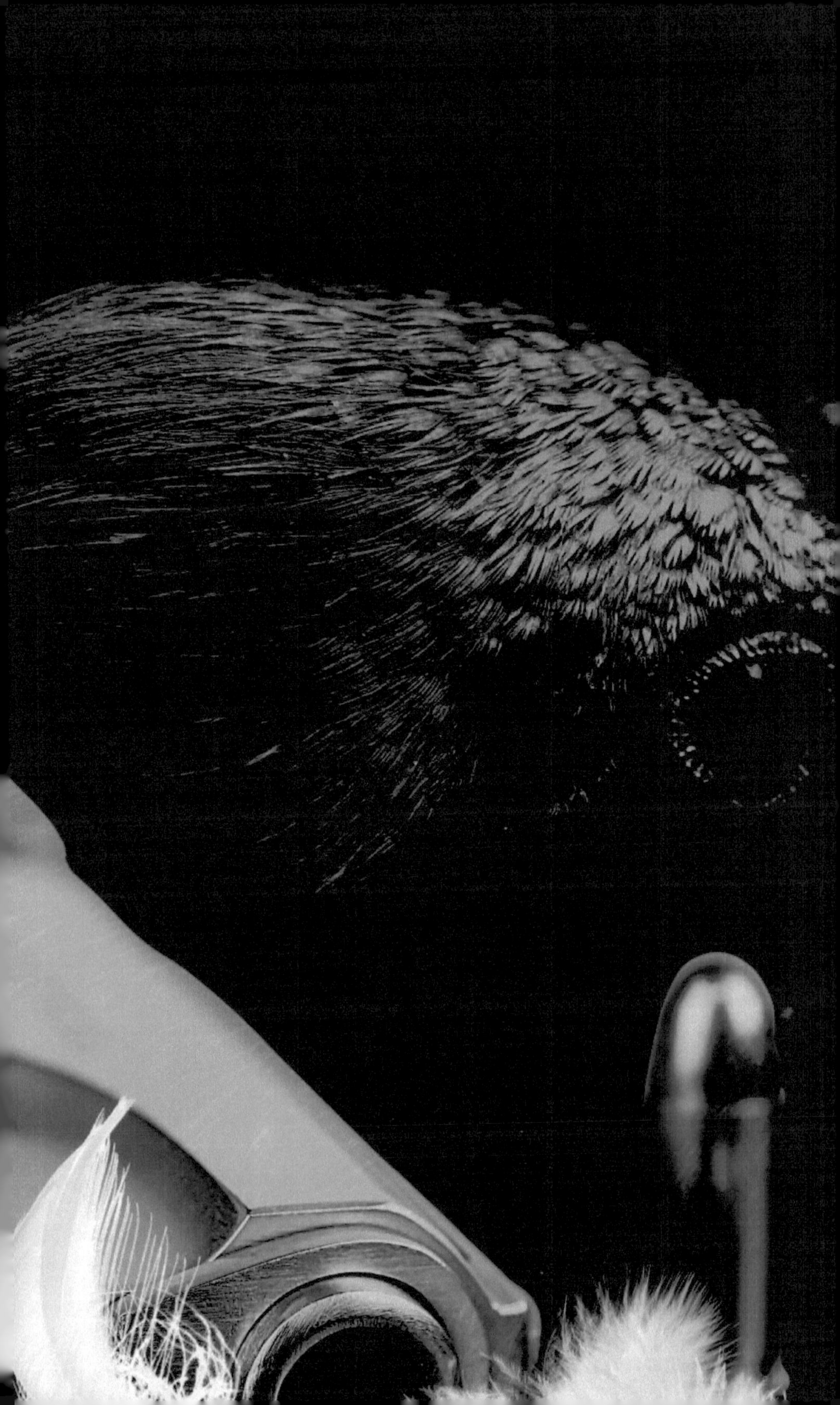

Chapter 18
Star

At night, Harper's house reminded me of the spooky castles back home that everyone claimed were haunted. Personally, I'd never seen any ghostly apparitions floating around at night. I'd also never snuck inside those abandoned stone structures.

I learned my lesson after what happened to Charlie. They never did catch the guy that held him hostage for three days. Nor did he talk about what happened to him. It was still enough to keep me away from those places.

This building was magnificent in the daylight, with beautifully sculpted shrubs and a trickling fountain with deep green leaves climbing the brick walls. I used to dream of houses like this when I was a child, twirling around the room in grandma's hoop skirt.

Sometimes Mum and Grandma would join me. We'd have tea in the garden while pretending we were members of the O'Hara family.

Harper's house was giving off a very different vibe right now.

The moon shone down on the roof's peaks, casting eerie shadows across the lawn. Instead of being a societal belle at the ball, I was an interloper in a nightmarish abyss. It felt like those inky black tendrils were spreading over the grass, getting ready to snatch me.

As I made my way to the front door, I couldn't help but think of poor Charlie. The breaking news headline that day read *'Lost Child Found,'* but it was the terror displayed on his face that I'd never forget. Even under the blanket the paramedics wrapped around him, I could see Charlie shaking.

I stepped up to the dark blue door and gingerly reached for the heavy handle of a big brass door knocker. The deep-set eyes of an intricately carved wolf stared back at me as I announced my arrival.

Each knock caused his menacing growl to vibrate loudly on the other side. Only when the door swung open, pouring light on the deck, did I allow myself to breathe.

An older woman dressed in a black skirt and white blouse looked down her nose at me. "Can I help you?"

"I'm here to see Harper."

"I see." Her cold stare ran disapprovingly over the gold sequins of my dress. "Is she expecting you?"

I lied. "Yes."

She stared at me for a few seconds before stepping to the side and waving me in.

"Miss Callaghan is in her room. I assume you don't need assistance getting there."

"No," I shook my head, "I know where it is."

Only because I had to drag her in there earlier to find her swimwear.

She didn't say anything else. Simply spun around—with perfect poise, might I add—and waltzed away.

Wow. Snooty much?

That woman could put some of the nobles back home to shame.

Anxious to get the night started, I marched across the black marble flooring to the right and headed for Harper's room. No one would guess people actually lived here, though I suppose personal space was one of the upsides to living in such a large place.

Alone time was something I could appreciate with having five little brothers. Less than an hour ago, the twins scared me half to death when they burst into my room. It didn't matter how many times I told them to get out. They continued swinging their sticks around in a mock gladiator fight.

A fight that I won by smashing Elm in the face with a pillow. I'd be the last person to argue for more space. So long as it didn't amplify sounds like this.

Good lord. The clicking of my heels, and even my breathing, rang through the air like the thunder of drums. As did the voice I heard coming from an ajar door down the hall.

"I have no investment in your war, nor do I care about the outcome."

War? That was an odd word to use, which was precisely why I tiptoed across the hall to peek through the open crack.

"I'm not one of your lackeys, Jax. So, I'd watch my tone if I were you, or I'll burn down that club of yours."

Harper's dad was pacing around what appeared to be an office, with a phone held up to his ear. He looked agitated. A business thing, perhaps? Harper said her dad dealt in equity and assets. I'm not sure what that meant, but it sounded very business-like to me.

"Be glad I told you she was in Miami. I didn't have to give you any information at all. Now I suggest you get off your ass and find her."

Was he looking for someone? Why?

"I don't care what you do. Ship her off, put a bullet in her head, whatever. She's your problem now."

I couldn't stop the gasp from slipping past my lips. Despite throwing my hand up to muffle the sound, Harper's dad heard me. My heart stopped as his eyes met mine.

His nonchalant attitude was more disturbing than the conversation he was having. Mr. Callaghan didn't threaten me or yell. He didn't even narrow his eyes as he walked over and pushed the door shut.

The last thing I heard him say was, "I'd start by watching Chase Mathers if I were you."

Maybe it wasn't what I thought it was? If he was planning some kind of hit, then surely he would've said something. Or, at the very least, threatened me into silence.

Deciding to go with that theory—it was the only thing that made sense—I straightened my shoulders and continued down the hall. The more I thought about it, the more ridiculous it sounded. Of course, Mr. Callaghan wasn't planning on having someone 'knocked off.'

"Come on, Star." I snickered at my own stupidity. "Just because you're in America, doesn't mean you're in the middle of a mob movie."

But how fascinating would that be? Living in a world where the laws weren't determined by men with badges, but those with power. Not that I would want to be part of that life, but I wouldn't mind the chance to observe it. I'd always been interested in the finer intricacies of the human psyche.

In particular, the dark parts. Richard Ramirez, Manson, and Bundy. They all had one thing in common. An uncanny ability to pull the wool over people's eyes.

One minute they'd be bathing in the blood of their victims. The next, they'd be kissing their girlfriend on the cheek, and she'd be none the wiser. What kind of person could do that?

It was that divine deception that drove me into my current mission. One that started with Harper Callaghan. Silas and Mason thought they had all the power.

Walking around like royalty, and the people in this town let them. I tried going to the police. Showed them the ping pong ball and told them about the assault in the woods. Know what the officer said?

"I don't know what to tell you, Miss Chadwick. Perhaps you should just steer clear of those boys."

Steer clear of them. That's all I got. As if I hadn't been trying to do that already.

I paused in front of Harper's bedroom door and smirked.

Let's see what the kings of Ashen Springs do when their drowned rat fights back.

Retribution was coming, and Harper would be the avenging angel. Come hell or high water, I'd pull her out of that pit of despair and show her how much power those boys really had.

When she pulled them off their thrones, Emily's tormented spirit would finally have some peace. I may not be able to save her bright light, but I could make damn sure Harper's shone brighter than the sun.

That would be my penance.

Filled with determination, I swung open the door and sauntered into Harper's bedroom, where I found her tucked into the corner of her bed, staring back at me with wide eyes.

"Star? What are you doing here?"

I've come to save your soul.

"Get up," I announced. "We're going out."

The decorations in here had to go. Harper wasn't a seven-year-old child. She didn't need to be surrounded by hordes of stuffed animals and pink ruffles.

This room should be filled with flair and pizzazz. It should depict the fierce creature I was going to pull out of her.

"W-what?" She shuffled back on the bed. "I-I can't."

Alright, maybe not fierce. I could settle with a cute little snarl.

"Sure you can."

"B-but my father... I-I can't."

Yes, her father was unusually strict, which was exactly why I'd brought an extra dose of charm. And some oatmeal cookies.

For once, the universe seemed to be on my side.

A knock rapped from the other side of the door as Harper's dad announced, "I'm going out. I'll be back in the morning."

Well, that solved that problem.

I listened to his footsteps echo in the distance and smiled. "Crisis averted."

Now Harper was really panicking.

She hopped off the bed and held up her tiny hands. "But... I don't have anything to wear."

I was prepared for that issue too.

"That's why I brought this," I said, holding up the bag in my hand.

I could sense an argument coming when her face paled. So, I passed her the bag and pushed her into the bathroom before she could start. She hesitated, naturally, but I knew enough about the girl to take care of that situation.

"If you refuse to go out with me," I pulled out my phone and sighed. "Then I guess I'll have to bring the party here."

If a gasp could suck all the air out the room, then Harper's would've done just that. She didn't like crowds. I had a feeling the threat of bringing one here would be worse than taking her to one.

"Well, what's it gonna be?"

She answered me by clutching tightly onto the bag and ducking into the bathroom.

While she got dressed, I occupied myself by shuffling around her room and humming in satisfaction. My intent was to explore. Delve deeper into the personality she fought so hard to keep hidden.

I didn't make it far.

A picture displayed proudly on her bedside table caused my brows to knit. The heart-shaped frame was nestled around two children.

A little girl with deep red hair–clearly Harper. The other was a boy with sparkling green eyes and an olive complexion.

Mason?

Sitting on the edge of her bed, I picked up the picture. It was definitely Mason Kessler. I'd recognize that mischievous smile anywhere. The expression on his face was almost as bright and happy as Harper's. But it was the love shining warmly in his eyes that kept me staring.

He couldn't be more than nine or ten in this picture, and he was gazing at Harper like she was the most precious thing in the world.

I looked over at the bathroom door. How did two people go from this to what they were now? What happened to these bright, happy children?

Harper tugged on the skirt of her dress yet again, making me sigh. She'd been fretting over it since she stepped out of the bathroom. I told her she looked fabulous, which she did. Black was her color, and the way the silk hugged her curves would make any man lose his mind. If I was her, I'd never take it off.

She didn't see it that way. One little dress was the end of the world. I swear she thought people were waiting outside to egg her. Her lack of self-confidence was possibly the most depressing thing I'd ever witnessed.

Quite frankly, I was surprised I got her in the car, especially after I brought up that picture. The door to her vault slammed shut faster than I could take my next breath.

She hadn't said much since then. Mason Kessler was clearly a sore topic, and not because of how he treated her. That much I knew.

Luckily, I had the perfect way to take her mind off it.

I'd overheard some kids in school talking about a club. Apparently, they had a great salsa band and good food, which sounded fantastic to me. After the week I had, I needed a little fun.

A place where I could go and dance my troubles away. The legal age in America was twenty-one, a problem great cleavage could remedy. One thing I'd learned about men, they'd do just about anything for a pair of breasts.

When I pulled into the parking lot, lit up by the large Mallum sign, I swear I literally heard Harper's heart drop.

Her voice rose to a high pitch as she shrieked, "We can't go here!"

"Why not?"

I didn't see the problem. It looked like a classy place. One of the walls was made entirely of glass, allowing me to see the deep red interior. Rustic wooden tables sat on clean black tiles next to a sleek bar.

Even the people inside were dressed to impress. Good thing I dusted off a couple of my competition dresses. We should fit right in.

Harper leaned in and whispered, "This is Mason's dad's bar."

"So?" I glanced around the parking lot. "I don't see Mason's dad anywhere."

"We can't go in there," she insisted with a headshake.

Once again, the question of what happened popped into my head. Why was she so afraid of him? Whatever it was, she couldn't go on this way. I'd seen firsthand what fear and loneliness could do to a person.

I not only watched Emily's destruction. I reveled in it. Fed my monster with each tear that sprang from her eyes. And she was a ravenous creature, that beast inside me. She devoured pieces of Emily's soul until there was nothing left. Nothing but the aching hollow void that came for me one day in the bathroom…

Knock…

Knock…

"Piss off." Good Lord, couldn't a girl go to the washroom in peace?

Knock…

Knock…

I rolled my eyes to the closed bathroom stall. "Go away."

It was probably Madeline. Everyone knew she fancied girls. I wouldn't be surprised if she was trying to spy on me.

"You're in the wrong spot to sneak a peek, Madeline. If you want to see the really juicy bits, you should be in the next stall."

Just last week, Alice caught her looking over the top of the stall. What kind of pervert did that? Then again, Madeline was always a little off.

Knock…

Knock…

I sighed at the black shoes visible under the door.

Knock…

Knock…

Alright, that's enough of that.

I stood up and threw the door open, prepared to give the incessant twat a piece of my mind. What I saw caused the ground to fall out from under me. A pair of broken brown eyes stared back at me as the barrel of a gun lifted. The first shot tore through flesh with a thundering bang. My body barely had time to register the pain slicing through my chest before the next shot rang through the air.

I stared down at the bright crimson stain seeping in through my shirt and coughed out more blood.

"You were right, Star," Emily tipped her head as I collapsed on the cold tiles. "I am worthless."

I couldn't talk, couldn't move, or suck in enough air. All I could do was stare up at Emily as a coppery tint choked away the words stuck in my throat.

She lifted the gun and pressed the barrel to her temple, "But you'll never forget me."

Bang!

That last shot rang through my head like the death bells I heard calling for me that day. I couldn't let that happen to Harper. I refused to sit idly by while the light faded from her eyes.

"You can't let Mason keep doing this to you. You need to stand up for yourself." *Before it's too late.*

Her head ducked, hiding the frown on her face behind a curtain of red curls. "I deserve it."

There was only one person in this car that deserved to be tormented. And it wasn't her.

"Whatever it is you think you've done," I twisted around and cupped her face, forcing her to look at me, "you've more than paid your penance."

Tears sprung up in her eyes, tugging at the remorse in my heart.

"You don't understand what I did."

"I don't care what you did."

And I didn't. This sweet, scared girl couldn't have done anything that bad. Not that warranted this kind of treatment.

"Harper," I sighed and swept a tear off her cheek. "I know something about guilt. If you let it, it will eat away at your soul until there's nothing left."

Emily was a happy child, bouncing around on the playground with a smile on her face. I took that from her. Permanently wiped the joy out of her life and stole her from the people she loved. The exact same thing Mason was doing to Harper.

"Now," I released all my frustration in one long breath and forced a smile on my lips, "we are going to go in there and have some fun because you deserve to have fun."

"But… what about Mason…"

"Fuck Mason Kessler, and fuck Silas too." I released her face and tugged on the handle of my door, "This is our night, not theirs."

If I could pull Harper out of her despair, then perhaps I could save both her and Mason.

Chapter 19

Silas

Oy, that little fuck. He threw my cousin under the bus, and there wasn't a thing I could do about it. Why did it feel like I just lost a war to a ten-year-old? Payback was coming.

I just had to figure out what said payback would be? I don't think knocking around a kid would go over very well with anyone. That could wait until later after I relieved some frustration.

"Really?" Mase cocked a brow at me when I pulled into the parking lot. "Mallum?"

"Yes, Mallum."

I told him I needed to let loose. Mallum did not fall under that description. Especially for him. Don't get me wrong, Lou's bar wasn't my first choice either, but it was the one place I wouldn't have to watch Mase like a hawk.

Everyone here was under strict instructions not to serve him alcohol, and no one, and I mean no one, went against Louis Kessler's orders.

Except for Derek Adams? Look how well that worked out for him. Riley was still Micha's, and he had even less credibility with his daughter than before. Too bad. Personally, I thought he was an outstanding father.

How many parents would give up their kids to an alcoholic, because they thought they'd be safer. Then again maybe, I just sympathized with him?

Mase let out a long groan and rolled his eyes. "Don't tell me you're worried that I'm gonna drink?"

My brow arched. I was always worried about that. And the constant fights and girls. Fuck, I was just worried. Since we were kids, I'd been watching him slowly deteriorate. Sooner or later that that last thread of sanity Mase was hanging by would break.

"Look," Mase sighed, "I swear I won't touch a drop."

"Like you didn't touch a drop last night?"

He opened his mouth to say something but quickly snapped it shut.

That's right, Asshole. I saw you sneak that beer.

Probably shouldn't have had that party, but coddling Mason is what got him in this mess in the first place.

Mase's head fell back with an exaggerated eye roll. "You know, I'm starting to become concerned with the seriousness you've taken in my sobriety."

Someone should take it fucking seriously—he sure as hell wasn't.

"Doesn't matter," I threw open the door and stepped out, "we're not here for the alcohol."

I was more interested in the private club underneath, than I was in getting shit face. Let's be honest, I should probably stay away from alcohol too. My common sense clearly went out the window when I drank. Last time, I kissed the Little Witch.

Mase hopped out and followed me. "Does this mean you've given up on a certain British Chippie next door?"

Should've known he'd bring her up.

"She was never an option."

"Sure," he snickered. "Keep telling yourself that."

Bastard.

Mase brought up Star just to get under my skin, and it was working. I lived my life resisting the urge to slap the asshole. The motherfucker had a barber shop quartet follow me around our school. But when he brought up that little witch, I was really tempted to give into that urge and slap the shit out of him.

The sad fact was, Mase was right. I didn't just want to fuck Star —I wanted to use her hard until there was nothing left for anyone else. It was my need to give into the desire that pissed me off more than anything else. Which was the exact reason we were here.

Most girls couldn't handle the shit Logan and Preston craved. Mallum was where those two fed that beast. However, Logan was banned last year. Mistress Vivi was a hard madame—if a girl stepped out of line, it was her wrath they got.

The customers got it just as bad. She only had one rule: don't mess with her girls. Logan had broken that one too many times. Before she banned him, the Mistress tied him down and gave Logan a taste of his own medicine. If anyone could shake the little witch from my head, it was Mistress Vivi.

Mallum was a popular spot in town. By this time of night, there was a fairly large line gathered on the other side of the velvet rope. Blue spotlights shone down on the crowd, a few of which were already dancing to the music wafting out from inside.

Getting in wouldn't be an issue for us. The only thing Stan, the bouncer, did when we wove our way towards him was nod and open the door. A couple of the more impatient people weren't too happy about that. They groaned and called out protests.

"We've been waiting for an hour."

"Why are they being allowed in?"

I was content to ignore them. Mase, however…

"People, people," he spun around with his hand raised. "It's not our fault you dress like shit."

I shook my head along with Stan, who also grumbled, "asshole."

"Except you," Mase pointed at a blonde in a red dress. "You are looking fine, sweetheart. Come find me if you want to ride my dick later."

"Prick," I snorted and shoved him inside.

The guy standing next to the blonde didn't look impressed, which would only taunt Mase into poking at him next. Getting caught in the middle of a fight was not how I wanted this night to go.

"Why do you have to be such a dick?"

"Hey man, the truth hurts," Mase shrugged and walked over to slap the bar.

I took a second to pinch the bridge of my nose and sigh before following. The mantra, woosah, echoed in the back of my mind.

The salsa band had the place bustling with people. I had to admit Lou had a nose for business, for a shrink. So many people were crowding dance floor that a few tables had been moved aside to make room.

I wasn't complaining. There was nothing wrong with watching a bunch of chicks swing their hips.

Especially the one in the gold dress—damn, that girl could move.

Wait…

My gaze narrowed, zeroing in on the sequins covered hips

twirling around seductively. I knew that ass and those hips. I recognized the way they moved. Just like I did that triangle birthmark.

Motherfucker.

Mase must've seen her too because he threw his back with a chuckle.

"Oh man," he rested his elbow on the bar and wiped the amusement off his face. "If that isn't a kick in the nads, I don't know what is."

A kick in the nads was right. What the fuck was Star even doing here? This was my turf, not hers. Did she want to get hurt? I had half a mind to go over there and slap that sparkle off her face. Drag her ass out of here and tell her not to come back.

My eyes slid down her raised arms, over the swell of her breasts, and down to her slim waist moving in time with the music.

Well, I wasn't a complete asshole. She could finish this dance, but as soon as this song ended, she was out.

Star's light hair fanned through the air as she spun around and kicked. Flexing her thigh sent a ripple of firm lines down her slender leg to the gold heel strapped around her foot.

What really caught my attention was the curve of a firm creamy cheek exposed when her skirt lifted.

Fuck me—she was wearing a thong.

I leaned back and signaled the bartender to bring me a beer. It wouldn't be the end of the world if I let her dance for a couple of songs. Nothing wrong with enjoying the show, right?

"I gotta say, Bro. Your girl's looking pretty fine."

My glare slid over to the smirk on Mase's face. "She's not my girl."

The warm light glowed around Star as she arched her back, bowing her body with the grace of a feline on the prowl.

She could be mine? At least until I was done using her.

No, I shook my head and sucked back my drink, letting the

whiskey burn a path down my throat. That little witch didn't deserve my dick. A fact I wish my dick would listen to—fucker was hard and ready to go. Good thing I wore jeans—there was no hiding this shit in dress pants.

"So," Mase grunted and swung the mug in his hand, "I guess you won't mind those guys dancing with her, then?"

What guys?

Two smarmy ass motherfuckers thought they were suave. Dancing up on Star, like she wouldn't see them trying to slip in. But she did see them. And what did she do when one of those sons of bitches ground up behind her? She threw her arms up and entwined her fingers behind his neck.

My hand crushed around the beer can I was holding, sending Mase into another laughing fit as beer spewed out. It was my turn to laugh a few seconds later.

Star took her hands off that prick, moving them to a girl in front of her. A girl we saw clearly when they spun around.

The smile instantly fell of Mason's face.

What was more, Star saw us. Her eyes widened for a split second before narrowing to match the mischievous glint curling the corner of her mouth. The next second, her red painted nails slid around Harper's hips, pulling her into sway with her.

Careful, Crumpet, you're playing a dangerous game.

It'd been a long time since I'd seen Harper smile like that. Eight years to be exact. Even though I thought she deserved everything she got, a part of me missed that happy sparkle in her big brown eyes.

Mase was a different story. He mourned the girl we knew a long time ago. Now, the only thing that smile on Harper's face did was piss him off.

"What the fuck does she think she's doing?"

"Harper?" I asked, despite knowing which *she* he was referring to.

"Yes, fucking Harper."

"Well," I tipped my head back to the girls. "She appears to be dancing."

His stern glare met mine.

Not so funny now. Hey motherfucker.

Mason Kessler gave new meaning to the term short fuse. Something I contributed to the genetics of his biological father—an interesting trait when you threw the Kesslers ability for self-control in the mix.

Because Lou had raised him, Mase wasn't the powder keg Logan was. In most instances, he knew when to tone things down.

This was not one of those instances. The thing I could see shining in his green eyes was the burning wrath of Ryker Hudson.

I might've been able to calm him down. Convince Mason to just kick the girls out and go on with our night if one of those assholes hadn't decided to slip up behind Harper.

The prick put his hands on Harper's waist, spurring Mase to push off the bar and charge forward.

That thread of sanity my best friend had been holding onto just snapped. All I could do was mutter a curse under my breath and follow.

Mase was on a mission. He pushed people out of his way, knocking them on their ass, as he made his way to his target, which he violently shoved. The guy stumbled back with a shocked look on his face. An expression Harper shared. Realization flooded her eyes as rage took over Mason.

"You got a fucking problem?" The asshole's friend slid forward.

"Yeah," Mase growled, puffing his chest up against the guy. "I got a fucking problem."

These two idiots obviously weren't from around here. Everyone in Ashen Springs knew who we were. A fact that was evident in the way everyone else ducked their heads and moved out of the way. Even the band stopped playing.

"Oh my God, Mason," Star shrieked, "what the hell is wrong with you? You can't go around shoving people."

Star wasn't from around here either, but she'd learn how things worked.

"Shut up, Crumpet." I yanked her back because I honestly, I couldn't guarantee Mason would deck her.

"You can't tell us what to do."

I bent over, getting right in her face, and growled, "Watch me."

All that did was cause her face to screw up in defiance.

"We're free to go wherever we want."

"That's where you're wrong. You see this," Mason's arm shot out, grabbing a fistful of Harper's hair. She cried out as he roughly pulled her over to him. "This is mine, and I don't appreciate her being dressed like a fucking slut."

"Let her go," Star shot out, lunging with her claws drawn.

I caught her before she could do anything. Wrapping my arm around her waist, I slammed her back against me. Luckily for her, Mase's attention was quickly rerouted. The prick that was dancing with Harper decided to step in.

"Hey man, that's no way to treat a lady."

I had no doubt the onlookers could hear Mason's teeth grind as his neck twisted back.

"Do you hear this shit?" Mase said to me before looking back at that asshole. "Motherfucker wants to die.

I was with him. His friend was staring at Star. Sliding his gaze over her curves as if he had the right to enjoy them.

My grip on Star's arm tightened. "I think they both do."

"Arsehole," Star snarled while trying to pry my hand off her arm. "You have no right to come in here and…."

"I suggest you shut up," I cut her off, curling my lip at the anger tugging on her expression. "Or you'll find out how much of an arsehole I can be."

Though she wasn't impressed, she shut the fuck up. Which was more than I could say for the prick squaring off with Mase.

He made things worse by nodding at Harper, whose hair was still wrapped tightly in Mase's fist. "You need to leave her alone."

"Mason," Harper whispered. Even she could sense that fuse on his powder keg lighting.

"Shut the fuck up," he barked out so loud that the words echoed through the room like a twanging bell, counting down doomsday.

This wouldn't be the first time I'd seen my best friend snap, but this was different. It wasn't some spout of pent-up rage coming out in a fight. It was years of misery and hatred pouring out of his broken soul.

This time, Mase wasn't going to just beat some asshole down. He was going to fucking kill him, and there was no coming back from that. Harper broke him once. I couldn't let him destroy what was left.

"Mase…"

But it was too late.

The prick to the left of Mase peeked around his arm at Harper. "Why don't you come with me, Honey? I'll take care of you."

Stan and the other bouncers burst in just as Mase grabbed a mug off the table and brought it down on the prick's head.

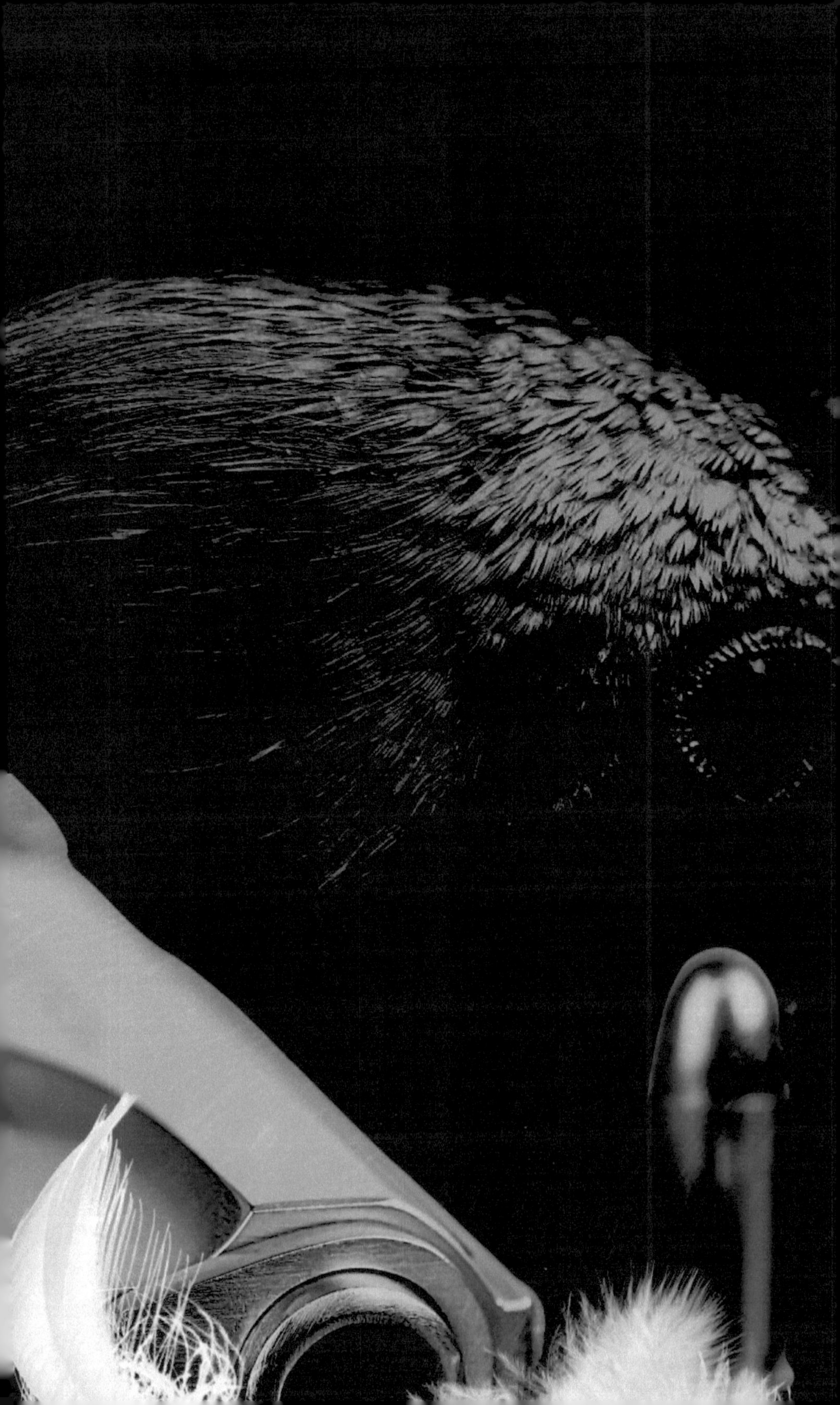

Chapter 20
Star

Harper and I were enjoying a nice night out until stupid Mason and Silas came along. Behaving like barbarians, puffing their chests up and growling.

They ruined everything. I finally got Harper to loosen up—she even smiled a little. Then Mason showed up and smashed a glass over someone's head. What the bloody hell was wrong with him?

And then there was Silas. What he did to that bloke—my dress was ruined. I was never getting the blood out. Just like I was never going to forget the look on that poor lad's beaten face. Or the way Silas's arms bulged as he threw punches.

Big masses of muscle swinging through the air. I don't know why some girls found that appealing? I sure didn't.

I looked over to a black couch against the far wall, where Silas was seated. He hadn't said much since the bouncers pushed us into this room. Nothing, actually. He just sat there, staring at me with a scowl on his face.

Well, he could stare at me all he wanted. The only thing I was sorry about was the terror on Harper's face. I didn't blame her. What was supposed to be a fun night out had turned into the start of our juvenile record. I can't imagine that would go over well with her strict father.

"Don't worry," I tucked Harper's hair behind her ear and swept the tears off her cheek. "Everything will be okay."

I'd tell her dad that this was all my idea—which it was. Mr. Callaghan may be a bit of a stickler, but I could be pretty charming.

"Stop coddling her," Mason growled from the corner he sat in. "She's fine."

"She's not bloody fine."

Who loses their shite like that over someone they clearly dislike? I'm not sure what happened between them or why Harper thought she deserved this kind of treatment, but enough was enough.

The girl couldn't even enjoy a simple smile. Mason deserved that cut on his lip, and Silas deserved the one on his cheek. Helping his friend destroy her life like that.

Arseholes, the lot of them.

"You're a pain in my ass, London."

"Good," I snarled back. "And I'm from Windsor, you bloody wanker."

Mason cocked a brow at Silas. "Did she just call me a wanker?"

Yes, I bloody well did.

Silas tipped his head, zeroing his icy glare in on me. Why was he looking at me like that? Did he expect me to apologize? Because that wasn't happening. At least he was growling insults my way.

"You know what you are, London?"

I sighed, "please enlighten me."

Why couldn't Mason take a hint from his friend and shut the hell up?

"You're a bad influence," Mason lifted his hand and pointed at a vacant chair across the room. "Harper, go sit over there."

The seriousness displayed on his face made me shake my head. Tosser was more entitled than I thought. I couldn't believe he expected Harper to do what he said.

"She's not a puppy!"

"Yes, she is. She's my puppy." Mason glared at me.

I glared back at him.

A silent challenge passed between us. One that came to an end with two loudly barked words. "Now, Freckles."

I don't know what pissed me off more. The gall of Mason Kessler? Or the fact that Harper jumped and scurried across the room. I literally felt my jaw hit the floor as Mason's mouth spread in a victorious smile.

I didn't know which one of them to yell at first. Harper for being such a pushover, or Mason for being Mason?

"You can't—how could—you're such a—" My finger flew from one to the other and ended with my foot stomping down in a frustrated growl, "Arsehole."

"Sit down, Crumpet."

I stopped cold. Now he decided to speak? And not to defend Harper or tell his friend to shut up, but to order me around.

Oh, hell no.

"Did you just tell me to sit down?" This situation had me so angry that I couldn't even bring myself to yell. "I don't know who you think you are, Silas Creswell...."

I was cut off by the sound of a new voice.

"He's the person in this room you should be listening to, Little Girl."

My brows knit as Mason rolled his eyes and muttered under his breath.

I turned expecting to see a police officer standing behind me. Perhaps one that Mason had encounters with before. It would come as no surprise to me if the lad had a criminal record. A man in a uniform and handcuffs was not what I saw.

My confusion grew as I eyed the three men following another in a finely tailored black suit. He strutted in, pushing his fingers through his thick chestnut hair.

There was an unmistakable aura of authority around him. That wasn't what scared me. For the first time in my life, I couldn't read the expression on someone's face.

Who was this man?

"Hey Lou," Mason sang in a mocking tone. "Come to join us for a drink?"

I jerked back a wee bit from the man's deeply growled, "Do you think this is funny, Mason?"

Mason shrugged, "A little."

A part of me wanted to warn Mason about talking back. I grew up going to school with aristocrats. I knew something about people in power—which is what I assumed this man was.

The men accompanying him walked with their heads held high and shoulders back, while also keeping an eye on the things around them. Bodyguards didn't follow someone around for no reason.

"I just had to send two of my customers off in an ambulance," Lou threw his finger up, pointing at Mason. "Because once again, you couldn't keep your cool!"

Customers?

Suddenly, I remembered what Harper said when we first arrived, *'This is Mason's dad's bar.'*

Oh my God, this man was Mason's father. I couldn't help but once again look over the others in the room with us. From what I'd heard, Mr. Kessler was a psychiatrist. Why would he need body guards?

Mason crossed his arms and grumbled, "Should've been a hearse."

"I've had enough of your shit, Mason," Lou cut him off by waving his hand through the air. "You will either control yourself or take her now." His finger pointed at Harper, making her squeak and shrink back in her chair. "Do you hear me?"

Mason's jaw twitched at the scared girl. "Yeah, I fucking hear you."

"So, what's it going to be?"

Without a word, Mason rose, shot his father a glare, and stormed out of the room. That was the truly scary part. One thing I'd learned about Mason Kessler: he not only enjoyed making people's lives difficult—he reveled in it. When his dad gave him an order, he didn't argue it or give him some smartarse remark. He just left.

Not only that but the order itself—take her now? As if Harper was a commodity already promised. Maybe she was? Maybe Mr. Kessler was more than a psychiatrist?

I'd studied various organizations, and there was one thing that all mafias had in common—arranged marriages.

That was crazy, right?

My mind went back to the various people I'd seen disappear in one of the backrooms. Originally I thought it was a poker game or something. Now, I wondered about the bouncer standing guard.

Everyone who went in that room handed him something. I don't know what it was, it was too small to make out, but anyone who didn't have it was turned away.

Why?

What was in there?

"Marco," Mr. Kessler waved at one of the guards. "Take Harper home."

Harper also obeyed. She stood up and quickly scurried over to the large man who stepped forward.

I stood there stunned, unable to force my mouth to form words. They were there, stuck in the back of my throat. I just couldn't make them out. Not until Harper paused to give me a meek smile.

"See you at school."

"Wait," I threw my hand out to stop her. "This isn't right. Shouldn't they be calling our parents?"

Harper stopped and peeked over her shoulder.

"It won't do any good," she said while sliding her gaze to Silas. "They can't help you."

What the bloody hell did that mean?

"Of course they can. This man doesn't have any authority over us."

That made Mr. Kessler cross his arms and cock a brow. I didn't care who he thought he was—he couldn't do this. What right did he have to decide anyone's fate?

Harper disagreed. She merely shot me a smile and left.

I could feel the walls closing in around me as the door clicked shut—locking me in here with them. This was wrong—all of it. I wanted out.

"I want to see my parents," I demanded.

I was their daughter. Not his. They would tell Mr. Kessler where to go.

Silas sighed, "Sit down, Crumpet."

"You can't keep me here." I shrieked, because well, I was afraid.

"I suggest you do what he says, little girl," Mr. Kessler's hard eyes met mine, "I don't have much patience left."

And I did.

I obeyed him because my thundering heart wouldn't allow me to do otherwise. Especially when one of the guards shifted, and I saw the handle of a pistol tucked under his jacket.

I didn't like guns. They made the ghosts louder. I could already hear Emily snickering in the back of my mind.

For some reason, I headed for the empty cushion next to Silas. He cocked a curious brow my way. I couldn't explain it either, just that he made me feel a little safer. Not much, mind you, but I'd take any modicum of security I could find.

Mr. Kessler nodded at me. "Is she yours?"

"No," we both said in unison—Silas out of anger and me, out of fear.

I got really scared when Mr. Kessler tipped his head. I could feel him studying us. Every second of his silence dragged on—ticking in the hard beatings of my pulse. By the time he did speak, I was ready to jump out of my skin.

His dark eyes locked onto Silas, "Prove it."

"How am I supposed to prove it?" Silas snarled back.

Maybe sitting beside him wasn't the best choice?

"Kiss her."

"What?" I screeched, "No, no, no."

The last time Silas kissed me, I wound up on the ground, thoroughly humiliated. That wasn't going to happen again.

"With all due respect, Sir, you can't make me…."

"Oh for fuck sakes," Silas ground out and grabbed the back of my head, bringing his lips to mine.

It was short and entirely too sweet. A simple press of his mouth on mine, and that's where I thought it would end.

I was wrong.

He pulled away and stared down at me with heat blazing in his bright blue eyes. The intensity in those brilliant orbs had me pinned. I couldn't look away, not even when I saw his control snap. Silas dove back in, swallowing my objections with his mouth.

This kiss was different. It was hungry, demanding, and completely feral. I was powerless to stop him, and I tried—shoved on his chest and slapped his shoulders, but my strength was no match for his. Silas pushed me back on the couch and crawled over me as if I was nothing more than a toy.

That was when my body betrayed me, giving in to the fear pulsing through me. I melted into him and parted my lips. Because as much as I tried to deny it, I liked the way he controlled me.

The heaviness of his weight pressing me down caused my heart to flutter in anticipation.

When he forced his knee between my thighs, I groaned and swept my tongue over his, needing more of his masculine taste. He had me. I was lost in the sensations pouring through my body.

And then someone cleared their throat.

Logic snapped back in my mind as Silas pulled his mouth off mine and muttered, "Fuck."

"I'll ask you again, Silas," Mr. Kesslers' voice boomed through the room. "Is she yours?"

At first, Silas didn't say anything. He just tipped his head and studied my face. What was he looking for? I didn't know. Maybe he wanted me to spit or call his name? I might've done, if I wasn't out of breath.

Whatever he was seeking out, he found when he pressed his knee up against my core, sending a twisted shock of pleasure up my spine. That gasp I couldn't hold back.

"Yeah," his breath washed over my face, heating my skin. "She's mine."

What?

I opened my mouth, but Silas cut off my argument by leaning in to growl. "This is *my* dress. Don't wear it out in public again unless you want to see more blood on it."

He couldn't tell me what to wear.

"How dare you," this time when I shoved on his chest, Silas didn't resist. He sat back down, allowing me to spring off the couch. "I am not yours, Silas Creswell."

"She's your problem now," Mr. Kessler sighed and smoothed down his suit jacket. "I suspect you can handle this little spout of defiance."

Handle it?

"Excuse me, but I'm not anybody's problem. Except for maybe my parents—and my brothers—and the birds sometimes. But Roger keeps getting out of his pen, and Andi's always running off. Bloody ostrich is going to give me a heart attack."

"Enough," Mr. Kessler barked, making me snap my mouth shut. "Does she always talk this much?"

Silas slid his intense stare my way. "She has control issues."

I did not have control issues.

"See that you work on that," Mr. Kessler said.

In response, Silas nodded at him and shot me a look. "We will."

My brow rose. "*We* will not be doing anything."

"You're right, Crumpet. *We* won't be doing shit."

Good. I'm glad we got that sorted.

"*You* will be doing what *I* say when I say it."

Oh, is that what he thought?

I snorted out a chuckle. Silas was seriously misguided if he thought I'd ever do what he said.

"You will do what he says, little girl."

My glare snapped over to Mr. Kessler. "Is that what you think?"

This whole town was corrupt, but I wasn't about to let anyone intimidate me, even if he was involved with the mafia. If I could hold my own against the aristocracy back home, then I could surely withstand the threats of a common criminal.

"No, it's what I know." Mr. Kessler stepped up and glared down at me. "I'm the last person in this town you want to fuck with.

I fucked up and did exactly what I told myself I wouldn't do—I gave into my desire. And in front of Lou of all people. He meant it when he said Star was my problem now.

Asshole probably already had a contract ready to go. My plan was to take the night to come up with something, an excuse or story that would appease him enough to back off.

That went out the window with the phone call I received in the morning.

"Micha's been shot."

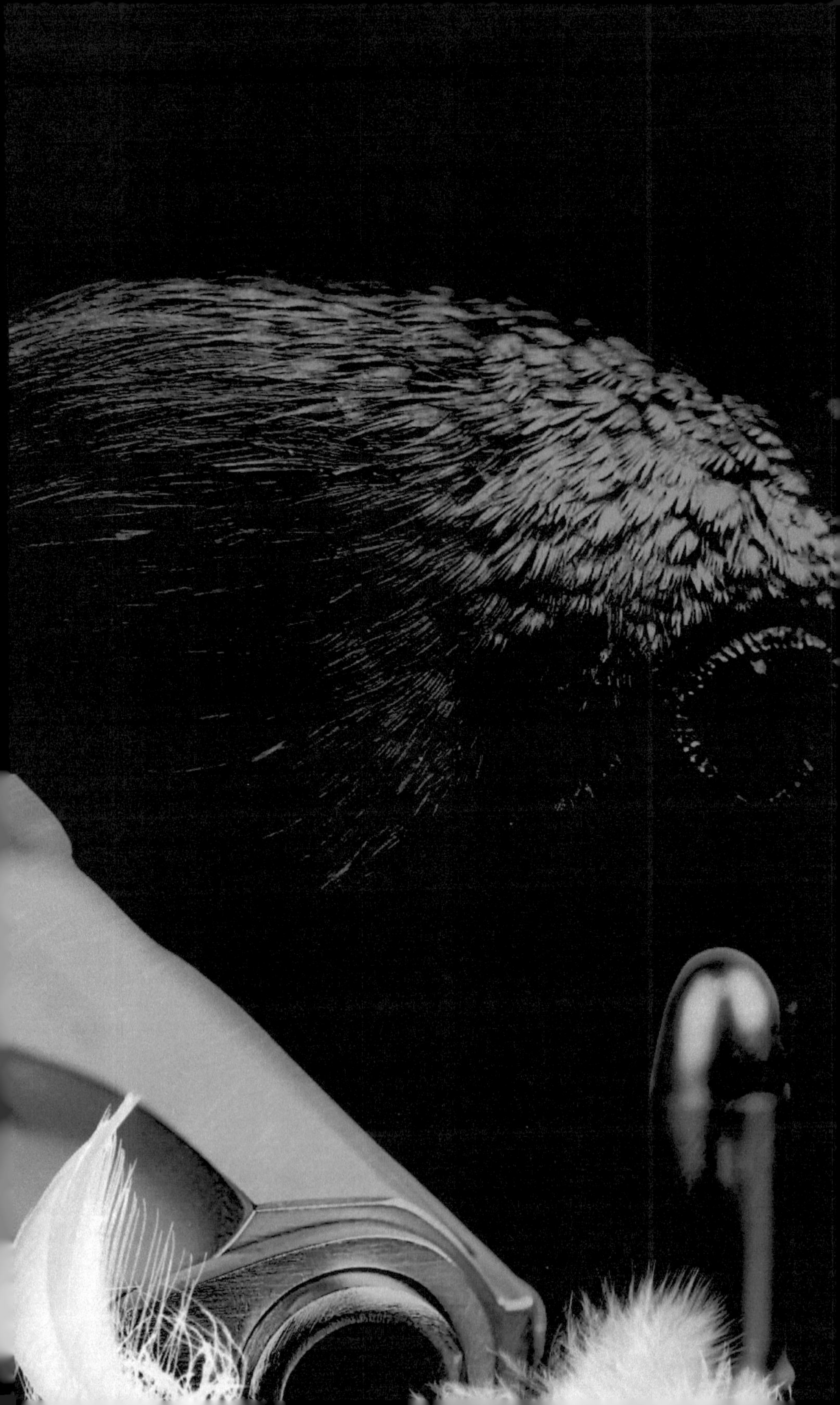

Chapter 22

Star

The twins burst into my room, pattering their feet loudly against the hardwood.

"Star, Star."

Grumbling, I rolled over to toss my blanket over my head. I don't know what time it was, but I did know it was too early to deal with the likes of them. They, however, didn't agree.

One of them climbed on the bed. Cedar, I assumed, based on the high-pitched giggle burning through my ears while the other poked head under the covers.

"Star," Elm continued to tap my covered forehead. "Guess what?"

"I don't care."

Cedar jumped on my mattress, jarring my body, "But Roger laid an egg."

That made me stop. I even fluttered my eyes open under the

blanket.

"Roger's a boy bird," I pointed out. "And boy birds can't lay eggs."

"But he did," Elm argued.

"Yeah," Cedar agreed. "Maybe he was a girl all along?"

Roger was a peacock with big beautiful tail feathers that only the males of that species have.

"That's not possible."

"Then how come we found an egg in his pen?"

Elm repeated our brother. "Yeah, how come we found an egg?"

Alright, let's see the stupid egg.

I threw the blankets back and screamed. Elm was holding up a lizard less than an inch from my face. Its long tail flicked as he opened his mouth, slurping his tongue.

"He fell out of a tree," Cedar sang while bouncing around.

"Mum said his name is Guana," Elm pet the vile things head. "Isn't he cool?"

No, he wasn't cool.

"Oh my god, I'm gonna kill you two," I called and sprang from my bed, chasing the screaming twins out of my room.

What the heck were they thinking waking me up with a bloody lizard? They wanted to scare me—that's what they were thinking.

I slammed my door shut, muttering. "Bloody shites."

Maybe I would help Cy with his clown costume after all. The twins had one fear: which our brother liked to play on. Normally, I wouldn't encourage him, but those two were asking for it.

Yesterday, they woke me up by trapping me under my blanket with their farts. Just thinking about that horrid odor made me gag. How two little humans held in that kind of toxicity was beyond me.

I thought about going back to sleep. After the night I had, my bed looked extra inviting, but I quickly decided against it.

There was only one thing I dreamt about, and it wasn't my

inevitable damnation, never thought I'd miss the ghosts haunting my mind. Emily's voice I could deal with—Hell, I deserved her daily taunts. The tingle Silas left on my lips—that I couldn't handle.

My morning didn't get any better when I headed downstairs to find something to munch on. It was too quiet.

Meaning the twins were up to something, Ash was into something, and Cy was somewhere evilly plotting. None of which outweighed what was really on my mind.

Mainly Louis Kessler.

That was his name. Louis, not Lou. I found that out last night during some research. And let me just say, it was seriously scary how angelic the media made him out to be.

The man I met last night was nothing like the savior the papers claimed he was. That meant one of two things, he owned the media. Or he had enough power to control them. Neither of which was a particularly comforting idea.

Particularly considering his claim that I was Silas's problem now. Did he expect Silas to marry me? Keep me like some kind of pet? Pfft. If that's what he thought, he was wrong.

The boy utterly despised me, and even if he didn't, my parents would never agree to some arranged relationship. They considered grounding imprisonment.

There was absolutely nothing the so-called King of Ashen Springs could do to change their mind.

"Sorry, Mr. King," I smirked. "You just met your match."

"Who's Mr. King?"

I jumped at the suddenness of Ash's voice.

"No one." I peeked over my shoulder at my baby brother, who was swinging something through the air. "And you shouldn't sneak up on people."

"Sworry," he sang while making pschew, pschew sounds. "Jedi's are quiet."

My eyes narrowed on the neon green object in his hands. His back was to me, and all I could see was a flash here and there as he swung it around.

What is that?

My question was answered when he swung it to the left and smacked it off the wall, causing a loud buzzing sound to ring through the room.

"Oh my God, Ash give me that."

"No," he dodged away from my reaching arm and took off across the room. "It's my lightsaber."

"That is not a lightsaber."

It was one of my parents' toys. I told them to lock those up, and did they listen? Of course not. Instead, they left me to chase my three-year-old brother around the house. Trying to snatch the fake cock away from him.

Thankfully, I managed to corner Ash in the kitchen and grab the vibrator.

"Hey," he whined.

"How many times have I told you to stay out of Mum and Dad's room?" my hand flew through the air, waving the green dick scoldingly. "Now, go play."

He stuck his tongue out and stomped away.

I sighed and dropped my face in my palm.

I bet other families didn't have these kinds of problems.

"Good morning. You must be Star?"

I spun around to see a man with sandy hair, and bright grey eyes smiling at me. "Who are you?"

"I'm Dean," he held out his hand.

Without thinking, I returned the gesture, lifting my arm before realizing what was still held tightly in my grasp.

Shite.

I quickly tossed the phallic object and prayed he wouldn't see the flush heating my cheeks. That hope went out the window when the dick bounced off the floor and started vibrating again.

Lord, kill me now.

I don't' know what possessed me to try and explain myself, but for some reason, I blurted out, quicker than my brain could think, "It's not mine."

"It's alright," he waved his hand and went about pouring himself a cup of coffee. "I've seen worse."

Mum walked into the kitchen, scooped up the dildo, and smiled at me. "Honey, if you want to experiment, that's fine. But you should really have your own toys."

"Oh my god, Mum. Eww," I'd never wanted to throw up more than I did right now. "I wasn't using it. I took it away from Ash."

"You know your father, and I don't have a problem buying you these things," her brows tipped disbelievingly.

"Masturbation is completely normal." Dean agreed and sauntered up to kiss my Mum on the forehead.

That explained why he was wearing her flowery bathrobe.

"At one point, I thought my youngest son Parker had an addiction to jerking off."

Was this seriously happening right now?

"I do not have…."

I stopped to eye my dad as he entered the room, slapped Mum on the bum, and kissed Dean on the cheek.

Did he just say, Parker?

"Like Lana and Parker?"

"Ah, you've met my daughter-in-law." A bright smile swept across Dean's face, lighting up the silver flecks in his eyes. "Isn't she lovely?"

"Mum," my jaw dropped. "This is my friend's dad."

Well, not Lana's dad, but close enough.

"Tell your friend his father is amazing."

I don't know what made me gag worse? Mum's statement, or the way Dad nodded in agreement. This couldn't be happening right now. As if I didn't have enough to deal with, how was I supposed to look Lana in the eye on Monday, knowing my parents did the dirty with her father-in-law?

This whole situation was so messed up—I couldn't even find the right words to yell back at them.

I stood there like a wanker while Dean announced that he had to go and walked away to get dressed.

Get dressed. Those words alone stunned me, speechless. My friend's dad's willy was currently rubbing on my Mum's bathrobe.

"I can't deal with this right now," I muttered and marched outside.

It'd been one hell of a morning. Maybe some air would help clear my head?

I sat down on the step and lifted my head. Enjoying the way the sun warmed my skin. At least there were no annoying little brothers or overly sexual parents to bother me—just the breeze carrying the fresh scent of cut grass.

My peaceful serenity only lasted a moment before Dean stepped out the front door, tugging the bottom of his shirt over his stomach. Not before I got a glimpse of the sharp lines of his abs.

I could see why my parents *had some fun* with him. He was a handsome man. That much I'd give him.

"Hello again," Dean smiled down at me.

I couldn't think of him as Mr. Whitley, not after I'd seen him in Mum's bathrobe.

"Hello," I sighed and pressed back my urge to tell him to go away. There was no reason to be rude.

"I imagine this is a lot to take in."

You can say that again.

"Especially after the night, you had."

My eyes snapped up to his, which looked silver in the light. "Nothing happened last night."

"That's not what I heard." He tipped his chin down at me, "Louis is a friend of mine."

Of course, he is. Louis Kessler was everybody's friend, according to the paper.

"So I snuck into a club," I waved my hand through the air. "I'm not the first teenager to do it."

"Louis was right. You are stubborn." Dean blew out a breath and stared up at the clear sky, "Lucky for him, I'm not as nice. I'll give you eight hours."

Was he messing with me? All Mr. Kessler did was puff up his chest and bark some orders. That didn't mean anything. And if it did, why would Dean know? Or even care?

"Eight hours for what?"

"You know what I mean."

Unconsciously my eyes flickered in the direction of the Creswell household.

"See, I knew you were a smart girl," he skipped down the steps and strutted over to a green Porche parked in the driveway.

Last night's events flashed through my mind. Is she yours? Silas's feral kiss and the way Louis stated that I was his problem. I knew what he was insinuating.

That didn't mean I was going to obey him. Mr. Kessler wasn't anything more than a man with too much power and an inflated ego.

"Remember, Star," Dean called out while shooting me a wink. "Eight hours."

"Whatever," I grumbled and leaned back against the deck.

Silas Creswell was a tosser that had been nothing but rude to me since the day I met him. There wasn't a man on God's green earth that could convince me otherwise. Surely not Dean Whitley.

I'd find out just how wrong I was when I met Dean's other son.

Chapter 23

Silas

Parker sat at the island drumming his fingers on the black quartz countertop while I paced around the kitchen for the hundredth time. Neither one of us knew what to say. And what could we say? Micha was currently in surgery after being shot protecting Riley.

Lou told me that the doctors said Micha would pull through. It wasn't him I was worried about, though.

This wasn't the first time he had been shot, and the fucker not only survived his own mother but he also saved Mase. Micha was a tough son of a bitch. Probably the toughest I knew.

Mase, however, was not.

He spent his life teetering the edge of broken and destroyed, and last night didn't help. By the time Lou let us go, Mase was nowhere to be seen.

I eventually found him sprawled out on the floor in his father's office. He was drunk out of his mind, muttering shit about betrayal, Harper, and how everyone lies to him.

What the fuck was Star thinking bring Harper to Mallum? Nothing good ever happened when that girl was around. I used to think Mase was overreacting, but I got it now.

Hating Star while wanting to fuck her was hard enough. I couldn't imagine loathing the person you loved, and Mase did love Harper. At least he loved that sweet, kind girl she used to be.

Happy little Harper Callaghan, the girl could make anyone smile. She was dead now—murdered by betrayal. Now every time Mase saw her, he was reminded of what he lost.

We were finally starting to pull him out of that hole he'd sunk himself into, and now I had to tell him that his brother was shot. Not only that, but Micha was shot on the night Mase broke his sobriety promise. Neither Parker nor I were looking forward to telling him. The guilt alone might kill him.

"Should we wake him up?"

"No," I shook my head. "Let him sleep."

My answer was purely selfish, just like my choice to drag his ass back here last night instead of leaving him for Lou to find. When Lou called, I told him Mase was down by the bluffs working on something for a class project.

Honestly, I was surprised he bought the excuse. He was probably too worried about Micha to over-analyze shit.

I didn't want Mase going back to rehab because, well, honestly, I'd miss the fucker. That and I didn't know if he'd survive it again? Mase was already broken. Locking him up with his thoughts would do nothing but cause more damage.

Dread flowed through my bones and settled in my heart when I heard Mase's footsteps skip down the stairs.

"Good morning," he yawned and scratched his head before

cocking a brow at Parker. "What are you doing here? Don't you have diaper duty or some shit?"

Parker didn't say anything, just shot me a look. He didn't have to speak for me to see the disappointment in his eyes. Anyone could tell Mase had been drinking. I could smell the scotch on his breath from here.

Our silence went unnoticed by Mase, who was probably hungover. Good, I fucking hoped he was. Hell, I was tempted to bang a couple of pots by his ears to make the asshole's head ring. Then maybe he'd feel a modicum of the headache he gave me daily.

"Whatever, I'm glad you're here. Now someone can laugh at this fucker with me," Mase slapped my back on his way to the coffee pot. "You should've seen his next-door neighbor last night— all dressed up in a skimpy dress."

Fuck the pots—I was gonna knock his head off the counter.

"I thought Silas was going to kill someone."

Funny how he left out the fact that Harper was there too.

Asshole.

"I gotta say, the girl's got some serious moves," he swung his hips around, making me shake my head. "I can see why you want to tap that shit."

"I don't–" I pinched the bridge of my nose and let out a mediative breath. Slapping the shit out of my best friend could wait. We had more important things to deal with. "Mase, we need to talk to you."

"Hey, man, I told you anytime you need advice on guaranteed orgasm moves, I'm your man."

"I don't need fucking advice."

"You sure?" he cocked his brow and waved a finger over me. "Cause I'm not sure that little girl can handle what you're packing."

Motherfucker.

Smacking my lips together impatiently, I looked over at Parker.

Pretty soon, we wouldn't have to worry about telling Mase shit because I was gonna fucking kill him.

Sensing my mood, Parker barked out, "Now's not the time, Mase."

"Wow, must be serious. Okay," Mase leaned against the counter and took a sip of his coffee. "What's up?"

Parker and I looked at each other before he said, "Maybe you should sit down?"

That made Mase's brow rise. "Is this some kind of intervention?"

"No."

Though it should be. Not that I thought an intervention would work.

Parker waved at one of the empty island stools, "Seriously, Mase, have a seat."

"Are you two having an affair?" Mase's finger waved between us. "Because it is way too early to deal with that shit."

Son of a...

"It's about Micha," I snapped.

That got his attention. All signs of amusement washed off his face as Mase pushed off the counter and stood up straight.

"What about Micha?"

I'd replayed this moment over and over for the last two hours. My plan was to just rip the band-aid off and get it over with. Now that the time was here, I couldn't do it.

Despite all of the flack Mase gave his brother, he loved him. More than he did anyone else. Micha wasn't just his brother—he was his hero, which was why it had hurt so much when he found out about Ryker.

Logan and I keeping the truth from him, he could handle. But knowing Micha knew for years and didn't say anything—that tore his heart out.

How could I do it again?

Parker was just as incapable of breaking the news as I was. His lips parted with unspoken words, then quickly clamped shut.

Our reluctance to say anything only pissed Mase off.

"Somebody better tell me what the fuck is going on with my brother," he slammed his mug down on the island between Parker and me. "Right fucking now."

I stared at the splashes of coffee sliding across the countertop and said, "He's been shot."

I didn't just see Mase's soul break—I felt it as he dropped down on one of the stools.

"He's okay," Parker added. "Well, not okay, but he'll pull through."

Pull through. That could mean a lot of things. All of which I saw in the various emotions flashing across my best friend's face. Sorrow, pain, anger, and finally guilt.

"Where is he?"

Parker and I both answered, "Miami."

That was all Mase needed to hear. He was up and out of the room before either of us could stop him. Good thing Parker was a running back and fast as fuck. He managed to catch up to him and slam the door shut.

"Where are you going?"

"Where the fuck do you think?" Mase barked back at him. "I'm going to see my fucking brother."

When Lou called, he explained that Chase Mathers's MC and his brother Jax's MC were at war. There was a hit out on Riley, who Micha was shot protecting.

An MC hit was much more dangerous than hiring someone like Preston to take her out. Bikers didn't give a shit about doing the job quietly—they'd open fire in the middle of a busy street just to hit their target, which was exactly why Lou wouldn't let them in

Ashen Springs. When MCs got in a war, blood rained on the streets.

So, until Chase's brother, Jax, could be dealt with, Riley had to go into hiding. And since there was no way Micha would let her go anywhere without him, so did he. Meaning we couldn't see them, couldn't talk to them, we couldn't do shit, but sit here and wait.

I stepped up behind Mase, "We can't let you do that."

Lou wouldn't even tell us which hospital they were at—all we knew was that Micha and Riley were in Miami somewhere, registered under different names. If Mase went looking for his brother, he'd lead Jax right to them.

"Why the fuck not?"

"The assholes that shot Micha were after Riley." I huffed and scrubbed a hand down my face, "just… call your father."

"He's not my father."

I looked him dead in the eyes. "He is today."

Mase wanted to fight me, it was written all over his face, but he didn't argue. He knew when I wasn't budging.

The only retort I got was a grumbled, "Fine," as he pulled out his phone.

It didn't take Lou long to answer.

"Dad, where's Micha. I want to talk to him."

At least he was calling him dad.

"Oh, don't give me that shit," he snarled and walked away with the phone pressed to his ear.

"Well," Parker let out a breath and fell back against the door. "That went better than I thought."

I slid my gaze his way. "When it comes to Mase, better isn't a good thing."

Better just meant the fall out was yet to come. The longer he went without talking to his brother, the more his guilt would build until he snapped. On the upside, I had the perfect excuse to get out of Lou's expectations with Star. Someone had to watch Mase.

At least that's what I thought.

Parker and I were in the kitchen when Mase came back and thrust the phone in my direction.

"He wants to talk to you."

I was expecting this. The inevitable keep an eye on him speech. So much so that when I put the phone to my ear, I said, "don't worry, I'll watch him."

The smirk on Mase's face should've been my first clue that Lou had something else in mind.

"I've got that handled," Lou said. "Your only job is to claim your girl."

"What?" I shrieked, like a little girl, making both Parker and Mase snicker.

"No one knew Riley was coming to Miami, not even Micha," Lou explained. "Which means someone told Jax she was here."

I failed to see how that had anything to do with Star. "So?"

"Think about what I'm saying, Silas. Someone told Jax that Riley was coming here. Someone in Ashen Springs."

"That doesn't mean anything." If anyone knew where Riley was going, it was Shelby, and that girl never shut up. One shopping trip downtown and half the town would know. "It could've been anyone."

"Would anyone leave a note at the crime scene from *The Piper*?"

Well, fuck.

Lou suspected that Ryker had someone working with him besides for his illegitimate son Luke. Who, by the way, made a miraculous escape from prison. Wonder who arranged that?

For all we knew, Luke had something to do with it. Micha was out for blood, and it would make sense for Luke to take him out first. Then again, if I was right and Lou had hidden his oldest son, then he would know if he had anything to do with the shooting.

"I need you focused right now, Silas."

"I am focused."

"No, you're not," Lou growled from the other end. "That girl is a distraction. One you need to take care of."

This was bullshit.

"Or I will. Do you understand me?"

"I got it," I growled back, knowing exactly what he meant by take care of it.

Yeah, I didn't like the girl. That didn't mean I wanted her fucking dead. Actually, I was kind of pissed off that Lou would even suggest it. A large part of me wanted to jump through the phone and strangle the shit out of him.

I could feel his brow arch in that judgemental way. "Do you?"

"Yeah, I fucking got it."

"Good. I sent you her school file. It might help." He added, "I'll be back in one week, I expect to see some progress by then." and hung up.

Fuck.

Well, I guess it was time to reign the little witch in—all I had to do was fuck her out of my system, then Lou wouldn't see her as a 'distraction' anymore.

It was kind of ironic when I thought about it. How many girls ran from my dick, and now it was gonna save someone's life?

Mase chuckled as I slid the phone over to him.

"Want me to go next door and grab her?"

My face dropped, spurring a loud laugh from him. "Go fuck yourself."

Parker swung his gaze between us, "Am I missing something?"

"You miss a lot."

We all turned to see Preston standing in the doorway. It was seriously scary how silent that prick could be. I once woke up in the middle of the night with him in my room.

He'd gotten past the alarm and made it up to my bedroom without waking my dad—who was the world's lightest sleeper. The asshole woke up if someone sneezed.

Parker didn't even bat an eye—he did grow up with him, so he was probably used to his surprise appearances. And let's not forget Ava. That girl gave new meaning to the term wrong.

Mase's brows knit, "What are you doing here?"

"I'm your shadow for the next few days."

It was my turn to smile. Mase wasn't getting away with shit now, a fact that his expression told me he knew.

"What? I don't need a babysitter."

"Apparently, you do," Preston flicked his Zippo open and arched a brow. "Let's go. I'm hungry."

"I'm not," Mase argued.

"Like I fucking care."

We all thought we knew what Preston was capable of, but I'd seen it first hand. He called me one night to come and help him clean up a body or what was left of the body.

I don't know what the guy did to piss him off, but whatever it was, it convinced me to never poke Preston's buttons. That was the only time death made me throw up.

So it was no surprise that Mase only hesitated for a second once Preston spun around and waved for him to follow.

"Have fun," I sang and waved as Mase flipped me off over his shoulder.

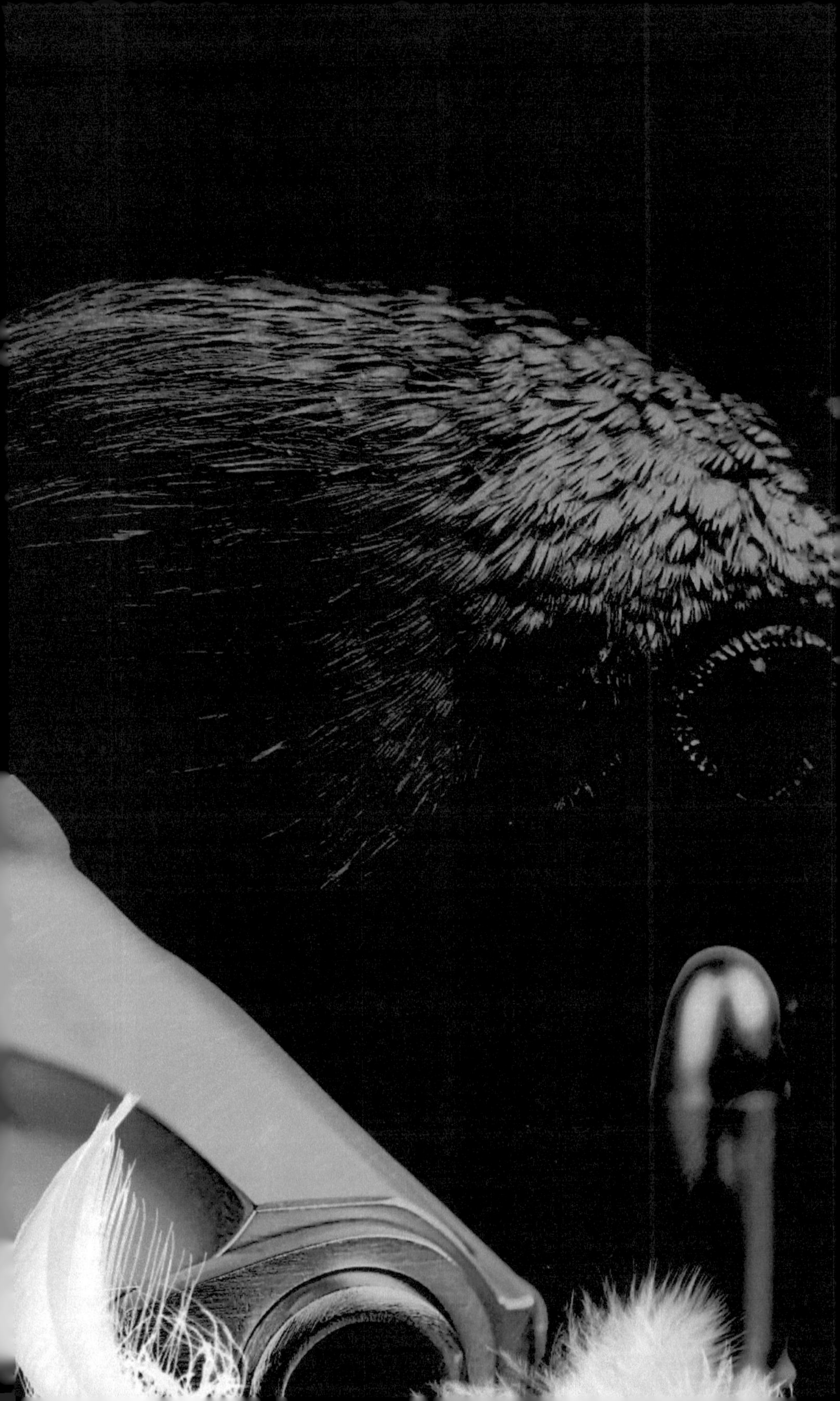

Chapter 24

Star

"Girl," Tico clicked his tongue at the silver sequins pillow I brought. "You have some flare."

I shrugged. "I just thought this place could use a little sprucing up."

Sprucing up was a nice way of putting it. Mind you, the Causegrove, wasn't exactly a house which is where I thought Tico should be sleeping. Since he wouldn't listen to reason, I decided to make this place as cozy as possible.

I stopped here every day on my way to school and back home to bring him blankets, clothes, or at the very least something to eat.

Harper wasn't too happy about me dragging her along and had

yet to get out of the car. She'd just sat there and watched Tico, and I chat. I blamed Mason Kessler for that.

The poor girl was so scared she avoided human contact, even with a guy like Tico–who, by the way, couldn't hurt a fly. I literally saw him talk to a mosquito sucking on his arm like they were best friends.

Tico nodded at my car, "no shadow today?"

"I think she's in lockdown," I rolled my eyes. "Her dad's a little strict."

When I tried calling her last night and today, my calls went straight to voicemail. Maybe her dad took away her phone? I just hoped she was okay?

After seeing Mason go off like that, I was worried about her, and not just because of last night. My concern was with what he'd done to her that no one knew about—the lad was clearly unstable.

"Hopefully, she's out of lockdown soon," Tico leaned closer to the firepit to light a cig. "Otherwise, I'll have to find someone else to stare creepily at me from a car."

"Harper's just," I trailed off. *Scared? Intimidated by a giant arsehole? Utterly terrified?* I opted to go with "Shy."

"Well, whatever she is, she's absolutely adorable."

I could agree with that. Carefully crafted dolls weren't as cute as Harper. I was itching to get my hands on those beautiful curls of hers and really knock Mason Kessler on his ass. If she ever spoke to me again, that is.

"One of these days, she'll talk to me."

I sighed and shifted my glare Tico's way, "Good luck with that."

He leaned back on the rundown couch and kicked his feet up, "I could always climb in the car with her?"

"Oh lords, don't give the girl a heart attack." I could imagine the look on her face.

"Hey," he tipped his dark eyes my way. "You got over your fear of the geysers."

Not really. I still jumped every time those bloody things went off. I just learned how to hide it better. Silas Creswell helped with that. The crafty bugger was popping out of nowhere constantly. One of these days, I was going to respond with a swift kick in the bullocks.

"Oh, I almost forgot." I jumped up and ran over to my car to retrieve the paper bag resting on the passenger seat, "I brought cinnamon buns."

Tico was talking about how much he was craving one, so I stopped at a cute little bakery on the way here.

His face lit up, "I told Riley you were cool."

"You know Riley?" My brows arched as I passed him the bag.

"Are you kidding?" He pulled out a cinnamon bun and took a big bite, "I've known that girl since she was running around the docks in diapers."

Huh? That explained why some of the girls at school referred to her as docksider. There were a few things I'd learned about Ashen Springs. Firstly, the high school football teams were rivals.

I was a little excited about that at first until I realized that football in America and back home were two different sports.

Secondly, no one in town had the balls to stand up to people like Louis Kessler. And finally, people who lived by the docks were looked down on.

Honestly, I was a little surprised to find out that Riley lived there at some point. I guess I never really thought about it until now. Not that it mattered where she came from, but it did explain a lot.

"What did she say about me?" I asked out of curiosity.

Riley and I didn't talk.

"I believe her exact words were, knock off Malibu Barbie with Rapunzel hair."

Gotta say I wasn't really surprised by that.

"Yeah," Tico sighed, "Riley takes some getting used to."

"I'm not sure I'll ever get used to her. Honestly, she kind of scares me."

"Riley scares everyone," he tipped his head to peek over the bag at me. "Including Riley."

Not everybody would be afraid of her. Cy had Urbach-Wiethe disease. He was incapable of feeling fear. Literally. Which made keeping him safe as a toddler almost impossible. He'd walk into traffic, touch hot stove burners, and try to pet snarling dogs.

Now that he was older, Cy understood that some things could kill him, but it was still a constant worry that he might do something because that danger sense in the back of his mind didn't go off.

Speaking of fear…

My lip curled at my ringing phone. Dad was calling. The last thing I wanted was another 'masturbation is normal' speech. Before I left, they made me look through a catalog of sex toys.

The fact that I now knew my parents had a sex swing tucked under their bed truly terrified me.

With a groan I answered the call, dreading what other disturbing things I was about to hear.

"Hello."

"Honey, I don't want you to worry."

What? Why would I worry?

"But your mother was in an auto accident."

Panicked, I shot up from my seat. "Oh my God."

Tico cocked a brow and mouthed the words, 'Everything okay?'

I shook my head. No, it wasn't okay. What if she was hurt? Or worse?

My heart dropped into the pit of nausea swirling in my gut. I didn't care if I had to watch a hundred dirty movies or order a million sex toys. I'd do anything. I couldn't lose Mum.

"She's alright, Honey," my dad reassured. "We're just at the hospital."

I was already on my way to my car before he finished.

"I'm on my way," I said and hung up.

I glanced over at Tico, who nodded at me and waved, "Go."

That's what I did. I got in my Sunfire and sped away. The entire time I felt the weight on my chest pressing in. I couldn't breathe. I couldn't hear cars honk at me as I rushed past or see anything but the road in front of me.

The only thing I could hear was that voice in the back of my mind, laughing.

The more I imagined worst-case scenarios, the louder Emily got. She mocked me with taunts of divine retribution.

Saying things like, *"You feel your heart pounding, that's how my parents felt."*

"You deserve this."

"You should suffer as they did."

By the time I pulled into the hospital parking lot, I couldn't stop the guilt from flooding in my chest. Quite frankly, I was surprised I remembered to drive on the right side of the road. Mum was all I could think about.

Was she laying in there hurt because I was a selfish, spoiled child? Had karma taken my sins out on Mum?

I'd never been more scared to walk through a door in my life. What would I find on the other side? Mum's bright eyes smiling back at me, or would I be helping Dad pick out a tombstone?

Thankfully, Dad was waiting for me when I rushed inside.

I flew into his open arms and let the tears fall.

"Oh honey, don't cry," he shooshed and kissed the top of my head. "I told you Mum was fine."

That didn't make me feel better.

I sniffed back a sob and blinked up at him. "Promise?"

"Yes, she's a wee bit scraped up, that's all." He smiled and tucked back a strand of hair that had fallen out of my ponytail. "The other car just skimmed her."

Thank God. Still...

"Can I see her?"

"Of course."

Dad led me down the hall and into a room, where I saw Mum sitting in a bed surrounded by my brothers. Even Cy was curled up under her arm, which did not help calm my nerves.

Cy didn't get afraid. If he was clutching onto her, then the accident had to be worse than Dad had said.

"Star," Mum's bright eyes lit up with a warm smile. "Don't' look so sad sweetheart, I'm perfectly fine."

She was not fine. She could've died. I sprang across the room and jumped on top of the twins, joining the pile. It didn't matter if she was hurt or needed space. The only words ringing through my head were, 'I could've lost her.'

"Hey," the twins cried out. "She's our Mum too."

"She's been mine longer," I argued and squeezed tightly onto Mum's waist.

We lay there for a long time. Listening to the doctor come in and explain Mum's injuries. Which were minor, but they still wanted to keep her overnight for observation.

There was a lot of moaning and groaning about that. A night hadn't gone by where Mum wasn't there to tuck us in.

The worst was Cy and me. I didn't want to leave Mum here all alone while Cy argued that he should be the one to stay. Though I think he was arguing with me to argue.

That's when Dad stepped in. "That's enough. Your Mum needs her rest. If you two can't get along, then you can go wait out in the hall."

"Kick Cy out," I shrieked and kicked Cy. "This is all his fault."

His dark eyes narrowed on me, "You're the one that's hogging Mum."

"Enough," Dad yelled, cutting me off before I could argue. "Both of you out now."

My parents didn't get angry often. So, when Dad thrust his finger at the door, we all knew he was serious.

Grumbling, I slid off the bed and stormed out of the room with Cy stomping behind me.

"I should be the last one kicked out."

"Why?" Cy rolled his eyes. "Because you're the only girl?"

"Exactly. Girls have a special bond that boys will never understand."

"Pfft," Cy snorted. "Just cause you have boobs doesn't mean you're special."

"Mum has boobs," I huffed and crossed my arms.

"Yeah," A smirk tugged on the corner of Cy's mouth. "But hers are bigger."

Little shite. My boobs weren't that small. At least I had cleavage, which was more than I could say for some girls.

"Girls can do anything boys can do."

"Yeah?" Cy arched a brow, "Go knock someone up."

My mouth opened, but nothing came out. Okay, he might have me there.

"That's what I thought," he said and strutted away.

I had half a mind to chase him down and make him say uncle like I used to do. Instead, I stomped over to a row of chairs, like an insufferable brat, and flopped down to pout.

The guy next to me cocked a brow, which made me cock a brow in return. What the hell was this guy looking at. Hadn't he ever seen siblings fight before? And who wore a jean jacket in this day and age?

Unable to take his staring anymore, I snarled, "Can I help you?"

"I doubt it." He snorted, "But I can help you."

Oh yeah, he'd help me alright. Creep.

"Oh yeah," I sang mockingly. "And how's that?"

"Depends whether or not you want your mom to survive the next crash?"

I thought he was joking for half a second. Then he turned to look at me. I never knew true fear until that moment. His eyes reminded me of another pair.

The lifeless brown pair that haunted my dreams. Except his weren't just lifeless, they were empty. Worse still was the lack of emotion on his face. No hint of remorse or anger. Just a mouth, nose, and eyes. No sign of a soul whatsoever.

The only thing I could say was a stuttered, "W-what?"

"What's so hard to understand? You were given eight hours."

Dean's threat this morning smacked me in the back of the head, as did the color of his eyes. They were very similar to the ones I was currently looking at, minus the lifeless voided abyss, that is. Did he have another son?

The deep baritone of his voice echoed through my ears. "Have you gone to see Silas yet?"

I glanced over at Mum, who was laughing with Ash, and back to him. My stomach sank deeper and deeper with each passing second. Something told me lying to this man would be a mistake, so I shook my head.

"I suggest you don't wait too long." I shifted away from those void-filled grey orbs as he leaned in. "All kinds of things can go wrong in a hospital."

I couldn't stop myself from looking back at Mum. Her accident wasn't an accident at all. It was a warning—a very clear and threatening warning.

My throat bobbed with a heavy swallow. "What do you want from me?"

"I'm not the one you should be asking." He rose from his chair and glanced over his shoulder to add, "Tick Tock," before walking away.

Emily was wrong, and this wasn't divine retribution. It was a day of reckoning. And I just met the reaper's avenging angel.

Chapter 25

Silas

When Star let the name Emily slip, I thought maybe she was a rival. All girls seemed to have them. I swear it was ingrained in their DNA that anyone with tits was competition.

Examples of this were everywhere. Naomi and Riley, Shelby and some chick named Chelsea, and Tiffany and Amy.

They liked to blame us for their hatred. He looked at her, or fucked her, or talked to her. Whatever the issue was, they always managed to track it back to some poor asshole, but there was nothing a man could do to a girl that compared to what they did to each other. Chicks were ruthless.

And it appeared that the witch next door was their queen.

I couldn't help but smile as I read through the file Lou sent again. I knew Star wasn't as sweet as she pretended to be, but damn. This I was not expecting. She didn't just destroy this girl. She fucking obliterated her. Pushed Emily past the point of sanity until she not only took her own life but tried to take Star with her.

I hated to admit it, but I kind of admired the girl. That kind of mind fuckery took some serious dedication and skill. My little witch had teeth.

Big sharp snarling fangs that would make girls like Naomi Prescott cower. Ironic considering all the shit she gave Mase. My best friend didn't have shit of perfect little Star Chadwick.

Was it wrong that I kind of wanted to play with that version? That girl was a force to be reckoned with. How long would it take me to break her? There was no doubt in my mind that I could do it.

They could play all the evil little games with each other they wanted. Every heterosexual chick on this planet had one weakness.

Men.

Wealth and success weren't the ultimate games in life. It was love. I'd seen best friends tear each other apart because they wanted to ride the same dick. If a guy could make a chick care about him, then there'd be no stopping her, and in turn him.

I snapped my laptop shut and headed down the stairs. My father wanted me to marry the right girl—someone pure and strong from a well-respected family. Well, I may have just found her.

If Dean could put up with Lillianna, then surely I could handle Star. The only question was, did I want to? What kind of lesson would that be teaching Finn? I saw how happy Micha and Logan were. I wanted that for him.

My cousin deserved to be happy, not fall in line with the family name. That's why I did what my old man asked. I got good grades, took the courses he wanted, and kept my public image clean, so Finn wouldn't have to.

As long as Finn could be free from the obligations of the Creswell name, nothing else mattered.

I stopped at the bottom of the stairs and glanced at my watch. Star should be feeding her fucked up birds right now.

Normally, I'd be sitting in my room, watching her strut around the backyard in a pair of shorts. My favorite days were the ones when she had to chase the peacock around.

That bird was a stubborn prick. I liked him, though. Not only did he make Star workout, but half the time, she wound up falling in the mud. There was something sexy about a chick covered in dirt. Especially Star Chadwick.

There was nothing stopping me from going over there and seeing it up close and personal. Lou did say he wanted me to claim her, and I'd hate to go against the King of Kings.

Ding, dong.

My brow cocked. No one I knew rang the doorbell. They just walked in.

The chime rang again, making me sigh and walk over to the door. It was probably one of my old man's patients—pain in my ass. They were always showing up here, looking for the good doctor. He had office hours for a reason.

My brow arched further when I threw the door open. It wasn't a patient standing on the other side. It was Star. Her wide onyx eyes sparkled up at me, but it was the way she bit her bottom lip that interested me. I couldn't tell if she was angry or worried.

"I swear to god, Silas Creswell, if you send one more person after my family, I will gut you."

I was going with angry.

"Listen, Crumpet. I don't know what you're talking about."

The curl in her lip deepened. "Don't pretend you didn't know about the creepy guy in the jean jacket."

Huh? That explained Preston's text. May as well go with it.

"What about him?"

"I don't know what you want from me, but if you think threats will work," she threw her finger up in my face. "You're wrong."

Star was a smart girl. She knew Preston was a scary mother-fucker. Fuck, a random person walking down the street could see that, and here she was. Getting in my face and acting all tough. The girl had some balls, didn't hide the fact that her knees were shaking.

I crossed my arms and leaned against the doorframe. "So, why are you here then?"

That shut her up. The snarl fell off Star's mouth as she let out a long breath. She didn't want to admit it to herself, but I could see defeat pulling at her features.

If pretending made her feel better, who was I to argue? I won. She knew it, and I knew it. Besides, it might be fun to make her admit it.

"Maybe you should come in," I said while pushing the door open.

She peeked up at me through her lashes, imploring me silently with her eyes not to do this, but I had every intention of doing this. The only thing that look on her face did, was make me hard.

All it took to make her step across the threshold and into the lion's den was a single arched brow. It was then that I realized just how much I was going to enjoy this.

I led her into the lounge and waved at one of the plush red chairs. "Have a seat."

"I think I'll stand."

"Whatever," I shrugged and strode over the bar. "You want a drink?"

"You'd like that wouldn't you?" Star huffed and narrowed her gaze, "Get me inebriated, so my judgment is down."

"Honestly, I don't give a fuck how sober you are." I pulled out a crystal decanter of single malt scotch and poured myself a glass. "It won't change anything. I know how this will go, and so do you."

I swirled the ice cubes around and sipped slowly, taking my time so my words could sink deep in that stubborn head of hers. I could tell the second it clicked.

Star's shoulders slumped as the corners of her mouth tipped. She looked pretty when she smiled, but that frown on her face made me lick my lips in anticipation.

One word rang through my head as my gaze rolled up her bare legs to the deep navy skirt wrapped around her hips. *Virgin.*

I'd never had a virgin before. I'd never touched a girl that some other asshole hadn't touched before me. Experienced girls sometimes had a problem taking me. The idea of someone pure hadn't really crossed my mind. Pain wasn't my thing, but I wanted to hurt Star.

Bracing my elbows on the oak bar, I leaned forward and watched her mouth open and close. If she was waiting for me to say something, she's been sorely disappointed. Why would I make shit easier on her now?

After a few minutes of silence, her eyes began to wander around the room.

"You have a lovely home." She nodded at a bookshelf in the corner, "Do you like to read?"

I shot down her attempt at small talk with a muttered, "Not really."

To my disappointment, she wasn't easily detoured. Star walked around the room, pointing out various things and asking questions about them.

All of which I ignored or gave a simple yes or no to. Why did girls insist on rambling on about useless shit when they were nervous? It was fucking annoying.

Finally, she threw her arms up in frustration and blurted out, "What do you want from me, Silas?"

There it is.

"I want your panties."

"What?" her jaw dropped. "Why do you want my knickers?"

"Because I want to jerk off with them tonight."

If someone's mouth could hit the floor, Star's just did.

"I-I-I," it was adorable how red her face was getting. "You can't say stuff like that!"

"You asked what I wanted, and I told you," my brow arched. "If you don't want the answer, don't ask the question."

"I asked what you wanted."

"That's what I want." I pointed out.

"My knickers?"

"That's right."

How hot was it that she called them knickers? I could listen to her say that all day.

"So if I give you my knickers," Star paused to eye me suspiciously. "You'll leave me alone?"

I couldn't help but laugh out loud. "I didn't say that was all I wanted."

She stamped her foot on the ground. "God damnit, Silas. Stop playing games and just tell me what you want."

God, she really was naive.

"Give me your *knickers,* and I'll tell you."

Her face morphed from embarrassment to anger as her hands twisted under her skirt. She was actually going to do it. I thought she'd fight more, but I had to admit, I liked it this way better.

Her obeying my demands was so fucking hot, I was mesmerized when the black lace material slid down her legs. I couldn't look away from her, carefully stepping out of them. I couldn't do anything but taste the salvia filling my mouth until she took that first step.

"Ah, ah," I held my hand up, stopping her, then waved a finger at the floor. "Crawl."

Star reared back. "I will not crawl."

"Your choice." *it wasn't, really.* The second Lou ordered me to claim her—she lost all free will. "But don't blame me if you get another visit from creepy jean jacket guy."

For years, we all listened to Micha talk about breaking Riley. How much he wanted to see her cower beneath him.

Even when he was busy pretending to hate her, we could all see how much he wanted her, same with Mase, but I never really understood how conflicting those emotions could be until Star slowly sunk down to the ground.

Every shuffle her knees made against the hardwood pulled at the lust raging inside me. I was a man starved. Hunger tingled on the tip of my tongue, tearing apart that fraction of control I had left. There was nothing more beautiful than the sight of her perched on all fours in front of me.

My last coherent thought came when I wove my fingers in her hair. Next thing I knew, those silky locks were twisting in my hand, pulling tighter and tighter until Star was forced to lift her chin.

"You want to know what I want, Crumpet?"

Her tiny hand lifted, holding up a scrap of lace. "I thought you wanted these?"

All my plans to toy with her, and torment the little witch for a while, flittered away the second her tongue darted out to moisten that plump bottom lip.

Feral. That's the only thing I could feel. The desire to claim my female seeped out of my pores, vibrating through my growl.

"Why would I want those?" I lifted her off the ground and roughly folded her over the bar. Slamming her face against the hard wooden top. "When I can go directly to the source?"

"Silas," her dangling feet kicked as her hands flew back, slapping at my chest. "Stop it. What are you doing?"

There was no reason or thought behind what I was doing. Just animalistic need. I needed to touch her—needed to feel her come apart. I needed it all. Every last inch of her. More than I needed my next breath.

"Shut up," I growled, pressing my palm down harder on the back of her head.

She could yell at me and fight all she wanted. I didn't fucking care. Hell, I liked the sting her sharp little claws sent across my skin, almost as much as I liked the way her thighs quivered when I slid my other hand under her skirt.

"So fucking soft," I purred and stepped in, pressing my cock up against her firm ass.

All of it was mine. Her ass, her slender legs, even her fucking hair. All mine. But most of all…

I twisted my fingers over the curve of her hip and forced my hand between her thighs to cup her mound. "This is fucking mine!"

Star sucked back a stuttered breath and released a whimper that had my cock begging to be let out.

"Silas, I don't–"

"You don't what, Crumpet?" I slid my finger between her folds and groaned as her wetness slicked my skin. "Cause it sure feels like you do to me."

The only thing she was fighting now was her orgasm as I swirled my finger over her clit, again, and again, and again.

I watched her fingers tighten around the bar's edge. I felt her entire body quake and still managed to hold onto a small string of sanity.

Then she moaned.

Felling her come apart wasn't enough anymore. I needed to taste it.

I flipped Star over and forced her thighs apart as I pushed her up the bar. The sight of her glistening pink pussy, cut that final thread. I dove in, dragging my tongue along her slit. I didn't know how starved I was until I started feasting.

Star hit me, I think. Yelled something and tugged on my hair. None of that mattered because I had the sweetest, most intoxicating flavor exploding in my mouth. My mind was gone, lost completely in the magnificence of her hot little cunt.

It was Star that pulled me back. More specifically, the scream she released as her pussy pulsed around my tongue. But I could still hear that beast demanding I take more. His growling, snarling fangs were quickly devouring my common sense.

"You need to leave."

Star's chest heaved as she stared up at me with her brows knit.

"Now, Star," I slammed my hands down on the bar next to her trembling form. "Or I will fuck you. And trust me, you're nowhere near ready for that."

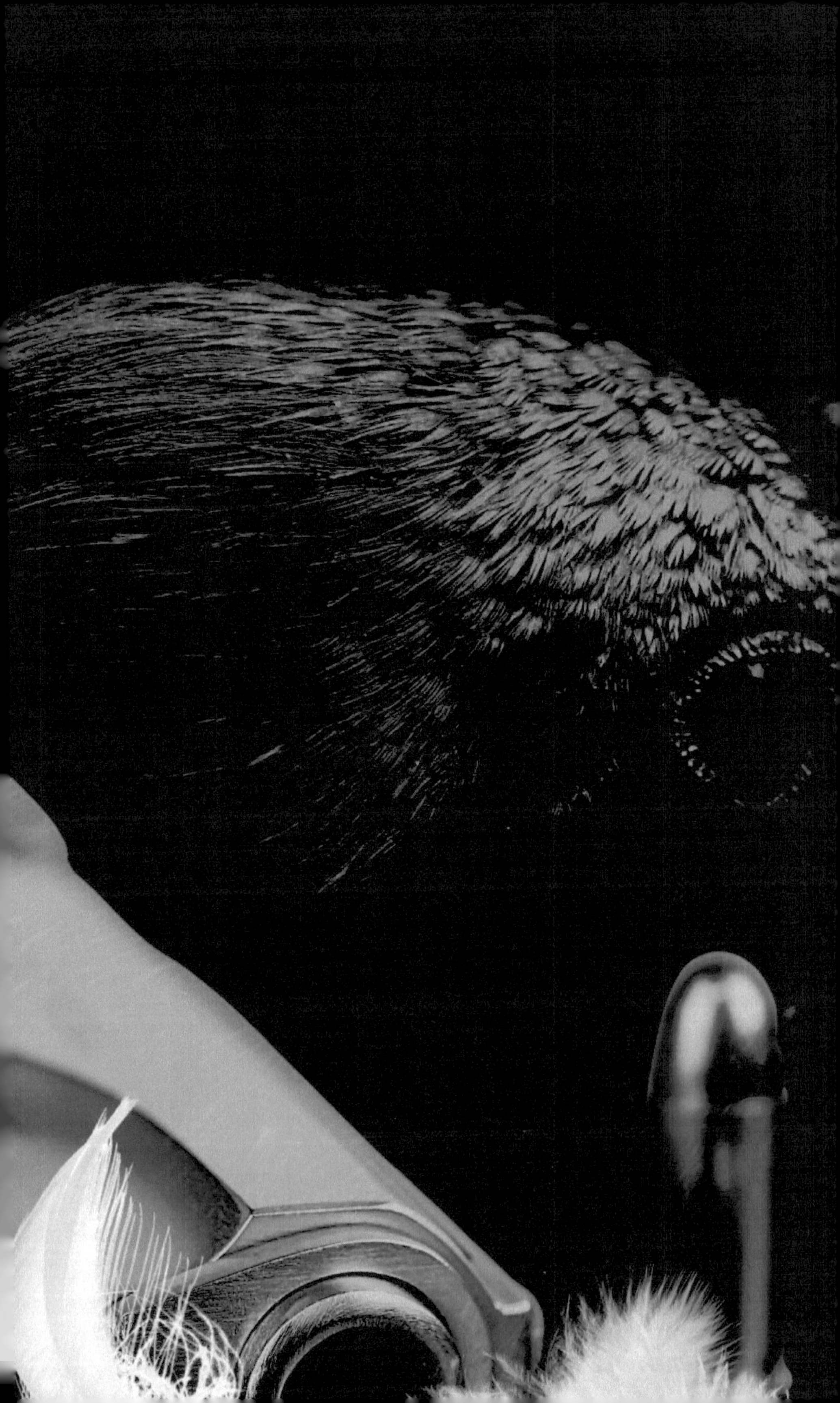

Chapter 26
Star

My ghosts didn't visit me that night. I didn't hear Emily's voice or see her dead eyes when I closed mine. I saw something much worse.

A mischievous smile and vibrant blue eyes. No matter what I did, I couldn't chase away the heat from Silas skin.

Every breath I took held his spicy scent. Every shadow was a reminder of his silhouette. Every thought in my head revolved around what he'd done.

When I did finally fall asleep, he was there too—waiting to taunt me in dreamland.

The next morning, I woke up and moved through my regular routine as if my life was nothing more than a simple checklist.

Step one, get up.

Two, have a shower.

Three, do hair and make-up.

Four, get dressed.

That's when I got stuck. Instead of heading downstairs for breakfast, I stood in front of the mirror, staring at the red tie around my neck. I don't know why or what kind of answer I thought would mystically fly out at me? Of if I was even seeking an answer at all.

My tie couldn't tell me what happened last night. It couldn't explain why my knees trembled when I thought about it or where Silas went at that moment? I'd seen that 'there but not there' look once before on a rabid dog.

A friend of Mum's brought it over, hoping she could save it. She tried. I watched her fight for days to just get him to eat. But nothing she did worked.

The thing that I remembered most was the wild sparks swirling in that dog's eyes. That's why when Silas told me to leave, I did.

I ran out of there so fast that I thought my legs were going to fall off. And even in the safety of my room, I could still feel his eyes on me.

I must've scared Dad because he spent half the night knocking on my door to see if I was alright. I told him that I was, but I'd veered so far from alright that a wrong turn wasn't a strong enough description, and not because of what Silas did.

Or how he held me down and forced my legs apart. But I enjoyed it. Not only that, I orgasmed.

Of course, I fought him. Yanked on his hair and punched his shoulders. At one point, I even slapped him across the face. Not one single thing deterred him. He simply dug his fingers into my arse and held on tighter.

I had the bruises to prove it. Marks that should trigger a traumatic reaction, not the memory of how hot his tongue felt against my flesh. He forced me to do something I didn't want to, and I came so hard I could still feel his mouth on me.

That's why I was standing here, staring at my tie. I didn't

know what else to do. If I left my room, then I'd have to eat breakfast. After that was school, where he was. I was terrified to face him.

That depraved part I tried so hard to hide reared her ugly head, and Silas pulled her out. He knew she was there. The scary part was, I think he wanted to feed her.

"What are you doing?"

Snapping myself out of my weird trance, I turned to roll my eyes at Cy. "Why are you in my room?"

"Um maybe because you missed breakfast?"

I did? Shite.

Glancing down at my watch, I let out a sigh. I was going to be late. Maybe that wasn't a bad thing? If I showed up a few minutes after lessons started, then I could avoid Silas.

Cy's eyes narrowed. "Is that bloke next door giving you trouble again?"

"What do you know about that?"

"I pay attention," he shrugged.

My head tilted as I eyed him. My little brother was shite to everyone, but when it came to the people that picked on us, he was an absolute arse. My parents refused to put him in the same school as Will.

His quiet, shy demeanor was a magnet for bullies. Last year, Cy got expelled for putting one such bully in the hospital. They'd already been called into a meeting once this year. Thankfully, he wasn't the one to start that tussle.

Maybe he was?

I glanced down at the bandage on Cy's arms. The timing of that altercation was way too convenient. Cy came home from school crying that someone had stabbed him the day after Silas filled my locker with rubbers. Which I told him about.

"What were the names of those lads you got in a tiff with?"

Cy crossed his arms and glared back at me. "Why? They got what was coming to them."

But did you?

"Was one of their name's Finn?"

It was just an assumption I made based on Finn's age and family standing. There were only two private schools in Ashen Springs. Ashworth and Midgarden. My suspicions were affirmed when Cy forced an innocent spark on his face.

"Don't you try that shite on me." Unlike Mum, who wanted to believe her son was a perfect little angel, I was on to his games. "You stabbed yourself, didn't you?"

It wouldn't be the first time Cy did something like that. I loved my little brother, but sometimes his diabolical nature scared me.

"Why would I do that?"

"Drop the act, Cy," I threw my hand up and pointed at him. "I'm telling Mum."

"Go ahead," he sang with a smile on his face. "But good luck explaining the bruise on my cheek."

"You wouldn't."

Cy locked glares with me, fisted his hand at his side, and cried out, "Mummy, Mummy. Star hit me."

Son of a...

"Fine," I hissed and snatched my bag off the bed. "But be warned, Cy. You go near Finn again, and I will get you back."

"I look forward to it," Cy called out as I walked down the stairs.

The battle for dominance had been an ongoing war between him and me. I blamed myself for part of it. I wasn't exactly the best role model. He grew up watching me destroy people, but unlike old Star, there was still time to save my brother and his possible victims.

Poor Finn. I know I only met him once, but he seemed like such a sweet boy. How he was related to Silas, was beyond me.

Silas was a grumpy arsehole, while Finn was full of life, but the resemblance was uncanny. Having a guy like Silas in the family was bad enough, and now he had to put up with Cy?

Finn was no match for my brother's malevolence. Some itching powder in Cy's bed should help steer him away. If that didn't work, I could always resort to good old fashion sibling violence.

My brother's diabolical plans were the least of my worries. That was made clear the second I opened the door.

Standing in my driveway, next to a large Hummer, was Silas.

My gaze shifted to the closed door behind me. Did I have time to duck back in the house?

"About fucking time."

Guess not.

"Get in the fucking car," he waved at his Hummer. "We're going to be late."

My brow rose. "Late for what?"

"It's Monday."

"Okay?" I had no idea what he was talking about—were we supposed to go somewhere? Because I sure as hell didn't remember making any plans, especially with him.

Silas sighed and shot me a dirty look, "We have school."

Oh yeah, that made sense.

Wait...

"You don't think I'm going to ride with you?"

I had my own car, thank you very much. I was perfectly capable of getting myself to school. Not to mention having the ability to leave whenever I wanted. An important factor to have when one was dealing with the Silas Creswells of the world.

"We don't have time for this, Crumpet," Silas released a breath and pinched the bridge of his nose. "I don't like being late."

"Well, don't let me stop you. I have my own car, and if I did need a ride, you would be the last person I'd ask."

I'd walk to school before I got in his vehicle. Even if that meant I had to get up at four AM.

"I didn't ask what you need," he pushed off the Hummer and marched my way. "Now, get. In. The fucking. Car."

"No," I crossed and lifted my chin, reaffirming my refusal.

I wasn't going anywhere with him.

Silas had other ideas. He walked up and scooped me up, tossing my body over his shoulder.

"Put me down, you Arsehole," I demanded while slapping my palms against his back, which was far too firm for my liking.

It was extremely hard not to focus on the way his muscles flexed and tensed. It was wrong how visible those firm lines were under that white cloth. Hard ripples moving in time with his steps. He smelled good, too, like rosewood with a hint of cinnamon.

Maybe he had cinnamon buns this morning? I bet his mouth tasted really sweet right now.

My body was dropped down in the passenger seat of his Hummer, snapping my mind back to the problem at hand.

God damnit, Star, pay attention.

I slid forward, moving to get out of the car. Silas stopped me.

He slammed his hands down on either side of the doorframe and growled, "Don't."

"I am not going anywhere with you."

Despite my refusal, my eyes were stuck on one thing. Those thick lips, twisting in a frown. Even while frowning, his mouth looked soft, supple, and entirely kissable.

"You better stay in that seat."

I lifted my chin to meet his gaze, "Make me."

That was the wrong thing to say.

Silas leaned in the car, making me shrink back from the wave of heat pouring through me, and clicked the seatbelt across my chest. After that, he twisted his neck, bringing his mouth next to my ear.

"Keep pushing me, Crumpet," his hot breath washed over my skin, causing a tingle of goosebumps to race down my arm. "And you'll find out just how lucky you were when I let you leave last night."

That was enough for me. I stayed put and didn't say a word as he drove me to school. I did, however, make sure to smack him in the face with my bag when we got there.

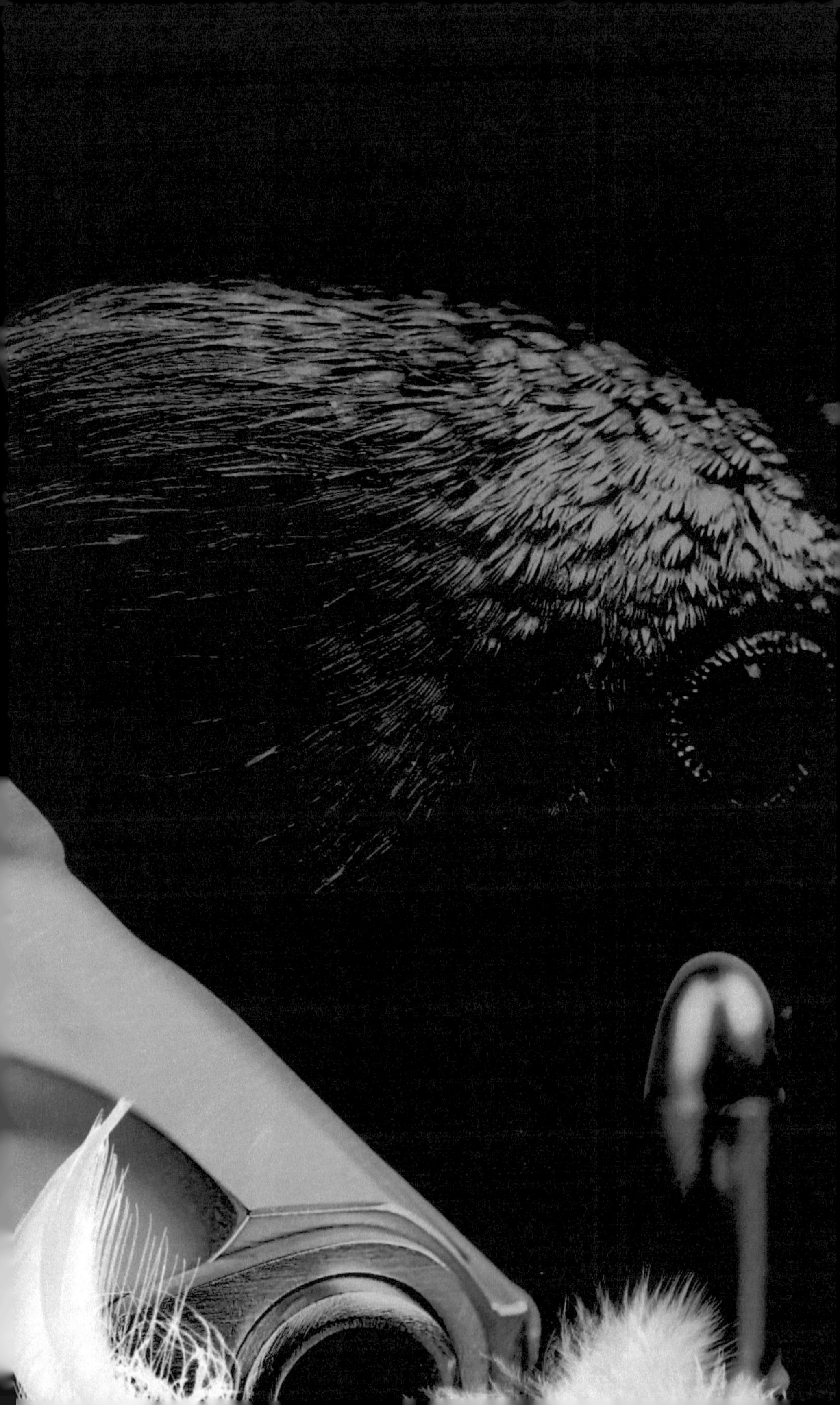

Chapter 27
Star

School was weird. Silas seemed to be everywhere I went. He insisted on walking me to my lessons, sat next to me in class, and kissed me on the cheek before I left for drill team practice.

I slapped him naturally, which was when he pulled me in and reminded me of what was at stake.

I don't know why he was suddenly acting like he was my fella? Nor did I know what to do about it? I couldn't really do anything.

Not without putting someone I cared about in danger. The only thing I could do was play along and prepare myself for whatever his endgame was.

One thing I'd noticed was how Mason and Silas steered clear of Riley. Maybe if she was here, Silas wouldn't be acting like a cocky arsehole, but she wasn't, and neither was Shelby. I thought at first they skipped school until people kept changing the subject.

I'd say something like, *'I bet they're having fun,'* or *'I wonder what Shelby and Riley are doing right now.'* And Lana would start talking about random shite.

We were only partway through the day, and I now knew way more about a baby's bowel movements than I ever cared to. Wherever those girls were, it wasn't worth trying to get the information out of Lana.

And yes, I was curious. Who wouldn't be? Everyone was clearly hiding something. I even asked Mason and Silas about it. All they said was that Riley and Shelby had to take a trip, and they'd be gone for a while.

Where did they go? No one seemed to know. Why did they leave at the beginning of the school year? Why not? Apparently, two girls taking off out of the blue was a normal thing. At least that's what everyone acted like.

Something was definitely up. There was one person who shared my skepticism. A pair of twins started at Ashworth today. I wasn't particularly fond of the one. She reminded me of the girls I used to call friends. But the other twin…

That girl was smart. She may not have openly asked questions, but I saw her sitting in the background watching everyone, and I'm pretty sure she was taking notes on that pad of hers.

Lana told me her name was Marnie, and the other Trina. Trina I didn't care too much to talk to, but Marnie… If anyone could tell me what was going on in this town, it was her.

Which is why I almost chose not to go to practice. I wanted to talk to that girl, but Harper was more important. I'd gotten her to peek out of her shell twice now.

Backtracking was not an option. One thing teams were great at doing was building up confidence. Something Harper was in dire need of.

"Come on, Harper," I tugged on her hand, dragging her out of the locker room.

She made a whimper of protest and tugged on her shirt. I rolled my eyes. She'd been doing that incessantly since I made her put it on. It wasn't that revealing.

All anyone could see were her legs and a touch of her stomach. I swear, the only place she's be comfortable was in a convent, surrounded by nuns in their long drab habits.

Harper shook her head, bobbing the ponytail I'd painstakingly fought her to put in, "I shouldn't be here."

"Yes, you should."

Her eyes shifted nervously, as I opened the door, letting the afternoon sunshine into the locker room.

"Harper, I've seen you dance. You belong to be here just as much as any of them. Don't let anyone tell you otherwise."

"B-but I-I don't belong."

"Says who? Mason Kessler? That blighter over there?" I tipped my chin at the team jumping around the field. "None of them have half the talent you do."

In the short time, I'd been watching them, I'd counted half a dozen simple dance moves that the drill team fumbled, but Harper wasn't convinced. She chewed nervously on her lip and shifted on her feet.

"Trust me, Harper," I slapped my hands down on her shoulders, gave her a smile, and pushed her toward the team. "Now, get over there and shake that cute bum."

I gave her a tap on said bum and skipped behind her.

Tiffany's eyes lit up with a smile when she saw me. I couldn't say the same about Harper. The smile fell off Tiffany's face and got stomped under her unimpressed footsteps.

"I see you brought *her*."

Harper stopped dead at Tiffany's statement.

Bitch.

"That was the deal wasn't it?" I sang and pulled a wary Harper past our stuck-up captain. "And *she* has a name. Harper. A proper team captain would know that."

Tiffany's mouth dropped. "Are you insulting me?"

Dear lord, this girl was so daft that her ears probably whistled when the wind blew past. Thank god she was pretty.

"In case you haven't noticed, your friend is a reject." Tiffany's glare zeroed in on Harper, "And drill team is not about rejects."

I was not about to let another person in this place make Harper feel like she was less than perfect.

"Fantastic," I said and grabbed Harper's hand. "Then neither of us need to be here."

This team didn't just want me—they needed me. Tiffany wasn't lying when she said I was a world-class dancing champion.

Having someone with my knowledge and experience would propel the drill team from mediocre to excellent. I knew my worth. I wished Harper did as well.

Two steps. That's how far we got before Tiffany called out, stopping us.

"Wait," Tiffany sighed and rolled her eyes. "Maybe we could use her in lifts. She's small."

A satisfied smile curled my lips. That's more like it.

Everything started fine. We were introduced to the rest of the team. Practiced some of their routines and touched them up with more complicated moves. It took a bit of persuasion on my part, but eventually, Harper participated.

She even started having fun. My heart lifted every time she smiled or giggled. Then, just like that night at Mallum, everything took a violent left turn.

I should've seen it coming. Should've recognized that evil glint in Tiffany's eye when Harper was being lifted off the ground.

Instead, I was too busy enjoying the rare moment of happiness my friend was having.

Vince tossed Harper through the air. I saw Tiffany drop her hands just as Harper reached her. Saw the smile on her face as realization and terror filled Harper's eyes, and I tried to make it to her, but I was too late. Harper's body hit the ground with a thud that vibrated through my soul.

I rushed to her side to cradle her groaning from as Tiffany snidely sang, "Oops."

The blood coming from Harper's nose and the tears streaming down her face didn't anger me as much a that one word did.

I could feel old Star bubbling up when my glare locked on Tiffany. "You did that on purpose."

"I would never."

I couldn't believe her gall. She actually sounded insulted.

"I saw you. You dropped your hands."

"I don't know what you think you saw, but you're mistaken. I would never intentionally hurt someone." Tiffany flicked her hair over her shoulder and smiled down at me. "I told you Harper wasn't drill team material."

The rest of the team stuck up for her. Nodding while saying things like, "She wouldn't do that," and "Tiff takes care of the team."

The evil locked away in my mind heard none of it. It bled through its cage, focused on one thing, the glittering eyes and a sly smirk looking back at me.

Destroy her.

Make her pay.

Make her bleed.

Crush everything she holds dear.

The only thing that stopped me was a small voice in the back of my mind.

'That's right, Star, show them who you really are.'

Tiffany hurt Harper. She needed to pay. I had to do something.

'Go ahead, take your revenge. And then take a little more, and more, and more. Until that girl is laying dead on the washroom floor like me.'

I wouldn't do that. I wasn't that person anymore.

'Aren't you? Look at Harper. She got hurt because of you.'

Guilt tugged at my chest as I swept the hair off Harper's face and held her close. I didn't mean for this to happen.

I wanted to give her a little confidence and make her see that she was worth something. That people would miss her and wanted her in this world. That I needed her. I just wanted to help her.

'You can't help her. You can't help anyone. People like you never change.'

Was Emily right? Would Harper be better off if I left her alone? What if I did and she followed the same path? I couldn't let that happen. I couldn't watch Harper's light fade from the world. I had to do something.

My head tipped toward the school.

Maybe, it didn't have to be me?

Chapter 28

Silas

"What's wrong with you?"

"Trying to enjoy my lunch." That obviously wasn't possible. I dropped the rest of my sandwich on the tray. The food was really going downhill in this place.

"That's not what I mean," Mase gave me a sideways glance. "You gonna kiss me on the cheek too?"

That wasn't a big deal.

"You know how my old man is."

"Ah, so this boyfriend crap was for his benefit?"

I shrugged. It was easier than trying to explain this shit to him. The only thing my old man cared about was public image.

He used my grandpa and mom as an excuse, but it was all about his reputation and how I made him look. Having a whore for a son wasn't exactly good for that.

Besides, if I was serious about taking a contract out on Star, I may as well find out if I could stand being around her now.

Better that than end up with another Julia Kessler. Lou hated spending time with his wife, so he ignored her. Look how that turned out.

"So what?" Mase cocked a brow at me. "Is she your girlfriend now?"

"You were the one that said just because I hate her doesn't mean she's not mine."

"So she's yours?"

"Until I decide otherwise, I guess so."

He slapped me on the back, "Well, it's about fucking time."

Really? It's about time? Was he seriously going to say that shit to me?

"I know where my girl is," I sat back and popped a grape in my mouth. "Do you?"

Mase's brows furrowed at the table where Lana sat with the twins. It hadn't occurred to him that Harper wasn't there. Then again, most people missed Harper. She was always quietly tucked in a corner.

"Of course, I know where she is."

No, he didn't. Otherwise, we wouldn't be eating in here.

"I figured you'd know about her joining the drill team."

"What?!" Mase's eyes went wide. "What the fuck do you mean she joined the drill team?"

"Yep," I let out a satisfied breath. "She's out there right now. Jumping around in that uniform—in front of the football team."

"Son of a bitch," Mase slammed his fist down on the table and then pointed at me. "Keep your girl away from mine. She's starting to rub off on her."

He stood up and stormed across the cafeteria.

"Where are you going?"

"To beat the crap out of the football team. Wanna join me?"

An image of Star dancing around in that tight uniform flashed across my eyes.

"Yeah, I kinda do," I said and stood up, causing my chair to screech across the floor.

I was going to go for that idiot Brandon first. I didn't care if he was just the water boy. He was still out there—watching her. I'd seen the way he looked at her. That motherfucker was mine.

We didn't make it that far because Star cut us off in the hall, and she looked like she'd been through hell. Her hair was sticking out of her ponytail. There was dirt on her legs, and dried tears stained her cheeks.

But it was the blood on her shirt that made me cock a brow. What the fuck was that drill team practicing out there? Ninja martial arts with actual swords?

Mase must've agreed because he leaned back and gave her a once-over. "Jesus Christ, girl, what kind of dancing are you guys fucking doing?"

Star huffed and rolled her eyes.

"Seriously," I growled while waving at her shirt. "What the fuck happened to you?"

If someone hurt her, I was going to fucking kill them. That was my job.

"It's not my blood. Tiffany didn't catch Harper."

That got Mase's attention. He pushed off the wall and narrowed his eyes. "When you say she didn't catch her…"

"I mean, she purposely let her fall," Star explained.

"Little fucking slut."

My best friend calling anyone a slut was kind of ironic. Though I had to agree. Tiffany Metcalf had aspirations to take over Naomi's spot at the head of the food chain.

Aspirations she tried to accomplish by sucking her way to the top. I fucking hated Naomi, but at least she had class. She'd never stoop that low.

Star crossed her arms and eyed Mase. "What do you care? I thought you hated her?"

"Hey, I told you she was mine." Mase flung his arm up and pointed at her, "If anyone's going to make her bleed, it'll be me."

Mase's mind was already going through possible payback scenarios. I was more interested in what someone else did.

I nodded at Star and said, "What'd you do to her?"

"To who?"

"Tiffany."

My interest was piqued when her throat bobbed with a heavy swallow.

"Why would I do anything?"

Because it's in your nature. "Uh-huh?"

That made her mad. Star charged forward, waving her finger at me.

"Just because you're an arsehole," she snarled. "Doesn't mean everyone is."

"I think Mr. and Mrs. Perkins would disagree."

I'd never seen guilt flood someone's face so fast, and I was best friends with Mason Kessler. A man who was the living definition of self-hatred.

Interesting. Maybe her sweet-as-pie act wasn't complete bullshit after all? Was my little witch trying to turn over a new leaf? I almost laughed at the thought.

Star backed off and whispered, "I don't know who you're talking about."

She knew exactly who the fuck I was talking about, and now she knew that I knew. In fact, it pissed me off that she was suppressing a part of herself. I wanted to see the real her. That fierce wildcat I knew was inside there. That girl would've torn Tiffany apart.

"Okay, I know exactly what to do to get the cunt back." Mase dropped his elbow on my shoulder. "You still got that video?"

"The one with Jenny and her dad?"

Mase nodded.

I liked where this was going. Jenny was Tiffany's best friend. Last year we caught her sucking Tiffany's dad off under the bleachers at a football game.

"Maybe we should just let it go?"

We both looked over at Star, who looked terrified at the idea of humiliating someone. I didn't like this side of her. This was the same girl that raised her fists against three full-grown men. She wasn't a fucking coward.

"Fuck that," I barked out, surprising even Mase. "We aren't dropping shit."

A person could grow, change, and evolve, but their soul was eternal. Tainted or not, eventually, it would come out. It was up to her to either embrace it or let it eat her alive. You can't fight who you are.

Star straightened up and lifted her chin definitely, "Well, I want no part of it."

That shit wasn't happening. Come hell or high water, I was going to pull that wildcat out of her. And make her fucking embrace it.

"Oh now, Crumpet. You're gonna come with us and watch this shit go down." I threw my arm over her shoulder and leaned in to add, "You wouldn't want your new best friend finding out about Emily, would you?"

Star's body stiffened.

"Who's Emily?" Mase asked as we headed down the hall.

"No one," I grumbled while steering Star to follow him.

She didn't fight. Didn't even argue. I had her, and she knew it. If I wanted her to suck me off right here in front of everyone, she'd get down on her knees. All so Harper Callaghan wouldn't find out her dirty little secret.

"Aww, man, no one tells me anything," Mase whined.

"Shut up," I shoved my phone in his chest. "Find that video."

We had a show to put on, and I'd bet my left nut that perfect Star Chadwick would enjoy every second of it.

***

"You bitch," Tiffany shrieked while pulling on Jenny's hair.

Goddamn, girls were mean. This shit had been going on for a couple of minutes now, and there were already clumps of hair on the floor and blood staining their clothes.

We didn't just send the video to Tiffany. We sent it to the whole school. It was the best way to guarantee a crowd, which meant more girl-fight for us to watch before the teachers broke it up.

Jenny squealed and threw her hand through the air, raking her fingernails across Tiffany's cheek.

"We shouldn't be watching this," Star whispered. "It's wrong."

"Then why are you smiling?"

For the first time since she moved here, it felt like I was seeing the real Star Chadwick, and it was truly a sight to behold. he smug arrogance surrounding her.

The high and mighty way she carried herself, and that evil little smirk curling her mouth, had me wanting to throw her up against the wall and fuck her hard.

This girl could handle what I had to give, and I was more than willing to give it to her.

Star tipped her brow at me. "Why are you looking at me like that?"

"Because right now," I bent over and growled in her ear. "You're the hottest fucking thing I've ever seen."

She gulped back a gasp and shyly ducked her head away, but the only thing that flush filling her cheeks did was call to the hungry beast inside me. I had to step away and fist my hands to keep him at bay.

After what happened last night, I couldn't afford to lose control again. She was a virgin, and a man my size couldn't rush things.

If I took her too hard, there'd be no coming back, and one thing was for sure... I was going to use Star Chadwick until she had nothing left to give.

Even if it broke me in the process.

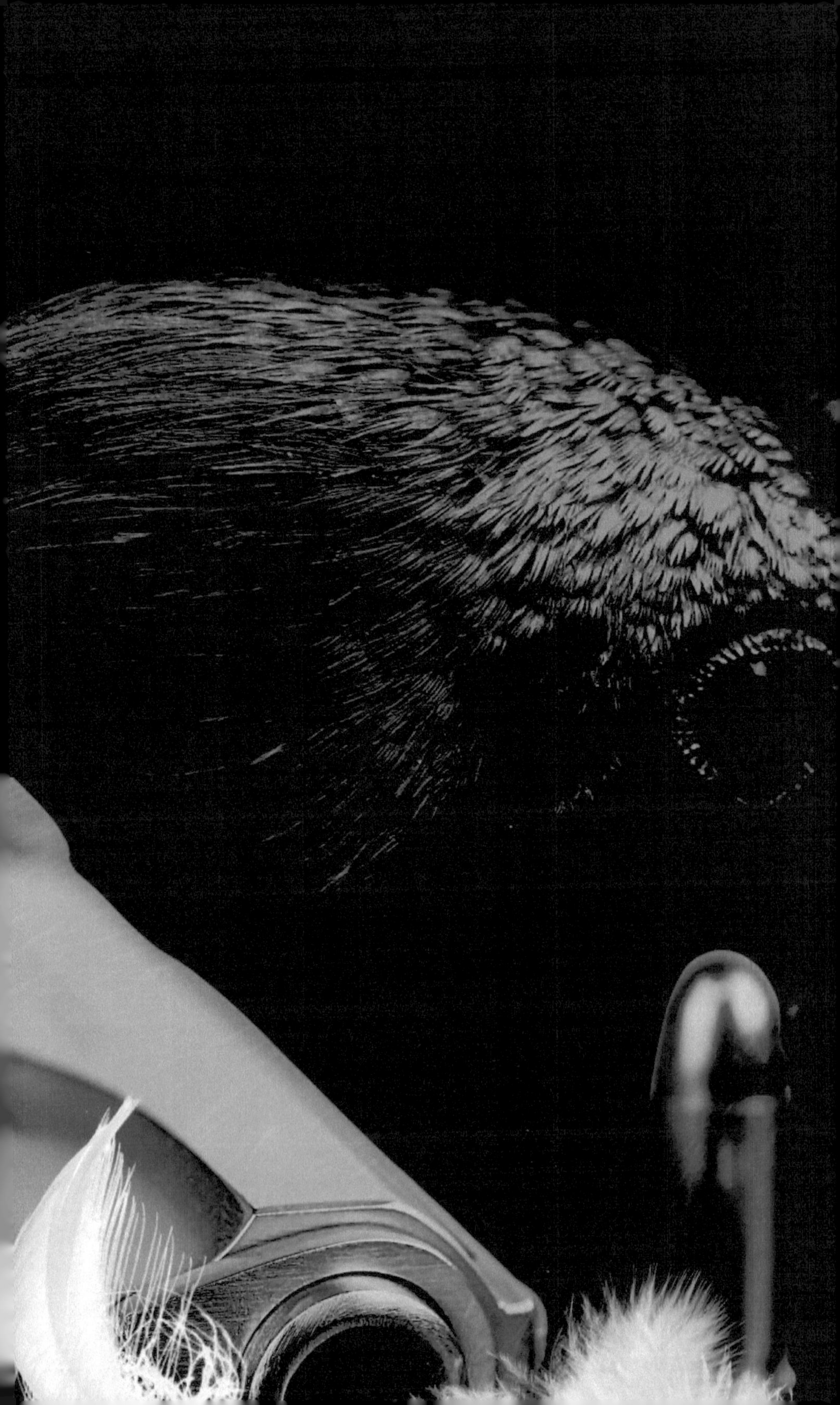

Chapter 29

Star

It was much later than I intended by the time I got home. The sky was already dark and full of stars. I hoped Will wasn't waiting up for me.

Normally we'd have read our chapter by now, but I had to run down to the Causegrove and check on Tico. Since someone insisted on driving me, I couldn't do it after school. That same someone was the reason I stayed so long.

Silas knew about Emily. I don't know how he found out. Tico didn't even know about that, and I had a full blown break-down in front of him. He knew something happened, but he didn't know what.

I thought about telling him tonight, but I was too ashamed. What would he think of me? What would Harper?

So I sat there, listening to Tico talk about the latest graffiti craze for as long as I could. I felt safe there, by the glowing fire, with my friend. Huh, friend. I couldn't stop thinking about that term.

Last year it meant something completely different. I never really knew any of my old friends. I merely socialized with them because they were in the right clique, or looked the right way.

I didn't know what they liked to do, who their hero was, or what they were afraid of. Heck, I didn't even care what their favorite color was. As long as they could do something for me, it didn't matter what kind of person they were.

With Tico, Harper, Lana, and everyone else, I wanted to know those things. I cared about how they felt and what they liked. I wanted to see them happy, not scared or sad. And what was more, they wanted the same for me.

What if I had given Emily a chance? How different would things be if I warmed up to her instead of beating her down?

I hopped out of my car and looked up at the bright moon.

It's funny how much things could change in a few months. This time last year my main concern was shopping. Now, I wondered why the lad next door always seemed so grumpy.

Yes, Silas was a tosser. And yes, he made my life hell. But today I saw something else in him. The way he escorted me around school, and how he reacted to Tiffany was almost… protective.

That was crazy, of course. Why would he care? But still…I couldn't shake that glint in his eyes when he was staring at me.

'You're the hottest fucking thing I've ever seen.'

I shook my head and headed inside. "Silas doesn't care about you, Star."

He only wanted to hurt me.

"Isn't Silas the bloke next door?"

Mum nodded at Dad. "I told you she fancied him."

They were cuddling on the couch in the family room and should not have overheard me. Did all parents have super-sonic hearing, or was it just mine? Oh, well, it didn't matter. I was just happy to have Mum home.

I dropped my keys on the table by the door and smiled over at them. "How are you feeling?"

"Oh, don't worry about that," Mum waved her hand through the air and propped her grinning face up on the back of the couch. "I want to hear about your fella."

"He's not my fella," I groaned and rolled my eyes.

"But you want him to be."

"I do not." *Did I?*

I mean, Silas was cute… okay, more than cute. But he wasn't exactly a nice guy. I wanted someone to look at me the way Dad looked at Mum. As if the sun rose and set in my eyes. Kind of like how Silas was staring at me this afternoon.

Stop deluding yourself, Star. The bloke hates you.

"Ah, I saw that," Dad piped in.

"Saw what?"

"That dreamy way you drifted off," Dad explained. "You were thinking about him just now."

Mum nodded in agreement, while my jaw dropped.

"I was not."

"Classic deflection," Mum smirked at Dad. "She's got it bad."

What was happening right now?

Dad scratched his chin. "Think we should stock up on Magnums? He's a pretty big bloke."

Dear lord.

"I don't know," Mum turned an inquiring eye my way. "Darling, have you seen his package yet?"

"No I have…"

I stopped and thought back to what Mason said in class, and the thickness I felt that day in the pool. Was he really as big as people said? I heard the rumors of a giant monstrous cock that some girls were terrified of. But that was just rumors. Right?

"Oh, oh," Mum slapped Dad's arm excitedly, "our Baby's going to pop her cherry. Get the camera."

I grumbled under my breath and headed up the stairs. "I'm going to bed."

"Wait! Come back," Mum called, "Dad got the camera."

"No pictures," I yelled back and closed my door.

Why couldn't I have normal parents? You know, ones that didn't put me on birth control the day I got my menstrual cycle, and who encouraged me *not* to have sex.

I grumbled out a few curse words and went about getting ready for bed. Perhaps tomorrow things would go back to normal and Silas would continue hating me from afar. My wish didn't come true.

When I crawled into bed and reached over to turn off my lamp, my phone dinged with a text that sent my heart racing in my chest.

Unknown: Leave it on.

Was someone watching me?

I scoured the dark corners of my room, searching for a hidden menacing figure. I found nothing. No body lurking under my desk, or eyes peering in from the darkness.

I pinched the bridge of my nose and let out a calming breath. Maybe I really was going mad.

No, I wasn't. Because when I reached for my lamp again, another text came through.

Unknown: I said leave it on Crumpet.

I picked up my phone and furrowed my brows down at the screen.

Me: Silas?

Unknown: It's not fucking Santa Claus.

Me: How did you get my number, and
more importantly, where are you?

My gaze was drawn to my window when a light clicked on in the distance. Suddenly, Silas was all I could see. A very shirtless Silas sitting in front of a window.

The light bounced off him, illuminating every dip and groove in his chiselled torso. I may have tilted my head to see if I could look below the window edge and see his stomach.

If the rest of him was any indication of what his abs looked like, then they must be glorious washboard muscles.

My heart leapt out of my chest as my phone chimed in my hand, loudly singing out the melody of my generic ringtone. That's when I noticed the phone pressed against Silas's ear.

Was he calling me? Why? What did he want?

I considered ignoring him, but then I ran the risk of him coming over here. Then Mum and Dad would answer the door, and they'd probably ask him for his cock measurements.

Or if he knew how to properly break in a virgin. Sweet Jesus, they had a camera. They were going to take pictures of him, weren't they?

Ring, ring.

Dear God, Star, answer the damn phone before it's too late.

"Hello."

Hello? Who says hello anymore?

"Why do you look so scared, Crumpet?"

You'd be scared too if you had my parents.

"I'm not scared," I snapped back at him.

Silas tsked, "Testy, testy."

I groaned and rolled my eyes. "What do you want?"

"I want to watch you finger fuck yourself while I jerk off."

I threw my phone. Literally tossed it on the bed because I was so shocked. Who says that? Seriously? Who calls up a gal at night and says they want to watch her finger fuck herself?

Silas Creswell, that's who. I suppose I shouldn't be surprised. If I'd learned anything, it was that the gobshite was blunt.

My wide eyes shifted from Silas to the phone, where I could hear him demanding that I pick it up. Did I want to pick it up? Did I want to go down this road? The thought alone had my chest heaving with quickened breaths.

I can't explain why I reached out to scoop up my phone. Perhaps it was the anticipation tingling low in my belly, or sheer morbid curiosity that drove me to do it.

Either way, I knew the instant I pressed the phone to my ear, there was no going back. The weird thing was, I didn't want to.

"That's good, Crumpet," Silas's deep tone sent a shiver down my spine. "Now get rid of the blanket."

The only thought that went through my head as I kicked my blanket on the floor was, 'why am I doing this?' While I refused to look at him, I felt every word he said.

"Put your knees up and spread your legs."

Against my better judgment, I slowly bent my knees. Cool air grazed up my bare legs as my nightdress slipped down my thighs.

I shouldn't be doing this, it was wrong. Silas Creswell was my enemy. I should be telling him to go to hell and hanging up. Not reveling in the dark yearning swirling in my soul.

Silas released a deeply penetrating groan as I slowly spread my legs.

"Do you have any idea how fucking hot white cotton panties are?"

Other than deciding which pair I'd wear, I'd never given much thought to my knickers.

"Take them off."

The very visible wet spot on my knickers filled me with shame. It burned a path down my neck and into my chest, snapping my mind back. What the bloody hell was I doing?

Silas barked out, "Don't fuck with me when I have my dick in my hand."

What?

My eyes snapped over to him. I couldn't see what he was doing. I could see the muscles in his arm flexing, though. But it was the twisted look of pleasure on his face that caused my breath to hitch.

"Hurry up, Crumpet." His eyes met mine, "Show me that pretty pussy."

And I did.

I pushed back my mortification and slipped my knickers off. And the rumbling groan that vibrated through the other end was worth it.

"Touch yourself."

I did that too.

I slid my finger through my folds and toyed with my clit. Silas's soft grunts and heady breaths had me powerless to do anything else. He hadn't even touched me and I was completely at his mercy. A puppet for him to control, and I loved every second of it.

I swirled my finger and pinched that bundle of nerves, working myself into a tightly wound ball of tension. All while staring directly into his piercing gaze.

I couldn't breath, couldn't talk, couldn't see past the heat flooding his eyes. My body was on fire. I needed release, but I couldn't find it. No matter how hard I worked my clit, or how many times I felt my orgasm crest, I couldn't make myself fall off that edge.

"No," Silas growled when I dipped my finger down towards my opening, "keep your fingers out of that hot little cunt. It's mine."

I frowned and whimpered into the phone.

"You heard me. Fuck," he grunted and dropped his forehead against the window, fogging up the glass with his breaths, "I'm gonna come. I want you to come with me, Crumpet."

That's what I'd been trying to do, but my body wouldn't cooperate. I was so close I could taste ecstasy, and still that tension kept building.

Then Silas growled loudly, "Fuuuck, now! Come for me, Baby. Let me hear you fucking scream."

My whole body seized as a cloud of euphoria bowed my back. All I could do to muffle the squeal escaping my lips was clamp my hand tightly over my mouth.

Afterward, I lay there limp and out of breath, riding out the aftershocks. Completely forgetting Silas was still on the phone, until I heard his voice.

"The next time I come, it'll be in your mouth."

Chapter 30

Silas

"**P**reston threatened to cut Mason's balls off."

Fucking Preston. What the hell was he thinking, saying shit like that in front of Finn.

I grumbled under my breath and turned down the road towards Dell's Dairy, Finn's favorite ice cream shop.

"Will Preston hurt Mason?"

Probably. Depended on what he did to piss him off.

"No."

Finn didn't buy my lie. He crossed his arms and shook his head. "He was pretty mad."

"Well, maybe Mase shouldn't have done whatever he was doing."

Fuck knows what that was. Prick could've hired a barber shop quartet to follow Preston around. Can't imagine he would've liked that too much. Neither would the barber shop quartet, who was probably six feet under right now.

Preston's mood was the entire reason I brought Finn here, instead of staying at the house like Lou suggested. When I got to Oakleigh Manor, Preston was going off. I could hear him yelling at Mase.

It was the first time I got to see Finn in over a week. The last thing I wanted to do was take on the impossible task of calming his ass down. That was as fruitless as trying to understand Ava's weird spring roll obsession. All the Whitley's were fucked.

Besides, I had other things to worry about. Like Star's attempt at avoiding me. Little witch called in sick today. Never took her for a coward. But that was a problem I could deal with later.

Finn's worried eyes swung my way. "We shouldn't have left them alone."

It was sweet that he was worried about Mase, but… "Preston won't do anything to him."

Nothing serious, anyway.

"He held a knife to Mason's nuts."

Or maybe he would?

"Seriously?"

Finn nodded.

Huh? Preston was usually calm. Scarily so. There was nothing more eerie than watching a guy casually munch on a sandwich while chopping a body up. That shit was fucked up.

"So we should go back, right?"

I pulled to a stop and looked over at my cousin, contemplating what he said. Preston was… well Preston, but he was loyal. Especially to our generation. He'd kill Lou before he would Mase.

"Mase will be fine." I gave Finn a reassuring smile. "How about we go get some ice cream?"

"Okay, but can you do me a favor?" Finn opened the door and climbed out. "Keep Mason away from those twins."

My brow arched. "Twins?"

"He was talking to one of them when Preston got mad."

I joined Finn in the parking lot and steered him towards the Dell's.

We all knew Mase was a slut. Fuck, his track record made Logan look like a goddamn nun. Since when did Preston give a shit about Mase's flavor of the week? Unless…

Fuck me. Was that crazy son of a bitch interested in one of those girls?

"Silas?"

I tipped my head at my cousin, who waved at the door.

"Ice cream?"

"Oh, right."

I pulled open the door and pushed Finn inside. I couldn't stop thinking about Preston. I just couldn't see him with one of those girls. One was frumpy, and the other flighty.

Fuck sakes, the flighty one walked in on me banging a chick at a party and stood there staring at my dick, licking her lips. If Preston got pissed at Mase for talking to one of them, I sure as fuck wasn't going to tell him that story. I wanted to keep my balls.

Was that why he killed that guy? I wondered why the fuck he gave a shit about some asshole in public school.

The twins transferred from public school. I never asked Preston about it. Learned that lesson when he made offing a kid sound logical. I'll say it again, every Whitley was fucked.

I shook my head and led Finn up to the counter to place our order. The last thing I wanted to do was get in Preston's head. There was no coming back from that shit.

Dell, the kindly elderly man who owned the shop, smiled

warmly at my cousin. "Hey Finn, did you bring me any rocks today?"

"No, but I found this really cool one." Finn's eyes sparkled as he placed his hands on the counter. "It was black with an orange stripe."

"Hmm," Dell tapped his finger against his chin. "Well, that could be a gneiss, gabbro, or basalt. Was it smooth or bumpy?"

Finn went on to explain the texture of his rock. This was an ongoing thing between these two. Dell used to be a geologist, which Finn found fascinating. Finn found everything fascinating.

That was the curse of my cousin's mind. Everything in this world had equations behind it. He once spent three hours breaking down the mathematics of a tea party.

Rather than try and understand what the hell those two were talking about, I spun around and looked at the space. Dell took pride in his place. It was one of the nicer shops in this side of town.

It reminded me of one of those ice cream parlors I saw in fifties style movies. Red titles on the walls with matching pleather booths and stools, and the staff was always smiling.

My favorite things were the nautical decorations he had hanging on the wall. Compasses, an anchor, ring and other things that had washed up on shore.

I didn't notice anything new today because I was too busy staring at the people sitting in the back corner booth.

Son of bitch.

My gaze rolled over the little boy with curly platinum hair, to the girl sitting across from him. Star looked pretty good for being sick. In fact, she looked great, in a red tank top and jean shorts with her hair piled on the top of her head.

What the fuck was it about messy buns that got guys hot and bothered? One look at that mass of hair and my dick was ready to go. Good thing I wore a hoodie today. In about two seconds, my dick would be playing peek-a-boo with the waistband of my jeans.

"Hey," Finn called out, "isn't that your neighbor?"

"Don't know why the fuck she's here." She should be at home, in bed, waiting for me.

Finn tipped his head, "Should we go sit with them?"

The corner of my mouth tipped up. "Yes, we fucking should."

Finn skipped over with a smile on his face. An expression Star returned when she saw him.

"Hi Finn. What are you doing here?"

"My cousin brought me," he said, slipping into the booth next to the little boy.

Well, they seemed pretty happy to see each other. Not as happy as I'd be in a minute, though. I scooped up the tray with our milk-shakes and sundaes and strolled over to join them.

Star's eyes sparkled over at Finn. "Is your cousin going to join us?"

"Don't mind if I do."

Her face instantly dropped. "Silas?"

Yeah, Silas.

I set the tray on the table and slid in beside her, jealous that my cousin got a smile and I didn't.

"What are you doing here?"

"I could ask you the same thing." My cold glare snapped her way. "Don't look very sick to me."

She dropped her head and muttered, "I had a headache."

I bet she did.

"I guess it's a good thing I didn't bring you chicken soup then."

That got Finn's attention. He stopped shoveling ice cream in his mouth and looked up at me with big wide eyes.

"You were going to bring her chicken soup?"

I don't know why he was so surprised. I wasn't that much of an asshole. I did nice things. Like every day when I didn't kill Mase, for example.

"Is she your girlfriend?"

"What?" Star shrieked while shooting the kid, who I assumed to be another one of her brothers, a look. How many kids did these people have? "He's not… I mean we're…"

Oh, she wanted to play this game, did she?

"Come on honey," I threw my arm over her shoulder and pulled her into me. "Don't be shy. I want everyone to know we're together."

The fucked up part was that I wasn't lying. I really did want everyone to know. That way, other assholes would stay away from her.

The little boy with curly hair looked at me, and then Star. "Do Mum and Dad know?"

"Stop it, Will," Star grumbled.

There might be hope for this kid. At least he had a normal name.

"There's nothing for Mum and Dad to know."

Did she think I was going to make it that easy? "How can you say that after what happened last night?"

Her brother's interest was definitely peaked now. "What happened last night?"

"Nothing happened," Star insisted.

"You sure about that?" I slowly licked some ice cream off my spoon and shot her a look. "Because I distinctly remember…"

She slapped her hand on the table, cutting me off. "Silas, can I talk to you?"

"I wouldn't want my ice cream to melt. You know how much I like licking things."

Finn and Will exchanged furrowed brows, while a flush crept across Star's cheeks.

"Please," she sang while giving me a fake as fuck smile. "It'll only take a minute."

I looked over at Finn, wondering if this could be a teachable moment for him. He let Shelby's little sister, Maggie, run all over him. He needed to see what it was like to wear the pants in the family.

Even a strong spirited girl could be tamed. It just took a firm hand. He didn't need to see how I turned her attitude around. Just the outcome. Which the sweet act Star was pulling off gave me the perfect opportunity to do.

"Sure, Crumpet." I stood up and held my hand out for her. Mostly because I knew she wouldn't slap it away. Not in front of her brother. "Let's talk."

Though she wasn't happy about it, she took my hand and followed me around the corner to the bathrooms. That's when shit went sideways.

I pushed open the door to the women's bathroom, and she lost her goddamn mind. Started slapping my hand and trying to pull away, as I yanked her into the tiled room and locked the door.

"Let me go!" she screamed and slapped me across the face so hard I stumbled back. "I can't be in here!"

My brow arched as she flung herself at the door and frantically tugged on it, like the devil himself was coming for her. I'd never seen anyone look so terrified in their life.

All the color had drained from her face and her entire body was shaking. Fuck sakes, she was so panicked, she forgot the door was locked. She just kept tugging on the handle, and when that didn't work, Star clawed desperately at the wooden door.

What the fuck?

And then it hit me.

Emily shot Star, and then killed herself in the school bathroom. I wondered why I saw her coming out of the office bathroom at

Ashworth. I intended to teach Star a lesson, and instead threw her into full blown PTSD panic mode. Well, that shit was going to stop now.

I charged forward, spun Star around, and pushed her back against the wall. "Calm down."

That's the opposite of what she did.

Star reared back and wildly flung her arms at me. Clawing at my exposed skin.

"Let me go! She's going to get me. I can hear her."

I did the only thing I could. Lifted my hand, and slapped her across the face. Not hard enough to leave a mark, but enough that she would snap out of it.

She calmed down just as her brother started pounding on the door.

"Star! Are you okay? Let me in."

"She's okay, Will."

She wasn't. Actually she was pretty far from fucking okay. She was seconds away from hyperventilating.

Fuck.

"Look at me, Crumpet." I cupped her face and pressed my forehead to hers. "You need to tell your brother you're okay. You don't want him to worry."

That seemed to get through to her. The desperation didn't leave her eyes, but she called out, "I'm okay, Will. Go sit with Finn. We'll be out in a minute."

Even though I doubted he believed a word she said, Will sighed out an, "okay," and walked away.

Star's dark eyes locked on mine. "Can we leave?"

"No, Crumpet, we can't leave."

Like I said, this shit ends now.

"She's in here." Her chin started to tremble as tears dripped from her eyes.

"The only people in here are you, and me."

She leaned in and whispered, "I can feel her watching me."

"Can you feel this?" I took her hand and slipped it under my hoodie, pressing her palm against my chest. "Feel me breathing?"

I expanded my chest and slowly let it fall with a long exhale.

Star licked her lips and nodded.

"Good. Now breathe with me. In… and out… in… and out…"

I didn't realize how worked up I was until my body relaxed when she calmed down. The world melted away as we stood there, staring into each other's eyes, moving our chests in sync.

It felt like I was seeing a part of her soul. Like she was sharing a part of herself with me, that no one else knew existed. That scared little girl that ran from monsters.

Except she didn't need to run anymore because, I'd crush any monster that came at her. Including the ghosts that haunted her mind. If Emily wanted to come for Star, she have to go through me first.

This little witch was mine.

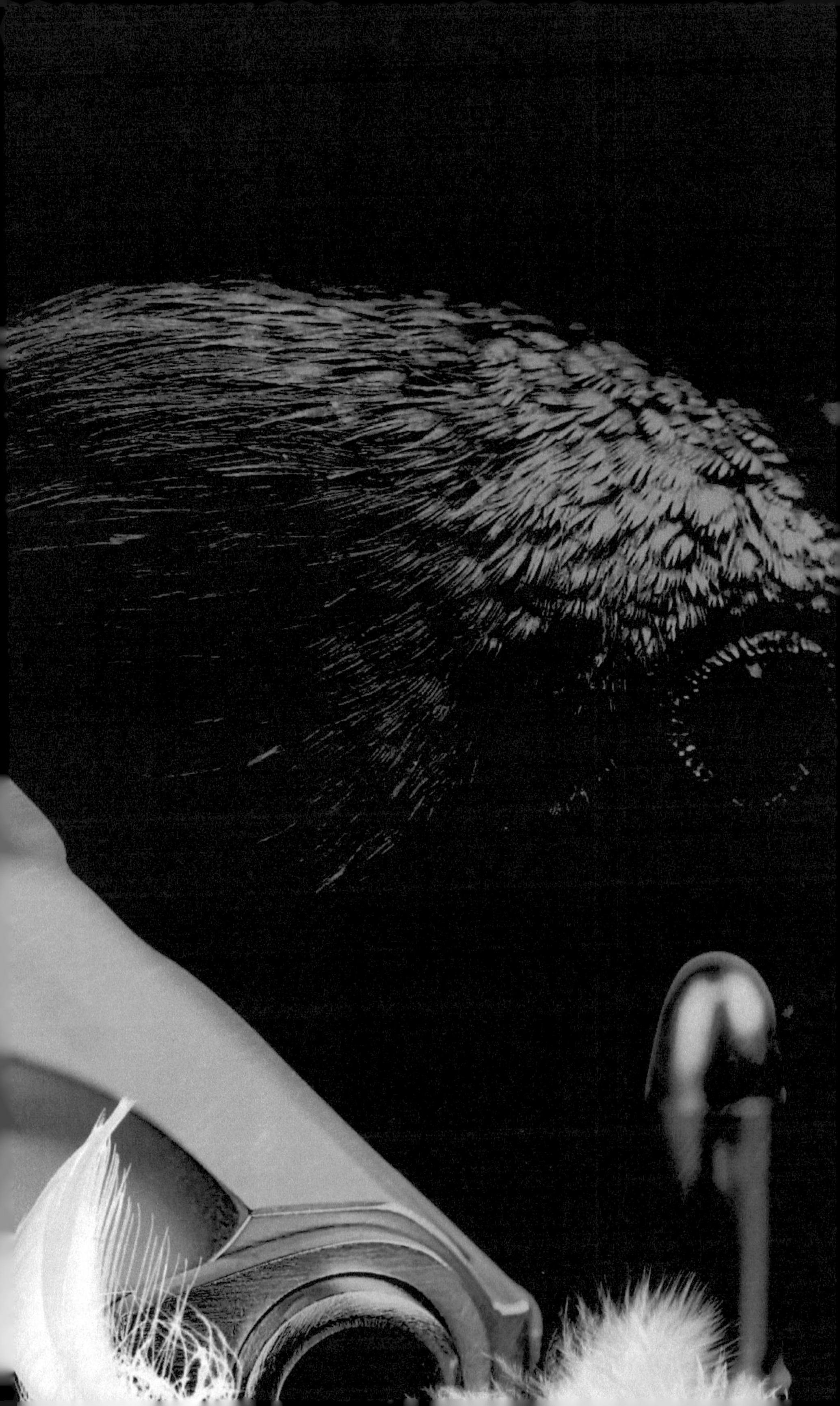

I lost it. Acted like a psycho in the bathroom, in front of Silas Creswell of all people. The worst part was, he pulled me back. Like I was some pathetic, fragile girl. I wasn't weak.

I was perfectly capable of taking care of myself. Silas and his dumb friends chased me through the woods for Christ sakes, and I stood up to them. I didn't need his help, or anyone else's. Exactly why I gave him all the 'attitude,' as he called it today at school.

I smacked him with my book bag twice. Sacked him, slapped him across the face, openly flirted with Brandon, and this morning when he texted me to be ready to go, I was already on my way.

He grabbed me at the end of the day and demanded I show up at the party at his house without my attitude. Oh, I lost my attitude all right. Put it all in a red silk dress that barely covered my arse, with a stunning Harper by my side.

"I don't think this is a good idea." Harper clicked up the walk, tripping on her heels.

Okay, maybe not stunning, but I did manage to convince her to put on some strappy heels with her jeans and t-shirt. And I happened to think her arse looked great in my Apple Bottom jeans. That is what they were made to do, after all.

I could hear music blaring from out back, but I wanted to make an entrance. So I looped my arm in Harper's, and stepped up to ring the doorbell.

"Can't we just slip in the back," Harper whispered. "I don't think they'll hear the doorbell."

"Oh, they'll hear it," I growled, and pressed the button again.

Silas was far too uptight to not pay attention to his front door. He probably had some app on his phone that let him know when someone was walking by his house. A minute later, the door was thrown open by said uptight tosser.

Silas rolled his eyes over my dress then cocked a brow at Harper. "Really?"

Yes, really.

I stepped up, tapped him on the cheek, and looped my purse around his neck. "Be a good boy and put that somewhere safe for me, will you?"

"I see you brought your attitude."

You have no idea.

"Come on, Harper," I tugged her into the house. "Let's go get a drink."

"I don't drink," she whispered back.

"You do tonight."

We made it three steps before Silas grabbed my arm. "You think I'm gonna let you drink when you're acting like this?"

"Listen, arsehole," I spun around and poked him in the chest.

"You might be able to make me come here, or go with you to school, but you cannot tell me what I put in my body."

Silas sighed and clicked his tongue.

"Alright Baby, you wanna play who's the alpha, I'm game." He waved his hand down the hall. "After you."

That's right, after me.

I looped my arm back in Harper's, rolled my shoulders back, lifted my chin, and sauntered us down the hall to the open patio doors. Heads turned to look as we walked out. As they should. We looked great. But it wasn't us they were looking at.

That was clear when Silas bellowed out, "No alcohol for these two."

I glared over my shoulder at him.

Silas simply smiled, said, "Have fun, Crumpet," and walked away.

He didn't seriously think that would work, did he? This was a high school party. Teenagers didn't care who drank what.

Turns out, I was wrong. When the almighty Mr. Creswell spoke, people listened. Not only was I blocked from reaching the bar, but some arsehole kept ripping the keg's spout out of my hand. The only thing I did manage to grab were two cans of soda.

I flopped down beside Harper on one of the patio couches and passed her a can. "Here."

"What is it?"

"Soda," I sighed.

She smiled and took the can.

Well, at least someone was happy.

I glared over at Silas, who tipped his brow at me and raised the drink in his hand. Arsehole.

Determined to salvage the night, I straightened up and looked at Harper. "We don't need alcohol to have fun."

That statement was wrong. Because Mason Kessler was here,

Harper didn't want to do anything but sit there and watch everyone else. I kind of wished Silas had a band again.

Since that night I was caught spying on him, I couldn't get the image of Silas out of my mind. The way he looked up on that stage, strumming his guitar as if he was making love to it, took my breath away.

I couldn't stop myself from searching the crowd for his icy-blue eyes. The same eyes that helped ground me yesterday. The way he looked at me, and how firm his chest felt under my hand…

Stop it, Star. The guy is an arsehole.

I shook my head, clearing my thoughts, and searched for something else to think about. That's when I saw Mason Kessler making out with some girl by the bar.

Speaking of arseholes.

And I wasn't the only one that saw him. Harper ducked away, chewing on her lip. She was clearly trying not to look at Mason's overly affectionate display. He knew she was here. I know he did. No one could miss the look he gave me when we arrived.

"I'm sorry, Harper." I let out a breath and swept her hair back. Maybe she was right, and we shouldn't have come?

"It's okay."

No it wasn't. The last thing I wanted was for her to get hurt. Bloody Mason Kessler. Couldn't he let her have one good day? No. He had to say Harper belonged to him one minute, and then suck face with some random girl the next.

My brow rose. Who says Harper couldn't do the same? She deserved to feel some affection. To know that someone cared about her.

I pressed my finger under Harper's chin, tilting her head to look at me. When I leaned in, she reared back.

"What are you doing?"

"Shhh," I hushed while cupping her face and pulling her in.

I pressed my lips to hers. Soft little peppers at first. A gentle sweep here, and tender lick there. Until Harper released all her tension in one long breath and melted into me. Then I really dove in. Sweeping my tongue over hers, enjoying the sweet taste of her mouth.

I told her everything she needed to hear with that kiss. How wanted and beautiful she was. A perfectly innocent creature, too good for the Mason Kessler's of the world.

Not even the loud, "what the fuck!" yelled across the way could pull me away from her.

But the pair of strong arms could.

One second I was kissing a sweet girl, and the next I was face to face with a very pissed off Mason Kessler.

"What the fuck do you think you're doing, London?"

"I-I was… just…"

I couldn't find the right words. Honestly, I was a little afraid Mason was going to hit me. The glint in his eyes wasn't right.

Mason's eyes narrowed as he stepped in on me. "I suggest you find the ability to speak coherent sentences real fucking fast."

"Back off." Silas came out of nowhere and shoved Mason back.

But he didn't back down. If anything, he took it as a challenge and puffed his chest up.

"Did you see what she did?"

"Yeah, I fucking saw it." Silas wasn't backing down either. "That one might be yours, but this one is mine. Now back. The fuck. Off."

"You gonna make me?"

Silas and Mason may be grade A arseholes, but I didn't want this. I didn't want to come between two friends.

I held my hands up and said, "Please stop this…"

"Go wait inside." Silas's cold glare snapped to me, and when I didn't move fast enough, he barked out, "Now, Crumpet."

I jumped and looked back at Harper, "Come on…"

"No," Mason interjected. "She stays here."

I didn't like that. No way I was leaving Harper out here with these animals.

Silas rolled his eyes, "She'll be fine. Now go inside."

I don't know why I trusted him, but when Harper nodded at me to go, I did.

"And don't even think about leaving," Silas growled as I stepped through the doors.

* * *

I'm not sure how long I waited there–pacing back and forth in the dining room–but it felt like forever. Thankfully, I didn't hear the sounds of a fight, or any more yelling. Just footsteps of people leaving. That didn't stop my gut from churning.

I used anything I could for a distraction. Studied the intricate lacing on the tablecloth. Counted the dinner ware in the oak cabinet, and studied the painting of wildflowers so closely, I knew which flowers had eight petals and which had six. I even thought about leaving.

Which was the current thought on my mind when Silas walked in. And he wasn't alone. Mason strutted in right behind him.

I swallowed and pressed my back against the wall, attempting to escape their angry glares. At least they weren't mad at each other anymore.

"Tell me, Crumpet." Silas bent over and flattened his palms on the table. "What the fuck do I have to do to get you to understand this isn't a fucking game?"

"You could slit her mom's throat."

That's when I noticed him. Creepy jean jacket guy. Why was he here?

340

He leaned against the doorframe and pointed the tip of a pocket knife at me. "You *were* warned."

Panic poured through me, making me cry out, "I'm sorry. I won't do it again. I promise."

"Relax, no one's going to hurt your mom." Silas shook his head and cocked a brow back at jean jacket guy. "Jesus Christ, Preston. Slit her throat? Couldn't have gone with something a little less devastating?"

Jean jacket guy, who I now knew as Preston, shrugged. "Micha got pissed when I threatened to beat his girl with her own arms, so I figured I'd go with this option."

His choices were between beating someone with their own arms, and murder? Who the hell was this fella?

"No one asked for your opinion." Silas rolled his eyes. "Feel free to leave anytime you want."

"No can do. I'm his shadow, remember." Preston nodded at Mason, who looked anything but pleased.

Why did Mason need someone to follow him around at all?

Preston pushed off the doorframe and eyed Mason. "You have anything to drink?"

"No, motherfucker, I didn't have anything to drink."

"Good boy. You need to stay sober." Preston walked up to Mason and squeezed his cheeks, making his lips puff out in a fish kiss. "I, however, don't."

He smiled, tapped Mason on the cheek, and left.

I wasn't sure what was going on here, but I was pretty sure it didn't include me.

"So… I can go now, right?"

Just like that, both Silas and Mason's attention was back on me.

"No you can't go," Silas growled. "You think I'm gonna let you off easy?"

Well damn. I was just starting to like Preston. Aside from the whole threatening to kill Mum thing, he was a good distraction.

"Don't give me that look, Crumpet." Silas wagged his finger through the air, "Actions have consequences."

Clearly he'd never met my parents.

"You're the one that decided to pull an attitude all day…"

I tipped my head and watched his hand fly through the air, emphasizing his anger. Is this what it was like to be lectured?

"Prancing around school, acting all high and mighty…"

Shouldn't I be intimidated right now? Isn't that what lectures were supposed to do? My friends dreaded getting them. But I didn't hate this. Actually, I kind of liked it. Silas's scowl. The way his jaw ticked with each firm statement, was kind of… hot.

"I'm tired of your lip." Silas slammed his hand down on the table, causing the vase to rattle. "You will fall in line, Crumpet."

If I didn't, would he spank me?

"You know what, your mouth got me into this shit." He stopped and cocked a brow at me. "I think it should get you out."

Mason smirked and left the room, sliding the dining-room doors shut behind him. My mind didn't register what was happening until I heard the lock slide in place. My pulse picked up as Silas slowly made his way around to my side of the table.

"Silas." I don't know how I made my feet move, but I somehow managed to back up and keep some distance between us. "Just wait."

"I'm tired of waiting, Crumpet."

He ever so gracefully stalked forward. Shoulders back and muscles tensing with each step. But it was the determination in his eyes that caused me to falter.

That one second cost me.

My heel caught on the leg of a chair, sending me sprawling back on the floor. Silas was on me before I could right myself. Looming over me with that scowl on his face.

I did the only thing I could think of and lurched back. Scurrying my ass across the floor. That was a mistake. The only place I had to go was into the wall, and by then, it was too late.

Silas lurched forward, straddling my legs, while slamming his hands down on the wall on either side of me. I was trapped.

"Silas–"

He cut me off by pressing his finger against my lips. "The only thing I want to hear come out of that mouth is the sound of you gagging on my cock."

My eyes dropped down to the very visible bulge in his jeans, and despite the cold spike rushing up my spine, I licked my lips. "I won't."

"Let me put it to you this way, one of your holes is gonna be filled with my cum." He cupped my chin, twisted my neck, and leaned in to drag his tongue up the side of my face. "It's your choice which one I fill."

"I could bite you," I snarled back.

"You could, but then I'd fuck your ass," he growled in my ear. "And trust me, you don't want my dick anywhere near your ass."

I couldn't just hear the truth in his words, I could feel it. I pulled at his last thread and he was ready to snap.

"What's it gonna be, Crumpet?" He sat up, swept his thumb over my mouth, tugging on my bottom lip, "Your mouth?" His hand dropped down, forcing its way between my thighs to cup my mound, "or your cunt?"

I gasped at his touch and pressed back into the wall. Suddenly, I had the very real fear that what Mason said in class about Silas's size was true.

"Mouth," I whispered as his finger grazed along the seam of my knickers.

I really had to stop wearing dresses around this bloke.

That was all he needed to hear. Silas pulled his hand off my pussy and rose to his knees. He was so much bigger than me that that was all he had to do. One small lift, and I was face to face with that massive bulge.

My stomach flipped as I watched his fingers work to unbuckle his belt. I was nervous. And not because I was scared.

It was more than that. Each step closer I came to doing the actual deed, thoughts that made no logical sense flooded my mind.

Belt unbuckled… How do I do this?

Top button of his jeans popped open… Would some natural instinct kick in?

Zipper slowly unzipped… What if I do it wrong?

For some reason, I sought reassurances from the man who put me in this situation. Looking up at Silas, I blurted out, "I've never done this before."

I swear I saw his pupils dilate, as if he enjoyed hearing that.

"Don't worry," he threaded his fingers through my hair and softly stroked my scalp. "I'll tell you what to do."

As odd and wrong as it was, that made me feel a little better. Until he shifted his jeans and boxers over his hips and his hard dick sprang out at me. And I meant sprang. That thing lurched out at me like an anaconda hunting in the jungle.

This was not a cock. It was a weapon of mass destruction sent to destroy pussies around the world. The term 'third leg' came to mind as I gawked at the glistening bead of precum sliding down the tip.

"That is never gonna—"

Silas cut me off my thrusting forward, pressing the head of his cock between my lips.

"Yes it will," he groaned and inched forward a bit. "You won't be able to swallow all of me, but you'll take enough."

Was it weird that my only thought as my mouth was being

stretched to the point that my jaw ached was, w*ell, son of a bitch, would you look at that.*

It was softer than I thought. Like warm silk wrapped around hard stone. I didn't even mind the taste. Actually, I kind of liked it. I swirled my tongue around the tip, testing more of his essence.

"Fuuuck," Silas growled and snapped his hips forward, shoving so much of himself down my throat that I choked and gasped for air.

His shaft throbbed inside my mouth while I slapped and clawed his thighs. It was too much, I couldn't breathe.

Just as blackness started to seep into my vision, he finally pulled out. Letting me greedily cough oxygen back into my lungs. Was he trying to kill me?

I'd barely pulled a full breath back in my body when he grabbed my hand and wrapped it around his shaft, holding it at midpoint.

"Keep your hand here," he said, "or I'm going to go in too deep."

I recognized that look in his eyes. It was the same one he had that night when he feasted on me. I couldn't help but feel flattered that he wanted me so bad that, his sanity slipped.

Then again I felt comforted by the fact that he wanted to make sure I was safe before that happened. Maybe he wasn't such a bad guy after all?

"Okay," I nodded.

He let out a sigh of relief. "Good girl. Now put me back in your mouth before I lose my goddamn mind."

I did. Slowly pulled him back in my mouth, making sure I kept my hand at the marker. He liked that. Silas's eyes rolled in the back of his head as a groan rumbled through his chest.

"That's it Baby, suck me."

Oh, that's what he liked.

I bobbed my head, increasing the suction. That's when his face really twisted. I liked the way he looked with his thick lips parted and glistening. I liked the way his chest heaved, and how sweat beaded down his forehead.

I liked everything about it. Getting him off was getting me off. I couldn't help but wriggle on the floor and squeeze my thighs together. I needed relief.

But more than that, I needed to see him come apart.

So when Silas's thrusts increased and he grumbled, "Stroke me with your other hand," I did.

It wasn't long after that. Three more pumps and he was exploding in my mouth. Now that taste I wasn't fond of. A little too salty for my liking.

That didn't stop me from swallowing back every drop. Because the way Silas stared down at me when he dropped his forehead on the wall…

Was the same way Dad looked at Mum.

Chapter 32
Star

The rest of the week passed by without incident. Silas still escorted me to class and made me sit with him at lunch, but for the most part he left me alone.

He didn't even drive me to school anymore. I wasn't sure how to take that. Should I be happy that he was somewhat leaving me alone? Or insulted?

The last time I was alone with him, I had him in my mouth. I couldn't help but wonder if I'd done something wrong? Didn't he enjoy it? Because I thought he did.

Not that I had much experience to go off of, but he came. That was a good thing, wasn't it? And what was more, why did I care?

I tried to tell myself that I didn't care. That it was my first blowie and I just wanted to make sure I did it right. But that was a lie.

I was having a nice Saturday playing games with the boys, and then Silas texted, telling me to get ready. We were going to a bonfire. Now I was trying on my fifth outfit.

We didn't exactly have a lot of bonfires back home, and I had no idea what one was supposed to wear. That wasn't the problem. Every time I changed my clothes and looked in the mirror, I thought, would *he* like this. Was this what insecurity felt like? Because I didn't like it.

I didn't even know what to do with my hair. I switched from putting it up to down, braided to rolled, brushed to tussled. In the end, I just threw it up in a messy bun to get it out of the way.

I blew out a breath and scanned my reflection. Black jeans and a red top. I used to love this shirt. It had a plunging neckline and was all soft and flowy, but right now, I hated everything about it.

"This is stupid, Star," I grumbled and grabbed my sweater on the way out of my room. "It's just a dumb bonfire."

It wasn't anything special. Just another excuse for people to get knackered. I stopped halfway down the stairs. Unless it was? Oh my God… was Silas planning on…

I shook my head. That was ridiculous. Silas had basically ignored me all week. Of course he wasn't thinking about that.

But what if he was?

"Star, darling, is that you?" Mum called out from the kitchen.

"Yeah, Mum, it's me."

"Can you come here for a minute?"

I skipped down the stairs. There was time before Silas got here. Besides, talking to Mum might take my mind off the possible destruction of my vagina.

Mum's honey eyes brightened up as I joined her in the kitchen. "I hear you're going out with your fella."

Oh dear lord.

"Your father went to get you some condoms. Do you need anything else?"

"No Mum, I don't need condoms or anything else." *Why was this my life?* "It's just a bonfire."

"Oh, a bonfire." Mum clapped her hands and hopped over to pull open a cupboard. "I have the perfect thing."

I was truly terrified of what she was going to pull out. Which turned out to be a container of brownies.

"I am not taking those with me."

Mum arched her brow at the containers. "Why not? They're just brownies."

Those were not just brownies.

"Mum," I walked over, held her hands in mine, and looked deep in her eyes. "I love you, but some parents get upset when their children use drugs."

The second that dreaded words left my lips, I regretted it.

"Cannabis is not a drug, Star. How many times have I told you…"

I flopped down in one of the stools and propped my elbow on the counter. The 'Marijuana is natural' speech typically took around five minutes. Ten minutes and fifty-three seconds, if Mum was really trying to prove her point.

She'd explain how hemp was used to make all kinds of things, like bags and clothes, but I bet no one ever smoked their shirt.

Maybe I should eat one of those brownies? It would help relax me, which would definitely come in handy if Silas was planning on doing something. Wait…

Why was I even thinking about this? Who cared if Silas wanted to do something. That didn't mean I'd let him.

That thing was not coming anywhere near my vagina. I may not have a lot of experience to draw from, but I knew enough to know there'd be no coming back from that.

It did fit in my mouth though. Logically, it should fit in other places. Women did birth babies, after all.

"Is there such a thing as too big?"

Mum cocked a brow. "What do you mean by 'too big?'"

Shite. I didn't mean to say that out loud.

"Um… I meant… too big… for…" *Come on, Star, think.* My eyes landed on a eggplant resting on the counter. "An eggplant."

A slow clap rang through my head like rolling thunder.

"Uh huh." A smirk spread across Mum's face, "So your fella is well endowed, is he?"

I thought about arguing, but Mum looked so excited. I never talked to her about this stuff. I was lucky that way because, I *could* actually talk to her about this stuff.

"He's not gonna fit, Mum," I blurted out, and instantly felt like a weight had been lifted off my chest.

"Oh honey," Mum reached out and placed her hand on mine. "I know you're scared, but you have to trust that he knows what he's doing."

I snorted. That was easy for her to say. She wasn't threatened with a weapon of vagina destruction.

"I don't think you understand how big he actually is."

"It doesn't matter," Mum argued. "He could be as small as your pinky, or as big as your arm. It's all about preparation."

I cocked a brow at her. "Preparation?"

How does one prepare for something like that?

"Hang on."

Mum turned around and rummaged through the fridge, returning with a large squash and a box of donuts. The squash she slammed down on the counter. I couldn't stop staring at it, or hearing the resounding bang it rang through the room.

"When you don't prepare," Mum picked up a donut and slammed it down on the squash, "shite can go wrong."

My jaw dropped as I watched pieces of the pastry fall down on the counter around the squash. If that was meant to represent my vagina, then I'd hardly call having it ripped apart going sideways. What the bloody hell did she consider right?

Dear lord. That's it, I was never letting Silas anywhere near me. There was nothing in the world that could convince me otherwise.

No bloody way.

"Oh, pick up your chin, child," Mum tsked, "it was just an example."

An example? Example? That's what she had to say?

"Bloody hell, Mum, I don't want to see the real thing."

Or experience it.

Mum shook her head and picked up another donut. I waited for her to smash that one down and try to convince me that everything would be fine.

Fine just took a left turn and jumped out the door before getting hit by a car, rolling down a ditch full of cacti, and falling off a cliff.

Instead of destroying it, Mum pinched and pulled the pastry through her fingers because apparently slamming it down on that giant squash cock wasn't enough.

Now she had to prolong the poor thing's destruction. Slowly dragging out it's torture by pulling on the dough and stretching it.

Wait...

"When you take the time to prepare," she lifted the donut up and slipped it down the tip of the squash, "things are much easier."

My jaw dropped again. This time in astonishment.

I thought back to the numerous times Silas said I wasn't ready, and how he yelled at me to leave. Was that his way of trying to protect me? Make sure I was 'prepared,' as Mum put it?

Come to think of it, he did a lot of that lately. Bloody Christ, he almost got in a fight with his best friend. Not because he was mad at me or Mason. Because he didn't like how rough Mason was being with me.

Why didn't I see it before?

I was so focused and the arsehole crap he did, I was blind to everything else.

"Honey, are you okay?"

I looked up at Mum. No, I was not okay. Silas was going to be here any minute and I was bloody terrified to see him. Maybe I could fake sick. I sure felt sick. The pit in my stomach was swirling with nerves that made me want to hide.

Bing, bong.

Shite. He was here.

Chapter 33

Silas

$\mathcal{I}$ swept my hands on my jeans and rang the door-bell. My palms had been sweating all day, it was fucking annoying.

All week I'd avoided being alone with Star and getting the inevitable 'your dick is too big' speech. Not that it would've mattered. She could tell me not to touch her all she wanted, she was still gonna get it. Regardless of what she thought.

The thing that really pissed me off was how long it took to tell myself that. I didn't sack up and act like a man, taking what I wanted.

No. I hid like a little fucking girl. Tucked away in my house with her words ringing in my head.

'No one will want you.'

Even after I face fucked her, the little witch could still taunt me. I balled my hands and glared at the doorbell. Jesus fucking Christ.

How long does it take to answer the damn door? They were probably out back playing with their goddamn birds again. Crazy fucking family.

My hand lifted, prepared to press the button again, when the door finally swung open. Star's mom looked up at me and leaned against the open door. My brow cocked at the smirk on her face. What the fuck was she so giddy about?

"Is Star ready?"

"She'll be right out. In the meantime, I thought you and I should talk."

Oh great. Shouldn't her father be giving me the 'don't touch my daughter or else' talk? Guess I shouldn't be surprised. Nothing these people did was normal. They had a pirate ostrich in their backyard for fuck sakes.

"Star's a wee bit nervous." Her mom leaned in and added, "She's never shagged before. But I trust you know what you're doing."

I tipped my head and opened my mouth, not sure what to say.

"Oh, that reminds me," she reached down and pulled a foil packet out of her pocket, which she promptly slapped in my palm with a wink. "XL for the well endowed lad."

I looked down at the condom in my hand and back at her. "Are you giving me permission to fuck your daughter?"

She clutched onto my arms and looked up at me with imploring eyes. "I'm begging you to fuck her."

Seriously, what the fuck was happening right now?

"She's still a virgin at seventeen." Star's mom leaned back and shook her head. "Honestly, we're a little worried about her."

Okay, it was official. These people were fucked.

"Hmm." Star's mom tipped her head and dropped her gaze, "You are a big lad, aren't you."

Was she checking out my package right now? Well, this just got a whole lot more awkward. Did Star say something? Of course she did. She was probably walking around talking about how the monster in my pants was never going anywhere near her.

We'll just see about that.

I should hate fuck her in front of everyone at the bonfire. I didn't even want to go to the fucking thing, but watching her scream while I impale her on my cock might make it worth the trouble. A thought that became more vivid when Star ran around the corner and grabbed my arm.

"Let's go."

Why was she in such a goddamn hurry? Whatever, it got me away from her crazy mother. Speaking of which…

I hopped in my Hummer and glared over at Star. "Did you talk to your mother about my dick?"

Her face paled while her hand froze on the passenger door handle. "What did she say?"

"It doesn't matter what she fucking said," I barked out, "why the fuck were you talking about my dick?"

"What's the big deal?" Star murmured and closed the door.

What's the big deal? Was that some kind poke at me?

"You think this is a fucking joke?"

"She's my mum," Star snarled. "I'm allowed to talk to her."

Like fuck she was.

"Talk to her all you want. Just not about me. I won't stand for…"

"I was scared, okay!"

I stopped and looked at her. "You were scared?"

Why did that bother me? Normally, I liked the way she blushed, but this was different. This time I wanted to reach out and wipe away her mortification.

"Yes." Star chewed on her lip and ducked her head. "You're

very big, but Mum said I should trust that you know what you're doing."

Huh?

I stuck my keys in the ignition and rolled down the driveway, onto the road. Star wasn't making fun of me, or talking about how I'd never touch her.

She was scared about when I did. I suppose that was normal for a virgin. Still, one question wouldn't leave my mind.

"Do you?"

Star sighed and flopped her head back. "Do I what?"

"Trust that I know what I'm doing?"

Star sat up and I could feel her studying me, but I kept my eyes on the road. Maybe I was afraid? I wanted to hear her answer. I didn't want to see it. Then I could keep that hollow ache out of my chest, no matter what I did.

One word slipped past her lips. "Yes."

I couldn't stop myself from stealing a glance at those beautiful onyx eyes, glimmering back at me. She wasn't lying. She did trust me. Why the fuck would she do some dumb shit like that?

We didn't talk much for the rest of the ride. Didn't really know what to say. I kind of wanted to slap her. Would it matter if she didn't trust me?

No. I'd still do what I was going to do and she could fucking deal with it. But self preservation was an important instinct.

One that she was apparently lacking. What if some guy came up to her on the street. Would she follow him into the back alley to find his dog?

That was it, I needed to have a serious talk with her. I couldn't spend my days worried that some creep had scooped her up because she was too naive to see danger.

I'd be bald by the time I was twenty. I was more angry that I was pissed at all, then I was at the prospect of losing my hair. And I had nice hair. By the time we pulled up to the bonfire, all I wanted to do was punch someone.

I pulled up to the beach and stared at everyone dancing around the fire with cups in their hands. Fuck, I didn't want to be here, surrounded by drunken idiots. Star, apparently, agreed with me.

She rolled her eyes and groaned, "Do we have to be here?"

"Yes." *Unfortunately.*

"Why?"

Did she have to make everything so difficult?

"Because," I sighed, "it's what kids our age do."

"So?" Star sat up and lifted her chin, "You clearly don't want to be here."

What the fuck did she know about what I wanted? Besides, appearances weren't optional for people like me. They were mandatory. One of the first lessons my old man drilled into my head.

"It doesn't matter what I want."

When I shifted to open the door, Star reached out and placed her hand on my arm. "I think it matters."

Was she trying to run a con on me? Get inside my head and tip the scales in her favor? Sorry little witch, but I own the fucking scales. Might be fun to play with her for a bit though.

"Is that right?" I sat back and crossed my arms. "Well tell me, Crumpet, what do you suggest we do then?"

"I don't know," she shrugged. "Take me somewhere?"

"Where?"

This should be good.

"Wherever you want to go."

She was definitely running a con.

I nodded at a nearby bush. "What if I want to take you behind that bush and fuck you stupid?"

The heavy sound of her swallow was like music to my ears. As was the way her face paled. Not so trusting now, are you Crumpet.

I looked over at the people dancing and let out a long sigh.

"Alright, Crumpet," I turned the key, firing up the ignition and backed away from the beach. "You want me to take you somewhere, I'll take you somewhere."

I'd play her little game.

For now.

* * *

I stared up at the dimly lit building, wondering how the hell we ended up here. When Star told me to take her somewhere, this wasn't what I had in mind. So, why the hell did I bring us here?

My eyes wandered up the brick column to the large Fender Strat hanging next to a museum sign. My old man wouldn't be caught dead in this place, so my mom brought me last time. I think that was six years ago?

It'd been at least that long since she'd been in town long enough to do anything with me. It wasn't her fault. She had a demanding job. Plus, I wasn't a whiney Momma's boy like Logan. I did still miss her though.

"What's this place?"

When Star leaned forward to gaze curiously out the windshield, I couldn't help but notice how the moonlight highlighted the delicate features of her face. She looked almost angelic.

"Rock and roll museum," I said, and tore my eyes off her to look at the building. "I think it's closed though."

"So? I'm sure we can find a way in."

I rolled my eyes at the mischievous smirk on her face. "We are not breaking into a museum."

"Oh, come on." She jumped out into the night air and glanced over her shoulder at me. "Unless you're afraid?"

I arched a brow. "Do you really think that shit is going to work on me?"

"Have it your way," she shrugged and took off into the night.

Shaking my head, I slumped back in my seat and watched her slink across the parking lot. She scurried back and forth, ducking behind poles and bins. Like she was in a fucking Mission Impossible movie.

That girl would not make a good spy. She sucked at being inconspicuous. First rule of sneaking around, stay out of the light.

I sighed and scrubbed a hand down my face.

The only thing Star was going to accomplish was getting a tick on her criminal record. Then I'd have to go and bail her out and explain to her parents what happened. That was more headache than I needed.

"Fuck sakes" I grumbled, and got out of the truck. Someone needed to keep her ass out of jail.

By the time I caught up with her, she was around the left side of the building, sliding a window open. Was she fucking crazy?

"What are you doing?"

"Shhh," Star held out her hand and looked up, as if she was searching the air for something. "Do you hear that?"

Did I hear what? "No."

"Exactly. No alarm."

She was bluffing. There was no way she was going in that window.

A smile spread across Star's face when she looked over at me.

Fuck, she was.

"Don't you do it."

"Just a little peek," she said, slipping her legs in the open window.

"I'm serious, Star," I pointed firmly at her, "get over here right fucking now."

"Come and get me." She blew me a kiss over her shoulder and disappeared inside.

Motherfucker!

Well, I wasn't going in after her. If the crazy little witch wanted to get herself arrested, that was her problem. Not mine. That's what I tried telling myself every time my tension built when I looked over at the window. Until I snapped.

"Fuck!"

I stormed across the grass and peeked in the window. All I saw was a dimly lit hallway with a couple displays. No Star in sight. I could hear her giggle echoing through the air though.

"Real fucking funny," I grumbled, while tucking my large body through the window frame.

Let's see how much she was laughing when I hunted her ass down. A task that proved to be a lot harder than it should've been. Would've helped if I could've turned on a fucking light.

Instead, I had to follow the sound of her footsteps and voice through the shadowed rooms. When I did finally find her, I stopped dead in my tracks.

Star was in the middle of a room surrounded by *Fleetwood Mac* memorabilia. Twirling with Stevie Nicks shawl on her shoulders while singing 'Rhiannon'.

I couldn't help but snicker. She was a terrible fucking singer. I'd never heard that song butchered so bad, but it was kind of cute.

I liked seeing her like this. Happy and carefree. So much so, that when Star spun around and locked her sparkling eyes on mine, I twirled my finger, silently telling her to continue.

The corner of her mouth lifted as she twirled around and sang, "Rhiannon sings like a sail through the night."

I couldn't hold that chuckle back. She even butchered the lyrics.

"Silas Creswell," Star tipped her head and gave me a fake pout, "are you laughing at me?"

"Yes, I am," I smirked back at her. "You are a terrible singer."

Her jaw opened with an exaggerated gasp. "I am not."

"Yes you are," I pushed off the wall and took a step towards her, "but that's okay. I don't need my ears to watch you dance."

"Oh, you like to watch." The seductive pout she gave me shot straight to my dick. Then she moved her hips, swinging them from side to side.

"Do you like that?"

Fuck yeah, I liked that.

"Or maybe you'll like this."

Star arched her hips through the air, and bent down to slowly drag her arm up the inside of her leg. I sucked in a breath through my teeth and followed her fingers trailing up the denim fabric of her jeans.

"It's missing something, isn't it?"

I'd say she had too much of something. Like clothes.

"Hmm?" She pressed her finger to her lips and slowly sauntered closer, increasing the sway in her hips with each step. "I've got the moves."

My teeth dug into my bottom lip as I rolled my eyes down the length of her. She fucking had the moves alright.

Two steps closer and she flipped the shawl behind her and rolled her ass into the flowery material. "I've got Stevie's shawl."

She was about to get fucked on Stevie's shawl.

"I know what I'm missing." She lifted her arms in the air, moving them in time with the rest of her. "There's one thing every ballroom dancer needs."

"Yeah?" I licked my lips. A few more steps and I could grab her. "What's that?"

Star kicked her foot out, spun around, and flattened her body against mine.

"A partner," she said, peeking up at me through her fluttering lashes. "Think you can handle me?"

She was about to find out just how hard I could handle her.

That idea was cut off when a beam of light flashed down on us.

"What are you two doing in here?"

Fuck. Guess playtime was over.

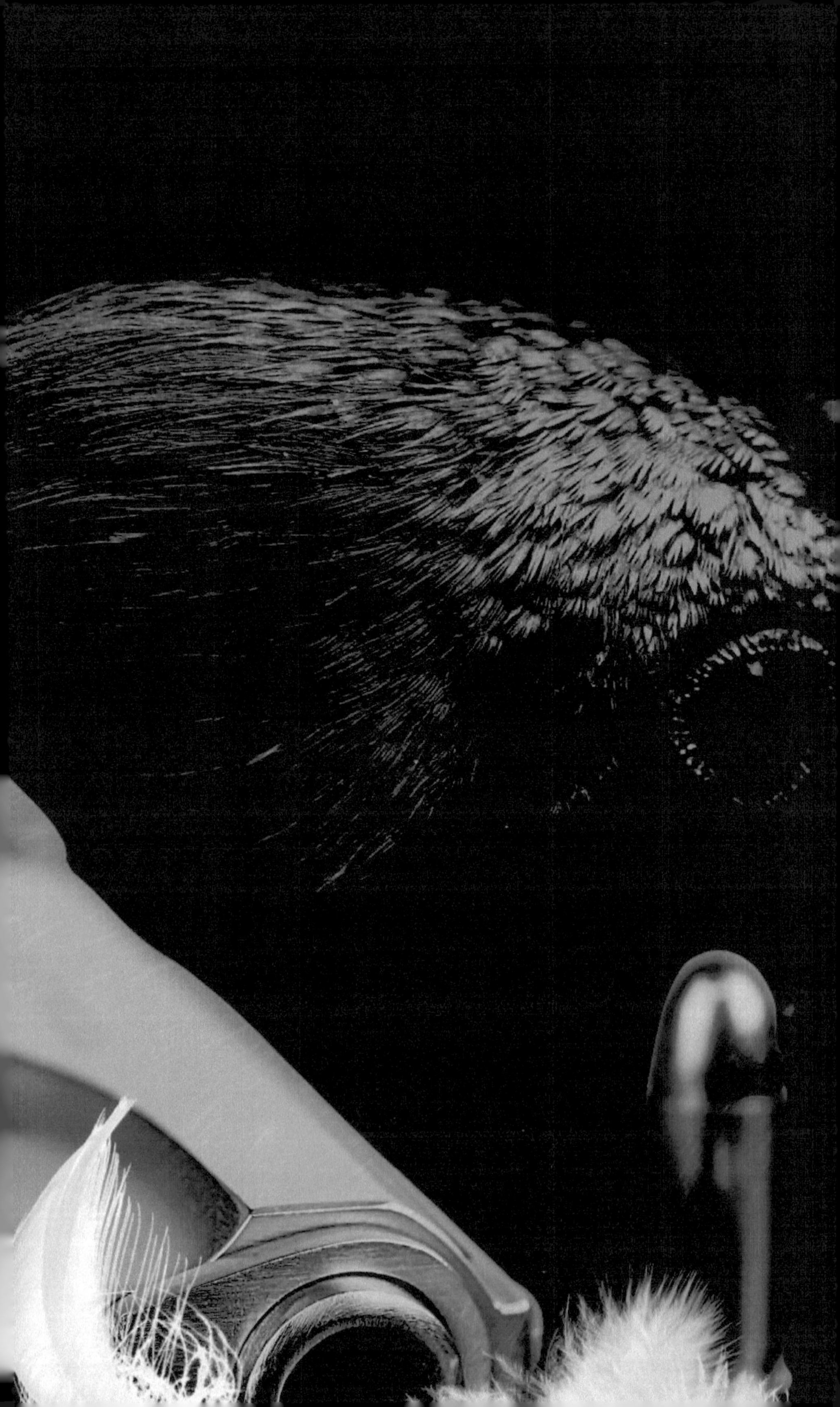

Chapter 34
Star

Silas chuckled. A genuine happy snicker. I couldn't get the way his entire face lit up out of my head. How his bright blue eyes sparkled as a smile spread across his face.

I twisted my neck and pulled my gaze over his thick black hair and down to the tick in his jaw. A firm muscle clenching next to his chiselled jawline. Silas was handsome normally, but when he smiled, he was downright breathtaking.

"What did you do to convince that guy to let us go?"

"I paid him off." He swung his stern glare my way, "Which I wouldn't have had to do if you hadn't broken in."

I rolled my eyes. So much for breathtaking Silas. Did he have something against having fun? Because it sure seemed like it. The arsehole was so regimented, I feared for his mental health. Why did he have such a hard time letting go?

"You had fun," I pointed out.

He didn't need to speak for me to know that made him uncomfortable.

"It's okay to let go sometimes."

Silas huffed out a sigh and shifted in his seat before pulling to a stop in his driveway. "I don't classify breaking and entering as letting go."

"What do you classify as letting go? Being two minutes late?"

"You sound like Mase," he grumbled and turned off the engine.

In this case, I happened to agree with Mason. Doing stupid things came with being a teenager. And despite what he said, I know he had fun tonight. Then again, the night wasn't over. There was still time to pull that breathtaking man out.

"Let me ask you a question," I said, crawling over the center console and onto his lap. "If that guard hadn't come in," I lifted my hand and trailed my finger down his jawline, enjoying the way his rough stubble scratched my skin, "would you have still made me leave?"

"No." He dug his fingers into my arse and roughly pulled me into him, "I'd have fucked you on Stevie Nicks' shawl."

The scary part wasn't the hardness I felt pressing up against my core, or the way his minty breath heated my face. It was how much I enjoyed staring into those ice-blue orbs.

It was that nervous fluttering behind my ribs that made me flatten my palms on his chest. My intent was to push away, but the second I felt the pulse pounding on the other side of those solid planes of muscle, I froze.

Was he nervous too?

"We should go inside." Silas leaned in and grazed his cheek against mine, "Unless you want me to fuck you here?"

My stomach flipped. I could feel the anxiousness sweating out of my pores. The only thing I could think about was that bloody donut falling in pieces around the squash.

He was going to tear me in half. I couldn't do this. But I couldn't move, either. Couldn't do anything but sit on his lap and tremble.

The corner of Silas's mouth lifted. "Scared now, Crumpet?"

Scared wasn't the right word. Terrified, petrified, completely and utterly panicked. Any of those would work. The only thing that saved me and knocked me out of my frozen state, was the clap of thunder that rolled through the air.

"It's going to rain" I said, and jumped out of the truck before Silas could stop me.

Instead of focusing on the rather large bloke climbing out after me, I closed my eyes and lifted my head to the sky. Back home, I didn't struggle to understand what people were talking about.

We didn't waste time on things like pep rallies, or worry about who was going to be captain of the drill team or cheerleading squad. We didn't have them because school was for learning.

We rode trams and put bags in the boot of our car. Things weren't little, they were wee. You could smell the ocean almost everywhere, and the royal family was a big deal.

Here, things were so different. People were rude and it was so bloody hot. Half the time I swore we'd moved to the ninth plane of hell. But the rain…

Until we came here, I didn't know rain could be warm. Ever since the first time I felt a drop hit my skin, I couldn't stop myself from running outside and spinning around in the downpour. Much like now.

When the sky opened up, releasing it's bath upon the world, I threw my arms out and spun around. It didn't matter if I was getting wet, or if Silas was watching me with a cocked brow. In this moment, I was free. Cleansed by the universe, washing away my sins.

I felt Silas's fingers wrap around my arm. "What are you doing?"

My breath hitched when I fluttered my eyes open. He looked really good with his hair plastered to his forehead.

He tugged me towards the door, "You're getting wet."

"So?" The rain helped me pull back and slip my arm out of his grasp, "Get wet with me."

He tipped his head and curled his lip, looking at me as if I had lost my mind. "What? No."

"Why not? It's freeing." I showed him how freeing it was by throwing my arms out and twirling around.

And what did the grumpy bastard do? He huffed and crossed his arms. But I could tell he wanted to let go. I could see the spark of yearning in his eyes. He just needed a nudge.

I stepped up to him and looped my hands around his neck. "Dance with me."

"I am not going to dance with you."

"Please." I lifted my chin and peered up through the rain at his scowling face, "Just for a wee bit."

Maybe it was the tone of my voice, or the pleading way I was gazing at him? I didn't really care why because the instant Silas let out a breath and wrapped his arms around my waist, my world was perfect.

I hummed and laid my head on his chest, enjoying how our bodies moved in sync.

Silas may not be the fella I dreamed about being with, but I never felt more safe than I did pressed against his hard body while gently swaying in the warm Florida rain.

Yes, he was an arsehole. An uptight monster that had made my life hell. But right now he was just a boy, and I was just a girl. There were no ghosts yelling in my mind. No reminders of the horrible things I'd done.

There was just him, and I, and the rain.

I wanted things to stay like this, but I knew that wouldn't happen. Tomorrow I'd wake up and this beautiful day would be nothing but a memory. Silas would go back to tormenting me, and I'd go back to pretending to be a good person.

That was the thing about lies. They made things look pretty and comfortable, but the truth always came out. No matter how tightly you wrapped it up.

I sighed and snuggled in closer to him. "I wish you didn't hate me."

Silas stiffened around me and grumbled, "We should go inside."

And just like that, the dream was shattered. I took one last look over my shoulder at the rain trickling in the night. I wished I could bring it inside because once we stepped through that door, reality was going to smack me in the face.

Silas pulled me into the house and up the stairs so fast I barely had time to look around. I'd been in his house before, but only one or two rooms.

I was curious if the interior was as cold and rigid as the carefully manicured outside. From what I could see, it was. The entire place had a cold, uncaring color scheme of whites, black, and greys.

Combine that with the properly placed decorations and it felt more like a museum than a home. The little table by the front door and pictures hanging on the wall—none of which were of family—did nothing to warm up the place. Needless to say, when he led me to what I assumed to be his bedroom, I was surprised.

This room did not match the rest of the house. I looked up and gawked at all the guitars hanging on the wall. They were all different makes and models.

Some old, some new, and others were restored. But each one was obviously cared for. Whether they were acoustic or electric, every guitar was displayed proudly.

There was only one instrument not hung up. Sitting on a black stand beside a four poster bed with a deep green bedspread, was an older acoustic Gibson.

On the oak bedside table behind it was an open package of strings and three orange picks. Leading me to believe that unlike the rest, this one was played.

"Stay here," Silas glared down at me, "I'll go get us some towels."

I nodded, barely hearing what he said. I was much more fascinated with this room. So much so that I couldn't help but wander around, running my hand over various surfaces.

In the corner was a mahogany desk stacked with papers filled with notes and lyrics. Next to that was a dresser and an open closet door.

I rolled my eyes at the rows of clothes organized by color. Everything in here gave me a small peek into the real Silas Creswell, but it was a large picture hanging on the wall that caught my attention.

It was a family portrait of a man, a woman, and a little boy I assumed to be a young Silas, on the beach. My eyes narrowed on the straight faced boy. Why did he seem familiar? So did the woman.

I walked over to get a closer look and gasped. "Oh my god, is that Sharon Monroe?"

"She's my mom," Silas called out from the bathroom.

What? Silas's mother was Sharon Monroe? The same Sharon Monroe whose face was plastered across every entertainment magazine in America?

Mum was going to lose her mind. We'd seen every one of her movies. Including the horrible B-grade horrors she started out making.

"Is it true that she doesn't like chocolate?" Who doesn't like chocolate?

"I wouldn't know." Silas walked out of the bathroom and handed me a large black towel. "I don't see her much."

I didn't think of that. Movie stars had a demanding schedule. It must be hard. I couldn't imagine not being able to see Mum every-day, or talk to her when I wanted.

"I'm sorry."

"It's fine. That's all most people want to talk about when they find out." Silas shrugged and bent over to rub his towel through his hair.

Well, now I felt like shite.

I dabbed the towel against my skin, running it up my arm and over my collarbone. "What about your dad?"

"What about him?"

I was momentarily stunned when Silas flipped back up. His damn hair was this tousled sexy mess that I wanted to run my fingers through.

Focus, Star.

"Do you see him much?"

"He works in town," Silas stated, while reaching over his shoulder to tear the wet shirt off.

My jaw dropped.

Oh. My. God.

I knew Silas was built well, but good lord… The deep cut lines in his torso were like crack to my addicted gaze. The wide spread black wing spanning across his collarbone only added to his appeal.

My brain fritzed out, losing control of my wandering eyes. Droplets slid across his tanned skin, carving a path of lust that had me licking my lips.

Even though my mind told me to stop gawking like a school

girl, I couldn't. I just stood there with the towel pressed against my neck.

The corner of Silas's mouth lifted. "See something you like, Crumpet?"

That snapped me out of it.

"No." I cleared my throat and concentrated on drying myself off.

"Really?" He cocked his head and rolled his eyes down my trembling form, "Because I do."

My heart skipped as the realization of who's room I was standing in hit me.

"I should go."

Determination settled in Silas's features. "You're not going anywhere."

It was that determination that made me back up.

"Silas," I held up my hands, displaying the towel as if the flimsy cloth could protect me. "We can't do this."

"The way I see it, you have two choices," he took another step, closing the distance between us. "You can play nice and I'll give you the rose petals and tender kisses fantasy all virgins dream of. Or we can do it my way, hard and rough."

If I'd been paying attention, I might've made it out of there. Instead, I kept my eyes trained on the predator ready to pounce.

So I didn't see the wall coming up on me, until my back hit it. By then, it was too late. Silas moved in, slamming his hands down on the wall and caging me in his arms.

He bent over and growled in my ear, "What's it going to be, Crumpet?"

I made a foolish decision then. Raised my hand and slapped him across the face. My fate was sealed with one sinister smirk from the man who had me cornered.

"My way it is."

I was tossed over his shoulder in the blink of an eye. Before I could so much as manage to slap his back, he tossed me on the bed. I tried to scurry away, but he stopped that too, and stripped me of my slacks in the process.

Silas grabbed my ankles, somehow managed to unfasten my jeans, and pulled me back down the bed.

Next thing I knew, I was laying under him on my stomach in nothing but a wet shirt and knickers. Shaking so hard the bed frame was rattling.

"Silas…"

"Shh," he hushed while folding his large body over mine. "Relax, Crumpet." He swept the hair off my face and pressed his warm lips to my temple. "I don't want to hurt you anymore than I have to."

I whimpered and pressed my face into the mattress. What else could I do? He was bigger, stronger, and far more determined than I was.

My body wasn't helping with the fight. It warmed up to the fear pulsing through my veins and melted back into him.

"Good girl," Silas purred while he smoothed his palm down my side and around my hip.

When his hand slipped inside my knickers, I tried to shoot forward, completely forgetting about the heavy weight trapping me on the bed. Silas answered my struggle by fisting my hair and holding me in place.

"Hang on, Crumpet, I'm gonna make you come hard." His finger pressed down on my clit, sending a spark of unwanted pleasure up my spine, "I need you good and wet."

Hang on was all I could do. Silas twisted, pinched and swirled my clit. Working me into a whimpering mess of need. I didn't argue when he lifted me up and tore my shirt off. Or fight when I heard his jeans hit the floor.

All I could concentrate on was the tension he was building, and that traitorous bundle of nerves. I didn't even notice he'd lifted himself off me.

Not until my hands fisted the blanket as a wave of ecstasy so intense that my vision blurred, bowed my body and he wasn't there to hold me down.

I didn't even have time to come down before Silas flipped me over, spread my legs, and dove in, growling out a groan as he lapped up my juices.

Violent trembles rocked my body with each swipe of his hot tongue on my tender flesh. I couldn't breathe. It was too much.

"I can't," I whined, while threading my fingers through his hair and yanking as hard as I could. "Stop."

"Not a fucking chance." He lifted his head and crawled over me.

I freaked out, not because I could feel his massive vagina destroying cock resting on my stomach, but because of the look in his eyes.

That feral spark I'd seen before was right there, waiting to come out in full force. Panicked, I shoved on his chest and tried to wriggle away. It didn't even phase him.

"Reach up and grab onto the headboard."

I shook my head and tried to shove him off me again. "Silas…"

"Now, Crumpet," he barked out, making me shrink back and wince, "I'm hanging on by a thread here. If you touch me, I'm gonna snap."

I saw it then. The strain in his face, and how his arms were tensed. He was desperately trying to hold himself back because he didn't want to hurt me. Mum's words rang in the back of my head.

'Trust that he knows what he's doing.'

I told Silas that I trusted him. Now it was time to show him. Didn't calm my nerves, or stop me from whimpering as I slowly raised my arms over my head to clutch tightly onto the headboard.

Silas, however, did seem relieved. He let out a breath and gave me a gentle kiss.

"Good girl," he breathed against my lips, then kissed a path down my chin and across my neck. "I want to fucking eat every inch of you."

I licked my lips and swallowed back a moan. His mouth moving across my skin felt so good. I almost sunk into his touch and forgot about the cold spikes lighting up my nerves.

Until I felt the smooth head of his cock press between my folds. I was instantly thrown back into full alert mode. Muscles tensing while I shook my head.

"I can't do this."

"Well, you're gonna." Silas propped himself up on his elbow, looked me dead in the eyes, and said, "Don't let go of the headboard. This is going to hurt."

That was all the warning I got. He surged forward, forcing his massive cock into my opening. I let the tears fall and screamed. Shook my head against the pain slicing up my core.

I couldn't breathe. Couldn't make myself open my eyes. Couldn't do anything but kick my feet. It felt like I was being ripped apart from the inside out.

"Jesus," Silas hissed and forced another inch inside me, "you're so fucking tight."

I hated him. Hated how he was taking pleasure in my pain. I wanted to claw his eyes out, but I wasn't letting go of that headboard. It was the only thing standing between agony, and utter destruction.

Each inch he fed me burned more than the last. My inner walls fought, trying to push out his uncompromising hardness, but he kept going.

By the time he finally stopped, my body was covered in a fine coating of sweat, and I was openly blubbering.

"Shh, Baby." Silas covered my body with his and peppered kisses across my face. "It's okay. That's all I'll make you take."

There was more!?

"You did so good, Crumpet." His hand kneaded a path down my side, while his mouth continued to place tender kisses on my skin. "I need you to relax now."

I wanted to yell at him, *you relax, arsehole,* but I could barely breathe. Screw Silas Creswell and his giant cock. I'd hate them both until the day I died.

"It'll get better."

My eyes flew open as I snarled, "This shite will never get better."

The arsehole smirked back at me.

"I bet I can change your mind."

"Like hell you can."

Oh, how wrong I was. Silas didn't just make me eat my words, he shoved them down my throat with a simple swivel of his hips.

I sucked back a gasp. Behind the pain of his cock moving inside me, was something else. Something dark and needy. A hint of pleasure so deep it called to the hunger inside me.

"You feel that, Crumpet?" This time he thrust his hips, pulling his shaft out and then sinking back in. "That's my cock in your tight little cunt."

God yes, I felt it. That hunger was quickly taking over. It drop kicked my pain to the background, leaving me with nothing but the pleasurable feeling of my pussy stretching. The only thing pissing me off now was Silas's slow rhythm.

"More," I moaned and arched my back, pressing my breasts into his chest.

Silas growled out a deep rumbling groan. He lifted his chest off me, wrapped his fingers around my neck, and drove into me, hard. The pain came back.

It sliced through my veins, mingling with the euphoria tainting my soul. But I didn't care. My beast was out, and she was ravenous.

"Look at you." His fingers tightened around the pulse pounding into my throat. "Three pumps and you're already my perfect little cock slut."

Yes, yes I was. If this is what being his perfect little slut felt like, then I'd happily do it all day. Every day.

I groaned and wriggled my hips, enticing him to give me more. And he did. Silas pounded into my pussy with the furry of a man possessed. My body ached and my chest heaved, but my soul sang.

The smell of sweat in the air, along with the hard grunts coming out of Silas's mouth, and the feel of his heavy body, was better than any rainfall in the world.

I felt wanted, needed, protected, and used. It was beautiful and dirty. Perfect. Like I'd never truly known myself until now.

"Fuck... Shit," Silas groaned, and thrust into me so hard, I moved up the bed, even with his hand on my neck. "Can't hold it..."

I didn't want him to hold it. I wanted to bathe in his essence. But he wasn't going to let go. He wanted me to come with him. The aches still rushing through me weren't going to let that happen. So I gave him what I knew he needed.

My touch.

I let go of the headboard and threaded my fingers around his neck, to pull his lips down to mine. Not only did I see the ecstasy in his muscles when his whole body seized, but I tasted it in his groan.

Felt it in the rough way he slammed into me, bathing my inner walls with his warm release. That's when I realized what my soul had been trying to tell me. Silas said I was his...

But he was mine too.

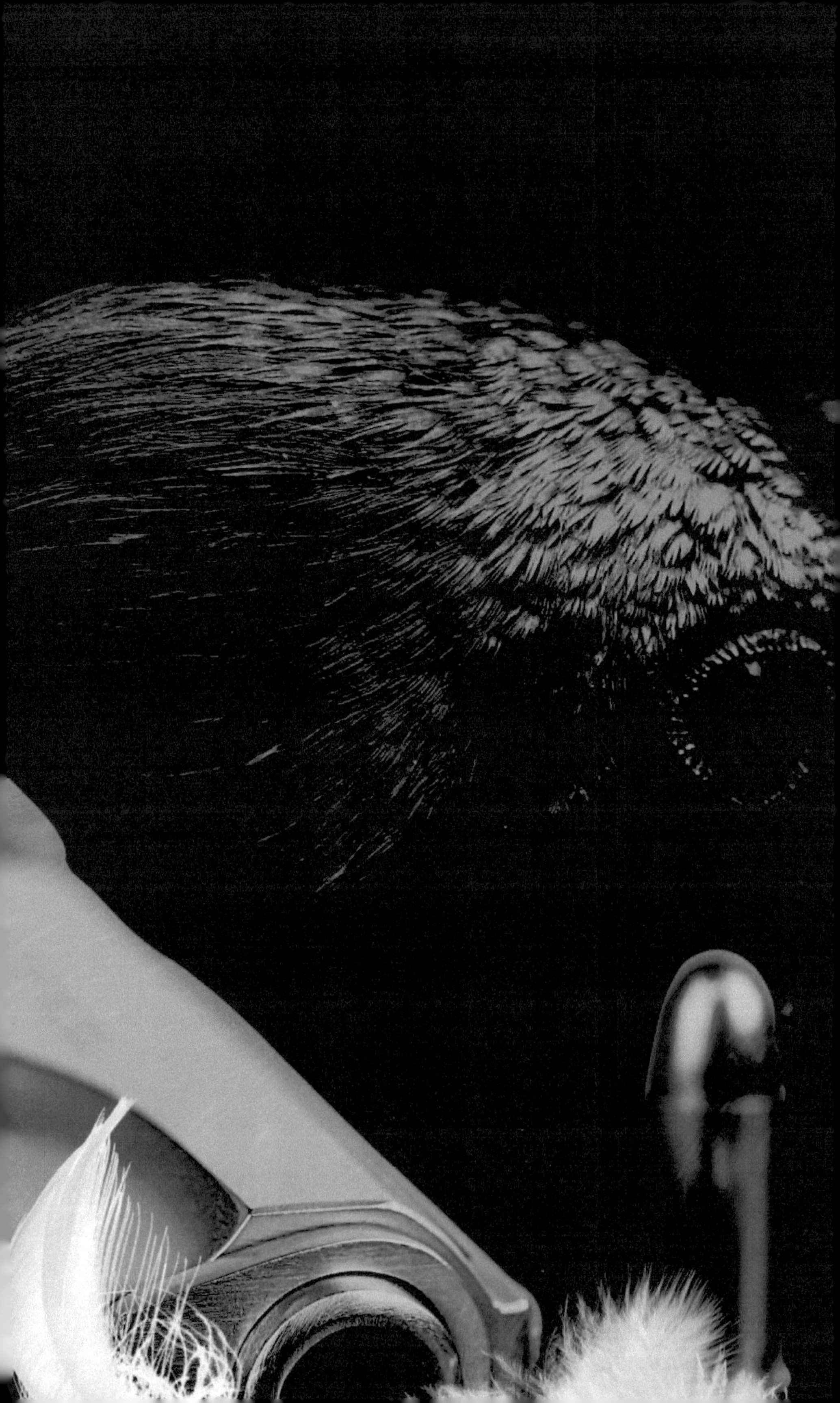

Chapter 35

Star

The next morning, I woke up wrapped in Silas's arms with him snoring lightly in my ear, and freaked out. I couldn't explain why. Just that what should've been a tender moment, made me feel like the walls were closing in on me.

I was laying there in a warm bed, next to a bloke that, despite being an arse, had proven time and time again that some part of him sought to protect me. And instead of enjoying it, I panicked.

I slipped away from him as carefully as I could, grabbed my clothes, and got the hell out of there.

My strange behavior didn't end there. I didn't go home like a normal person. Well, I did. But only long enough to snatch my keys off the counter and jump in my car. Mum and Dad cocked a brow at me when I burst in. Then again when I rushed out.

They may have tried to say something. If they did, I didn't hear it. I was lucky I managed to get my clothes on before they saw me. And even then, my shirt was only pulled down enough to cover my breasts.

I didn't know where I was going, or why. Just that I had to get far away from the strange feeling warming my chest. A feeling that followed me, no matter how fast I drove. Same as the ache between my legs.

Every bump in the road caused my pussy to throb and remind me that I wasn't the same person I was yesterday. My innocence was gone. Given to a man that I was trying really hard to hate.

Except, right now, I couldn't remember why I should hate him. Only how safe I felt curled up to him in the rain, and the sweet way he tried to kiss away my pain, even though he was the one that was ripping me in half.

Was it love that I was trying to run away from? Did I care more about Silas Creswell than I cared to admit? Was one good night all it took to make me fall for a cruel man? But he wasn't all cruel, was he?

Instead of walking away from me when I lost my bloody mind in the bathroom, he took the time to calm me down.

He went toe to toe with Mason when he grabbed me, and even though he wanted nothing to do with breaking into the museum, he followed. Silas could've left me there to get arrested, but he didn't. He came in after me.

Dear lord, I did care about the bloke. What the bloody hell was I supposed to do with that? Did that mean I had to play girlfriend now? Take care of the arse, and support all his arseish ways? I didn't know how to do that.

I tried doing that for Harper. Being a friend and shoulder she could lean on. A person in her life so she would know she wasn't alone, and look how that turned out.

I just made things worse. It was time to face facts, the only thing I was good at was destroying people. No one knew that better than Emily.

My phone buzzed in my pocket, making me jump and lurch the car to the left. At least I remembered to grab it. A thought that no longer seemed as pleasing when I read the text.

Silas: Where the fuck are you?

I didn't know how to answer that. 'Sorry, your comfort and warmth freaked me out so I ran away,' just didn't seem like the proper thing to say.

Silas: Answer me, Crumpet.

Nope, not going to happen. I'm busy driving to some unknown place.

Silas: Fine. Have it your way.

After that, my phone went quiet. I didn't know if that was a good thing or bad thing. Either way, he was leaving me alone. For now, at least.

I drove for lord knows how long. During which I mulled over everything. Let my thoughts and feelings swirl in hopes that they would solidify. They didn't.

Things only got more confusing the longer I spent trapped in my own head. Perhaps that was why I ended up stopping where I did?

Leaning forward, I stared through the windshield at the broken down bridge Tico called a second home. Though I'd argue that it was his home, since he spent more time here.

The only thing I knew about the place where my friend lived was that it was a brown and green trailer on the west end of town that he shared with his alcoholic father.

I asked him once to take me there. He said it'd be safer if I stayed away. Based on some of the bruises I'd seen on his face, I had to agree.

I tried mentioning foster care to him. Even thought about contacting a social worker myself. It had to be better than his current situation, but Tico insisted that foster parents were worse than his real parent.

So, I left it alone. Besides, he was two months away from eighteen. I doubted the system would waste their time on someone so close to aging out.

How ironic was it that after all the time I spent trying to take care of him, I was now here, hoping he could take care of me? It turned out, Tico wasn't the broken one in need of repair. I was. Couldn't help but snicker at that one.

I pushed open the door to my Sunfire and stepped out onto the grassy field. The way the sun shone down on this place highlighted the ground as if it was a divine sanctuary. Perhaps it was.

This was one of the few places I felt comfortable in this town. I didn't even mind the hint of sulphur mingling with wildflowers in the air. The geysers roared in the background, making me twitch. Now those, I could live without.

"Tico," I skipped towards the stone bridge, "I did something incredibly stupid."

Whether that stupid thing was sleeping with Silas, or running away from him, was yet to be seen.

I ducked under the archway and called out, "Tico."

No answer.

That was weird. He should be here. I walked over to the firepit and placed my hand on the metal barrel. It was cool. No sign that a fire had been crackling in it last night.

Did he go home?

I looked around, thinking I'd find him sleeping, but the couch was empty, and so was the sleeping bag in the corner.

What really got my heart pumping was the shoe I saw laying upside down on the ground. Tico didn't have a closet here, or a storeroom full of footwear. He wouldn't walk away with one shoe.

"Tico, this isn't funny." I threw the blanket off the couch and peeked under the cushions. "If you're here, come out."

Still no answer.

Something wasn't right. It was too quiet.

Bang!

I screamed and clutched onto my chest, silently cursing the geysers roaring in the background.

"Get ahold of yourself Star. Just because he's not here doesn't mean he's not okay."

That's when I saw it.

Dripping red letters scrawled across the stone wall.

Can you find the crow in the raven's nest.

It was a note. One that was written in blood.

Tico was definitely not okay.

I turned and ran for the passenger seat of my car where I'd tossed my phone. I had to call the bobbies or the FBI. Anyone that could come down and find my friend.

The person standing beside my car had other ideas. I stopped and reared back. What was he doing here?

Silas crossed his arms and narrowed his gaze. "What are you doing here, Crumpet?"

"How on earth did you find me?"

"Tracked your phone."

I stamped my foot on the ground and shrieked, "What? How dare you…" I took a deep breath and shook my head. We didn't have time for this. "We can talk about your invasion of my privacy later. Right now, I need to find Tico."

"Who the fuck is Tico?"

"He's my friend." I rolled my eyes at his arched brow and marched over to retrieve my phone.

The displeasure in Silas's brow deepened. "*He's* your friend?"

"Yes," *arsehole*, "he's my friend."

"Oh hell no."

Next thing I knew, instead of reaching in my car for my phone, I was folded over it. Bent in half with my face smashed down on the hood.

"Oh my god," I threw my hands back, reaching my claws out for him. "What do you think you're doing?"

"I should be asking you that." His heavy hand landed on my arse with a resounding smack that burned a path down my thighs. "Running out of my bed to come and see another guy."

Another smack. This one so hard my hips cracked against my car.

"Stop it." I slammed my hands down on the hood and tried to push myself up.

Silas pushed me back down and smacked me again. Three slaps and my arse was on fire.

"Please stop." I sucked back a sob and gritted my teeth, "I need to find Tico."

That was a mistake.

Silas went from angry to a snarling rage beast. His palm pressed down on the back of my head, further smashing my cheek into the hard metal, while his other hand made quick work of my jeans.

Unfastening the button and yanking them over my hips before I could blink.

"Silas, you need to let me go. Tico's missing and there's a note on the wall." I tried to look over my shoulder, but his grip was too firm. I couldn't budge. "I have to find him."

"The only thing you need to find, Crumpet," he kicked my legs apart and shoved a finger inside me, "is your way back into my good graces."

I winced from the intrusion and tried to wriggle away. His answer to that was to force another finger inside me. The ache from his rough use last night was reignited, making my pussy cry out as tears dripped from my eyes.

"It hurts."

"Good. Maybe now you'll remember who this pussy belongs to," Silas growled and pumped his hand, fucking me hard with his fingers.

I don't know what spot he was hitting, but oh. My. God. I didn't just see stars, I bloody well tasted them. Every nerve in my body lit up, sparking with the blissful electricity he was forcing through me.

"Oh yeah. Not so fucking concerned with finding your friend now, are you?"

Shite, Tico!

Silas added a third finger and pumped his hand harder.

Fuck Tico, I wanted more of this.

"Oh god, yes please," I moaned while scratching the paint off my hood.

"God isn't the name I want to hear."

He flicked his fingers and I went off. Screaming his name for all to hear.

"That's right Baby, you let everyone know whose dirty little slut you are."

Somewhere in the hazy cloud fogging my mind, I heard the jingle of a belt. But it didn't register until I felt his cock line up with my entrance.

"Silas…"

But it was too late. He surged forward, driving his cock deep inside me.

Silas released a long loud growl and pushed further into me.

"God fucking damnit." His hand rose and smacked hard against my arse. "This tight little cunt is squeezing the shit out of my dick."

This time he didn't stop and let me adjust. There were no whispered words or tender kisses. Just the deep seed of possession he was fucking hard into me. Silas Creswell surrounded me.

I felt him everywhere. In the heady scent filling my nostrils. In the taste of the grunts being forced out of my lips. And in the strong strokes of his cock against my inner walls.

Going deeper and deeper with each thrust until I was scrambling to crawl across the hood, away from him.

Silas fisted his hand in my hair and slammed me back down on the hood. "Where the fuck do you think you're going?"

"It's too deep," I whined and reached back to push on his abs.

"That's too fucking bad."

Silas forced me to take more of his cock and folded over me.

"You think you can leave my bed to come and see some other fucking guy?"

"I'm sorry," I whimpered and shrunk away from his deep growl vibrating through my ear.

"You'll be fucking sorry alright," he grunted and snapped his hips forward, "when I make you take every last fucking inch I have to give."

There was no possible way I could take anymore. I was so full already. But Silas didn't care. He continued surging forward with each thrust.

At some point, my body gave way and let him in. I never felt more relieved than I did when his pelvis met my backside. It even felt good. Like, really good. My nerves were still on fire, but the burn was different. More intense and full of need.

That's when he really fucked me.

His fingers dug into my hips, lifting my feet off the ground as he plowed into me with the fury of a man possessed. The first time Silas took me I didn't orgasm. This time, I exploded. I screamed as a wave of bliss stole my breath and seized my muscles.

"Fuck yes!" Silas groaned. "Soak my cock, baby. I want to feel your come dripping down my balls."

His words sent me over the edge again. By the time he roared out his own release, I was a puddle of exhaustion melted on the hood of my car with his cock twitching deep inside me.

"Fuck me." Silas collapsed out of breath on top of me.

I purred and stretched back into him, enjoying his calm state.

"The next time you leave me to wake up alone, I'll tie your ass to my bed and fuck you for a week."

Okay, maybe calm was a strong word.

"I'm sorry. I freaked out."

His chest lifted with a heavy sigh as he rolled off me and stood up.

"Come here," he said, lifting me up to sit on the hood and face him. "I'm scared too."

My eyes flew up to his. "You are?"

"Yeah." He nodded and cupped my face. "But I'm not going to be a coward and run away. And I'm not gonna let you do it either. Understand?"

I couldn't do anything but chew my lip and whisper, "I'm sorry. I won't do it again."

"Good." He kissed my forehead and pulled me down to shimmy my slacks back over my hips. "Now let's go see this note that has you so worked up."

Shite. I couldn't believe I forgot about Tico. I was a horrible friend.

I took him to the bridge and pointed out the things I'd found. The shoe and empty sleeping bag. But it was when he saw the note scrawled across the wall that his body language changed.

Chapter 36

Silas

Star wasn't happy with me. She made that very clear at school today. I swear to god I was going to burn that damn bookbag if she hit me with it one more time.

I was never interested in the ditzy girls, but right now I kind of wished the little witch had a few less brain cells.

She didn't fall for my 'there's nothing wrong and your friend is probably at home excuse.' She accused me of hiding something from her. Which I was.

That note on the wall was meant as a warning for The Order. What the fuck Tico had to do with us, I had no idea. But there it was. Etched in blood on a stone surface. So yeah, I was hiding something. But it was for her own good.

Just like keeping her by my side was for her own good. Well, maybe that one was a little more for me. I couldn't let her go home.

What if something happened? Her parents didn't strike me as the gun having type.

It was more likely that they'd offer to smoke up with someone who broke in than to beat the fuck out of them. Which was fine. That was their prerogative. But Star was mine. And Tico was her friend.

Exactly why I didn't want to let her out of my sight. It was hard as fuck to let her go home after school. Honestly, I just wanted a break from getting smacked in the face with her bag.

And now what was I doing?

Sitting in my driveway, staring at her house. Like some asshole was going to show up and kick in her door. I sent a picture of the wall to Lou, so I knew the Kings were on it, but still…

I sighed and looked down to type in my phone.

Me: What are you doing?

Witch: Having a bath.

Me: Want some company?

Witch: My vagina can't take any more of your company.

I chuckled at that. I didn't just keep Star by my side for the last twenty-four hours. I kept her under me, and on me. Bent over the bed. On top of the dresser. In the bathroom and kitchen, fuck, anywhere really.

Any excuse I could find to dive back in the warmth of her tight little cunt, I took. I'd die a happy man buried inside her.

"Fuck," I grunted and adjusted my cock. I wanted to be inside her right now.

Me: Come over when you're done.

Witch: No.

Me: It wasn't a question, Crumpet.

Witch: I don't care.

I loved it when she pulled attitude with me. It gave me a reason to do very bad things to her.

Me: Would you rather I came over there?

Witch: I'll tell my parents not to let you in.

I snorted. Considering her mom gave me a condom when I picked her up for our date, I highly doubted they'd turn me away. If anything, they'd welcome me in with open arms and maybe ask for details.

Me: I wonder what your parents would say
If they knew what you've been doing. Or
should I say who.

The seconds ticked by silently before my phone finally dinged.

Witch: Ugh, fine. But no shagging.

Isn't that cute. She thought she could order me around.
We'll see about that.
I smirked and hopped out of my Hummer to head into the house. If I got in the shower now, I could jerk one out before she showed up. Might stop me from attacking her the second she walked in the door. Sounded like a good plan to me.

That is, until I walked in the house and was met with a familiar face.

"Mom?"

"There's my Baby." My mom rushed forward and threw her arms around me.

Confused, I hugged her back and said, "I thought you had to stay on set in Tokyo?"

"I did, but I missed you and your father."

"Oh god, Mom," I groaned when she squished my cheeks and kissed me. Why did she always have to do that shit? Mom's should not kiss their sons on the lips. "Don't do that."

"Hey, I made you. So I can kiss you if I want."

I rolled my eyes.

"Come on." She grabbed my hand and dragged me into the parlor. "Tell me everything. What did I miss?"

She missed a lot. She always missed a lot. I didn't resent her for it. I was happy she was doing something she loved. It would just be nice if she was around a little more.

"There's not much to tell."

There was plenty to tell. Micha, and Riley, and all the shit that happened to them. Parker now had kids. Mason was in rehab. The list could go on. I didn't say anything because I didn't want to see that guilty look in her light eyes.

"There has to be something." she insisted and dropped down in the red velvet chair in the corner. "Do you have a girlfriend?"

"Actually… yeah."

I just made her day. My mom sat forward, eyes sparkling with glee, and clapped her hands.

"Is she pretty?"

She was beyond pretty.

"Where does she live? What's her family do? How did you meet? Do you love her? Come on Silas, give me something."

I would if she shut up for five damn minutes.

"What's she like?"

"She's a pain in my ass," I grumbled.

My mom nodded. "Good."

"What?" I cocked a brow at her. "Why is that good?"

"Because, if she's a pain in your ass," Mom pointed her finger at me and narrowed her gaze, "then maybe she can get you to loosen up a little."

I wasn't that uptight. There was nothing wrong with being organized. At least people knew I'd show up on time, in the right attire and at the right place.

Star would be lucky if she made it there a half hour late with one shoe on and fully clothed. She should be happy that she had me.

There was no being late when I took her places. And as for fully clothed… let's see her try and wear another dress like that gold one in public again.

Her ass would be so red, she wouldn't be able to sit down for a week. I'd be damned if I was going to let some other motherfucker enjoy her body. That was my shit.

Mom tilted her head and eyed me. "You really like her."

I didn't answer. Didn't need to. My mom may not be around much, but she could read me like a book. It was fucking annoying.

"Are you thinking it's contract time?"

"Maybe." That was a bold faced lie. Lou was already having it drawn up. I just had to figure out how I was going to convince her dad to sign the fucking thing.

"Have you talked to her about it?"

My brow arched at my mom. Have I told Star that I was taking out a contract on her that would bind her to me for life? And if she ever thought about breaking it, it would mean the death of someone she cared about?

"No." Did mom take a drink from the stupid well while she was in Tokyo?

"Silas," she sighed and sat back. "You have to talk to the girl about it. Let her make the choice."

"Why would I do some dumb shit like that?"

"Exactly." We both turned to see my father walking into the room. "If Silas wants the girl, that's it. End of story. Who cares what she wants."

Guess Lou told him about the contract. Can't say I was surprised.

While I was less than impressed to see my old man, my mom was ecstatic. She leapt out of her chair and sprang across the room, throwing her arms around him.

"Martin." She laid a big kiss on him that made me gag. "I missed you so much."

"I missed you too, Baby," my old man growled and buried his face in her neck. "Fuck, you smell good."

Fuck me, now they were making out like a couple of teenagers. That was my cue to leave.

Without a word I got up, slipped past their disgusting display, and headed up to my room. If I played some music I might be able to drown out the sounds that were sure to follow.

I picked up Lucy, sat on my bed and started strumming. I worked my way through a couple regular songs, but soon found myself plucking a different beat.

One that matched the way Star and I swayed the other night. I could hear the raindrops trickling in the back of my mind.

Star said she wished I didn't hate her, and I didn't say anything. I wanted to though. I wanted to tell her how alive she made me feel. How every time she smiled, my day got a little better. I just couldn't make the words come out.

That was the first time in my life that I felt free to be myself. I didn't have to wear a mask or act a certain way. I could just be.

Star didn't expect anything. She didn't want me to be a perfect version of myself. She was happy just being there with me, dancing in the rain.

"Wish I was dancing in the rain,
Feeling free enough to soar above the pain,
There's no one there to judge us,
Just the moon and stars above us,
With the crazy girl,
Dancing in the rain."

"That's beautiful."

I forgot Star was coming until I looked up and saw her standing in the doorway.

"I met your parents." She tipped her head to her shoulder and rolled those beautiful onyx eyes over me. "They're affectionate."

"Yeah." With a roll of my eyes, I set Lucy back in her stand. "Sorry about that."

"I think it's cute." Star smiled and sauntered slowly up to me.

I snatched her arm and pulled her in between my legs. "I think you're cute."

"Oh yeah?"

I damn near lost my mind when she bit her bottom lip. Watching her teeth dig into that supple flesh made my dick jump to life.

"Yeah," I breathed and trailed my hand up her arm and over her shoulder to cup the back of her neck. "I think you'd be a lot cuter without the clothes though."

Star gasped and tried to pull away, but I wasn't letting her go anywhere.

"Silas, your parents are home."

"So?" I slipped my hand under her shirt and pinched her nipple. "What do you think they're doing right now?"

I fucking loved the way her body flushed when I touched her. Almost as much as I loved the breathy way a gasp escaped her lips.

"I'm sore."

I spun us around, flopping her down on the bed under me. She was about to get a whole lot sorer.

"Silas, no." Star reached out and pushed on my chest in a feeble attempt to move me off her.

"Did you just say no to me?" I tsked and dove in, laving my tongue up the side of her neck. "I thought you'd know better than that by now."

"What if your parents hear?"

I forced my knee between her thighs and kissed my way across her skin to the swell of her breasts. "I guess you better be quiet then."

Like it or not, Star was getting fucked good and hard. All night long.

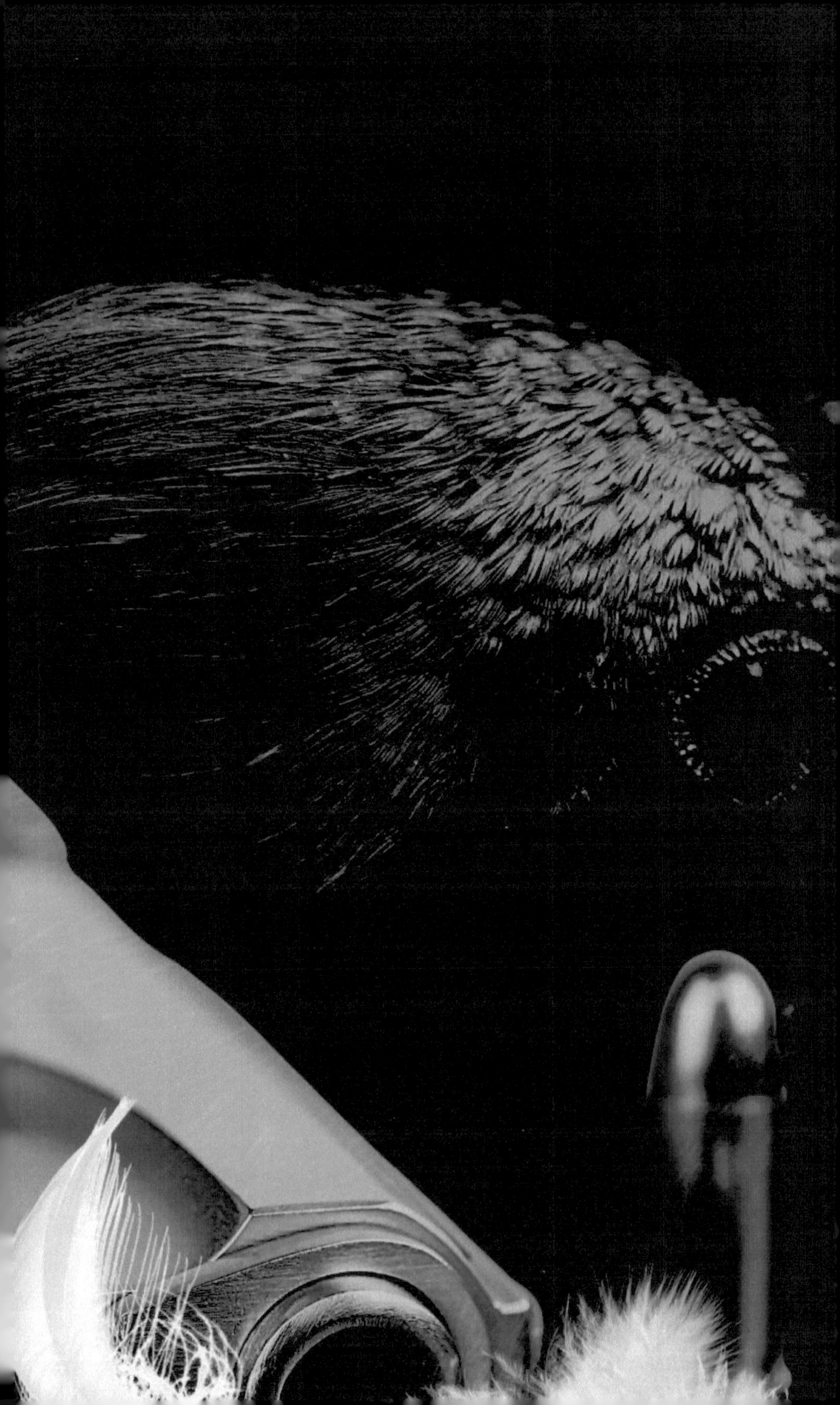

Chapter 37

Star

There was seriously something wrong with the people in this town. I'd been trying all week to get someone to listen to me about Tico. Silas kept insisting that everything was fine and Tico would be back soon.

He knew something, I know he did, but I'd be damned if I could get him to tell me what it was. I didn't press the matter too hard. What if it was something small?

Like Silas recognized one of the graffiti pictures on the wall. There was no reason to make a mountain out of a molehill.

So I continued to do what I could. Went back to the Causegrove everyday looking for signs that Tico had been there. Asked around at school. It turned out the new twins knew him. Only Marnie seemed concerned though. I even went to the cops. They were about as useful as a bag of smashed arseholes.

The officer I talked to told me Tico was in foster care and had probably just been placed with a different family. Well, that was complete and utter shite.

I bloody well knew he had a dad. He told me about the horrible things he did to him. And if he was being taken care of by the state, he sure as heck wouldn't be sleeping outside.

Since nobody seemed to want to look for him–I wasn't sure how much I trusted Marnie–I decided to investigate myself.

Hence the reason why I was driving around the west end of town looking for a brown and yellow trailer. Maybe Tico's dad would give a shite. Or at the very least have some answers.

My phone went off, ringing the doomsday bells I chose for Silas's ringtone.

"Yes," I sang into the speaker as I turned onto a dirt road around a patch of trees.

"Why the fuck are you down by the docks?"

I seriously needed to figure out how he was tracking my phone. Arsehole.

"It's such a lovely day out, and I thought, what better way to end my Thursday night than with a nice evening breath of ocean air."

And it *was* a beautiful night. The moon was out, the crickets were chirping, and there was a slight breeze in the air. The kind of night Tico would've loved to spend gazing up at the stars.

"Don't fuck with me, Crumpet."

"Why," I sang while glancing at the phone attached to my dash. "Do you have your cock in your hand?"

I was pretty pleased with myself for that one.

Silas was not.

"I'm about to have my hands wrapped around your neck if you don't tell me where the fuck you're going."

"Where did you go?" I shot back at him.

"What do you mean, where did I go? I'm at home," Silas barked. "Where you should fucking be."

I cocked a brow at the phone and clarified. "I meant, where did you go last night?"

The line went quiet.

Not so growly and demanding now, are you? Bloody tosser.

We were curled up enjoying a movie when Silas got a call. He jumped right up and said he had to go to a meeting. At ten o'clock at night. Know what kind of meeting takes place that late? Sketchy, dirty ones that take place in a motel.

"I told you I was at a meeting."

Yeah, sure you were.

"For what?" I snarled. "The next in line for your weapon of vagina destruction?"

Silas groaned. "I'm not fucking anyone else, Crumpet. Why would I, when I've got you?"

"Uh huh." Those were literally the same words every cheater on the planet said.

"Look, do you remember Lou?"

It was kind of hard to forget the man that threatened the people I cared about.

"I'm sort of in a club with him."

Well, now that was interesting. "Like a gentleman's club?"

"I guess it's more like an organization," he explained.

I thought back to the night I met Mr. Kessler. The armed guards that accompanied him, and how he barked orders at everyone. Orders to which they listened.

Maybe my original thought of him being in the mafia wasn't that far off. Mr. Kessler was clearly a bad man. He didn't even blink an eye when he threatened me.

I swallowed back the sick feeling in my throat and glanced at my phone. "Silas, do you hurt people?"

It was quiet for a second before he spoke. "Do you really want me to answer that?"

No, I didn't. I already knew. I think some part of me always knew Silas was dangerous. The truly odd part was how little I cared about the possible bad things he'd done.

Luckily I didn't have to dwell on it for too long. A block down the road, I could see a run down brown and yellow trailer.

"I have to go. I just found Tico's house."

"Star, don't fucking go in there…"

I hung up, cutting off his yelling. Silas could be mad at me later. The only thing that mattered right now was finding my friend. Even if that meant talking to his alcoholic dad.

"It's now or never, Star."

I took one last look at my phone, which was ringing again, and got out of the car. Tico wasn't kidding when he said he lived in a shite hole.

There was a torn apart car scattered across the yard of browning grass, and I think those parts were mixed with a generator? My lip curled at the peeling siding as I walked up the steps.

Honestly, I was just glad I didn't fall through. The wood creaked under my weight and I didn't weigh much. I was almost scared to reach out and touch the doorbell. Was it going to shock me?

It didn't, thank god. But it did ring this strangled screech through the air that I cringed away from.

I heard a commotion erupt inside. Something got knocked over, while something else rolled to the left. A second later, the door was thrown open. The only thing between me, and quite possibly the greasiest man I'd ever seen, was the outer screen door.

"You lost, girl?"

Jesus, I could smell the whiskey on his breath from here. "Um… I'm looking for Tico?"

He snickered. "You must be lost. My boy's a floopsie. He don't go for pussy."

When he tipped his head and sucked a whistle through his teeth, I took a step back. The way he was eyeing me sent a shiver up my spine.

"What do you want with him anyway?"

Maybe Silas was right? I shouldn't have come here. "Well… um… I was looking for him… and I thought you might…"

The door flew open and Tico's dad charged out. "Well come on girl, spit it out!"

"You don't have to be rude."

"Rude?" He reared back. "You're the one that came knocking on my door."

He took a large step and puffed his chest up against me. He wasn't a big man, Tico obviously got his height from his father, but he was intimidating enough that I had to stop myself from taking a step back.

"Now why don't you tell me what a girl like you," he paused to snake his gaze down the length of me, "wants with my boy."

I could see why Tico didn't spend much time at home. Questioning this man I'm sure would prove fruitless. But I came here for a reason. And I wasn't leaving until I had some answers.

"Honestly," I snarled right back in his face, "I came to see if you did something to him."

His eyes narrowed. "You want to repeat that?"

If I had it my way, I wouldn't just question the man. I wanted to slap him around like he did his son. I managed to keep my composure, until I saw the evil snarl on his face. That's when I lost it.

"It's people like you that should be locked away from the rest of us."

"Careful, girl."

No, I was done being careful. Tip-toeing around everyone,

afraid to let myself say what I really thought. Well, this man was going to get a mouthful. He deserved so much more.

"Other than your horrendous odor, what do you contribute to society, huh? What skills do you have? Drinking a bottle in less than a minute? Or how about what not to do when you're a parent?"

I saw his hands fist at his sides, but I didn't care. I rose to my tip-toes, got right in his face, and continued.

"What kind of man beats his own son? You waste of skin, alcoholic, greasy little…"

That's as far as I got.

Tico's dad raised his fists and punched me, causing my neck to twist as I stumbled back down the steps. For a drunk, Tico's dad moved fast. I'd barely landed on the ground and registered the pain slicing through my jaw before he jumped down after me.

"Your entitled ass should've stayed away." He kicked me in the stomach.

Pain violently shoved everything I ate that day back out, in a winced out cry of vomit and agony. I couldn't breathe or move. I tried lifting myself back up, but he placed his booted foot on my arse and shoved me back down in the dirt.

"I'm gonna teach you the lesson your daddy should've."

I cried out as his foot landed in my back. Every inch of my body screamed as blackness started to seep into my vision. This was it. This was how I was going to die. I could already see the bright lights of the afterlife calling me.

No, wait… that wasn't the afterlife. It was headlights.

Tico's dad lifted his head and snarled, "Who the fuck are you?"

The last thing I saw before darkness took me was Silas lit up like an angel in one of the bright beams.

And the gun in his hand.

Bang!

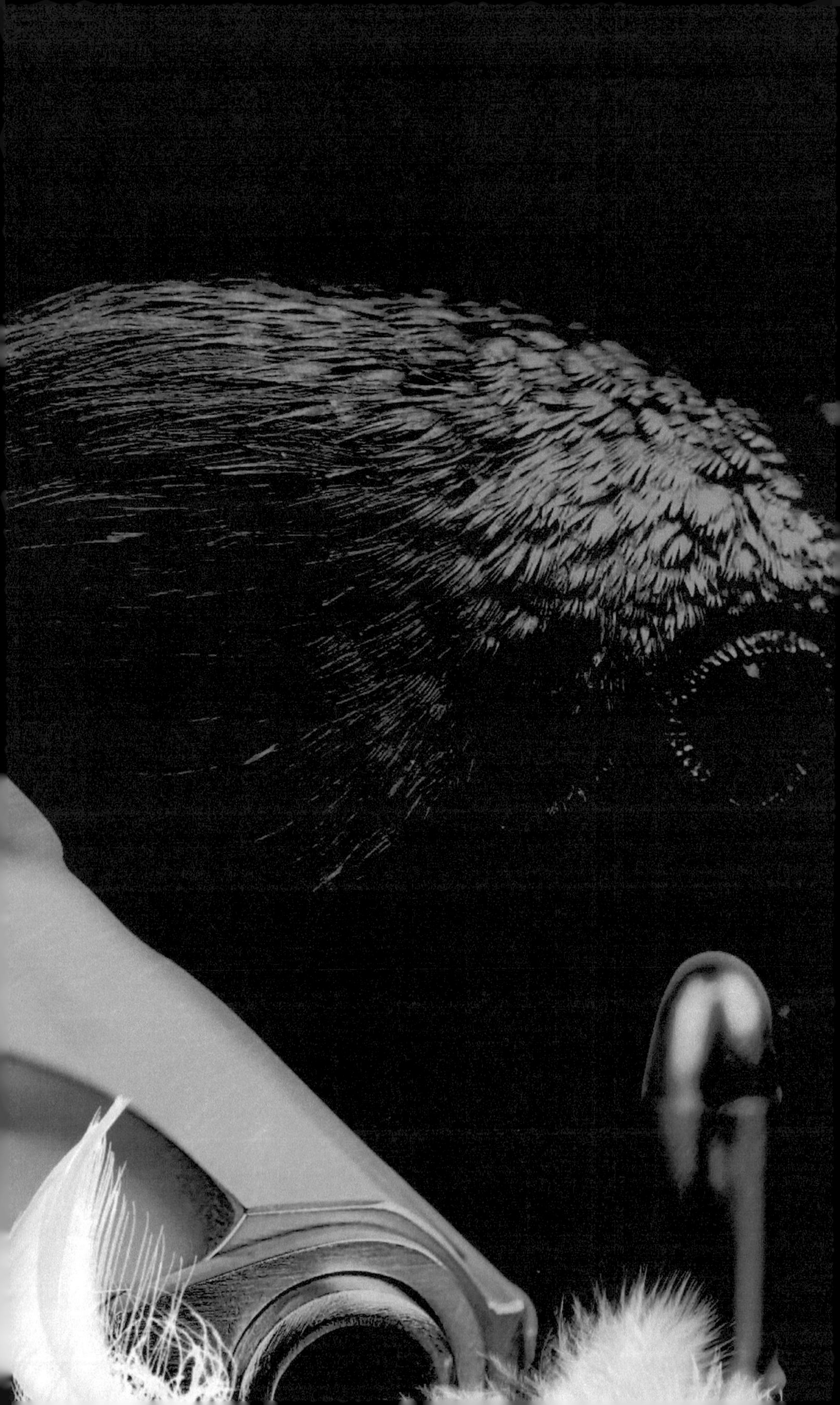

I rolled over and groaned. Why was I so sore? The last time my body ached like this was when I slipped from Craig's grip and fell during a lift.

Let me just say, dancefloors were bloody hard. I'd take the dirty forest ground over that any day. But I wasn't dancing anymore, so why was this ache flowing through my system?

'Your entitled ass should've stayed away.'

Tico's dad! That's why. He was leering over me with that greasy snarl on his face. I thought I was going to die.

I shot up and clutched the left side of my face as a searing burn tore through me.

"Careful now, Crumpet."

I twitched back from the hand that caressed my face.

What the hell was Silas doing beside me? I looked at the green

413

bedspread covering me and the room around us. Silas's room. How did I get here?

It all came back to me then. The headlights, Silas's silhouette, and the gunshot. I could hear it echoing through my ear, mingling with the same thundering sound from last year.

I sprang out of the bed and threw my hand up at Silas. "You shot him!"

His brow arched. "Shot who?"

"Don't give me that…" I paused to lean over, clutch my chest, and catch my breath.

Silas immediately scooped me up and pulled me back on the bed to cuddle in his warm embrace. "Take it easy, baby. You took a bad spill."

While the genuine concern in his eyes tugged at my heart, I couldn't forget about what I'd seen. I did not take a bad spill. I was beaten. By a greasy little man who Silas…

"You shot Tico's dad."

"No I didn't."

I rolled my head back on his chest and watched the muscle in his jaw flex. "I know what I saw."

"I don't know what you think you saw, but I didn't shoot anyone."

He was lying to me, just like when he saw that note in the Causegrove. Regardless of what he said, those words meant something to him. I had had no idea what he was hiding, or proof that he knew anything, but this… this he couldn't brush under the carpet with some convenient excuse. I know what he did. I was there.

"You had a gun, Silas."

Silas's chest lifted with a heavy sigh. "You're not going to let this go, are you?"

"No I'm not gonna let this go." I shrugged out of his arms and sat up. "You killed someone."

"Yeah, I fucking killed someone." He leaned forward and pressed his finger to my forehead. "Shot him right between the eyes. And I'd do it again, except next time I'd make him suffer a little first. He fucking hit you!"

I'd seen Silas mad before. Hell, I watched him beat the hell out of someone at Mason's dad's club. But the spark in his piercing gaze right now was truly terrifying.

The messed up part was, it wasn't him I was afraid of. It was the warm feeling flooding my chest. Yes, he took a life. Lifted that gun and pulled the trigger without so much as a second thought. But he did it to protect me.

That didn't change the fact that I was sitting in bed next to a murderer. I should've jumped and run away. Gotten as far from this dangerous man as I possibly could. But I didn't. Instead, I lurched forward and threw my arms around him.

Because despite what he did, I'd never felt more safe and protected than I did right now.

"I'm sorry," I sobbed into the crook of his neck. "I should've listened to you."

If I'd never gone there, then Silas's soul would be free of taint and Tico's dad would still be alive.

"It's all my fault."

Silas smoothed his hand down my back and pressed his lips to my cheek. "It's not your fault."

"Yes it is." I shook my head and let my tears fall.

Tico's dad, Mason's extra cruel treatment of Harper, and Emily. All of it was my fault. I was evil. A monster that only hurt the people around her.

Eventually I'd hurt Silas too. I'd tear him apart and leave nothing but a broken shell. Just like I did to Emily.

"If I'd been nicer to her, then maybe she wouldn't have..."

"Stop that." Silas grabbed my shoulders and pulled me back. "That shit was not your fault. You didn't put the gun in her hand."

I sucked back a sob and hung my head. "I may as well have."

"Don't do that. You are not a coward." He cupped my chin and forced me to meet his gaze. "Where's that fierce girl that was ready to take on three men in the woods?"

I couldn't help but snicker. The image alone was comical. Little five foot one me, raising her fists against the three of them. "That was pretty stupid."

"Yeah, it was." He chuckled and pulled me back into his embrace. "But it made me love you more."

I froze, and so did Silas.

"What?" Did he just say love?

"What?" he repeated.

I leaned back and looked up into his eyes. "You just said love?"

The clock behind me ticked by slowly as Silas stared back at me. Each tick, tick, tick, counting down the plucks of a flower.

Tick.

He loves me.

Tick.

He loves me not.

I could see the petals fluttering to the ground. Feel the wind blowing through my hair as I mentally played the childish game.

A game that came to an end when Silas said, "We're gonna be late for school," and got out of bed.

* * *

Neither one of us brought up that dreaded four letter word again. I considered it a couple of times, but lost the chance to say anything when we picked up Mason.

Never thought I'd be happy to see that arsehole. I was, though.

His presence meant I could sit quietly alone in the back and pretend that nothing happened.

Except, something did happen. Silas said he loved me and I couldn't stop thinking about it. I tried. I mulled over upcoming school projects.

Things that Harper and I could do this weekend, and possible paybacks for Cy. Nothing worked. I kept getting pulled back to that moment.

'It made me love you more.'

"Hey," Mason snapped his finger in my face. "Are you going to sit in the car all day, or are you coming?"

"Am I coming where?"

Mason raised a brow and waved at the brick building in front of us. "School?"

Oh right, school.

I blinked away the image of Silas's eyes and shook my head.

"Are you daft? Of course I'm coming."

"Whatever." Mason rolled his eyes at Silas. "How hard did she hit her head?"

"She's fine," Silas muttered and shot me a look before getting out of the truck.

I was fine, was I? Trying telling my muddled thoughts that, Mr. It Made Me Love You More.

I grumbled, "Arsehole," and followed.

It didn't take me long to pick up on the change in the atmosphere. People were gathered in groups outside the building. A clutch of three by the doors, another one of four by the shrubs, with a larger group in the parking lot.

Every single one of them ducked their heads in hushed whispers. Even more suspicious was the way they shifted their gaze away from us as we walked past. More specifically, Mason and Silas. No one seemed interested in me at all.

When we walked up to the doors, Lana stepped in front of us and looked at Mason. "You don't want to go in there."

"No, I don't, but school awaits so…" Mason shrugged and moved to step around Lana.

She once again blocked him, except this time it was Silas she plead with. "Don't let him go in there."

"Alright, Lana," Silas huffed and crossed his arms. "What's going on?"

"Just…" she paused to shoot Mason a look, "don't let him go in there."

It was the look on Lana's face that got my heart pumping. I'd never seen her worried, scared, or sad. All of which I could see tugging in the deep-set lines of concern on her face.

"Look, I get that you want me, but you're my friend's wife." Mason placed his hand on Lana's shoulder and gave her a fake frown, "Besides, I wouldn't want to make Edith jealous."

I rolled my eyes. Leave it to Mason to make a joke out of an obviously serious situation.

Lana tried to warn him once again. "I'm serious, Mason."

"So am I." There was nothing fake or joking about the look he was giving her now. "Get the fuck out of my way."

And she did. Can't say I blamed her. It didn't end well for the last person who caused that glint in Mason's green eyes.

The second we walked into the school, my hand flew up, muffling the gasp that flew from my lips. Pictures were pasted on every inch of the wall, covering the halls with a single grizzly image.

A man with dark hair, laying in a puddle of blood on the asphalt. There were four words written in black across each picture.

Where's your king now.

I didn't know who the man in the picture was, or where it was taken, but he was obviously shot. More than once. I'd had that same circular tear in my flesh.

There was one person in the picture I did recognize. Riley was hunched over the man with a look of anguish on her face.

Mason went wild. He tore one of the pictures off the wall and yelled down the hall. "Who the fuck did this!"

"Mason," Silas stepped up and grabbed Mason's shoulder. "Calm down."

I was a little scared for Silas when Mason turned around and glared at him.

"Don't tell me to calm down!" He slapped the picture in Silas's chest and growled, "Micha's fine, my ass. We're going to see Louis."

Silas sighed and held up his hand, "Mase…"

"Now, Silas," Mason barked out. "Or I swear to god I'll burn this town to the fucking ground."

After that, Mason stormed out, throwing the doors open so fast that they slammed against the school wall.

That's when Silas turned to me. "Stay here, Crumpet. I don't want you involved in this shit."

I wasn't sure if I wanted to be involved in it either.

"Who is that man in the picture?" I asked as he turned to leave.

Silas looked back at me and sighed. "Mason's brother."

Chapter 39

Silas

We made it back to Oakleigh Manor in record time. Most of which I spent hanging onto the door handle, prepared to either jump out of kiss my ass goodbye when Mase rolled us in the ditch. I knew I shouldn't have given him the keys.

Technically, I didn't give them to him. Fucker ripped them out of my hand. But I didn't fight him to get them back, either. I was a strong motherfucker, but when Mase was like this, the devil himself couldn't knock the bastard out.

He screeched the Hummer to a stop inches from the steps leading to the front door and jumped out.

I snatched the keys out of the ignition, muttered, "Here we go," and followed.

Mase's house made mine look like a poorly built one bedroom

cottage in the woods. If someone didn't know their way around, they could easily get lost in these walls.

A few of the Kesslers' maids had. By the time we found Loretta, she was a crying ball on the floor. Never did find out what she saw in Lou's wing of the manor, but whatever it was, she refused to come back.

I didn't have that problem. I spent more time here as a kid than I did at my own house. So I knew exactly where Mase was going.

I strutted down the hall to the left and climbed the stairs to Lou's office, where I could already hear Mase yelling.

"Don't give me that shit, old man!"

"Mason, you need to take a breath and calm down." Lou sighed and looked over at me as I joined them. "Did you let him drive here?"

Seriously?

"What the fuck did you expect me to do? Knock him out?" *Good luck with that.*

"Don't put this shit on him," Mase snarled and slapped the picture down on Lou's desk. "Where the fuck is my brother?"

Lou's leather chair creaked as he leaned forward to eye the picture. I had to hand it to the bastard, there wasn't so much as a tick in his straight-faced expression. No one would ever know he was currently looking at an image of his son, bloody and shot the fuck up.

"Your brother is fine."

Mason pressed his finger loudly down on the picture, "Does he look fucking fine to you?"

Finally there was a crack in Lou's icy exterior. A spark of anger flashed across his dark eyes. If it was sadness or guilt, then I'd worry. Anger meant that Lou was pissed because someone tried to take out his son. *Tried* being the operative word.

And let me just say, the last person anyone wanted to piss off was the King of Kings. Louis Kessler didn't just fuck you up. He destroyed everyone and anything that had the smallest involvement in your life.

"I want to talk to him," Mase demanded. "Right fucking now."

Lou leaned back and folded his hands on his lap. "No."

That didn't improve Mase's mood any. "What the fuck do you mean 'no'?"

"I mean no. What's so hard to understand about that?"

I don't know if Mase was shocked, or just stunned by his old man's flat out refusal. But whatever it was, he stopped and stared at him with his mouth hung open. Lou took the opportunity and leaned forward, bracing his elbows on his desk.

"Let me explain the situation, Mason. This thing goes deeper than someone putting a price on your brother's girlfriend's head.

Someone is out to get us, and I am not going to let you run your mouth to the wrong person and fuck up all my careful planning." Lou locked his stern glare on Mase and added, "So, no. You can't talk to your brother."

What Mase did next made me flinch. He let out a loud roar and flipped Lou's desk over. Shit flew everywhere, crashing on the floor and smashing against the wall as the desk rotated in the air.

Slamming down so hard the vibrations nearly knocked me off my feet. The entire display was impressive. It took four men to move that thing in here, and Mase lifted it as easily as he would a paperweight.

Lou, on the other hand, was not impressed. He shot out of his chair and dodged out of the way of the desk. After which, he lifted his hand and pointed at Mase.

"That right there is what I'm talking about. You can't control yourself, Mason."

"I didn't mean..." Mase huffed and looked around at the mess he made.

"Just like you wouldn't mean to get your brother killed." Lou sighed and scrubbed a hand down his face. "But you would, Mason. And you know it."

I didn't know what to say, or how to shake away the guilt flooding Mase's face. Because in all honesty, Lou was right. Mase was a twisted ball of guilt and anger. He couldn't control himself long enough to think rationally. Violence was the only thing that brought him peace.

When he was pounding on someone else, for a few seconds, he could concentrate on someone else's pain. He didn't have to feel his own. That's why he stuck that needle in his arm the first time. To numb himself. Overdosing wasn't a big deal to him.

Sometimes I think he wanted to leave this world. So he wouldn't have to see her face everyday and be reminded of the love he lost. Harper didn't just betray him. She crushed his soul. Ryker, and all the things we hid from him, just added to it.

My heart broke as Mase furrowed his brows and looked around the room. For the first time in his life, he was face to face with the reality of who he'd become. And it was tearing him apart. I didn't know how to fix that for him. Lou tried.

He reached his hand out and stepped closer, "Mason…"

"Don't," Mase shrugged away.

"We can work on this, son."

The anger was instantly washed back into Mase's eyes. "I'm not your son."

With that, he was gone, leaving me alone with Lou. Who dropped his face in his hand again.

"I shouldn't have said that to him."

"He needed to hear it." Someone had to knock some sense into him.

Lou sighed and kicked a broken lamp. "I suppose he did."

We both stopped and looked out the door when we heard a car start up and peel away.

Fuck. What the hell was Mase going to do now?

Lou had the same thought. I could see the wheels in his head turning. Right now, he was going through worst case scenarios. Mase in the liquor cabinet or worse, laying somewhere with a needle in his arm.

"Don't worry," I gave his shoulder a reassuring squeeze. "I'll find him."

"Is he ever going to stop hating me?"

"He doesn't hate you, Lou," I said and walked out. "He hates himself."

I spent all day driving around looking for my best friend. I checked all his regular spots. The beach, hot springs, and the hidden shack on the west end of the bluffs he used to hide in and get high.

I even checked Ashworth. By the time I found him, the sun had long set and the moon was shining down on the world.

Mase looked over at me as I walked across the sand towards him and lifted the bottle in his hands to his lips.

"You remember the last time we were here?"

I sat down beside him and gazed out at the glistening pond nestled in a clutch of trees. "Yeah."

Harper, Mase and I found this spot years ago while on one of our explorations of the bluffs. Back then it seemed like some magical oasis given to us by the fairy gods.

We spent the entire day here, running around and catching lightning bugs. It was our special place. A secret clubhouse no one else knew about.

The next day, Mason was arrested.

"I keep going over that day, trying to figure out when things went wrong." He frowned and sucked back the rest of his whiskey. "Did I do something? Or say something?"

"I don't know?" I sighed and looked up at the moon. "Maybe I'm not the person you should be asking."

Mase snorted and tossed the empty bottle on the sand. "I don't care what she has to say."

"That's the problem, Mase." I tipped my head towards him. "Yeah, you do."

His brows furrowed at the lake. "It's too late."

"You sure about that? Some asshole once told me, just because you hate her, doesn't mean she's not yours."

He rolled his eyes. "Sounds like a dumbass."

"Oh, he's definitely a dumbass," I nodded. "But he has his moments."

We both snickered.

"Besides," I nudged him with my shoulder, "I kind of like having the idiot around. He keeps me on my toes."

"Well, someone has to help remove that giant stick from your ass. Who organizes their socks by days of the week?"

Fuck sakes, here we go.

"Do you have days of the week panties too?"

Motherfucker.

I should leave him here to drown drunk in the pond. Last year, that son of a bitch stole all my boxers and replaced them with days of the week panties.

When I came at him for it, he told me to calm down and put my Wednesdays on.

"Well, come on Tinkerbell." Mase slapped his arm on my shoulder and pushed himself up. "You better take me home so Louis can give me his disappointment speech."

I'd take him home, alright. Might knock him around a bit first. Making me look all over town for his drunk ass.

Mase stumbled down the sand and smirked back at me. "You coming? Don't want to be late getting home to your girl. Who else you gonna feed that footlong to?"

I was definitely going to knock him around first.

I shook my head and followed. At least I found him in one piece, without a fucking needle in his arm. That was something.

The small shred of relief I felt went out the window when my phone lit up with Star's number.

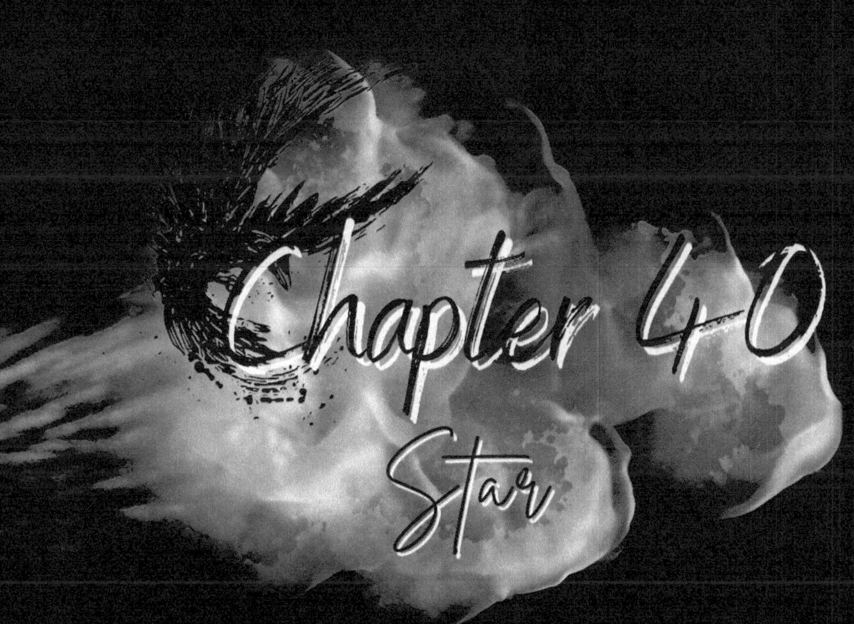

Chapter 40
Star

I stepped out of my car and sucked in a deep breath of night air. It was too loud in my house. I couldn't think with the twins and Ash running around. Here, it was quiet.

Nothing but me and the soft lapping of the lake. This was what I needed. A moment to myself so I could collect my thoughts. And there were so many swirling around.

When Mum and Dad said we were moving here, it was so I could start over in a place with a clean slate.

Well, this was the most messed up clean slate in the history of mankind. My name was tainted back home, but it felt like what was left of my soul was in danger here.

The taunts, ridicule and humiliation Silas put me through I could handle. After everything I'd done, I bloody well deserved it.

It was the other stuff that tore me apart. The tenderness that

Silas showed, and his insane protectiveness. I wanted it, but didn't deserve it.

Silas said he loved me. How ironic was that? One killer falling for another. What I did was so much worse than what he did.

Silas pulled a trigger. I destroyed a soul. Leaving her parents nothing but hollow holes wishing the ghost of their daughter would pay them a visit.

She didn't ignore me. Emily was a constant voice in the back of my mind. Or, at least she used to be. I hadn't heard her in over a week. Perhaps that's why I came here, to wander around the beach where I first saw Harper smile?

A part of me wanted to find her again. As long as I could hear her voice, some part of Emily was still alive. I needed that. Needed to know that her light wasn't completely snuffed out.

"Are you there?"

Nothing.

"Emily?" I gazed out over the moonlit water and sniffed back a sob. "Please come back."

The only answer I got was the unbearable silence in the back of my mind.

Of course Emily wouldn't say anything. She was gone, and no matter how desperately I wanted to change that, I couldn't. I couldn't take back what I'd done. But neither could she.

I fisted my hands against the anger I felt coursing hotly through my veins. Silas was right. I didn't put the gun in her hands. She did that. She chose to leave her parents alone.

"Why did you have to do that!" I yelled up at the sky. "You could've done something. Hit me, or fight back. Anything but what you did!"

It made no sense to stand here and scream at the stars. Emily wasn't there. She couldn't hear me, but I couldn't stop. I continued to rant while hot wet streaks trickled down my cheeks.

"I might be a bad person Emily, but you're worse. You tore apart everyone who loved you with one bullet. Why? Because I picked on you! You're selfish, Emily. A selfish spoiled person that only thought about herself." I collapsed onto the soft sand and whispered, "I hate you."

She should've just shot me.

I sat there in the sand while the breeze toyed with my hair, wishing that the ghost haunting my mind would come back. But she didn't. And I'd never felt more empty.

My ears perked at the sound of my name.

"Star?"

"Emily?" I looked up, searching for her familiar brown eyes.

What I found was so much worse.

There was a figure laying further down the beach in the sand. A cold shiver wracked through my entire body when the moonlight glinted off his left shoe. I had the matching one in my car.

No!

"Tico!" I screamed and shot up to rush over to him.

The closer I got, the more my heart dropped, replaced with heavy deep set dread. A patch of skin had been cut out of his arm, along with cuts and bruises all over his face, and one of his eyes was completely swollen shut.

Horror really set in when I saw his chest. Someone had carved a raven into his tanned skin, cutting so deep I could see one of his ribs.

"Oh my god." Warm, sticky fluid coated my hands as I scooped him up. "Who did this to you?"

His blood was everywhere. Seeping into the ground beneath my knees and dripping from the bird's wings. If I didn't get him help now, he wasn't going to make it.

I cradled him in my lap and pulled out my phone to call the only person I could think of. The longest seconds of my life ticked by as I watched Tico struggle for breath and listened to the phone ring.

"Miss me already, Crumpet?"

The sound of Silas's voice caused me to choke on my desperation. Because right now, I did miss him. Immensely so.

"Silas… he's gonna…" I sucked back a sob and looked down at the red staining my hand. "There's so much blood."

"What? Whose blood?"

But I couldn't answer. All I could do was cry and beg some unseen force to save my friend.

"Star!" Silas yelled into the phone. "Where the fuck are you?"

Tico's chest arched off my lap as he violently coughed out blood.

I threw the phone and rolled Tico over, trying to clear his airway. He spasmed and hacked up more blood, then went still.

No, no, no, no!

"Don't you die on me!" I screamed, slapping my palms down on the ground. "You stay right here with me, you hear me!"

Tico rolled over and fluttered his eye open. "Star?"

God, he sounded so weak.

"Yeah." I swept the hair off his face and smiled down at him. "I'm here."

"Harper…" He lifted his arm, pressed something into my chest and arched his back. "She's not…"

I watched in horror as the last breath hissed past his lips and his body settled onto the ground. He was gone.

As if the heavens could hear my anguished cry tear through the night, the sky opened up and rained down on us.

I don't know how long I sat there staring at his lifeless form. Or what drew my attention to something glinting in the sand. But when I finally tore my eyes off Tico, that orange shell glittering in the sand became my lifeline.

I could hear someone calling my name in the distance, but I didn't care. All that mattered was that shell.

And the bright blue eyes of the little boy who tried to give it to me years ago.

"Come on, baby." I ushered Star into my room and sat her down on my bed.

I damn near lost my mind when she called. Thought I was gonna find her mangled and dead somewhere. I'll never forget the anguished scream I heard ringing through the phone.

I felt my soul tear apart in that moment. And when I saw her staring into space covered in blood, my heart fell down that hollow hole with my soul.

It took me a second to realize it wasn't her blood. Then I thought the fucker on the ground had attacked her and she fought back.

I wanted to drag him back from hell and kill him all over again. Until I saw the raven carved in his chest. He wasn't some punk that attacked my girl. It was Tico.

My fierce girl had to watch someone else die. Except this time, it was her friend. The same one she'd been so worried about.

I should've done more. Insisted the Kings look harder for him. Anything that would've saved her the pain she was suffering now.

"Baby," I knelt down on the floor in front of her and tucked her hair behind her ear. "Can you tell me what happened?"

I wanted to take revenge for her. Make the asshole that did this pay. But Star wasn't talking. She wasn't doing anything but staring off into space.

I sighed and pulled my jacket tighter around her shivering form. "I wish you would talk to me."

I didn't need much. Just a simple nod, or one word. Something that told me I hadn't lost her. Lou said this was a normal reaction to trauma and that I should be patient with her. I called him while my dad was checking her out for physical damage. Thank god she didn't have any.

Mase was still at Cherry Lake, waiting for his old man and Derek. I got Star out of there. She was in no condition to talk to the cops. Besides, this was something that would be handled internally.

The note and raven all pointed to an enemy of the Order. I didn't care what Lou of the other Kings did, I was just happy Star was okay.

Seeing her face, even if it was unresponsive, gave me more relief than anything else. Right now wasn't the time to worry about me though. I needed to take care of her. And I'd start doing that by washing the blood off her.

"Stay here, baby." I stood up and kissed her on the forehead, thanking god that I could still feel her warmth on my lips. "I'll be right back."

I walked into the bathroom, grabbed a cloth, and turned on the water. As I stood there staring at myself in the mirror, a single tear rolled down my face and splattered on the marble counter.

What would I have done if I lost her? How could I have gone on without being able to see her beautiful face every day?

It was then that I vowed to make sure she was always protected and safe. I'd spare her every single ounce of pain I could. If I had to swim through the fires of hell and throttle the devil himself, then so be it. I'd take on every demon in that abyss just to see her smile.

With a cloth in hand, I headed back in the room to take care of my beautiful, perfect little English crumpet.

I knelt back down on the floor and looked up at her empty eyes. "I'm back, baby."

She didn't move when I swept the cloth over her cheek, gently wiping off Tico's blood. Didn't so much as flinch, or say a word.

She just sat there doing nothing while I cleaned her skin. That's what hurt the most. The nothing. It was like she was gone and nothing I did could reach her.

"You probably don't remember this, but I met you once before." I trailed the cloth down her left arm and furrowed my brows at the piece of bloody paper clutched tightly in her fist.

"I still remember the bathing suit you were wearing," I said, continuing my story as I carefully uncurled her fingers. "It was pink, with little yellow flowers."

The paper was an old missing poster from twenty-five years ago. It was so stained with blood that the only thing I could make out was a warped face with brown eyes and a name.

Niles Fenton.

What was Star doing with this? And who the hell was Niles Fenton?

Shaking my head, I set the poster on my bedside table and returned to cleaning my girl. I could worry about that later. This silence was killing me. I needed to hear something, even if it wasn't her voice.

"Do you know what I remember most about that day, besides for what you said to me?" She was a little spitfire back then too. "It was how the light shone around you. You were so bright, even the sun couldn't outshine you."

My heart damn near leapt out of my chest when she whimpered and rolled her eyes down to me. I was so excited I couldn't stop myself from rising to my knees and cupping her face.

"Do you remember that, baby?"

Please tell me you remember something.

Star held up her fisted right hand and whispered, "Penguins bring their wives rocks."

"What do you have there?" I reached out for her hand, and Star lost it.

Wherever she had gone, she came back full force. Kicking and screaming. "No, you can't have it! It's mine!"

I tried to calm her down, but she was having none of it. She slapped me across the face and scurried further up the bed.

What the hell was in that hand? Whatever it was, I was going to find the fuck out. For all I knew, she was holding onto one of her friend's ribs in some warped attempt to bring him back.

"That's enough," I barked and pointed at her. "You're gonna show me what you have."

"No," Star screamed and threw a pillow. "It's mine."

Alright, that was it.

I crawled on the bed after her. Not fast enough, though. She rolled into a ball, curling around her fist as if it was the goddamn Holy Grail. I had to pry her apart. Which wasn't easy.

I didn't want to hurt her, and her fucking dancer legs were strong. But I eventually managed to uncurl her and grab her arm.

"No, it's mine," she blubbered with tears streaming down her face.

My breath hitched when I saw what she was protecting so fiercely. Laying in the middle of her palm was an orange seashell.

The same one I tried to give to her ten years ago. Her whimpering cry sunk deep in my chest, making my heart sing.

"You can't have it. It's mine. You gave it to me."

"I'm not going to take it from you, baby." I looked deep in her eyes and curled her fingers back around the shell. "I promise. It's yours."

Just like I am.

She looked up at me with her chin quivering. "Tico's dead."

"I know." I pulled her into my arms. "I'm sorry, baby."

She cried in my chest as I held her. Tighter than I'd ever held anyone. I didn't care how long she cried, or what she said because she was here. With me. That was all that mattered. Ten minutes later and it could've been her body I found on the beach, and that thought utterly terrified me.

So much so that after I'd bathed her and tucked her into bed, I sat there and watched her sleep.

Memorizing every delicate feature of her face. How the moonlight cast an angelic glow around her head, and the cute way her nose twitched when she softly snored.

I told myself that earlier that day that love was just a slip of the tongue. But that was a lie. I didn't just love this girl. I needed her. She was the missing piece of my soul.

My little taste of freedom while dancing in the rain.

The next morning, I headed down the stairs with the Missing poster in my hand. While I was happy to sit there and watch my Crumpet, I couldn't stop thinking about it. The name Fenton picked at the back of my brain. When I woke up, it hit me.

We were all given a handbook when we were initiated into the Order. That's where I knew it from. Inside the book, all the family names were listed, from both sides. Fenton was one of the wolves' names.

Funny, considering we were told all the wolves except for Alexander Mathers were wiped out over a century ago. Yet there was someone named Fenton in Ashen Springs twenty-five years ago.

I believed in coincidences, but come on. My old man going to high school with a Fenton who conveniently disappeared? That was shady as fuck. And I intended to find out what the hell was going on. Right fucking now.

My old man looked up from his newspaper when I walked into the kitchen. "How's your girl?"

"Still sleeping." I tossed the poster at him. "I'm more interested in this."

"What's this?" he said while picking it up.

"Star had it."

I watched him read the letters and roll his eyes over the picture. A picture of a face that I had stared at for a long time this morning, I knew every inch of it. When he opened his mouth, I knew he was going to lie to me. So I cut him off before he could.

"Mind telling me why the same night I found my girlfriend crying over the dead body of her friend, she had a Missing poster of a wolf that went missing when you were my age?"

"Niles wasn't a wolf." My old man dropped the poster on the counter. "He was a fool."

"So the name Fenton is just a coincidence?"

My ass it was.

He sighed and rolled his eyes my way, but didn't say a thing. He was cut off before he could.

"Just tell the boy, Martin."

I turned and cocked a brow at the man in a suit with greying hair standing in the kitchen entryway.

"Grandpa?" *What the hell?* "What are you doing here?"

My grandpa's blue eyes twinkled as a smirk lifted the corner of his mouth. "Can't I come and see my favorite grandson?"

"No."

He didn't come when I received an award from the senator for an essay I wrote, or when Finn was born. He didn't even come when Finn's parents died—he merely made an appearance at the memorial.

My cousin had only seen our grandfather three times in his entire life. One of which was the fifteen minutes he spent giving some bullshit speech at my uncle's funeral.

"I'm sorry Silas, I know you think I haven't been there for you, but I have." He lifted his chin and gazed over at my old man. "Do you want to tell him, or should I?"

"Tell me what?"

I looked from one to the other, waiting for them to say something. It was my old man that spoke first.

"There's a reason your grandfather stayed away."

Now I was really confused.

"Twenty-five years ago, your father and his friends fucked up." My grandpa walked forward, eyes locked on my old man, whose jaw ticked at his statement. "They made a mess. Quite a big one, and we had to clean it up."

"Those asshole's raped Dean's girl," my old man argued.

"But did you have to flay them alive on the street?" My grandpa shook his head. "That explosion killed a dozen innocent people, Martin."

Explosion? What?

My old man hung his head. "We didn't see the propane tanks."

"I know." My grandpa walked around the island and dropped his hand on my old man's shoulder. "But it's done now." He then turned his attention back on me. "Part of the deal we made with the families involved was that we would step down from power and leave Ashen Springs. Hence why your fathers are Kings, and we aren't."

"We?" I asked. As far as I knew, none of the other knights had any grandparents. On their father's side, at least.

My grandpa nodded. "William Kessler and Charles Whitley will be here next week."

Micha and Parker's grandpas were alive. Did they know that?

"We don't need your help," my old man grumbled. Was that resentment I saw in his face? "We can handle things."

"Clearly you can't," my grandpa barked back at him. "Honestly, we should've never left. You boys weren't ready to take the reins."

I sat there watching them because I was too stunned to say anything.

My old man rolled his eyes. "We're doing just fine."

"Fine? Micha's girl has a hit out on her head. You guys let Ryker Hudson run amuck while all of you were vying for power, and your brother is dead. I'd hardly call that fine."

I mean, I couldn't argue with him. Grandpa did have a point. My old man did not agree.

"You can't just come back after twenty-five years and claim your thrones."

"The thrones were always ours. You boys were merely holding them for us. Don't worry," he slapped his hand on my old man's back and smiled. "We'll give them back when we feel you're ready."

The King of Kings having to give up power. Couldn't wait to see how Louis was going to handle this.

My grandpa arched a brow at me. "Go back upstairs to your girl, Silas. You father and I need to talk about a few things."

Was it wrong that I got a sick thrill watching my old man get chastised by his own? How ironic was it that the straight laced Dr. Creswell was getting scolded like a little boy. I liked this side of him. And as much as I would love to stick around and see this, there was a beautiful girl waiting in bed for me.

"Oh, and Silas," my grandpa called out when I got up to leave. "Remember to always put her first. That's a rule your father seems to have forgotten."

Couldn't help but smirk at that.

"Don't worry, Grandpa. I take care of the things I love." I headed upstairs to do just that.

Star was still passed out when I walked in. The drugs I gave her to sleep probably hadn't worn off yet, and I didn't want to wake her. So I grabbed Lucy and worked on a song I'd been playing with.

I sat at the end of the bed, so I could feel her feet pressed against my back, and started to strum. A few picks in and the words just flowed out.

"She's beautiful, she's the enemy,
She's a perfect catastrophe,
That crazy girl next door,
I sit at the window,
Hating the flawless way she moves,
The image of her graceful strides,
An image I can't remove.

Like that night out on the street,
Just the crazy girl, the rain, and me.

Wish I was dancing in the rain,
Feeling free enough to soar above the pain,
There's no one there to judge us,
Just the moon and stars above us,
With the crazy girl,
Dancing in the rain.

She's upside down, she's an absolute fox,
She's chaos in a pretty box,
That crazy girl next door,
I try to push her away,
Wishing she would just fall apart,
And still she glides her way into my heart.

Like that night out on the street,
Just the rain, the crazy girl, and me.

Wish I was dancing in the rain,
Feeling free enough to soar above the pain,
There's no one there to judge us,
Just the moon and stars above us,
With the crazy girl,
Dancing in the rain.

Do this,
Do that,
Be better,
Don't wear that hat.
Lies, betrayal and choices that aren't mine,
A future I can't see,
Except for the crazy girl, the rain, and me.

She's incomplete, she's all mine,
She's utterly divine,
An angel sent down to rescue me,
Open my heart and set me free.

Wish I was dancing in the rain,
Feeling free enough to soar above the pain,
There's no one there to judge us,
Just the moon and stars above us,
With the crazy girl,
Dancing in the rain."

I was so lost in the song, I didn't realize Star was awake until I heard her voice.

"That's beautiful. Did you write it?"

"It's just something I've been playing around with." I set Lucy down and crawled up the bed to kiss her cheek. "You should be sleeping."

Star's beautiful onyx eyes fluttered up to mine. "Is the song about me?"

Everything was about her. The wind, the sky, every breath I took, and the sun–all of it would be meaningless if she wasn't here.

"You said you loved me."

"I did."

There was nothing sexier than the cute little way she chewed on the corner of her mouth.

"Did you mean it?"

I tugged on her hips, pulling her to lie on her back, and grazed my nose up the side of her neck. Inhaling every last bit of her scent I could force into my lungs.

"I couldn't breathe when I thought I lost you. So, yes. I meant it."

More than you could ever imagine.

A groan rumbled through my chest when Star smoothed her palm under my shirt and up my chest. "Show me."

"Baby," I lifted my head and gazed down at her. "I don't want to hurt you."

I would love nothing more than to lose myself in her hot little cunt, but she'd been through an ordeal. She needed time to heal.

"Please, Silas." Like a cat in heat, Star arched her back, pressing those firm tits against my chest. "I want to feel you."

Fuck me.

"Baby, we can't…" I really fucking hated myself right now.

"I need you," she whined in a breathy tone that made my balls ache. "Make love to me, so I can make love to you."

I was trying really fucking hard to resist her tempting taunts, but when she reached into my sweats and grabbed my dick, I was done. Her clothes were torn off almost as fast as mine.

After that, we were a tangled ball of teeth, needily clutching hands, and panting breaths. Her wet pussy grinding against my shaft was the hottest fucking thing I'd ever felt. But this wasn't how shit worked, and she knew it.

I wrapped my hand around her neck and slammed her back on the bed.

"You want my cock, baby," I growled, while swiping my tongue over her bottom lip.

Star whimpered and nodded.

Yeah she fucking did. Her pussy was soaking my dick with her desire.

"Such a perfect little slut." I reached down and shoved my fingers in her cunt, reveling in the way her mouth parted with a gasp. Fuck, I loved that sound. "Always ready to take my cock."

I finger fucked her hard, inhaling every breath and moan that flew from her lips. When her pussy clamped down and her back arched off the bed, I slammed my mouth down on hers.

Eating up the scream that tore through her body, like a ravenous beast. Her cunt was still spasming when I slammed inside her and groaned.

Like the good girl I knew she was, she took every last inch I had to give. Only whimpering when I forced the last couple into her tight walls. That was okay. She'd learn to take me. She didn't have a choice.

I could feel her cervix hitting the head of my cock. It sent a tingle down my shaft and into my balls with each stroke. But if I could go deeper, I would. I'd fuck her womb and tear into her soul, imprinting myself on her forever.

Just like she'd done to me.

"Oh God," Star panted and swiveled her hips, matching my furious thrusts.

"You better stop calling out to God, Baby," I grunted, and slammed into her hard. "Or I'm gonna have to hunt the fucker down and slit his throat."

I'd do it too. I'd claw into heaven and slaughter my way to the ivory tower to end the creator. Star was mine. Every move she made and breath she took belonged to me, and me alone. All of it was mine.

The hands desperately clawing my ass. The goddamn sexy moans that rolled through her chest. Hell, I even wanted her pain. I'd take everything she had to give and demand she give me more.

"Silas," *that's better*, "please, I need more."

"You want more, Baby," I growled, then flipped her onto her stomach and slapped her ass. "I'll give you more."

Who was I to deny her?

I pulled her hips up and lined my cock up with her entrance, groaning out a loud, "Fuuuck," as I slowly slid inside her hot cunt.

I didn't need to storm the Pearly Gates because I was already in heaven. The divine kingdom was wrapped tightly around my cock. I stopped moving, wrapped her hair around my fist, and lifted her head off the bed.

"You said you wanted to make love to me." I slapped her ass, causing a squeal to mix with her panting breaths. "I'm waiting."

It took her a second to catch onto what I was saying, but she slowly started to move. Pulling her pussy along my shaft in tentative strokes.

"Come on, Crumpet." I slapped her ass again, this time hard enough to leave a nice red handprint. "Fuck me."

And she did. Bobbed her body back and forth, slamming her backside against me with each hard thrust. It wasn't long before I snapped. I pushed her head back down on the bed, grabbed her ass cheeks, and pulled them apart to watch myself disappear inside her.

I'd never get tired of that sight. Her glistening pink pussy hungrily swallowing my cock. There was only one thing I needed to make this moment perfect.

I slammed deep inside her and stilled. "Do you love me, Baby?"

Star whimpered out a nod and wriggled her hips.

I rewarded her by pulling out and slowly sinking back in.

"Say it."

"Silas," she whined. "Please."

"Nope, not what I want to hear."

She didn't like that.

Stubborn little thing grunted out a growl of frustration and pounded her fists into the bed.

Too fucking bad for her. I could stay like this all day, soaking up the warmth of her inner walls was enough to get me off. If my little witch wanted to come, she better earn that shit.

"Last chance, Baby. I don't need to fuck you to blow my load."

My breath caught in my throat when she pushed herself up and gazed over her shoulder at me.

"I love you, Silas."

It wasn't just her words that sunk in my chest. It was the devotion shining in her eyes.

"Come here." I grabbed her neck, pulled her up against me, and kissed her hard. "I love you too, Baby."

I showed her just how much I loved her all day long and well into the night.

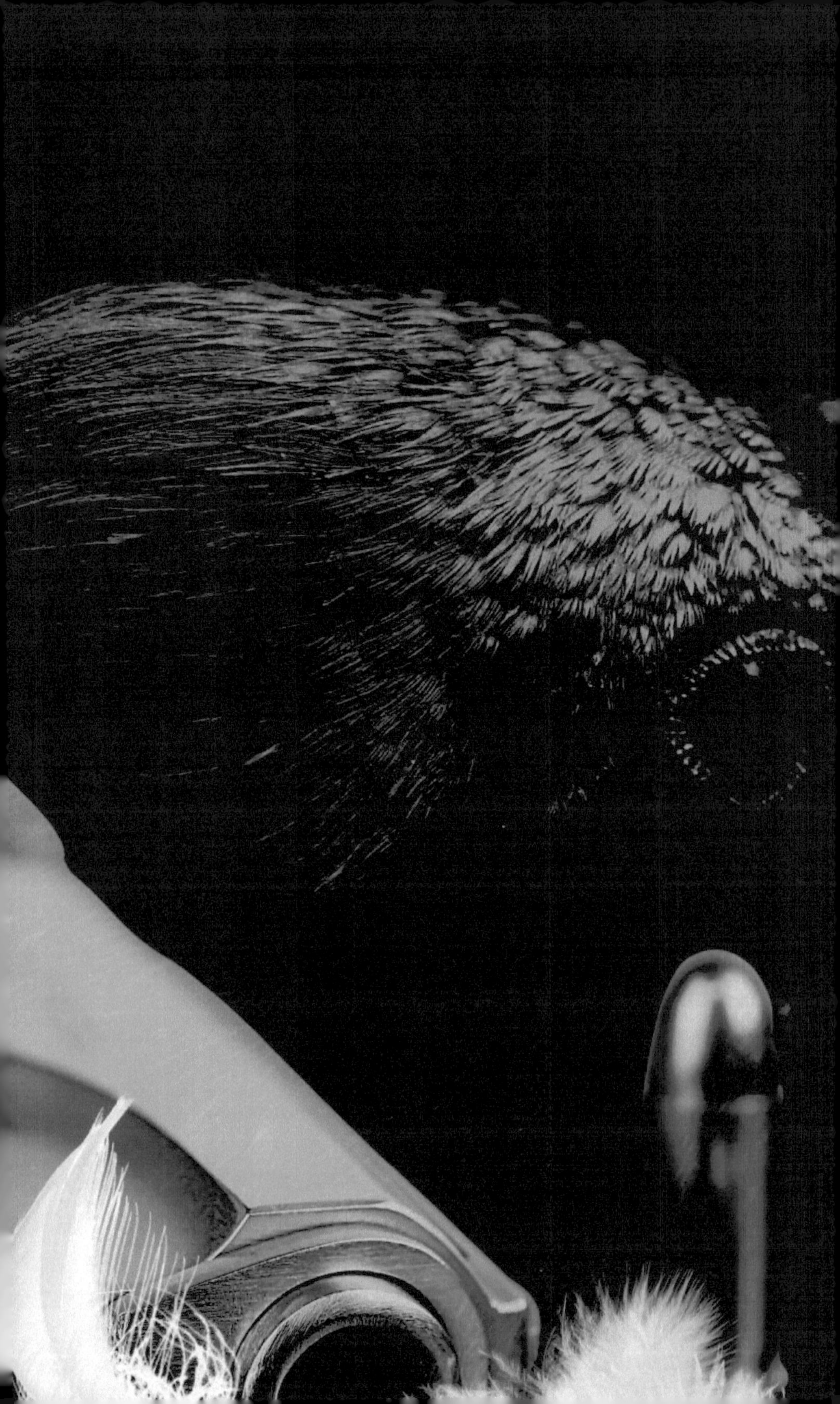

"Why the fuck are you looking at me like that?"

I followed Silas's glare to a pair of sparkling green eyes across the room. *Ugh, Logan Hudson.* I still hadn't forgiven him for chasing me in the woods. I don't care how sweet Shelby said he was. He would always be an arsehole in my books.

"Stop staring at me," Silas grumbled and wrapped his arms around me. "You're creeping me out."

Mason's gaze narrowed on us as he leaned in closer to Logan. "You thinking what I'm thinking?"

"Yeah," Logan nodded.

Shelby shook her head from her spot beside her boyfriend. "I don't want to know."

Silas had a full house today. Micha and Riley were also here, curled up on the couch beside Logan and Shelby. While I was happy Mason's brother was okay, I didn't know what to make of him.

There were exactly three people I hadn't been able to read. Preston, AKA jean jacket creeper, one of my former teachers back home, and Micha Kessler. From the little I had learned about him, I'd come to one conclusion. He was probably the only man on this planet that could handle Riley Adams.

She went ballistic when she found out about Tico. Threatened just about everyone she came across for two weeks straight. It was Micha that reigned her in. I shared her frustration.

They still hadn't found his killer. Silas kept telling me to be patient. They were working on it. And by 'they,' he meant the secret society he was part of.

Which he only told me about because he needed some stupid contract signed by my dad. That was easy enough to do. Dad didn't read it or ask what it was for.

He signed it because I wanted him to. Sometimes I was worried about my parents' trusting nature. One of these days , it was going to get them in trouble.

Did I care that Silas technically owned me? No. Because I owned him too. Though the whole crow in the raven's nest note made a lot more sense now.

Exactly why I started my own investigation into Tico's murder. If the Order did have a traitor in their midst, then he was currently working to solve his own crime.

I was going to get justice for my friend. Whether Silas liked it or not. Who knows, maybe I'd save him in the process. After all, he saved me.

I turned around and gave my gorgeous fella a kiss on the cheek.

"What was that for?"

I smiled and gave him another. "For being you."

Riley made a gagging sound while Logan cooed out an, "Aww. Isn't that cute."

"It's fucking disgusting, is what it is," Mason grumbled.

I stuck my tongue out at him and settled back in Silas's lap. "You're just jealous."

"Actually," Mason tapped his finger against his chin, "I'm curious."

"Yeah." Logan agreed. "What do you think she is? Like, five two, five three?"

"Nah man," Mason shook his head. "She can't be anymore than five foot even."

I rolled my eyes. "I'm five one."

Five foot two on a good day.

"Okay, five one." Logan's eyes slid over to Silas. "So that means…"

Silas held out his hand, cutting him off. "Don't fucking do it."

Was I missing something?

"Come on man, you gotta admit it's a miracle the girl can take you." Logan waved his hand at me. "Your dick's gotta be what… like a third her body weight?"

"That's what I've been saying," Mason nodded in agreement.

Dear lord, help me survive these boys.

"You two are fucking morons," Micha grumbled.

I couldn't help but wonder if he knew how to talk any other way. Don't get me wrong, Silas was grumpy, but Micha had that growl down to a science.

"Hey," Logan whined back at him. "I'm not the one that spent months complaining because he couldn't get any."

"No, you just complained about the cold." Shelby rolled her eyes at her boyfriend. "Like, constantly."

Logan puffed his chest up. "Do you have any idea how many sweaters I had to wear…"

Micha quickly cut him off. "I swear to fucking god, if you say one more word about the weather in Canada, I'll shove my fist so far down your throat you'll taste me when you shit."

Apparently Canada is where they went. Why Shelby and Riley disappeared with their boyfriends up there, I had no idea. All Silas would tell me was that they were on vacation.

Well, I knew that was bullshite. Especially since three days after they came back, Silas disappeared for the night and came back in the morning with blood on his shirt.

Whatever. He could have his secrets. I think it made him feel better, keeping me out of things. Since that day he found me on the beach, Silas had become super protective. Always needing to know where I was, and who I was with.

I didn't mind. It was kind of flattering that he worried that much. Anything I could do to set his mind at ease, I would.

"It's almost time." Silas pulled me in and nuzzled my neck. "You sure you want to do this?"

There was something else that came with his Order's contract.

"Yes," I reassured him. "You already branded my heart."

A mark on the back of my neck was nothing. I'd wear it proudly.

I gave him a kiss and hopped off his lap. "Let me go get Harper."

The fact that I convinced her to come here at all was a miracle. Harper tended to avoid places where Mason Kessler might be like the plague. His best friend's house definitely fell into that category. Though, I can't say I blamed her.

I skipped up the stairs and knocked on the bathroom door. When she didn't answer, I got a little concerned. She'd been in there awhile. My jaw dropped when I swung the door open.

Harper was standing in front of the mirror, holding her shirt up to inspect a large black and purple bruise on her abdomen.

"Harper! What happened?"

She jumped back and quickly tugged her shirt back down. "I fell."

Fell, my arse.

"Did Mason do that to you?"

Instead of answering me, Harper rushed by, slipping past me while muttering, "I have to go."

I wanted to chase after her and demand she tell me what happened. But I had a good idea of that already.

I pulled out my phone and texted Mason.

> Me: Leave Harper alone!

A few seconds later his response came in.

> Mason: Blow me, London, I haven't
> touched your friend.

> Me: Bullshite! I saw the bruises Mason.

This time it took a little longer for him to respond.

> Mason: What bruises?

> Me: You know damn well what bruises.
> Leave her alone! Or so help me...

I stood there waiting for some smartarse response. What I got didn't come in the form of a text. It bellowed up the stairs in the sounds of yelling and flesh hitting flesh.

Dear Lord, what did I start?

I rushed forward and froze on the landing.

Down at the bottom of the stairs, Micha and Mason were on top of each other, arms swinging in violent punches. Logan and Silas were trying to pull them apart, but it wasn't working.

Just as one would get tugged away, the other would lunge after him. I couldn't do anything but gawk in horror at the rage in their faces. Couldn't so much as breathe until finally Silas managed to pry Mason off Micha, who Logan fought to hold back.

"Fuck you, Micha," Mason snarled while attempting to lunge at his brother again. Thankfully, Silas managed to hold him back. "This is none of your business."

"Eat shit, Mase," Micha barked back. "You made it my business when you threatened my girl."

Mason threatened Riley? I looked over at Riley, who was standing back from the boys with Shelby. Why would he do that?

"Micha, calm down." Logan tugged back on Micha's shirt collar. "You how worked up he gets about this shit."

"Yeah Micha, listen to your friend."

I'd never seen darkness in someone's eyes like I did when Micha stilled and glared at his brother.

"You know what Mase, fuck you." He roughly yanked out of Logan's grasp. "You want to destroy yourself, go right ahead. I'm tired of cleaning up your messes."

Logan stepped up and put his hand on Micha's shoulder. "Micha…"

"Oh shut the fuck up, Logan. Stop fucking coddling him." He rolled his eyes back at his friend and shrugged out away from his touch.

"Here's an idea Mase," Micha charged forward, puffing his chest up against his brother. "Why don't you grow the fuck up and take some goddamn responsibility for once in your life."

I couldn't help but feel bad for Mason when his brow furrowed. "You sound like your old man."

Micha didn't seem to like that. His finger flew up, poking Mason roughly in the chest. "News flash, asshole, he's your old man too.

Just because you didn't spawn from his nut sack doesn't mean he's not your dad. He was there when you were growing up, dealing with all your shit."

"Yeah, sure." Mason rolled his eyes. "Next you'll be telling me to talk to Freckles."

"You know what, that's a good fucking idea."

"She betrayed me!" Mason yelled back.

"Yeah, she did." Micha leaned forward, getting right in his face. "You ever ask yourself why? You want the truth so bad Mase, then go and fucking find it."

Micha shook his head and stormed out of the room, grumbling, "Stop playing the goddamn victim."

I didn't know what to say. I don't think anyone else did either. We all just stood there staring with our mouths hung open. Except for Silas. His expression twisted in sorrow as he reached out for Mason.

"Mase…"

"Don't," Mason muttered and marched out the door, slamming it behind him.

I rushed up to Silas and threw my arms around him, wanting nothing more than to take away his pain. "Should we go after him?"

"No," he kissed the top of my head, "this is something Mase has to figure out on his own."

Spitfire

Fuck you and fuck Micha too.

Sincerely,

Mason

11 YEARS AGO:

There she was. The most beautiful girl in the whole world was building a sandcastle. I couldn't stop watching her smack more sand in her pink bucket. She was so much prettier than the picture I saw, even with her tongue sticking out to the side.

How come Micha got to pick through that book first? What made him so special? Just cause he was older didn't mean he should get to do everything first. Just the other day Silas and I hunted down a ghost in my basement. Micha never did anything like that. He didn't even believe in ghosts.

My brother was so dumb. Instead of picking a girl from the book, he picked some stupid one because he said she needed to be taught a lesson. Pfft. Why would he want to marry her just to give her a time out? Didn't make sense to me.

Standing up on my tiptoes, I shielded my eyes from the sun so I could see the girl in the sandbox better. I was glad Micha didn't pick her. She was so pretty, with big brown eyes like Bambi and freckles on her nose. I couldn't see her freckles from here, but I saw them in the picture.

They reminded me of the connect the dots games in my coloring book. What kind of picture would her dots make? Maybe a crown. The sun did make her hair shine like waves of rubies. That's what Mom called her red jewelry.

Huh? Could gems make waves?

That would be really cool if they could. It probably wouldn't feel very good to dive into a river of diamonds – they were hard. I knew because Micha cut me with one of our mom's bracelets. He got in trouble for that. Our dad took away his bike. Then he took away mine when he found out I threw a paperweight at Micha first.

That was a funny word. Paperweight. Why did anyone need to weigh down paper anyways? Yeah it fluttered in the wind, but how were you supposed to draw anything with a big rock in the way?

Rocks were dumb. They got in the way and hurt my feet when I tried to walk in the water at the hot springs. I bet diamonds wouldn't do that. Besides, no one would go swimming in water made from diamonds. What kind of sound would that make?

The docks had a soft lapping sound, but the water at the bottom of the bluffs smacked hard off the rocks. *Dumb rocks.* Then there were the geysers. They boomed out great big streams of red water. Micha tried to tell me it was blood 'cause there was a whale trapped underneath, but Silas and I looked and we didn't see no whale.

Anyways, I really liked her hair.

"Hey." Someone poked me in the back. "Are you gonna go, or what? You're holding up the line."

I turned around and eyed the girl's long black hair. Micha had been following her around since we got to the park. I wasn't sure why? I didn't really care. I was just happy he was annoying someone else.

"Hello," she sang and clapped her hands in front of my face, making me jar back a bit. "Go already."

No girl was going to tell me what to do.

"This is my slide," I spat and crossed my arms. "Go find another one."

"You can't own a slide," she argued.

"Can so," I argued back.

My dad said our family owned this whole town *which meant* this slide was mine.

The little girl grumbled and rolled her eyes before trying to slip past me. But I stepped in her way. She didn't like that. Her lips twisted in a frown while she glared up at me.

"You better move."

I smiled back at her. "Make me."

Her eyes got really small and her lips tightened, making them kind of pale, like when Mom put that skin colored cream all over her face. Girls did weird things. What was the point in putting stuff on if your face was already that color?

The girl puffed up her chest and crossed her arms. "Maybe I'll just push you down the slide?"

That made me laugh. I was way bigger than her, and Micha was bigger than me and I couldn't push him.

Speaking of Micha...

His head appeared at the top of the slide as he climbed up the ladder.

"Careful Mase, she's a dog killer."

That's where I knew her from. She was here the other day looking for her dog. Micha said he was dead, but I didn't find a body.

The little girl's mouth fell open with a loud gasp.

"I am not!" she propped her hands on her hips and waggled her head at my brother. "We found Charlie."

"Or," Micha charged up to her with his chest puffed out, "you took someone else's dog."

I was too mesmerized by her pigtails swaying to hear what she said. They moved back and forth like slithering black snakes. My hand shot out, yanking on a bundle of hair. I'd make a good snake catcher.

Suicide is a serious issues. If you or anyone you know are depressed or having suicidal thoughts please talk to someone. There are plenty of resources out there in every country. Suicide is never the answer, please remember you are not alone.

Thank you for reading Accident-Prone.
If you enjoyed this book please consider leaving a review. Reviews are always appreciated by authors.

If you'd like to be among the first to know about new releases and get an inside look into my world join my Facebook group T.L. Hodel's Murder Of Ravens.

For more information on the family at the garage check out Dylan Page's Torment duet. Please note: reading is not required for this series.
Look for more books in The Order of Ravens and Wolves.

Next in the series: Relapse

I would like to thank my beta readers. Ashley, Alexis and Bianca, you guys are great.

Also my work wives, Becky, Dylan, Evi, and Vivi, who sit there everyday listening to me yell at my computer or laugh evilly.

And my readers, I love you guys. Your support means the world to me, and look no cliffy this time.

Special note: If we can get 100 reviews for Accident-Prone, I'll write a novella for Micha and Riley on when she found out about Tico.

T.L. Hodel is a Canadian author, poet and artist. Through coming up from a difficult childhood she excelled at writing, having her first poem published in junior high. When not writing she occupies herself with numerous crafts, hobbies and is an avid gamer and horror movie fan. She lives in Calgary with her kids and cat, (who is a complete asshat), and may have a slight weakness for true crime shows.

Connect with T.L. Hodel online:
www.facebook.com/groups/2724029706612789/?ref=share
www.instagram.com/tarahodel
www.facebook.com/Author-TL-Hodel-102923044775313/

Also by T.L. Hodel

The Order Of Ravens And Wolves:
Aftereffect
Scartissue
Happenstance
Accident-Prone
Relapse
Panic-Button (coming soon)

Deviant House:
Innocence
Innocence corrupted (coming soon)

The Lost Souls:
Adversaries
Frenemies

Brothers Of Shadow And Death:
Backfire
Backstab (coming soon)

The Seven Sins Series:
Pride

The Buchanan Brothers
Twisted Abel
Twisting Tallon (Coming soon)